The Barbosa Legacy

ALSO BY ROA LYNN

The Barbosa Legacy

Roa Lynn

CORCOVADO PRESS

The Barbosa Legacy
Roa Lynn

CORCOVADO PRESS
corcovadopress@verizon.net

Printed in the United States of America

This is a work of fiction set against historical events. All the principal
characters and their actions are fictional creations.

Cover illustration of Little Brazil Street at Times Square by
Corcovado Press, all rights reserved.

For my husband, Bernard, of course.

CHAPTER ONE

I

It was a spectacular night of catastrophe. My father, Jorge Antônio Barbosa, was burdened by business debt and seduced by his appetite for cards. In the final round of his regular Wednesday night poker game, he bet and lost the vast coffee and cattle plantation that had been acquired by my family over six generations. Had we received the news in another age and place, a servant would have been told to lower the family heraldic banner and pack it away for protection from moths. But this was January 1969, high summer in Brazil. The next morning, with the ownership of Fazenda Maraíba in the hands of Bernardo Fernandes, my father's face bespoke defiance. There is always a little arrangement, a way out of the burdens imposed by duty and law. Even at the final judgment, a Brazilian expects to find a way to bend the rules.

"Do you want to leave me, Lucilia?" he asked my mother over breakfast. "I wouldn't blame you."

"You were mad to make the bet." She exaggerated her already erect seated posture and stared straight ahead.

"But if I'd won, Lucilia, we'd be free of debt. I had a magnificent hand."

"Where are we supposed to live?" She looked around the spacious, light-filled atrium of our manor house, with its graceful furniture and carefully tended flowering plants.

My father smiled and reached out to pat her hand. She quickly withdrew it. He pretended not to notice the rebuff. "In 31 years, have I ever failed to provide you with a roof over your head? And a lot more than a roof." He resettled himself in his chair unfazed, still smiling. "This isn't the moment for melodrama, Lucilia."

"If this isn't a drama, I don't know what is. A woman with good sense would leave you, Jorge Antônio."

"Bernardo didn't get everything. He thinks he did. I still have an asset or two."

My father noticed my surprise and continued. "I have no doubt Bernardo thinks I'll do something rash — like rush off to the station and board a train to Bolivia. Lick my wounds in some Godforsaken jungle town or go to La Paz, where nobody knows me. I wouldn't dream of disappearing. It's not going to be so easy for him to untangle the affairs of the *fazenda* and make a profit. I'll enjoy watching him try."

My throat was tight with emotion. I hardly recognized my voice when I spoke up and asked my father if he had sufficient funds to help me finish my architecture degree.

"We'll have to talk about that, Alexandre. I have some calculations to make."

"I'm not staying here in Bauru, *papai*, no matter what."

"That's been clear to me since you were 10. Coffee growing and cattle ranching are not for the likes of an architect? Agriculture is God's architecture, Alexandre. You resist the obvious parallels."

"Whether we own the *fazenda* or not," I said, trying to keep my voice under control, "I'll find a way to go back to school in Rio, even if you can't help with my expenses."

My father searched for the plumpest roll in the breadbasket, spread it with a giant scoop of guava jam and poured himself a cup of coffee with hot milk. Neither my mother nor I made a move to help ourselves to breakfast rolls, fruit or coffee. My sister, Maria Rita, picked up a finger banana and an orange and left the breakfast table in tears without saying a word.

2

Had my parents been able to peer into my mind, they would have found treasonable thoughts. I had been destined to take my father's place as lord over our *fazenda*. Thanks to my father's bet, the distinguished architecture practice I intended to create in Rio would be safe. Its anticipated interruption, possibly at the peak of my career, was forestalled. Now everything the *fazenda* grew and nourished and sold, either at a profit or a loss, was Bernardo's concern.

Two days after my father's grandiose wager, my thoughts returned to the quandary that had obsessed me all during my summer vacation. Family expectations were not the only threat to my career as an architect. I had to make a choice when I returned to school — either drop my sporadic, ineffective involvement in the student resistance to our military dictatorship or fully commit to the cause. If I decided to engage seriously and was caught, I would likely be tortured. I could be left to rot in prison, perhaps die at the hands of my captors. I examined my options and kept coming back to the same conclusion — either I was a bystander or I was in the fight. Participating halfway had no appeal.

II

For longer than any living person could remember, my family had grown coffee for export in the acid soil 15 kilometers from the center of Bauru, a small city in the state of São Paulo. My paternal grandfather, Heitor Barbosa, had added cattle for the domestic market. In hard times, property had been mortgaged, section by section, to liberate needed cash — and not just first mortgages, but second and third. When coffee prices improved, the mortgages were paid back in full. Forest fires, freezing winds blowing up from the South Pole, trees sickened by fungus or by insects, or a flooded world coffee market would set off a new round of borrowing. Recently the *fazenda* had borrowed money from the Bauru Ford dealership my parents owned in partnership with a wealthy notary.

Our land — sometimes completely free and clear, sometimes not — had been acquired by my family beginning in the 1850s. Aside from an ancestral passion for agrarian life, the gambling disease had also run in my family for generations, on both sides — the Machados, my mother's family; and the Barbosas, my father's. In 1929, a year of hard times, one of my maternal great-grandfathers, Raimundo Machado, lost his family property in a poker game. Eight years later Raimundo won his property back in another sweaty game with a string of successful bluffs and one final, genuine full house — three tens and two kings.

Like many of the farms in the interior of São Paulo state, my family's plantation had been christened generations back with an Indian name — Fazenda Maraíba. "Maraíba is far superior to being burdened with some saint's name," my father had said on more than one occasion. "Since no one can tell me the meaning of Maraíba in Tupi-Guarani, the name doesn't carry any expectations. Saints have the habit of imposing themselves."

My mother's father, Manoel Machado, was the one family member not interested in farming. He lacked the passionate attachment to the land. When, in 1941, the U.S. began building military bases in northeastern Brazil to support an assault on the Axis forces in North Africa, Manoel saw opportunity. He sold his property to his neighbor, my paternal grandfather, Alfredo Barbosa, who combined the two plantations into the present *fazenda*. Manoel invested the proceeds in manganese mining and textile manufacturing, which proved to be very profitable when, in 1942, Brazil entered World War II on the side of the Allies. Upon Manoel's death, ownership of these companies had been divided evenly between male and female descendants, with man-

4

agement responsibilities passing to his oldest son and namesake, my maternal uncle Manoel.

Our holdings included our house, a local adaptation of a Portuguese farmhouse, built in the late 19th century. Half a kilometer from the main house there had been a modest building that contained a family chapel as well as a sacristy and a bedroom reserved for visits by the local priest. Nearby was another building, a dormitory, with a row of small guest bedrooms with locks, curiously, on the outside. In the old days hospitality was obligatory, but it was just as well to be cautious.

Over the years these detached buildings suffered from neglect. Eventually they were pulled down. In 1961, when I was 15 and Maria Rita was 18, my mother had the house remodeled, one end to the other, by a French-born interior designer who lived in Rio. The reconfigured house had six airy bedrooms, a formal parlor, a large, wood-paneled library with a pair of tufted dark green velvet sofas and shelves of leather-bound books — the farm's connection to the sophisticated metropolitan world — a dining room that could be arranged to seat 30 and the sunny, burgeoning atrium, my father's preferred venue for breakfast. Surrounding the house on the north and west were wide, shaded dining verandas. Since, in my father's estimation, Bauru had no acceptable restaurants — a poor showing for a city of 100,000 — he had insisted that his house have varied locations for taking meals. Together with the working areas — kitchen, pantry, laundry, sewing room and servants' quarters — the house was almost 600 square meters, a little more than 6,000 square feet.

Not far from the manor house were enormous brick terraces where our workers raked the crimson coffee cherries — the ripe fruit of the Arabica coffee trees — to dry in the sun. Nearby was a complex of buildings for storing them when dry and a building that housed the machine for removing the cherries' outer layers. My mother had an architect transform another outbuilding into a chapel open to all. Nearly 100 farmworkers and their families lived on the property in dwellings nestled alongside a narrow river two kilometers from our house. A market selling homegrown goods served their everyday needs. The nursery bed for coffee seedlings, shaded by a bamboo roof, was also close to the river.

Bernardo Fernandes, the new owner of Fazenda Maraíba, the winner of our property, was my parents' lifelong friend, a fellow large-scale coffee grower and rancher and, like my father, a poker fanatic. It had been 18 months since my father had borrowed the equivalent of $2 million from Bernardo on a handshake. Fazenda Maraíba had needed a cash infusion and Bernardo had offered my father better terms than our local commercial bank. Most of the money was still owed on the night my father proposed the bet.

III

Every few years on April 23, the date when my great-grandfather won his property back, my family has commemorated that triumphal bet with an impressive series of events culminating in a dramatic re-enactment of the game as it was played that night. By the time of its first ceremonial recapitulation in 1939, the Machado and Barbosa families had been united by the marriage of my parents. The first gathering was held in the house where my mother was born. After Grandfather Barbosa purchased the Machado *fazenda*, the festivities were moved to the larger, grander Barbosa manor house. The occasion, coming as it did between Easter and Ascension Day, brought members of both families home from as far away as Europe. Aunts, uncles and all our cousins came — first, second and third — also the bishop, our parish priest, important local lawyers and notaries, physicians and dentists, the mayor and our representatives to the State Legislative Assembly

6

and to the National Congress. Everyone gathered at our *fazenda* for a noon Mass, followed by a lavish lunch, tours of the property to observe preparations for the coffee harvest, afternoon cigarettes and gossip, naps, brief rendezvous under the mango and avocado trees between cousins wishing to taste another's partner, cocktails at 7 and, at 8:45, a sumptuous dinner. The eldest member of the Machado family would tap a glass precisely at 10:40 p.m., the exact moment when my great-grandfather had plunked down his winning hand, re-establishing his ownership of land farther than the eye could see in any direction.

For this ceremony, it was our family's idiosyncratic tradition, exceptional for Brazilians, to call attention to the hour. Everyone agreed that observing the precise time was critical to the re-enactment but, in general, Brazilians belittle the northern European fetish for punctuality. The story was recounted for the assembled guests by various first-degree relatives: to begin, why Raimundo was in financial difficulty; a recitation of the pedigrees and business connections of the other cardplayers; what beverages and viands were served and finally how Raimundo had, all along, for eight years, cleverly hidden some assets. When it was his turn to narrate the story, one Machado uncle who was adept at drawing limned the crucial poker hands of those two fateful evenings — losing and winning — on cardboard panels propped up on a rococo easel. When the storytellers finished — it could take at least an hour, sometimes much longer with all the embellishments added over the years — champagne was poured and everybody toasted God, who both challenges and, in turn, protects us.

The last such reunion had been in 1964, 22 days after the coup d'état that threw out President João Goulart and put a military government in power. That year, talk at our family celebration had two themes: the caprice and lure of gambling and the lightning takeover of the government. Certainly everyone gathered in Bauru realized one thing — the nation had been seized by the scruff of the neck. I wasn't present at the 1964 reunion because I was a high-school exchange student in Minneapolis. I had told my American family the tale of my great-grandfather and they surprised me on April 23 with a party, food prepared from Brazilian recipes and champagne for a toast. Mr. Madsen tapped his glass at the correct hour and invited me to speak.

"Well," I said, "my English is definitely getting better. But I'm afraid not better enough to convey to you how outrageous my family is. Imagine losing everything in a poker game. Imagine my great-grandfather moving his family in with an immigrant Italian family who worked for him. It was a scandal. Imagine winning everything back in another poker game. Imagine that everyone in my family still loves to gamble — and for high stakes — my father, my aunts and uncles and cousins. I hope nobody here invites me to play poker or blackjack. I might lose my plane ticket home." I could have added that public gambling had been illegal in Brazil since it was outlawed by the Dutra administration in the mid-1940s. Of course, closing the country's 69 casinos had no effect on my family.

Indeed, my father's eldest sister claimed that as a young widow she had had an affair with one of President Dutra's close aides. "And I can tell you, he loved to gamble. We played jackpot poker in bed at seaside hotels." The family was astonished by this story because the aide was known to be a religious fanatic, ugly and dull.

IV

After the somber breakfast following the loss of the *fazenda*, whatever jolt of anger or fear my parents felt was not discussed in front of me. The atmosphere in the house felt eerily restrained. Three days after the calamity, our family had to make a point of showing up at the funeral of Bernardo's mother, *dona* Irene. My father continued in the same defiant posture he had adopted from the start. He actually had a discreet twinkle in his eye. As we settled into a pew near the rear of the Church of Santa Terezinha, he addressed my mother in his usual theatrical fashion: "My God, there he is, the little shark, greeting people as if he were the maitre d' at the Hotel Ritz. Imagine! At his mother's funeral! *Dona* Irene would be ashamed." He cleared his throat loudly and continued to observe Bernardo. "We shouldn't have come, Lucilia."

"Keep your voice down, Jorge Antônio. People are turning around to stare. This absurd predicament we're in has the feel of a bygone era."

"Really? What era? When were cards invented?"

Every important person in Bauru was present in the church. I didn't hear any muffled weeping as *dona* Irene was eulogized. After all, she was 89 and afflicted with all the infirmities that came with great age. The congregants, I imagined, didn't bother to reflect on her arrival in heaven. The earthly fate of the Barbosa family was far more absorbing. My father and mother bowed their heads and didn't speak again or look at each other until the requiem Mass was over. In edgy silence I sat between them and Maria Rita. It was a relief when *Padre* Eugênio Alves' dry, emotionless voice intoned the final blessing. As *dona* Irene's ornate coffin was borne to the main portal, two white lilies from the requisite spray on top fell to the stone floor. A subtle signal from my father kept us in our seats while the pews emptied. As we walked down the steps of the church, my father touched my elbow. "I suppose you overheard us. I've suspected for years Bernardo had a base nature."

I didn't respond. I wanted him to feel my reproach.

Padre Eugênio caught sight of our family as we walked around the hearse parked in the drive at the bottom of the staircase. Would he leave the side of the bereaved to greet us? He waved. "Jorge Antônio!" he called. He limped toward us.

"What happened to you, Eugênio?" my father asked.

"Soccer practice."

My father looked like a man who had not yet calculated his situation. In fact, if anything, his countenance of bravado had mutated into one of triumph.

"Jorge Antônio, I'm not going to pretend with you," the priest said. "I know all about the poker game. I'll say this much, it's Christian of you to attend *dona* Irene's funeral."

"Why shouldn't I come? *Dona* Irene wasn't involved. It's her son who has been waiting for his moment to steal Fazenda Maraíba. The moment came and he jumped. That's what happens when your close friend abandons you and takes up with Satan."

Padre Eugênio shook his head. "You've had a shock, Jorge Antônio. I'm going to discount your statement."

"What the hell," my father continued, ignoring the priest's remark. "Let him have it. If I hadn't played poker with him for the *fazenda*, he would have had it sooner or later anyway. But don't expect to see me standing shoulder to shoulder with Bernardo at *dona* Irene's interment. I'm going home to lunch."

"As you wish, Jorge Antônio."

The priest rejoined Bernardo and his family. The Fernandes women had removed their black mantillas and put on European-style sunglasses. Bernardo kissed the tips of his fingers and pressed them to the window of the hearse. We waited at a discreet distance while the bereaved entered three chauffeured Chevrolet sedans. With military bearing, my father turned on his heel and headed off to our car. We fell in behind him like recruits.

"What are you serving for lunch, Lucilia?" he asked as we drove past Rui Barbosa Park, where a photographer was posing a tense bride and groom in front of a giant *flamboyant* tree. Sitting in the back

10

seat, my father's window wide open, I felt the breeze coming from the muggy Mato Grosso jungles.

"Fillet of pork," she said in a flat voice. "And Jocy said there's some leftover heart-of-palm pie."

"You see, no one's starving," my father said. "Speak up, is anyone in this car starving? He tapped the steering wheel for emphasis. "Alexandre? Maria Rita?"

The morning after the funeral, I lay in bed lamenting the loss of our land that was so far-flung the boundary lines had not been precisely determined until the beginning of the 20th century. Though I didn't want to participate in the management of the *fazenda*, I took an owner's delight in walking among our coffee trees and contemplating our beloved Nelores at pasture — strange, hardy, long-legged white bovines with pendulous ears and a fleshy hump over the shoulders. The homely cows, a breed of Zebu successfully introduced into Brazil from the Nelore district of India, looked thoughtful as they grazed over huge tracts of land.

I roused myself, took a shower, slipped on jeans and an old shirt and joined my family in the atrium. Breakfast was silent. Jocy, our cook, didn't make her usual high-spirited morning appearance. Perhaps she was away arranging for a new domestic situation. My father feigned intense interest in a three-day-old newspaper. The milk for coffee was barely warm and the papaya wasn't ripe.

Maria Rita stared at her engagement ring. "Thank God I finished my degree last year. And doubly thank God I'm marrying Paulo, who's levelheaded." She turned her gaze toward my father. "If I told you, *pai*, what I truly think about our situation ..."

He interrupted: "I know for a fact the poker game was rigged. We aren't going anywhere. If you've started packing, stop immediately."

11

He went back to his newspaper. No one spoke. I peeled an apple and ate it, took several swallows of tepid café au lait and got up from the table to fetch my sketch pad. Tablet in hand, I left the house. I needed to calm down. A walk and some sketching *en plein air* might help. I looked out over the rows of mature coffee trees with their shiny, dark green, elliptical leaves and started drawing. The pattern of endless "avenues," roughly two meters wide, with trees planted evenly on either side, set up a pleasing geometric rhythm. I didn't sketch what I saw, I sketched what I felt — a melancholy, disquieting landscape.

In three months, when the coffee cherries were fully ripe, seasonal workers who lived on the outskirts of Bauru would be trucked in to augment our regular workforce for the harvest. By then the *fazenda* would be in Bernardo's hands. I fantasized that, in an act of loyalty to the Barbosas, our farmworkers would decide to leave their homes, drifting away to pick cotton or cut sugar cane up north or harvest grapes in the south rather than work for Bernardo. What rejoinder did my father have in mind against Bernardo's winning hand? Who was going to believe that the deck had been unfairly shuffled? Or that Bernardo had a card up his sleeve? Or that another player had slipped Bernardo the fourth seven he needed to win? Bernardo had four of a kind; my father had a full house. Games are games.

I never felt more attached to our *fazenda* than at that moment of loss. Maria Rita strolled over to me with a coffee cup in her hand. For two days she had barely left her room.

"Last look, Alexandre?"

"That's what I'm trying to figure out. Is this the last look at what used to be ours?" I put my sketchbook under my arm and we started walking. "What do you think?"

"I think I'm getting married in two months and Paulo's diplomatic career could take us anywhere — Europe, I hope. But I wouldn't mind

Japan. I have to disconnect from our family drama or I'll get deeply depressed. Father just told me my wedding's only partially paid for."

"Surprised?"

"Not really. He told me not to worry. It's incredible. I'm trying to stay steady for Mother's sake." We turned a corner and started down another avenue of trees. "After you left the table, the phone started to ring. It didn't let up, but no one had the guts to answer it. People must be dying of curiosity. What's your plan?"

"Go back to Rio after summer holiday and finish my last year of architecture one way or another. Mother and Father can have the proceeds of selling my car and my glider. I can get a part-time job doing some drafting. I'll have to move out of Pedro's apartment. He can find another roommate. I think Luis would let me stay with him for a semester without paying rent. It's a dump, not much good for entertaining girls, but ... "

"Beggars can't be choosers?"

"I'm infuriated," I said, "but at whom? At what? Competition on the world market? The high cost of production? The invasion of *bicho mineiro*? I wouldn't put it past the Africans to have deliberately released those insects into our coffee fields. But what Father did was crazy."

"And selfish." She dumped the last dregs of her cold coffee on the ground.

"Father knew he couldn't hold off repaying Bernardo much longer," I said. "He likes to think gambling is a way of defying logic. For me, frankly, there's a positive side to this mess. I can build my architecture practice in Rio in peace."

"He could win it back, Alexandre, like Great-grandpa." She touched my elbow. "Don't worry, I respect your secrets." Her eyes filled with tears. "I especially love it in spring when the coffee trees are in bloom. The flowers smell like jasmine, don't you think? We'd better go back. Somebody's got to answer the telephone."

CHAPTER TWO

I

One week later, my mother left my father. "Is this a permanent move or temporary displeasure?" he asked her as she put her last suitcase in the car.

"It's profound disappointment."

"With me?"

"With life."

"You think your *Bandeirantes* ancestors would disapprove of me?"

"What kind of joke is that? Anyway, Jorge Antônio, it was my grandfather who lost the *fazenda*. Not yours." She kissed him and drove off to her sister's house in town.

Both sides of my family descended from *Bandeirantes*, ruthless Portuguese explorers who expanded Brazil's borders in the 16th and 17th centuries with their expeditions into unmapped wilderness to enslave indigenous people and search for mineral wealth. I suppose, in my father's mind, his remark was a half-hearted recognition that his loss of Fazenda Maraíba shamed a proud family whose lineage went back to the founding of Brazil. This joke, as my mother called it, was as close as my father had come to contrition.

After lunch, to get away from the awkwardness at the *fazenda*, I went to the Bauru *Aeroclube* for a flight in my beloved silver L-13 Blanik glider. When I arrived at the airport cumulus clouds had gathered overhead, the kind of clouds formed by thermal currents — a perfect day for motorless flight. Several of my friends, also sons of prosperous families, were already in the air. In our family's changed financial circumstances, this might be the last time I could join them. I got a free tow from Hans, the founder of the gliding school. Hans, who had immigrated to Brazil from Germany, had been drawn to establish his school in Bauru because of its favorable meteorological conditions. We rattled down the runway and in a few seconds we were aloft, the roar of the Piper Pawnee towplane and the sound of rushing air filling my cockpit. When we reached our agreed altitude — 1,800 meters — I released the towrope. The constraints of gravity and the din of the Piper engine were gone. I was left alone with my thoughts, my predicaments and the currents.

Through the canopy I had a panoramic view of our grazing lands and the patchwork of our coffee fields. The uniform rich green corduroy disappeared in areas where diseased trees had been cut back or replaced with seedlings grown in the nursery. Even with nearly 200,000 trees damaged by insects or fungus, Fazenda Maraíba still had more than 5 million producing trees, each capable of yielding coffee worth about half a U.S. dollar per year, depending on growing conditions and the market.

I tried to dismiss my worries and enjoy soaring through the air, but my troubling ruminations kept after me. I could see my glider's silhouette surrounded by a rainbow-colored oval as it passed directly between the sun and a cloud. Making a series of tight banked turns I enjoyed the feeling of pivoting around my wing, chasing my silhouette. It was going to be a relief to escape my family situation in Bauru, return to the university and immerse myself in my studies. I had one month before summer holiday ended and I went back to Rio to start the academic year. I felt suffocated in my family's history; I longed to escape to anonymity — radical thoughts in a country, a society, where family is everything and autonomy is hard to achieve. I moved the stick to take full advantage of a thermal, but instead of executing aerobatic maneuvers, I found myself concentrating on the political outrages that had preoccupied me during my school holiday before they were crowded out by the loss of the *fazenda*.

In the winter of 1968 I had participated enthusiastically in several of the massive street demonstrations in Rio against the military. I had shared my fellow students' optimism that our demonstrations would spread to the population at large and sweep the military from power. Student politics and debates on mobilizing the masses distracted me from what had been the passionate core of my life — my architecture studies. In June, demonstrations as large as 10,000 strong had turned into riots. In one week alone more than 1,000 people were arrested. At one demonstration a police baton landed on my right wrist and thumb. I wasn't able to hold a pencil for a week.

By November the government had had enough. Demonstrations were banned. In retrospect, we should have realized it was just a matter of time before the president gave himself the power to declare a state of siege. On Friday, Dec. 13, 1968, the military regime imposed the infamous Institutional Act Number Five — an outrageous, sweeping decree by which the president, Artur da Costa e Silva, suspended the right of habeas corpus for "political" crimes, shut down Congress and assumed dictatorial rule. Hundreds of people were immediately picked up and jailed. Why not choose a day of bad luck, Friday the 13th, to eliminate the last vestiges of democracy in Brazil? Two days later, press censorship was imposed. I had a patriotic obligation to resist. What should I do? I feared that my father had been right when he had said that further student resistance was futile. The military had the upper hand; it controlled everything.

My father's attitude toward the military government and the resistance was complex — neither that of the majority of rich landowners around Bauru, blind to dictatorial dangers and grateful to the government for having lowered interest rates for farmers, nor that of a revolutionary determined to oppose the military at any cost. He viewed

17

totalitarianism, whether fed by fascist or communist ideology, as a curse you had to outlive. I respected him for having his own reasoned position. At the end of the 18th century, one of my paternal ancestors had been hanged alongside our patriot Tiradentes, the first of my countrymen to raise a revolt against Portuguese rule. At my father's insistence, a faded and damaged portrait, believed to be of our brave forebear, had always been displayed in our vestibule, and new visitors were told his story. After the 1964 military coup, the portrait took on new life. My father and I got in the habit of saluting the revolutionary on our way to the breakfast table.

The painting was not hanging in its usual place when I returned to Bauru for my summer holiday. I inquired. "We don't need another dead romantic patriot in the family," my father said. "I know more than you think I do about what you and your classmates have been up to. The portrait is retired." Later that afternoon he observed, "I'm deeply skeptical, Alexandre, that the underground resistance will accomplish anything." The open book on his lap was an analysis of John F. Kennedy's assassination. "But what I know will succeed is time. In the end, time is the Brazilian cure for every ill."

"Students I know are rotting and dying in prison while the clock is ticking," I said.

"I would forbid you to return to Rio if I thought you could end up in a jail cell. Your mother and I consider ourselves fortunate that the serious left regards our son as a class enemy. It makes them less likely to invite you to join their escapades."

"I believe their escapades, as you call them, are the only way to attack the dictatorship. If the armed resistance grows ..."

"That's dangerous talk, Alexandre. If you get picked up in a demonstration, no lawyer I can hire has the power to prevent you from being tortured or get you out of prison."

I topped out my glider at 2,300 meters, sharing my thermal with a flock of swallows. We parted company when I steered back toward the runway. By the time I landed, I had made up my mind that, despite my father's realistic fears, I was honor bound to resist the generals. I was no longer half in and half out of the fight. I was in!

II

Maria Rita waited only three days after Mother left home before she eloped to Uruguay. Her telegram announcing her marriage was telephoned from the Bauru telegraph office and later delivered by courier to the *fazenda*.

PAULO AND I MARRIED MONTEVIDEO. HONEYMOON PUNTA DEL ESTE BEACH RESORT. RETURN BAURU NEXT WEEK BEFORE MOVE TO RIO. WE ARE HAPPY. LOVE MARIA RITA AND PAULO

My parents were deeply disappointed that Maria Rita felt her wedding celebration, as planned, could not take place for financial reasons. They consoled themselves that in the long view, a wedding with 320 guests looking on didn't predict a happy or an unhappy marriage. What mattered was making the right choice for a partner. In that, Maria Rita had selected well. Everyone adored Paulo. He was attractive, thoughtful of others, terrifically bright, came from a good Rio de Janeiro family and had passed the highly competitive exams to be accepted into the foreign service. An interesting life of diplomatic work and travel lay ahead of him.

Since the fateful wager, my father had given no sign of facing his own reality. He should have been making plans about where he and my mother were going to live. When, three weeks after the game, Bernardo came to claim our house, no plan was in place for moving, for

19

protesting, even for making a joke. Bernardo and his notary arrived at noon, two hours after Maria Rita and Paulo had put her belongings into her car and departed for Rio. My father was in the library, still in his pajamas and maroon dressing gown. He hadn't shaved; his unbrushed, reddish-brown hair came to two points, like two forks on top of his head. He looked like a confused rooster when the two men walked in. In full sight of them I listened at the doorway, both appalled and amused.

"History repeats itself, Jorge Antônio."

"Does it?"

"I take no joy in this. Believe that. Your debt to me was ruining us both. It was a heavy hand."

"Is that meant to be funny?"

"It was unintended. I have some papers for you to sign."

"Why did you propose the wager, Bernardo?"

"I didn't. You raised my bet. I have to say, though, when it was just the two of us left in the game, you surprised me with your proposition that you put up Fazenda Maraíba against my forgiving your debt. You had to know I had a strong hand."

"Why cheat, Bernardo? Why take advantage?"

"Cheat? What the hell are you talking about? You calculated the odds, you bet and you lost. Story concluded. I could just as easily say that you cheated three years ago when you won my new Cadillac imported from Miami."

"That was different. And I didn't cheat. I normally beat you. I don't need to cheat."

"Is that what you told Lucilia — that I proposed the wager? Where is she? You look god-awful."

"She left me."

"Not seriously."

"She's at Claudia's."

"She asked me to meet her there yesterday. We had an interesting talk. She didn't say anything about leaving you."

"Really! Do you think you're moving in, Bernardo? I won't let you. I have a new deck of cards right here. Sit down, let's play. Alexandre can shuffle."

"What are you playing for?"

"Everything back to *status quo ante*. No hard feelings."

"No, Jorge Antônio."

"Scared?"

"You have no bargaining power."

"I have the furniture."

"You already lost it. It goes with the house."

The notary spoke up: "There's room for disagreement on that point. Did you mention it in the bet, Jorge Antônio?"

"Of course not. I didn't mention my cufflinks either."

I walked into the room. "*Papai* ... "

My father raised his hand. "Don't say it, Alexandre. We're dealing with a bad sport. A rematch in 18 months. Meanwhile we live in the house and you run the *fazenda*. It's all yours. Every coffee tree, every turd from my adorable Nelores."

"You can live in the house, Jorge Antônio."

Without another word my father got up, pulled the sash of his dressing gown tight around his expanding middle and left the library.

21

"He's an obstinate man, your father," Bernardo said. "I hope you realize, Alexandre, there was no cheating involved and Jorge Antônio knows it. Christ, he and I and Fausto and Renato have been playing poker nearly every Wednesday night for 20 years." He tapped me on the shoulder. "Your father will come around. He's always in a fit of high pique when he loses, even if it's small change."

I pulled away. "This isn't small change, Bernardo, and I know all about the euphoria of poker."

He nodded, avoiding my gaze. "I'm sorry, Alexandre. I still want him to sign some papers. To make everything legal."

Bernardo and his notary came back to the *fazenda* the next day; my father signed revised papers. We would continue to live in the house — no rent. Bernardo would own and run the *fazenda*. His ownership included the manor house (but not its furnishings), the chapel, all the outlying farm buildings, all the machinery and equipment, the livestock and the ripening crop on the coffee trees. Coffee in storage, waiting for world market prices to improve, still belonged to us. My father was relieved of all debt, he had no duties to perform but, if he wished, he could participate in the *fazenda's* management and Bernardo would pay him a small salary. He accepted, and promptly got Bernardo to agree to raise his compensation.

"After all," Bernardo said, "you know better than anyone the workings of Fazenda Maraíba. I don't hold you responsible for the underlying reason for the debt. I hold you responsible for the management of the debt. In that, in my opinion, you didn't pay proper attention."

The next Wednesday, as if nothing had happened, my father went into town to have dinner with my mother and play poker with Bernardo, Fausto and Renato. "A penny-ante game," he said. "I need to show my

22

strength." Because he hadn't been to the bank, he had to borrow some small bills from me.

He was dressed in his best British blazer and gray trousers. He wore the floral silk tie my mother had selected for him on their trip to Paris three years before. It was unlike my father's normal cautious choice of neckwear. His hair was neatly parted and brushed. We were almost exactly the same height — slightly over 6 feet — and we both have the same aquiline nose. His eyes are brown; mine, like my mother's and Maria Rita's, are hazel. I still had not had a discussion with my father about how I was going to pay my living expenses in Rio. My architecture curriculum at the Federal University of Rio de Janeiro, which everyone referred to as Nacional, was tuition-free, but students were responsible for their own textbooks, materials for studio classes and living quarters. In general parents paid for what the government didn't provide. I had always expected after graduation to make my own way in the world, not to live off my patrimony. Now I worried that my independence had arrived earlier than I expected.

My mother remained at her sister's and would not divulge her plans. My father asked me to have a private chat with her to see what I could learn. She greeted me in my Aunt Claudia's drawing room. The house, in the center of town not far from Rui Barbosa Park, was turn-of-the-century, magnificently restored and enlarged. There wasn't another private house comparable to it in Bauru. The drawing room was nearly square. Its original moldings, chair rails, double doors of jacaranda wood and window hardware were in perfect repair. The decor was adventuresome: chrome-yellow walls complemented a handsome tan leather sofa and four matching soft, oversized easy chairs designed by the architect Sérgio Rodrigues, the originator of modern furniture in Brazil. The adjoining peacock-blue dining room had a round birch plywood table designed by Alvar Aalto and eight glass-and-chrome

23

Charles Eames dining chairs, available only in Brazil. Colorful paintings of ripe, ebullient mulatto women, a seascape, a small Cândido Portinari of a black farmhand and a surreal metal sculpture were carefully placed for advantageous viewing.

"It's a wonderful space, isn't it, Alexandre?" my mother said. "I feel tranquil here. I'm ready to discard all my dark, solemn antiques."

"Have you really got the courage for that?" I asked.

I thought my mother looked younger, despite the alarming and angry thoughts that had to be running through her head. She chain-smoked and paced. I tried to appear unperturbed about her situation, but underneath I was very concerned.

"Your father sent you to pick me up, I suppose."

"He's unhappy. We all are. Are you ready to go home?"

"I'm going to Portugal with your aunt. Just for a fortnight, no extravagances. I have a bank account left from my inheritance that your father can't touch. You know, Alexandre, I saw this coming."

"You're not going to leave Father?"

"Of course not. And we're not broke, either. We've got money invested here and there."

"But no land . . ." I prompted.

"And no debt, Alexandre." My mother put out one cigarette and lit another. "Your father didn't have the cash to repay his loan to Bernardo on the schedule they had agreed to. The situation was tormenting him. He didn't want to worry the family, so your father kept his business troubles to himself. I knew what was going on. He didn't sleep. On the positive side, if I can force myself to think that way, we can still live in our beloved house. But I'm furious, more than furious, with your father. His intoxication with cards is the sword of Damocles suspended by a hair above all our heads."

"I can find you a buyer for my glider."

She cut me off. "Don't bother, Alexandre." She groped in her purse, found her checkbook, wrote out a check and handed it to me. She inhaled her cigarette as she watched me read the figure. It was enough to cover five months' living expenses in Rio.

"I really appreciate this, *mamãe*, but I can take care of myself." She held her hand up in the same way my father did when he wished to terminate a topic of conversation. "You know Bernardo came to see me. I talked some sense into him."

"About letting us live in our house?"

She nodded. "I know you admire your Aunt Claudia's house. When you finish your architecture studies, you can remodel our house with all the modern furniture you love."

During the next week, late in the afternoon, my father changed out of his dressing gown into elegant sports clothes and went to visit my mother. On Tuesday and again on Friday, he didn't return to the *fazenda* until midmorning the next day. I refused to talk to him. I was sick to death of his cards. When he returned Saturday morning he asked, "Do you know where I've been?"

"Yes."

"You don't know. I stayed with your mother." He blushed.

I wanted to ask about the strangeness of this honeymoon, but merely expressed my relief that it wasn't cards that kept him out all night.

III

The next Friday, five days before I was due to return to the university from summer break, my father broke a molar at breakfast by biting into a prune he thought was pitted. He held the broken piece of the tooth in his hand while he tried to place a telephone call to a well-regarded restorative dentist in São Paulo. He didn't trust our family dentist in Bauru to repair it because he hadn't been trained in the United States. It was possible to fly from Bauru to São Paulo in an hour and 40 minutes, but the flight was only available on Tuesdays and Thursdays. My father wanted to be in the dentist's chair Monday morning. He had to spend most of the morning attempting to get a dial tone from our telephone system. When he finally made the connection he was able to confirm a Monday appointment for 9:30. He had our Ford Galaxie prepared for the road trip. I suggested that I accompany him, since it would give me an opportunity to take photographs of downtown São Paulo to use in my urban-design studio. By driving one leg of my journey back to school (there were no direct flights from Bauru to Rio), I would save on plane fare, an economy neither of us mentioned. I hoped my father would frankly discuss his financial picture and whatever else was on his mind while he was confined with me in the car on a long drive. The hints he and my mother had doled out to Maria Rita and me about their investments did not convince us they were financially secure.

On Saturday my father's fellow poker player, Renato, came to the *fazenda* for lunch. Renato was retired and spent his time visiting friends, reading, playing cards and living vicariously the active lives of his children and grandchildren. He was a civil engineer by profession, but he also owned several businesses, including a small coffee farm that he had turned over to one of his sons. It was obvious from the moment Renato arrived that my father had no intention of rehashing his situation with his old friend.

Dessert of fruit and cheese was accompanied by second and third *cafezinhos*. It was my father's custom, unlike most Brazilians, to drink these demitasses of strong black coffee without sugar. He believed a coffee-grower should taste his product unadulterated.

26

Eventually, he brought the conversation around to "the most sinister terrorist plot of contemporary history." According to newspaper stories that had appeared in mid-October 1968, an Air Force brigadier had planned to explode the gasworks adjacent to downtown Rio in order to blame the catastrophe on Communists. The detonation was to take place at the height of Friday evening rush hour, killing perhaps more than 100,000 people. Since the story surfaced, it had been a recurring topic of conversation in our family.

Renato reached for his pack of French cigarettes lying on the table, but changed his mind and didn't light up. "I used to think we had more than an adequate number of clowns and misguided individuals on both sides — the military and the leftists," he said. "I have to say the *gasômetro* story changed my mind. How could something that evil even be imagined? The bus station is practically next door to the gasworks. It would have been packed on a Friday evening with weekend travelers. You still believe the story was true?"

My father and I answered simultaneously, "Yes."

"It would be impossible to comprehend the horror if he'd succeeded," my father said. "This Brigadier Burnier is manifestly an agent of the devil. I mean that quite literally."

Despite the depth of my feelings, I let my father carry the conversation. I helped myself to one of Renato's unfiltered cigarettes, lit it and took a deep puff. It tasted terrible. Normally I smoked only when I was studying for a tough exam. My father stared into space. "The truth, Renato, is that since Costa e Silva and the armed forces took over, the opposition has been powerless and they know it. The leftists just hope everybody else is as unhappy as they are. Maybe it's time for extralegal action."

"You're supporting the armed opposition, Jorge Antônio? You know what would happen if the Communists actually succeeded. We'd lose everything."

27

"I already lost it. I'm free to think like the hippies."

Renato argued that installing the Leninist philosophy of revolution in Brazil would be an assault on reason. I felt myself growing increasingly choleric. Almost shouting, I said, "Every student demonstration last year was in response to some brutal action by the police. Since censorship, we don't even know the extent of the repression." My disillusionment and anger spilled out. "Detention, torture, prohibiting demonstrations! We're in a state of siege, for sure! It's the only thing Costa e Silva said that's true."

My father put his forefinger to his lips. "Don't worry, Renato," he said, "I haven't fallen for the great Marxist fallacy, even though my son likes to spout about the promised land. Have you got time for gin rummy? No betting." My father became lost in thought and made no move to get the cards. He poured himself another *cafezinho*, but pushed the cup and saucer aside. He looked sad, subdued.

"You know, Renato," he continued, "while we're here living our lives as usual, a cousin of mine in Brasília, a brilliant young lawyer ... He was an aide to one of the Federal Supreme Court justices who was removed from office. A week ago Oswaldo was picked up for questioning. While he was in custody, he was beaten very badly. They held him for three days." My father shifted his unfocused gaze to his neglected coffee and spoke without looking up. "The beating left him blind in his right eye. We were just told yesterday that the doctors doubt he will ever see again with that eye." The men folded their arms and fell silent for several minutes.

Ten years my senior, Oswaldo was the older brother I didn't have. I wanted to copy him in everything, except when it came to my choosing to study architecture, not law. Oswaldo was the one who first took me up in a glider when I was 8 and gave me my first lessons when I was 13. I was still trying to absorb the devastating news of his beating.

The heavy emotion hung in the room. Finally my father said, "I'll get the cards." He and Renato didn't notice when I left the table. They were pretending to be intent on deciding whether to match all the cards or end a game when the unmatched cards added up to 10 or less. I needed air, a walk. In addition to facing up to the barbarity of our political situation, I was still adjusting to the changed circumstances of our family. Even before I found out that my parents were able to continue underwriting my studies, I had seen Brazil's political situation and my involvement in it as a greater threat to my academic plans than their financial troubles were. As I paced between rows of newly planted coffee seedlings, I vacillated between outrage and fear. Ever since the Minister of Justice announced Institutional Act Number Five on television, all dissent had been squelched by the military's oppressive hand. No one could predict what pressure might be building up underneath. It occurred to me to break down my hunting rifle and pack it in my suitcase to take back to school. I had no idea what I might do with it, but it would be no use to me in Bauru.

My walk was interrupted when Mario, Fazenda Maraíba's manager, intercepted me. His face was flushed. "Alexandre, is *senhor* Jorge Antônio ill? One of our pulping machines needs repair immediately. What authority do I have? *Senhor* Fernandes has come to see me every morning for the past three days, giving me orders. I heard the rumor. Is it true?"

"It is. Hasn't my father talked to you?"

"The last time I talked to *senhor* Jorge Antônio was eight days ago. He appeared quite well. Normally we talk at least three or four times a week."

Obviously my father had not told Mario the news and it wasn't my place to go into details. He had been our *administrador* for 12 years. He wasn't losing his job, but he needed to know that, in the future, he would be taking direction from a new *patrão* and that Bernardo would expect him to shift his loyalty accordingly. My father would look foolish — preposterous — in front of Mario. Of course he dreaded the conversation. "Don't wait for my father to talk to you, Mario," I said. "He has a guest right now, but tomorrow morning you should ask him your questions directly."

What could my father say? "Well, Mario, at the end of a long evening of overwhelming good luck at poker, I bet the *fazenda*. I had a spectacular hand, a full house. I could have won, should have. I was that close to Bernardo Fernandes renouncing my entire debt to him. You could have bought a dozen new pulping machines. There's really nothing for you to worry about. *Senhor* Fernandes will consult with me on every major decision concerning the *fazenda*. First thing, ask *senhor* Fernandes for a raise. You deserve it. Unhappily, I just couldn't afford to increase your salary." Or would he say, "Mario, I hired *senhor* Fernandes to help me run the *fazenda*" or some such obfuscation? In his present state of grand delusional thinking, anything was possible.

I continued my walk, reprising my responsibilities to myself, my family and especially my country. The *gasômetro* plot was a surreal horror, but it was only a symptom of Brazil's ghastly rule. The huge demonstrations in the winter of 1968 had not developed into an organized mass resistance. Only a handful of Brazilian revolutionaries who had traveled to Cuba were actually trained in guerrilla warfare. After the government's ban on demonstrations, many of the student groups spent more time arguing about ideology — Pro-Soviets versus Maoists versus Guevaristas — than actually accomplishing anything. The underground groups encompassed doctrinaire Communists who wanted land reform and a more equitable distribution of wealth as well as moderates who would be satisfied with free elections, the restoration of the political rights of people who had lost them, the immediate release of all political prisoners and a free press. Everybody wanted to see the torturers strung up immediately.

It pained me that, as my father had reminded me, the movement's leftist stalwarts had not been inclined to encourage my active participation.

My mother was due to leave for Lisbon in a week. My father was full of plans and threats about the future course of his life, which included moving to Mafra, a small town north of Lisbon, learning to play the piano, purchasing an International Harvester franchise and buying an apartment in Las Vegas, Nevada. "You know, Alexandre, Las Vegas is quite interesting," he said to me with a perfectly straight face. "You'd find the architecture there fascinating."

"Are you mad, *pai*?"

"I don't think so. Why do you ask?"

He then went on to tell me the story of Mafra's gigantic National Palace. "After three years of marriage, King João V was childless. He promised God that if Queen Maria Anna gave him an heir, he'd build a monastery at Mafra. The project started out small, but gold from Brazil let it grow into one of the biggest buildings constructed in Europe in the 18th century. Anyway, God took the bait. The king had a daughter."

"I hope you're not planning any bargains with God," I said.

"Not at all, not at all. I just thought I might like to live in a small town with an impressive narrative. Bauru is bereft in this department."

"Pelé started his career here. Didn't God take a special interest in him?"

"You're ruining my story. Bauru is mostly bereft."

CHAPTER THREE

Sunday morning, very early, my father and I left for São Paulo. An accident on the main roadway tied up traffic, so the trip took the better part of the day. Our conversation was disappointing. I didn't feel it was my place to interrogate him; he showed no inclination to discuss financial matters or anything to do with coffee production or cattle. At least we could talk about opposition to the military government — neither of us convincing the other to re-examine his position. As we got nearer to São Paulo we passed the time listening to the radio, commenting on the profusion of modern factories spread over the rolling hills of one-time coffee lands and weighing my inchoate ideas for a project in my urban-design studio. For several weeks, when I wasn't consumed with politics or my father's folly, I had been trying to settle on a proposal for that class. One of my leading candidates was a comprehensive plan for the chaotic center of São Paulo. It would be an extremely challenging project to execute well, and I wasn't convinced that I should attempt it.

Mother had arranged for us to use a suite that one of her cousins maintained as a *pied-à-terre* at the Hotel Jaraguá. Early Monday morning, still tired from our long drive, we went to the hotel dining room and ordered a large breakfast intended for tourists — fruit, croissants, eggs and sausage. "Fortification for your ordeal?" I asked.

Father grimaced and set off for his visit to the dentist. I draped my Nikon around my neck and left the hotel to take pictures. I was relieved to see the sun shining. The day before, as we drove into town, it had rained nonstop. In São Paulo, then a city of nearly 6 million, a million more than Rio, there was always a violent energy in the air. All the sentimentality that bound Bauru, and even Rio, to its past was missing in the city "that can't stop." How should I photograph this megalopolis that was out of control?

I began my inquiry on the bridge that crossed the vast Anhangabaú Park and led into Patriarch Square. Looking across at the buildings that flanked the bridge and the confusion of autos and people below, I wondered how I would regulate this Times Square of Brazil if I took on the problem for my class. Wherever I looked, an old building was coming down, a new one rising in its place. I roamed through the streets, photographing the white granite skyscrapers, the profusion of new construction. Was it really true, as some statistics suggested, that in greater São Paulo a new building was completed every eight minutes, 365 days a year? I took a half-dozen pictures of the classic Teatro Municipal. Then, following along Avenida Ipiranga, I photographed the huge movie theaters and the luxury shops on the side streets. In a bookstore I bought maps of the city. I used up nearly a whole roll of film on Oscar Niemeyer's graceful, enormous, S-shaped Copan apartment building. With more floor area than any other residential structure in the world, this famous building had come to symbolize São Paulo, just as the statue of Christ the Redeemer was the iconic symbol of Rio de Janeiro.

At 1 o'clock my father and I met back at the hotel. He was permitted tepid clear soup for lunch and nothing more. Dentist's orders. I planned one more short foray after lunch to take a few more pictures in Republic Square before catching the Air Bridge to Rio. Since the planes left for Rio every half-hour, I would jump aboard as soon as I finished shooting. My father would stay in São Paulo another week for a second session with the dentist, then drive back to Bauru alone. I had a substantial lunch and two different puddings for dessert — my favorites, caramel and mango. Finally, when he knew I was leaving in a few minutes, my father broached the subject of money. "I feel sorry about your sister's wedding," he said. "She didn't consult with either your mother or me before she and Paulo ran off to Uruguay to get married. Your mother is heartsick. She blames me, of course."

"Maria Rita didn't think you could pay for it. Neither did I. Certainly not the extravaganza that was planned."

"Precisely the wrong conclusion." My father took a moment to look longingly at my desserts. "I thought I had made myself very clear. I hope by now you realize my poker game didn't finish off the Barbosa family. Where's the ruination? You're going back to Rio to finish your architectural studies. Your mother's going to Portugal and plans to buy tiles to refurbish her bathroom. What is patently of concern to me is Paulo's career. He hasn't been assigned to a foreign posting. Without experience abroad, he can't be promoted. His bosses at the Ministry of External Relations keep telling him to be patient."

My father winced and reached for his jaw. "Christ, the anesthetic is wearing off. By the way, I didn't withdraw any of the plans we made for Maria Rita's wedding. Nothing was changed, from the size of the guest list to the French champagne. You know what she told me? She said if she and Paulo ever get into a serious dispute she could get a divorce, because they didn't marry in Brazil. I never thought of it. She has a point. It's an interesting way to start a marriage. I'm sure she got the idea from our cousin Sérgio. You remember he used to talk about how Brazilians should marry outside the country so they could get a divorce when they needed one. I suppose it makes sense. Sérgio managed to get a divorce in Switzerland when Lina Teresa misbehaved with one of his colleagues — I'm sure he misbehaved, too — and he wanted to marry that American girl. Lucky for him he was a diplomat posted to Geneva, so he could arrange a foreign divorce. And lucky for the girl that Sérgio changed his mind about marrying her. He always thought he was handsome enough, and charming enough, that he didn't have to be emotionally responsible."

"I think I'll do the same thing myself," I said, "get married in an enlightened country that grants a real divorce. Our legal separation is a joke, just like our fascist government."

"Not so loud. Pay attention! Especially here in São Paulo. You know as well as I do who put the military in power."

"I certainly do." I let my eyes roam the dining room full of portly men in dark suits wearing tinted gray glasses. "These São Paulo businessmen stuffing themselves — with assistance from Washington, of course."

"Let's be completely fair, Alexandre. Goulart's government was polarizing the country. Something had to be done." My father paused and dipped his spoon into the remainder of my caramel pudding. "Too sweet." His expression changed from dislike to enthusiasm. "I want you to know, my son, I'm working on my own plans."

"Piano lessons? Moving to Portugal?" I asked. I didn't try to hide the exasperation in my voice.

"One of these days, after Bernardo realizes he can't repay himself so easily and he starts losing money, he'll agree to a return game. He'll beg me. The Barbosa family will have two momentous dates to commemorate — April 23rd and the day I win back our land. Maybe I can fix it so the two dates coincide. I'll conduct the first celebration myself, including setting up that rococo easel to display my winning hand. You can do the drawing."

With that, my father and I said our goodbyes. I strolled out onto the street past the Biblioteca Municipal and continued toward Republic Square. It must have drizzled while we were having lunch. The sidewalks were slippery, a hazard to pedestrians. Their surface of small black-and-white mosaic tiles in geometric patterns was typical of Portuguese sidewalks, which had been widely copied in Brazil. It might be a design element I should consider reworking.

As I was crossing Rua 7 de Abril I was nearly hit by a speeding car. I managed to jump out of the way in time but another car, tires screeching from acceleration, brushed my hip as it flew by. I froze in the middle of the street, unable to react. Impatient drivers honked their horns and cursed me as they were forced to swerve. Three men burst out of an imposing bank building onto the sidewalk across the street from where I stood. One of them lugged a large cloth sack; he was having trouble running. A second guy grabbed the bottom to help. The third guy carried a smaller sack; its shape suggested a long-barreled gun. Still riveted in the midst of heavy traffic, I snapped pictures without thinking. The men jumped into a waiting sedan. As the car raced away from the curb, a policeman ran down the block toward the bank, drew his weapon and shot three times at the tires. He missed, but a ricocheting bullet shattered the window of a taxi. A man in a business suit screamed at the cop: "Don't shoot, you idiot! You want to hit a pedestrian?"

Some people trapped by the gunfire had dropped to the ground. Others tried to get out of the way by pressing their bodies against storefronts. As the sedan lurched into the stream of traffic, one of the men pointed a pistol out a rear side-window, then ducked down. Someone in the front seat threw a handful of white leaflets onto the street. Gaining speed, the car passed a group of students in jeans and T-shirts. I had the impression that the gunmen's car was trying to catch up with the two cars that nearly knocked me down. The three vehicles sped through a traffic light that had just turned red, barely avoiding collisions. Finally, with traffic stopped at the red light, I was able to retreat from the street onto the sidewalk.

Within minutes more cops arrived on foot and two cruisers with sirens blaring threaded through the traffic, pulling up in front of the bank. Some pedestrians scurrying about on their normal afternoon business stopped to take in the scene when they realized a bank had just been robbed. Others, just entering the scene, joined the crowd out of curiosity. Confusion and speculation overtook the sidewalk. I let myself get pushed into the growing throng.

"It was just a car backfiring," I heard a woman say.

"Didn't you see those cars speeding away?" someone answered.

"Lunatic drivers!"

"No! It was a bank robbery. Three guys. One of them was carrying a huge sack of money."

"Hurry! A man's bleeding inside that taxi."

"We have lunatic cops shooting with all these people so close."

People ran to give aid. I picked up one of the leaflets from the street:

> This is a transfer of funds from the agents
> of the regime into the coffers of the people.
>
> NLM

I glanced at the initials. If NLM was a political organization, it was one I had never heard of. I shoved the leaflet into my pocket. A young guy who looked like a student ran over to me. "I saw you taking pictures. What do you plan to do with them?" He was brusque.

"I wasn't thinking. I just shot."

Another police car, its siren blasting, slammed to a stop in front of us.

"Put your camera under your shirt. If the cops see it, they'll take it just on the chance you took incriminating pictures."

I turned around, slipped my camera inside my shirt and concealed its leather strap under my collar. It was a warm afternoon. I didn't have a jacket to hide the bulge. I held my arm awkwardly over it.

"That's good enough," he said.

A girl in jeans holding a notebook joined us. "Who's he?" she demanded. "What's your name?"

"What's it to you?" I asked.

"I don't have time for games," she snapped.

"Alexandre Barbosa, if it's so important."

"From where?"

"Bauru."

"Student?"

I nodded. "In Rio."

"What are you doing in São Paulo?" the guy asked.

"Errands with my father."

"Are you politically active?" the girl asked.

I nodded again.

"Are you a member of an organization?"

"Yes."

"Do your parents know?"

"They've got their own problems."

The pair reminded me to watch out for my camera. I asked if they wanted my pictures.

"Maybe. We have friends in Rio who can get them for us." The girl asked for my address and telephone number in Rio. She jotted it down quickly in her notebook. "Get lost, Alexandre, before the cops notice your camera."

"You guys are students?" I said.

"More like ex-students," the guy said. "When our country is free, we'll go back to class."

I told them I had joined a political organization because it was easier than explaining why I hadn't. As I walked away, merging with the crowd, police officers streamed into the bank. No one except the three robbers had come out. Other cops began questioning the spectators standing nearest the entrance. Some pedestrians had disappeared into a nearby movie theater before the cops could interrogate them. Other on-lookers, their curiosity satisfied, crossed the street and walked toward the Thomas Cook travel agency. I joined them. Military police with submachine guns took up positions every few meters in front of the bank. I wanted to take a picture of the soldiers guarding the premises after the money was gone. I didn't.

CHAPTER FOUR

I

For two years a cousin from Curitiba and I had shared a modest one-bedroom apartment in a nondescript building on a back street in Copacabana. Pedro Barbosa was also a student at Nacional. We divided the rent but, on the toss of a coin, he won the privacy of the minuscule bedroom that faced an airless shaft. The living room was big enough for an armoire, a double bed placed against a wall, a small sofa and my desk, which also served as our dining table. The apartment was furnished with castoffs we had acquired from students who had graduated.

Pedro studied civil engineering. The year before, in March 1968, when the enormous student demonstrations in Rio began, he joined the rallies before I did, and was the first person I knew to be tear-gassed. For a month or two Pedro would believe that one of his girlfriends, usually a ravishing philosophy or literature student, was divine. He would endow her with such expectations that disappointment would invariably build up. "Why is it," he would say, "when I get rid of one girlfriend, it turns out someone less interesting takes her place?" On several occasions I captured one of his former "divines" for myself when I stepped in to dry her tears.

Pedro's older brother, Heitor, named after our grandfather, left medical school and went underground to join an armed guerrilla group. Normally when someone went underground, he or she cut all contact with family, friends and lovers, except for an occasional, very brief phone call. Even so, during the previous spring semester, Heitor showed up at our apartment now and then, always after midnight. For nine months he was constantly on the move, organizing dissent, shifting from urban safe houses to rural hideouts, gathering information on the deployment of security forces and the storage of military weapons. The three of us would talk all night about how the trade unions needed to get re-energized by throwing out their regime-approved leaders and joining forces with the students and the left wing of the Catholic Church. Uncannily, after these discussions my father would telephone in the morning to bring me back to another reality. "You know, when you finish at Nacional you could go to Georgetown University in Washington for graduate school. I never regretted my two years there studying international economics."

"Georgetown doesn't have a school of architecture, *pai*. Besides, I'm not matriculating into the enemy camp."

"If you think you're going to study in the Soviet Union or Cuba, forget it."

My return to Rio felt far from routine. The excitement of the afternoon in São Paulo infiltrated my thoughts for the following few days. I had gotten a good look at the robbers' determined, youthful faces — they could have been my fellow students. I found myself hoping my interrogators would indeed send a colleague to collect my photographs. I developed my film in a friend's darkroom the morning after I arrived. Had some recognizable "subversive" concealed himself in the crowd? Perhaps Carlos Marighella himself, the Marxist writer and urban-guerrilla strategist, was driving one of the cars. I stared at the contact sheet in the cramped, smelly darkroom. The students who stopped me on the street were obviously integral to the robbery. In their officious way, they were showing off. Did they think I had a "cold foot" — someone who neither has good luck nor brings it? I had photos of the policeman firing his revolver and two motion-blurred pictures of the robbers dashing toward the car, but the dangerous photos I had taken were an unambiguous head shot of the driver of the getaway vehicle and a clear picture of the license plate. I concealed the negatives and the contact sheet between the pages of one of my art books and slipped it behind the armoire.

I plunged into my classes — Architectural Theory, Case Studies in Engineering, Pre-Thesis Research and my studio on Urban Design. Monica, an old girlfriend I first met when we were involved in a heated student union election, turned up in my Architectural Theory class. The last time we were together it hadn't worked because Monica was still recovering from a love affair with a former boyfriend who she thought was a genius. Monica and I got reacquainted during a leisurely dinner in a Chinese restaurant, strolled to my apartment and immediately went to bed. It was sublime. She was a slender brunette with small breasts, very uninhibited about sex.

The next morning a phone call from my father woke us. Monica slipped out of bed and strode naked to the kitchen, admiring herself in a long mirror I had leaned against the wall opposite our east-facing window to reflect the morning sun. "Make coffee," I called after her, muffling the receiver. I didn't want to get into a discussion with my father about whom I was talking to. I hoped Pedro had left for class — not that Monica would have been at all embarrassed to encounter him.

My father's voice was strained. "Your mother's still at Claudia's. I can't persuade her to come home, even though she's ordered some construction to be done on our house."

"Bernardo's house," I corrected. I waited a moment. I was not above letting my father feel my irritation. Finally I asked, "Did mother buy tiles in Portugal?"

"Thousands. Very beautiful."

"Blue ones?"

"No, yellows and pinks. I think she's gone a bit cuckoo. She says I'm the one who's cuckoo. Are you studying, Alexandre?"

"Furiously. Are you playing cards?" I asked without thinking. I didn't really want an answer.

"I still have my Wednesday night game. Sometimes Saturday, after lunch. Why change?"

My bus ride from Copacabana to the architecture building at University City was interminable, and I often had to stand all the way. It usually took an hour and a half. Sometimes, when I could get a seat, I would pass the time by sketching the scene I had witnessed in front of the bank in São Paulo. I was fascinated by the choreography — how the getaway car was able to join up to form a convoy with the two cars that nearly hit me, how the three cars were able to dodge heavy traffic and ignore a red light without causing an accident, the positioning of the student lookouts, finally the storming by the cops. The escape had come off flawlessly. When I finally reached the architecture building, I immediately ripped up the drawings and threw them in a trash basket on my way to class.

In the late afternoons I stayed at my drafting table at the university, surrounded by other students working on projects. Monica was there, one of the few women studying architecture and the only woman in my class who planned to have a practice rather than teach architectural history. Her firm body, long and lustrous hair and elegant clothes, which she designed and made herself, were distracting, and not only for me. To make matters more titillating, she fueled herself with bananas that she peeled and ate very deliberately, licking the soft, ripe spots, taking her time as if she were devouring a prick. The ritual, she knew, provoked comments around the studio. I watched her smiling to herself. Her demeanor said, "It's my pleasure to stimulate your fantasies." I wanted to believe that now she slept with me and no one else, but I wasn't sure.

43

Monica had been more active in leftist student politics than I. She had partaken fully in the activities of the student union in the architecture department and had also been an officer in the citywide federation of student unions. I had listened in on the student union debates about how to construct a more egalitarian society in Brazil, but I had not been persuaded by the talk of socialist revolution. I wanted the military government to be gone, but I did not believe that leftist dogma and cant were going to bring that about. The dictatorship wasn't going to be overthrown by a popular uprising. Our mass demonstrations had failed. I had a theory, not shared by my activist classmates, that the generals might be made to step down if they lost the support of businessmen and the rural oligarchies — people like my father's friends in Bauru. I didn't share my father's faith that time would cure every Brazilian ill.

The fourth glorious time Monica and I had sex was on a Sunday morning. We were lying in her small bed in her apartment in Leblon, the residential beach neighborhood adjacent to Ipanema. Her apartment was an all-white studio, its décor carefully thought out. Off to one side a low white coffee table fronted a small white sofa; a tailor's female form for fitting clothes occupied a place of honor in the center of the room. A Swiss sewing machine and a drafting board shared space on a long piece of white laminate that rested on cinder blocks. Monica was fanning her post-coital sweat with a cupped hand. She lit a cigarette. "Someday, Alexandre, you'll be in London or New York, someplace cold, designing a fantastic museum or a hotel, and you'll miss the South Atlantic — the year-round nakedness on the beach." She smiled. "Everything that makes up the intoxicating broth of Rio," she said in a theatrical tone.

"I'll send you a postcard of a depressing frozen lake, you can be sure."

"We keep trying to plant an inappropriate imitation of the Tuileries garden in Brazil," she continued. "It's stupid. I like your idea for cascades in a São Paulo park. It's our way. Brazilians have the instinct for creating beauty out of humble materials. We can use rocks instead of melodramatic statuary. Who needs a formal Parisian park in the tropics?" She was passionate about the work of Roberto Burle Marx, a Brazilian landscape architect famous for finding ways to balance bold concrete-and-glass structures with the welcoming greenery of native plants in gardens and parks. We both enjoyed the experience of walking into the architecture school building through the grove of exotic trees and plantings Burle Marx had selected.

Still sweaty, contentedly spent, we were savoring a few more relaxed moments before plunging into an afternoon of class assignments. We knew our screwing was a diversion, not a grand passion. We had said so explicitly to each other. Neither of us had time to tend to a lover's emotional needs and demands. The phone rang. Monica reluctantly roused herself, ambled to the coffee table and answered it in a low, sexy voice. She turned to me and said, "It's Pedro, calling for you."

I pulled on my briefs and took the phone from her. "A guy telephoned half an hour ago, Alexandre," Pedro said. "I've been trying to get a damn dial tone since he hung up. He says he urgently needs to see some photographs. He didn't give his name. I thought you'd want to know."

"What did you tell him?"

"I said you weren't home and I didn't know when you would be back. He said he was going to come here and wait for you."

"I'll be there in 45 minutes."

Monica was focused on getting her first cup of coffee of the day and on ideas for the cemetery she was designing for her landscape

45

studio. I didn't explain why I had to rush home. No need to involve her in the details of my life. We soaped each other in the shower, got dressed quickly and went out to get a *cafezinho* with lots of sugar at her neighborhood *botequim*. Standing at its convenient sidewalk counter, we gulped down our coffee and kissed goodbye. I took a taxi to my apartment. Pedro wasn't there when I arrived. I had missed him by two minutes. He had propped up a note against some books on my desk where I would be sure to see it:

> 10:33 a.m. — I waited, but the guy didn't show up. Spending the morning on the beach. Fed up with looking like a ghost.
>
> P. S. Careful what you say on the phone. They have ears everywhere listening.

I retrieved my contact sheet from the art book where I had hidden it, studied the tiny pictures with a magnifier for several minutes and put it back. No one showed up at our apartment. Pedro came home from the beach, showered and left to go to a matinee movie and to dinner with a girl. My only relief from fitful reading and drawing was recollecting the lavender scent of Monica's hair. Around 8 p.m., irritated with waiting, I pinned a note on our front door and went for a walk, always restorative to my spirit. I strode along Avenida Atlântica, the wide, crescent-shaped avenue bordering Copacabana's beach, stopping to buy a cheese sandwich, a coconut drink and an ice-cream cone from street vendors along my route. When I got home an hour later, my note was still attached to the door.

Pedro arrived around midnight, looking very pleased with himself. The girl, coyly, had allowed herself to be screwed at her apartment. Pedro really liked her. While he settled himself on the sofa to read *Jornal do Brasil's* Sunday sports pages, I played with ideas for my senior thesis. Unable to concentrate, I invited Pedro to play cards. Normally

46

I wouldn't let myself be distracted from school projects by cards, but I made exceptions. After an evening of unproductive pacing, feeling frenzied because of a looming deadline on an important assignment, I would sometimes suggest a game as a soporific before going to bed. Pedro never had to be coaxed. We never bet money; the loser had to shop for food, a chore we both hated. We were constantly running out of staples. "Just one game of 10-card gin?" I said. "We stop at 100 points. Think of it as our first game this semester. I've had a weird day. I need to unwind."

"One game, Alexandre? Who are you kidding? Barbosas never play one game. With what just happened in your family, I'm amazed you still own a deck of cards."

Pedro showed no sign of wanting to stop playing after it was clear he would win the first game. A discreet rap on the door interrupted my adding up the score.

"Alexandre Barbosa?"

I nodded at the stocky stranger at the door. He quickly entered our narrow foyer and shut the door. He was older than I, maybe 25 or 26. He wore jeans and a white T-shirt. "Someone from São Paulo asked me to look at some pictures you took. I'm Celso." We shook hands. "The cops have been tailing me all day. I had to make sure I lost them."

His manner was weary. I remarked that he looked exhausted.

"I haven't slept more than four hours a night in the last week. And never in the same berth."

"You're a seaman?"

"Used to be. What made you guess that?"

"You said 'berth.'"

Pedro got up from our game, introduced himself and disappeared into the kitchen, offering to make sandwiches. I said, "Pedro and I

47

are cousins. Maybe you know his brother, Heitor? He was in medical school until last semester. Now he's underground."

"I don't think so. We all change our identities. Let me see the pictures."

Celso sat down on the sofa. I retrieved the contact sheet and handed him the magnifying glass. He scanned the pictures first cursorily, then intently. I saw him pause on the image of the license plate. I said, "Anyone nearby could have memorized the license number and given it to the cops."

"Those cars were stolen and abandoned immediately. It's your pictures of the guys that matter. Who's seen them?"

"Only me and Pedro."

"You didn't show them to a girlfriend?"

"Hell no."

"Other than you and Pedro, who's been in this apartment?"

"Girls from the university. Maybe three or four."

"Maid?"

"Don't have one."

"If the police got hold of these, they'd be plastered all over the country in hours. Why'd you keep them?"

"The girl in São Paulo said someone might want to get in touch with me —"

"Laila should have captured your film. She's new. Give me a match." Celso burned the negatives and the contact sheet in our glass ashtray. The smell of smoke brought Pedro running. He saw the evidence smoldering and went back to the kitchen. He returned with sandwiches and mineral water. "We've got beer," he said to Celso. "Do you want one?"

"Thanks, I don't drink alcohol. Water's fine."

"The robbery was three weeks ago," I said. "How come it took you so long to worry about my pictures?"

"Two days ago, one of the drivers thought he was being followed. We're checking every possible way he could have been identified. He's not the one you photographed." The newspapers had not specified the amount taken in the robbery. Pedro and I were curious. "Something around 68,000 *cruzeiros novos*," Celso said when I asked. In those days that would have been worth about $17,000 — four *cruzeiros novos* to the dollar.

"Whoo . . . not bad," Pedro said. "My group at the university is broke and frustrated, but nobody's got the guts —"

Celso cut him off. "One miscalculation . . . " He drew his forefinger across his throat. He got up to leave. I invited him to spend the night. "Too dangerous for you. I can't guarantee the cops didn't follow me to this building. If they figured out I stayed here — you know the rest." Celso finished his sandwich and slipped out into the night.

While Pedro was collecting the sandwich plates, he said, "You need to become a famous architect, Alexandre. Oscar Niemeyer gets away with his communist sympathies only because the world has its eyes on him."

"At least, so far, it's working for Niemeyer," I said.

We were too jumpy to go to bed. We went back to playing cards — gin, hearts, casino — until dawn. At first light I made *maté*, the strong tea *gaúchos* drink to keep awake in the saddle. It had been a parting gift from one of Pedro's girlfriends. At 7 we put the cards away and got ready for class. "My group is endless talk," Pedro said on the way to the shower. "All we do is hang out, drink beer and plan things that never come off."

"Like what?"

"Getting some guns."

"Have you ever had target practice?" I asked.

"No. I didn't grow up on a *fazenda* like you."

"Ever shot a gun, at least?"

"Alexandre, you're getting bogged down in details that can easily be solved. You're missing my point."

But I wasn't missing his point. Not many who mouthed a commitment to restoring democracy in Brazil had Heitor's steady courage. Or Celso's.

II

The next day I sat in my class on architectural theory, feeling I should be studying Mussolini's Rome. Or Hitler's Berlin. Architecture under dictatorship. When my father telephoned the following Sunday morning, I reeled off my comparisons.

"You're forgetting a very important example," he said. "Stalin's Moscow. Or do you consider Stalin on the plus side of your ledger? When you've lived as long as I have you learn that not all oppression comes from the right. Nothing would make me happier than to see Costa e Silva and his supporters backed off. And the Americans, too, for that matter. I hope you're not feeling romantic."

"What's that supposed to mean, *papai*?"

"Simply that I hope you aren't still thinking too much about that portrait of my ancestor."

"He's my ancestor, too. He's inspiring."

"He was hanged. *Point final.*" There was a long silence on his end. "Has your mother told you her latest plan? She wants to study architecture in São Paulo, at the university. She thinks she's missed her calling. I told her she was doing a superb job remodeling her bathroom. That was my undoing."

"She's serious about moving to São Paulo?"

"She hasn't moved home. Your aunt is supporting her agenda. The two of them are nuts. The piano tuner was here. I started my lessons. If your mother can have a calling, so can I. In a few years, who knows, I could give a concert. Don't underestimate my resolve."

"That's the last thing I'd do."

"I might have to give up cards to really practice. I'm going to send you some money. Bernardo's started paying me to manage the *fazenda*. He's not really interested in overseeing day-to-day activities."

"Let me know when Mother starts discussing the structural systems of ferroconcrete."

"My God, Alexandre, do you think it could come to that?"

By mid-April, my father had adopted a schedule of calling every Sunday morning to complain about my mother's increasing independence. I had to agree with Pedro that my parents' situation resembled grand opera. My mother called erratically at any hour of the day or night, but only to discuss impersonal matters: "I found Portugal stuck in the past, Alexandre. Maybe it's because of their climate that they don't take chances on new buildings. We're so fortunate we don't need heating systems or have to worry about earthquakes. And they don't have a giant like Oscar Niemeyer. I should have studied architecture. Your talent comes from my side of the family, you realize. I'm considering visiting Brasília. What a dream it is. This country of ours can keep your eyes busy. You're lucky to be a Brazilian."

"But born in Washington, *mãe*."

"Only by accident, because we were there while your father was studying."

Saturdays I had lunch with Maria Rita and Paulo at their apartment in Ipanema. It was the only time I allowed myself a few hours off to relax, eat an unhurried, well-balanced meal and forget studying. Since returning to school in March, I never had time to loaf on the beach. No hardworking architecture students did. I even had to hide from the sun because I wasn't accustomed to it. "You like looking white as plaster?" Maria Rita teased. "A good-looking guy should have a tan."

Paulo had been expecting his first overseas assignment from the Ministry of External Relations at any time. They had rented a small apartment, thinking it would be a temporary arrangement. They got an unpleasant surprise when it was announced that a handful of diplomats at the ministry were losing their political rights and had been forced to retire without pensions. Orlando Pacheco, Paulo's friend and mentor, was one of them. This rebuke, coming after Orlando's 18 years of distinguished service, meant he couldn't vote for 10 years or express political opinions in public. He had been singled out by the military government for punishment because of his well-known leftist leanings. Maria Rita had telephoned me with the news as soon as she learned it.

When I arrived on Saturday for lunch Paulo said, "Even dunces can put two and two together. Everyone knows I was Orlando's protégé. At the moment Orlando's scrambling to find work doing translations of Shakespeare for some publisher in Lisbon. It's monstrous. The ministry never should have caved in to the military."

The family worried how this outrage might affect Paulo's career. At the ministry Paulo was stunned into an enraged silence. I mentioned to him that my father never failed to ask what I knew about his prospects for an overseas posting. "No word yet," Paulo said. "I sincerely doubt my employment's in danger, but I got switched from the political section to administration, which I hate. Believe me, I watch what I say around the ministry and I'm not pestering anybody to get assigned to one of our Elizabeth Arden posts — London, Paris or Rome.

That would definitely antagonize certain diplomats who I wish would forget I'm around."

III

Monica Paiva was unsettling me. One minute her open, generous sensuality belonged to me, but an hour later I felt her aloneness, a sort of middle-of-the-night desperation. Her conversation would be consistent and clear for a while then, suddenly, out of focus, as if she were abruptly astigmatic.

"Did you read that feminists burned their bras and marched outside the Miss America Pageant?" she asked.

"You don't even wear a bra," I said.

"I do sometimes."

"I like it when you don't."

"Alexandre, do you ever feel like you're being sucked in by dark thoughts?"

"Sure. Doesn't everybody feel that way once in a while?"

"No, I mean really sucked in. I have a dark, irrational space I retreat to."

"It takes irrationality to create," I said.

"No, artists should have clear heads. It's the interpreters who need to be irrational so they can criticize." She reached into her purse for a cigarette. "You've been distracted lately," she said.

"I can't make up my mind what I want to do for my senior thesis. I have to jump one way or another soon." I left it at that. I didn't see any reason to burden her with my internal struggle over how to join the resistance in a serious way.

"We're living under subtle repression," she said. "Bras are a part of it."

"There's nothing subtle about the Brazilian military, Monica."

I knew the source of her black moods and dark thoughts. It was a story known to everyone in the architecture department. Her brother, Jayme, also an architecture student, one year ahead of us, had disappeared. "Disappeared" was the euphemism for someone vanishing while in police or military custody. Referring to someone as disappeared carried the strong possibility that the person would never be seen again. Jayme had helped a group of student protesters overturn a police van at a demonstration in June, a few weeks before fall semester ended. The driver fled, but a truckload of *Policia Militar* happened to be passing by. Jayme was arrested. It had taken Monica's family three weeks to find out that he had been taken to the Navy barracks on Cobra Island. They didn't know where he was now, or even if he was alive. Although I didn't know Jayme well, we had attended some of the same student union meetings where the political philosophies of Brazil's different guerrilla organizations were debated. Just eight days before he disappeared, we had stood shoulder to shoulder at a downtown student rally.

Some people would have talked endlessly about such a tragedy. Monica didn't. I thought Jayme's disappearance had broken her spirit and left her with unspeakable sadness. It had been months since she had been involved in student union activities. When I asked her if she was afraid for herself, she didn't answer. My numerous reasons for hating the military multiplied when we started dating. Now my last thoughts when I drifted off to sleep and my first upon awakening were of Jayme and my beloved cousin, Oswaldo, who had shown me the wonders of seeing the earth from a glider, his eye now beaten blind by police thugs.

One night, lightheaded from hours of studying, Monica and I felt entitled to an extravagance. It was nearly midnight when we arrived at

Rio's most soigné and expensive hotel, the Copacabana Palace, to have a beer at its poolside café. Tourists floating on plastic inner tubes were laughing loudly and splashing each other. Their shouts in a jumble of languages carried over the water. A bow-tied waiter seated us and I ordered two expensive Dutch beers. Monica waved her hand at the people in the pool. "Jet-setters having fun in romantic Rio."

"Something we've had taken away from us," I said. "We're compelled to go around succumbing to our dark thoughts."

"Don't be serious tonight, Alexandre. I wish we could make love over there behind those palms."

"I dare you," I said.

"Is that a bet?"

"No. You've read too many fairy-tale novels. 'The animate night, satiny music drifting over the dance floor, weightless bubbles of color held in the air ...'"

"That's it, Alexandre, the perfect romance-novel sentence. Did you make it up or memorize some trash?"

"Half and half."

Monica got up, reached for my hand and pulled me to my feet. As we walked toward a collection of tall plants, she rubbed my hand over the full curve of her buttocks. I was aroused. "They'll think you're a prostitute and throw us out," I said.

"Want to back out?"

I didn't answer.

We reached a dark corner midway between the main hotel and the separate, high-rise annex on the opposite side of the pool. Sentry palms and philodendron were planted in large decorative tubs. The concealment was scanty. I put my hands under Monica's sweater and stroked

55

her breasts. She wriggled her hips against my pelvis. I could hear waiters taking orders and dishes being set down on glass tabletops not far away.

"The staff is too occupied to notice us," she whispered.

The free-and-easy tourists got out of the pool. One of the girls had left her towel on a chaise directly in front of our hiding place. I started to move away from Monica, but she put her hands firmly over mine on her breasts. I could see the girl wrap a towel around her shoulders. A young man walked over to her. "Cold?" he asked in English. "I'll warm you up in the room." They walked away toward a side entrance of the hotel. I pulled Monica's miniskirt up and slipped my hand inside her bikini pants. She was wet. I kissed her nipples, her neck, caressed her buttocks, slipped my finger inside her. Monica unzipped my trousers and fondled me.

The couple came back. I froze. "Do you see it?" the woman tourist said.

The man bent down and retrieved a bathing cap. "I found it." They hurried away.

I recovered my equilibrium, took the chance and entered Monica. She balanced on my bent knees and set up a rhythm against me. "Slow down," I said, "or I won't be able to wait."

"Shush, darling."

"You're milking me."

We moved together. It was delirious. I buried my face in her neck. If someone was watching, I wouldn't see. It was almost impossible not to come quickly. "Is this what you had in mind?" I asked, still trying to hold back.

"Exactly what I had in mind."

I stroked her buttocks. She was miraculous. "I hope you came too," I said after I couldn't wait any longer.

"I did, with you."

My legs felt unsteady from too much pleasure. I kissed her, licking inside her mouth, still feeling an intense sensation. She broke off our kiss in soft laughter, whispering, "Now we can finish our pricey beers and go back to studying. Damn, I left my purse at our table and I don't have a tissue." As we walked back to our table, my legs still wobbly, we held hands. I didn't care whether we had been seen. Would the house detective ask us to leave immediately? Okay, we would.

Monica was testing me.

CHAPTER FIVE

I

No one I knew had intended to become a full-time militant. Certainly I didn't. It just happened to some of us because there wasn't any space where political ideas could be expressed. All roads were blocked. By 1969 the formula to resist the generals was to get funds by robbing banks, buy arms — better yet, break into military arsenals and steal weapons — disrupt universities, disrupt whatever you could get away with. The bank robbers didn't think they were stealing — they were expropriating money in the name of justice. The enterprise of opposition was built on an elaborate structure of theory and intense rhetoric that collapsed years later when it was undermined by *glasnost* and *perestroika*.

My complicated existence was exacting its toll. Celso had come after my photographs, but he made no attempt to recruit me and I never expected to see him again. At the same time that I was looking for a way to join the armed struggle, I demanded of myself that I be an academic star. I felt overloaded with class assignments, and I still had not settled on a topic for my thesis. If these problems weren't enough, I could always rely on phone calls from my parents to set off additional rounds of worry.

In spite of the government's strict enforcement of its ban on demonstrations, Heitor's group organized a "lightning" May Day rally on the very day the Communist world was parading its immense show of infantry and armaments. Pedro decided to participate in the taunt. I couldn't persuade myself to take time from my studies for a symbolic pinprick.

Shortly before the downtown demonstration was to get under way, someone — perhaps a university official — tipped off the police that two members of Heitor's group were duplicating a manifesto in the university's Engineering Building. The cops arrived, rounded up the student mimeographers and beat them savagely in the men's room. Pedro heard their cries from his laboratory down the hall. Sickened, he knew he could do nothing until the police left. From his lab window he could see the police van parked in front of the building. When he saw the cops depart he, along with other students, ran to the men's room. Pedro managed to put the two most severely injured students into a taxi and he climbed in after them. He told the driver to take them to the emergency room of Souza Aguiar Municipal Hospital nearby. One of the students mumbled, "No, no hospital." It was rumored that the police would sometimes follow injured students to a hospital, only to arrest them there. As the cab threaded through traffic, Pedro watched out the back window. When he was confident that no police car was following them, he redirected the driver to our apartment. After dark, Heitor appeared with his medical bag and sewed up their cuts. I assisted. I had thought repairing a body was related to architecture — both required careful solutions to three-dimensional problems — but with these wounds, cleanliness was the main concern. Heitor told the students that they needed to go a hospital as soon as they could to be checked for internal injuries.

Heitor's rally had been calculated to irritate the government, but it did more — it ignited a progression of reciprocal sallies. Under orders from the government, the University's Institute of Social Sciences locked out its students. In response, students in diverse departments boycotted their classes, which, in turn, provoked the administration to suspend all classes for the rest of the week. I went to the beach with Monica and got a sunburn.

Pedro dropped the girl he had been seeing and began dating a very attractive sociology student who aspired to celebrity as a journalist. We both thought Silvia had a winning personality. Within two weeks of their first date, she was sleeping in Pedro's bed every night. Exhausted

59

from studying, the three of us would debate our proper role in the fight for freedom. One evening, after yet another circular discussion, I stayed up to play solitaire after Silvia and Pedro had gone to bed. I liked to let winning or losing at solitaire foretell my future: If I won a game, it meant I would finish a difficult project on time. A second win predicted that my professor would think my solution was brilliant. If I lost, my future as an architecture student was in peril. In a semi-robotic state, I won two out of five games. I decided to take a chance and pose the most urgent and momentous of the many questions on my mind. Winning would be a signal from God — it was time for me to join the fight against the military right now. My first time through the deck, I liberated three face-down cards, including two aces. The last 18 hidden cards were easy to uncover.

Around 2 in the morning, mulling the consequences of my victory, I took a bus downtown to Mauá Square, the beginning point of Rio's kilometers-long expanse of docks. I had left the apartment with the ridiculous idea of looking for Celso where sailors hung out. My plan was unfocused, to say the least. Rattling at high speed along the Aterro, the giant park that flanked Guanabara Bay, no traffic on the road, no passengers on the bus but me, every window wide open, I tried to suppress thoughts of my parents' reaction if they found out about my resolve. "Joining the resistance, Alexandre! We'd sooner your glider made a crash landing. At least you'd have a chance to walk away." As the bus approached the port, thoughts of what to say to Monica and how she might respond preoccupied me. Monica and I no longer regarded each other just as casual lovers, although we insisted we did. My political activities could endanger her. I was duty bound to break off our relationship.

I got off the bus on Rua Dom Gerardo and walked into the square, stopping Brazilian merchant seamen along the way to describe Celso and ask if they knew him. "What line does he work for? Lloyd

Brasileiro? Linea C?" I didn't know. I didn't even know if he was a merchant seaman or an ex-Navy man, though as I thought about it, the latter was more likely. The Navy was known to cashier sailors suspected of having Marxist sympathies.

I walked past block-long, impregnable warehouses that barred access to the wharves. Behind the gate at the Mauá pier, a passenger ship's superstructure glittered. A few bars of muffled music drifted toward the city. The autumn night was unusually cool. Shivering, I returned to Mauá Square, with its juxtaposition of the sacred and the profane: To the east of the square, situated on a hill commanding a magnificent view of the bay, was the 17th-century São Bento Monastery. Along the western edge of the square was a row of rowdy strip joints. Most of the bars were drearily emptying out. I entered one — the Scandinavia Bar — that still seemed to have some life. Inside were foreign seamen and libidinous cruise-ship passengers. A tame sex show kept them sipping their beers. I drank several, too, before I left to take a bus to Monica's apartment.

It was close to 6 a.m. when I knocked on her door. While I stood waiting for her to open it, I worried about how I would handle the situation if she had a man in her bed. My stroll around the docks had served to break my routine, but it did nothing to clear my head. I worried that I was mythologizing myself into someone I wasn't. Was I being honest? Was getting involved in the armed resistance really a patriotic imperative or just a form of gambling? I wasn't looking forward to the scene with Monica. Would she care one way or the other? She might say, "We were just having fun, Alexandre. If we don't see each other anymore, it's no big deal." Or she might say, "Please don't do it. I really love you and it's dangerous." I even fantasized that she might say, "I'm proud of you. How can I help?" I was beginning to feel sleepy and foolish.

"Couldn't sleep?" she said when she opened the door, almost as if

61

she were expecting me. "Have you tried counting backward from 100? It really works." She slipped her arms around me and kissed me on the mouth. Her breath was sweet. Her robe fell open.

"I wasn't sure I should come," I said, relieved to see she was alone.

"Just because we haven't made commitments to each other?"

"Something like that."

"Want some coffee? We'll have to get some on the street. I haven't got any. I hate housekeeping."

"I've been up all night."

She took my hand and led me to her bed. Bits of luxurious fabrics were scattered around the room and on top of her sewing machine. I realized that the robe she had thrown on was actually a half-sewn evening gown. "I'm designing costumes for a play," she said, reading my mind. "I get paid if they sell enough tickets." She took off her gown and slipped into bed.

"Can I use your toothbrush? I've been drinking beer."

"I noticed. Use the one on the right. I save it for visitors."

I made a face of revulsion.

"Just kidding. It's brand new."

I brushed my teeth and washed my face. When I sat down on the edge of the bed to take off my jeans, Monica reached over and undid the buttons on my fly.

"No erection," she said.

"I've got things on my mind."

I got into bed and embraced her. She massaged my shoulders. I was beginning to relax when her alarm clock went off. "*Merda.* Have you got an early class?" I asked.

"A meeting."

"I need to talk to you."

She kissed me. "I'm sorry, Alexandre, I've got to go. You can stay here."

"Is your meeting that important?"

She got out of bed, but not before she teased me until I was aroused. "Now what am I supposed to do?" I watched her put on a brown miniskirt and a brown T-shirt. Except when she wore jeans, her outfits were monochromatic — either all black, all brown or all white. She picked up a tortoiseshell comb and drew it quickly through her long, silky hair. She came over to the bed, pulled back the sheet and placed her hand on my still-erect prick.

"Do you know what Chairman Mao said?" she asked.

"On what subject?"

"'Revolution is not a dinner party.' I'll be back in three hours. Will you be here?"

"No. I've got studio."

We agreed to meet at my apartment in the evening. "Have you got an unused toothbrush, Alexandre?"

"I'll buy one."

I fell asleep in Monica's bed. I could smell the perfume of her body on the sheets, mixed with the scent of her English lavender soap. I drifted fitfully into and out of sleep, each time returning to the same bizarre dream about a fat man from Buenos Aires trying to sell Fazenda Maraíba to my father. I woke up disoriented, thinking I was in my bedroom at the *fazenda*.

Monica arrived at my apartment much later than I expected. I had been tense waiting for her. She kissed my cheek, brushed by me and sat down on the sofa. "What do you want to tell me?"

"When I came to your apartment this morning, I'd spent the night downtown at the docks, just wandering, thinking things through. I don't think we should see each other anymore outside of class, Monica. I've made up my mind to join a militant group. Being close to me could put you in danger."

She said nothing for what seemed like several minutes while she considered my statement. "I didn't take you for that kind of subversive," she said at last. Then she fell silent again, gathering her thoughts.

I wasn't obliged to explain my reasoning to her. I imagined giving her an excuse to be glad to be rid of me: "I've enjoyed fucking you, Monica. You are an exciting, talented person. But I have to be frank — for me it was nothing more than fun. Let's not complicate things."

Before I made up my mind what to say, she finally broke the heavy silence. "Besides, Alexandre, there are other, less dangerous ways to participate. You could join a support group on the media side."

"All they do is mimeograph leaflets and distribute them at factory entrances," I said.

"You're wrong about the importance of what they do. With censorship, how else can people know the truth? We have a moral duty to publicize what our government is up to."

"We? Are you in a media group?"

"Eight months ago I joined AP. I haven't told you because I didn't want you to join just to get my approval."

AP (Popular Action) was a militant Maoist organization. All the weeks we had been together, I had misjudged her! She had not been frightened off by Jayme's disappearance, not paralyzed — rather the opposite. She had been taking risks while I had been making disparaging remarks about the futility of Heitor's efforts to change the country and Pedro's beery sessions with his garrulous Trotskyite group. Compared with Monica, I was less than a raw recruit. I felt a mixture of embarrassment and awe. It took me a minute or two to get my bearings. "When you talked about feeling sucked in by dark thoughts ... now I

64

get it. They just let you join? What's it like? How did you do it? I thought you had to prove your commitment. Criticize your bourgeois family — be ashamed of them."

She explained how AP had indoctrinated her in stages. At first she participated in lecture groups and debates. Later she was placed in a group of new recruits and put through an intense period of ideological training. She was given a code name and tasks to perform. Little by little, AP introduced her into their hierarchy of secrets. "It's a pyramid structure," she said, "with one person from each cell being the only contact with the cell above it. A cell is supposed to dissolve if one of its members is caught. We have emergency arrangements to reorganize after a cell shuts down."

"You have more patience than I do to sit through an indoctrination of Marxist ideology," I said. "It seems to me the Maoist organizations do more talking than acting. Am I wrong?"

"First you have to build a wide front among the common people before the revolution can spread. The Maoists understand that."

We agreed that there were strong reasons why I shouldn't join her organization, even if I could persuade them to accept me. We would be endangering each other if one of us were caught and tortured to reveal information about the other. We both valued our independence, our self-determined schedules. We weren't ready for vows.

In the early morning I heard Pedro and Silvia leave for class. Monica awoke and, as usual, she walked naked to the bathroom, then, still naked, to the kitchen to make coffee. She returned with two coffee cups, sat on the edge of the bed and pointed to a scar on her hip. "When I went to the Navy barracks on Cobra Island to try to see Jayme, a lieutenant took me into a room, pulled down my jeans and my underpants, put me over his knee and spanked me. He was getting off — I could feel his erection. He wore a ring with a big stone. It broke my skin, and he spit in the wound."

"Jesus Christ, Monica! Why didn't you tell me?" I felt sick. I didn't know how to respond. Should I caress her scar? I had noticed it before, but never made anything of it. I looked directly into her eyes. "You took a terrible risk going to Cobra Island. You're the bravest person I know."

She shook her head slowly. "As far as my beating is concerned, it's over, Alexandre. We have to move forward." She got up, put on one of my shirts, lighted a cigarette and retook her seat on the bed. "I don't believe in adopting a survival strategy and waiting for more favorable times. It's been 10 months since Jayme disappeared. He's enormously talented, everybody said so. We planned to have our own architecture firm together. For his senior thesis he was designing an aquarium in Flamengo Park with a fantastic connection by pedestrian tube to the Museum of Modern Art. He could be in a prison anywhere in Brazil — or dead." She leaned against me for a moment, then abruptly sat up straight, full of energy. "By strategically starting the fight it can spread out, Alexandre. A spark can set a prairie on fire."

II

A few evenings later, while Monica went to the theater to make last-minute adjustments to her costumes and Pedro and I studied at home, my mother telephoned. It was going to be my first exercise in concealing my intentions from my parents. "When I drove out to the *fazenda* last week to take care of a few things ..." she said, then hesitated. "My herb garden is in desperate need of attention ... Your father is so miserable without me ... Even Bernardo encouraged me. So here I am. Home."

"Father said you had plans to study architecture in São Paulo."

"Did he mention that?"

"Yes, and he said he was astonished by your design for your bathroom."

"Really! I'm glad he was impressed. I've hired an architecture tutor. I'm not sure he knows more than I do. So far we've had one discussion about Le Corbusier's sketches for the Ministry of Education and Culture. Have you chosen a thesis project?"

I told her I had decided to design affordable housing for the Amazon. She immediately began to envisage the horrors of my traveling to that pestilent place. "With good reason, no Machado or Barbosa has ever set foot there, Alexandre. I sincerely hope you don't plan to be the first in our family to take the risk. And on the subject of dangerous activities, thank God those street demonstrations in Rio are finished. When your hand was injured last year in one of those marches, your father and I almost told you to come home."

"Well, things are quiet now, *mãe*. So don't worry."

The next afternoon I stopped by Monica's drafting table to look at her cemetery project. I made several suggestions, which she quickly rejected. We walked outside to buy a Coke at a food trailer and stood under its awning. We argued about who had left stray hairs on the bathroom sink, whether we needed more time apart to study, the most reliable way to fund the resistance, when and where weapons should be used. We were surrounded by dusty weeds that passed for grass. To avoid her glower, I scanned the vast, ugly, empty space that surrounded the university's functional, but unattractive, buildings. The landscape of University City on Fundão Island was gray, and everything — natural and man-made — needed upkeep and repair. Still upset, Monica returned to her drafting table. When my last class was over, I went home.

After midnight I was washing dishes, brooding over the asinine argument I'd had with Monica. It was spawned, I knew, by the burdens

67

we carried. Pedro and Silvia were out. Before I realized he had entered the room, Heitor was standing beside me at the kitchen sink. "Christ, Heitor!" I dropped a glass and it broke in the sink. Weeks earlier, Pedro had given him a key.

"Sorry. I guess I'm getting too used to walking on cats' feet."

Heitor accepted my offer of a beer. We stood in the kitchen, chatting. "I'm through being a spectator, Heitor."

He looked at me quizzically. "That's a surprise."

"It shouldn't be." I told him about meeting Celso and that I thought he belonged to an underground group composed of former Navy men.

"If your parents had any idea what you're contemplating, Uncle Jorge Antônio would give up cards for the rest of his life to stop you."

"I think these Navy guys really know how to execute a robbery."

"Is that meant to be an invidious comparison?" Heitor stalked off to the living room with his beer.

I finished throwing away the pieces of broken glass and followed him. "I'm not undervaluing your group's contribution, Heitor."

"Forget it. I'll ask around if anybody knows a Navy group."

Three days later, Heitor reported that he had come up empty-handed. I took this as a sign that Celso's group was committed to rigorously protecting its security.

III

During the second week of May two newspaper stories caught my attention, although I didn't recognize their significance immediately. I clipped the first one Wednesday and filed it with my notes for my urban-design project. On Friday I clipped the second. The first article described robberies on consecutive days at two branches of Banco do Brasil in downtown Rio:

On May 14, a daring bank robbery at Banco do Brasil on Rua Primeiro de Março was conducted in paramilitary fashion. Five men with submachine guns held pedestrians at bay along the heavily trafficked street. Seven armed men strode past them into the bank. The holdup, witnesses recalled later, was conducted in silence and was over in less than 10 minutes. The robbers made off with 116,000 *cruzeiros novos*. The next day a second branch of Banco do Brasil was robbed on Rua Senador Dantas using the same strategy. Pedestrians outside the bank were held at a distance while the robbery took place. The robbers escaped with 80,000 *cruzeiros novos* in the second robbery.

Authorities say at least some recent holdups have been carried out by a shadowy group of longtime Communists and young radical recruits led by Carlos Marighella, a 58-year-old former Congressman who bolted from the Communist Party in August 1967 and founded ALN (National Liberation Action).

The provisions of the national-security law have been extended to apply to bank robbers as well as persons charged with guerrilla warfare, terrorism and sabotage. Bank robberies, which used to be rare in Brazil, have become frequent in São Paulo and Rio since late 1967. It is believed that many of these holdups were staged in order to fill revolutionary war chests. In cases of bank robberies for anti-government purposes, penalties are to be increased by half.

Friday's news story reported that on Thursday a neighborhood bank had been robbed in Rio's North Zone and that inflammatory pamphlets were found at the scene. The same pamphlets had been left at the two downtown Banco do Brasil branches robbed earlier in the week. The story did not report how much money had been taken.

By Sunday evening my quarrel with Monica was forgotten. She was in my arms asleep when I suddenly awoke with a thought. I didn't need to join an existing group to participate in the resistance. I could rob a bank myself and contribute the money to the armed fight. I would give the money to Heitor's group. And to Monica's. I crept out of bed to fetch the news articles and read them again in the kitchen, then went back to bed and fell asleep.

In the morning I kept my plan to myself. I fantasized that one afternoon I would simply walk into the apartment with a sack full of money. My contribution. Monica would be completely astounded. I would propose a celebratory grope in the Copacabana Palace Hotel pool, right under the noses of the paunchy bankers whose money I had expropriated.

Away from the commerce of downtown and the beaches of the South Zone, Rio's North Zone neighborhoods were sleepy, working-class and remote. Because of the growing number of robberies in central Rio, the big downtown banks had begun taking steps to guard their money. As soon as cash deposits coming through the front door began to add up, the cash was rushed out the back door to the Central Bank of Brazil via armored truck. It had been clever of the robbers to shift their focus from downtown, even though at first their strategy seemed to run counter to logic. While the city's financial activity and cash were concentrated downtown, a bank robbery in the North Zone would meet little professional resistance although the haul would, no doubt, be less. I didn't know my way around the North Zone, and neither did any of my affluent *carioca* fellow students. They were born in the South Zone, raised in its pleasure-seeking beach environment,

70

and would sooner go to Europe than visit the North Zone. I set out to explore.

After classes I started taking buses to the neighborhoods of Méier, Vila Isabel and São Cristovão. I found what I was looking for in Méier: a small private bank, Banco Boavista, located on a corner directly across from a farmers market that operated Tuesday and Friday mornings. If I couldn't make it to a getaway car, I could play hide-and-seek among the beef and pig carcasses. For three days I skipped classes and watched the activity in the neighborhood. On the commercial streets, housewives in loose housedresses and rubber-thong sandals shopped and ran errands. Sometimes they stopped at a *botequim's* outside counter to drink a *cafezinho* and have a chat. Their small children fussed and tugged at their bare legs.

I observed Banco Boavista's activities and layout from a counter reserved for customers needing to fill out forms. There were few women patrons. Skinny men in shoddy shirts and shiny pants did the banking. They looked like porters, postal clerks, pensioners, bookkeepers. I ducked into the bathroom to see if it had a window. It didn't.

Halfway down the block I stopped to ask a woman the location of the nearest police station. She didn't know. A man overheard my question. Waving his arm in a wide, meaningless direction, he said, "It's no use going with your complaint. The cops are worse than lazy." For my planning purposes, there was no such thing as a lethargic cop. I located the station. During three hours roaming the neighborhood, I didn't see any cruising *Policia Militar* cars.

I should have been questioning my motives and worrying about the consequences for my studies, but at that moment what I really felt was exhilaration and release. Finally I was moving from endless talk to action. I started staying up very late to study, or I never went to bed at all. Random thoughts interrupted my concentration. I was running

71

on a combination of catnaps, self-confidence and adrenaline. Without telling Monica why, I let my beard grow so I could instantly change my appearance by shaving. "It makes you look older," she said.

I had begun my double life.

IV

Where should I look for accomplices? The obvious person to approach was Pedro. I asked him, "Are you willing to rob a bank with me? I've picked out a good candidate in Méier."

"I'd love to. And afterward we can attack Army installations and police stations and remove their weapons."

"I'm serious."

"You've got the wrong guy, Alexandre. Talk to Heitor. You want to know what I really think? I think the armed struggle is crap. It won't work in Brazil."

"What choice do we have? Should we give up? My nutty father — and we both know how impractical he can be — says we should just wait till the military get bored and go back to their barracks. He says the resistance just keeps them interested and postpones the end of it. He won't face the fact he lost Fazenda Maraíba, either. If you won't do it, I'll find someone else. Not a word about this to Monica or Silvia."

The next day Pedro surprised me. He introduced me to one of his engineering classmates who was acquainted with a group that was impatient with the pace of militant action. They had read Marighella's *Minimanual of the Urban Guerrilla* and wanted to follow his decentralized strategy for armed rebellion. They were considering everything — kidnapping, bank robbery, fabricating dynamite. Roberto, their leader, a mathematics student, was interested in my plan.

CHAPTER SIX

I

The following morning, Tuesday, Roberto and I took the bus to Méier to observe the bank on a day when the farmers market was open. I had brought a string bag, the kind that food shoppers used, so we could blend in with the crowd. Roberto slipped his yellow English sunglasses into his pocket. They were out of place in Méier.

We got off the bus a block away from the bustling market and threaded our way through streets temporarily closed to traffic, taking note of where the market ended and normal traffic resumed. The shoppers and the vendors seemed to have long-standing relationships with each other; they shouted good-natured greetings and bargained. We wandered, taking in the friendly atmosphere, noticing a collection of large storage boxes where we might hide briefly if we were being chased on foot. I filled my string bag with okra, mangoes and star fruit, but avoided unnecessary conversation with the vendor. I didn't want to be remembered. "It's your normal neighborhood market," Roberto said. "It could be anywhere."

I pointed out the cluster of more substantial stalls selling refrigerated food. If we had to run, they would block our way, but we could easily vault over the displays of produce spread out on low cardboard boxes and on blankets covering the sidewalk. We scouted the small side streets radiating off the market for places to hide the money. If we were chased by the police on foot, our plan was to dump the money and get lost in the crowd.

"Don't worry," Roberto said, tapping the side of his head with his index finger, "the location of every useful detail is filed away in here."

Even on a market day, the street in front of the bank carried traffic, though a few vendors had set up flimsy stalls on the sidewalk directly

73

opposite the bank. We perched on the outdoor stools of a *botequim* where we could survey the activity in front of the bank and ordered two shots of *cachaça*. Roberto worried about the bank's large smoked-glass front window until he realized that it functioned in daylight as a one-way mirror. No one could see inside from the street. At a second *botequim* we switched from raw rum to *cafezinhos* and ate ham sandwiches while I sketched a map of the neighborhood on a napkin and suggested a plan: One man would loiter on the street to warn us if he saw the police. We would have two escape cars — one to head southwest toward Encantado, the other north toward Cachambi. Roberto and I would rob the bank. Roberto said it was our obligation to make a political speech in the bank, in addition to scattering leaflets demanding an end to the dictatorship.

In 1969 Rio's banks didn't yet have security guards, locked doors, timers on vaults and cameras. The political left, fighting against the dictatorship, started the trend of robbing banks — unintentionally showing the common criminals how it could be done. Five or six guys carrying heavy artillery in cloth sacks would walk into a bank, calm everybody down and tell them to stay quiet. They wouldn't wear masks. Their getaway car would be waiting in front with its doors open. We didn't think we had to follow the left's prevailing formula strictly. I had my hunting rifle and Roberto could get his uncle's Colt .45, which had not been fired since World War II. Roberto's uncle had been a major in the Brazilian Expeditionary Force, fighting alongside the Allied forces in Italy. An American officer had given his uncle the sidearm as a souvenir.

We decided to rob the bank at 10:15, when the market would be in full swing. We planned the robbery for a week from Friday, which gave us 10 days to rehearse.

The following morning, I telephoned my father. Because of the unreliability of the phones and my father's unpredictable schedule, I

74

was never sure when I could reach him. It was important that I talk to him because this might be my only chance for a leave-taking in case we were caught. I tried to keep emotion out of my voice.

"This is unusual, Alexandre. I normally call you Sunday morning. Do you need money? I'll send you some."

"I don't need money, *papai*, thanks for asking. How are the Nelores?"

"Ugly and beautiful as ever. How's your reorganization of central São Paulo coming along?"

"I present my plan in class tomorrow. I think my solutions really work. I just hope my professors agree."

"And your Amazon village?"

"Right now I'm just doing research on the local conditions and sketching preliminary ideas. I have until the end of next semester to finish."

"Your mother's here. She wants to talk to you."

"Wait."

"Something wrong?"

"Let's finish talking."

"Your mother's making plans to sell most of our antiques. And the religious art. I don't care if she does, as long as she leaves my piano and the library alone."

"I'm getting more involved politically, *papai*."

"Is that why you called? You want my approval?"

"It's up to the students now. I've decided to join a serious group."

"Serious groups do serious things."

"That's the point, isn't it?"

"I'm coming to Rio, Alexandre. I won't tell your mother why."

"*Papai* …" He rang off. I called back. "It's not necessary, *papai*. I'm really busy."

"So am I."

He rang off again.

Twenty minutes later the phone rang again. It was Roberto. "Change in schedule. It has to be this Friday."

"Fuck! Why the rush? We need time to reconnoiter the escape routes. We're amateurs."

"An opportunity's come up, and it won't wait."

"I need to know the justification for the change."

"Are you having second thoughts?"

"It's not that. In the midst of all this, I'm still trying to be a student."

"We all are."

We met at the Mathematics Building at noon. Roberto outlined the situation: Fifteen 9 mm Uzis were sitting in cartons labeled "textiles" on a Rio dock. If we acted fast, we could buy them through a crooked customs inspector. "This chance won't come around again, Alexandre. The shipment's en route to Bolivia. Think about it. If we rob the bank now, we might have enough to buy all of them! Fifteen Uzis! The world's most famous firearm — light, simple to load, compact. The butt folds up so it's easy to hide." Roberto beamed.

The prospect of getting the Uzis won out over my trepidation. Roberto had picked three members of his group to be our accomplices. He suggested we all meet on Thursday after my presentation in urban-design studio to discuss the final plan.

"They're totally dedicated to the cause," Roberto said. "Plus I'd trust any one of them with my life. César and José study classical

Greek; don't ask me why. Adolfo studies mathematics with me. We've been friends since elementary school. César and Adolfo will be the drivers. José will be the lookout. We always kid him that he's got eyes in the back of his head."

Late that afternoon my father telephoned. "I've just checked in at the Leme Palace. I got a good rate."

"What!" I struggled not to show my alarm. "I thought you intended to come in a few weeks."

"What gave you that idea?"

"I told you, *papai* — I've got my São Paulo presentation tomorrow and classes all day Friday. This isn't the best time for a visit. Anyway, how did you get here so fast?"

"Simple. Hans at the glider school knew someone who was flying a twin Cessna to São Paulo at noon. With six seats, there was room for me. From there I just took the shuttle to Rio. We'll have dinner tonight. You know I've never seen this famous apartment you share with Pedro."

I was impressed by my father's resourcefulness, managing to fly on a Wednesday when there was no commercial service from Bauru to São Paulo. Clearly our conversation had worried him deeply. We agreed to meet at his hotel at half past 8.

I couldn't allow my father's arrival less than 48 hours before the robbery to jeopardize the schedule. Suddenly everything seemed much more risky, the time available totally inadequate. When I walked into the Leme Palace Hotel, my father was waiting for me in the lobby. He looked the opposite of the dazed, barely groomed man I had left moping around the house two months earlier. He wore a well-cut black suit, white shirt, maroon-and-black paisley necktie. His wavy hair was neatly cut and combed. For the first time since the fateful card game, I felt my father was regaining his balance. When he stood up to embrace

77

me, he was again a man who obviously enjoyed being tall — half a head taller than most Brazilian men.

"You look very well, *pai*."

He released my shoulders, stepped back and surveyed his son. "I wish I could say the same for you, Alexandre. Late hours, too much beer and coffee, no time to shave, ill-advised thoughts — I suppose you'll recover. What do you feel like eating? Fish? We can go to the Yacht Club. I might as well get some benefit from my membership. Or do you prefer something else? Le Cordon Bleu right here in the hotel has a good reputation."

We took a taxi to the Yacht Club. My father suggested one of my favorite Portuguese dishes, codfish with caramelized onions and raisins. "Wine?" he asked. "A nice Chablis to go with the fish? A red from Portugal could also work. You choose."

"I'd better not drink alcohol. I've got some work to finish up tonight. I can't afford to get sleepy."

After we ordered, my father said, "You know why I'm here and I know what you're going to tell me before you say it. I'll say it for you." He lowered his voice. "The country is in the hands of military thugs and censors. Nobody's free to find out what's going on. They've installed a police state to support the traditional structures of a backward society, which in turn is dependent on money and markets in the United States. Brave urban guerrillas with revolution on their minds are committed to saving us. The poor are politically invisible and the wealthy are conveniently oblivious or support the regime. Did I leave anything out?"

I had to smile. He was magnificent. "Only Tiradentes and our ancestor," I said.

"I'm not here to bolster your arguments with a family legend from the 18th century." He drew in his breath. "So the issues are clarified.

78

But it's not politics that concerns me right now, Alexandre, it's your actions."

My father had come a long way to deliver his lecture. His concern and love were not to be minimized. We traded rambling talk — the quality and preparation of Rio's codfish compared with São Paulo's, the robustness of Brazil's coffee crop compared with Africa's, our student movement compared with those in France. Impatient, he finally said, "Okay, Alexandre, let me put it plainly. You feel joining the resistance is the correct thing to do. Don't think I'm unsympathetic. I share your outrage, but not your interest in futile gestures."

"I think it's an obligation, *papai*."

"As an active member, sooner or later you'll be in situations where you're exposed. It's more than risky. It could be a death sentence. As your father — "

"You're going way beyond my intentions."

"Am I? I'd be relieved if I believed you. Not that I think you lie. I know you don't. But I also know how you behave when you're determined. Remember when you wanted to swim in the ocean without first learning the basics? Like how to float and tread water? You were about 7. Your mother and I took you and Maria Rita to Rio for a beach holiday. I wanted to teach you to swim. You said you didn't need instruction, and you ran right into the water. I had to chase after you or you would have drowned. I can't remember how many times that happened until I convinced you to take lessons. I gave up trying to teach you myself."

"I was right. You don't need lessons to learn to float. The talent is inborn."

"Christ, you have your great-grandfather Machado's stubbornness. I can imagine you doing what he did — losing the *fazenda* and moving in with his farmhand, despite the family's pleading."

"What options did he have?"

"As it happens, several. But he was thumbing his nose at everybody."

I smiled. "Should I now be the one to say it?"

My father smiled, too. "I know I have my own keen interest in cards. I'm not in Rio to discuss that kind of game."

"You think that's what this is, *papai*? That I'm playing a game?"

"If I thought that anything you could do would actually improve our situation, I would encourage you. Unfortunately, I don't think you can help our nation." He leaned over, drew in his breath and patted my hand. At last he said, "I'm terrified the military will take you and I'll never see you again. And if I do, you won't be the same person I'm talking to right now. All you can do by joining the resistance is risk losing one of Brazil's best and most promising citizens."

My father's anxiety was understandable and affecting. But I was not convinced by his argument.

II

The next morning, my father visited our apartment. Pedro skipped his 9 a.m. class. He hadn't seen his uncle in over two years. We got up at 6 to wash a pile of dishes left in the sink, straighten our jumble of books and clothes and make our beds. My father looked over my shoulder while I made minor adjustments to one of my drawings. I had concentrated my efforts on the square kilometer surrounding São Paulo's Teatro Municipal. My plan envisaged closing off one block of the narrow Rua dos Timbiras to vehicular traffic and transforming it into a pedestrian shopping arcade. I also converted a small square that was choked with cars into a lush park and designed a three-level municipal parking garage underneath it. To unite the core area visually,

I designed a rhythmic pattern of street benches, sleek light standards and kiosks for flower and newspaper vending.

"*Impressionante*," my father said. "São Paulo is a city built for robots. It needs a rational plan for humans. The city fathers should seriously consider yours, Alexandre."

From the beginning of their schooling, architecture students are trained to present and defend their work in front of the faculty, and sometimes outside judges, and to take their criticism in the spirit in which it is offered — as helpful suggestions. We were supposed to remember that our current projects were being judged — not our past work, not our personalities, not how we looked. Nevertheless, at least once a semester an overfrenzied and underbathed student would be told that, in future, he should take a shower before defending his project. Never far from our minds was the importance of satisfying our professors. Our work had to show versatility in attacking an architecture problem as well as skill in creating beautiful buildings and inviting streetscapes. An architecture professor could boost a former student's career by mentioning his talent at a dinner party. The reverse was also true. Careers could be damaged, plum commissions lost, because of a less-than-enthusiastic remark. I had taken on a tough problem, worked hard. I had to be prepared to receive disapproval or praise.

My father left to have lunch with Maria Rita. After he had gone, I couldn't stop myself from speculating compulsively about what could happen if we got caught. It was conceivable *Jornal do Brasil* would carry the story of the robbery of Banco Boavista in the North Zone and the arrest of the robbers while my father was still in Rio. Pedro would have the unenviable task of telling my father that I was one of the robbers and trying to offer hope that I would survive incarceration.

Most political prisoners were brutally beaten from the beginning to the end of their incarceration. Women detainees were subjected to punishment that included sexual violation. We had heard, though, that the

81

CIA had taught our Department of Political and Social Order (DOPS) an alternative method to get accurate information. This approach was psychological rather than overtly physical. Detainees would be separated immediately. Each one would be interrogated nonstop in isolation. No food, no sleep, no going to the bathroom. No sense of day or night. The DOPS interrogator would state, "Your friend Luis has told us this story." The DOPS agent would have fabricated a story that he thought roughly corresponded to the activities under investigation. "We already know your crimes. Cooperate and everything can go so much easier." The story would be repeated over and over in a drone. Shifts would change. Two questioners in rotation would go over the same ground again and again. "Your friend Luis spilled his guts. Your friend Luis didn't care about you — why should you care about him? We now have the same story from another prisoner. Your friend Fábio. Maybe we should say your former friend Fábio. He has betrayed you. You might as well validate his story. Or possibly you have another version? We're listening. We dislike torture."

Eventually the prisoner, exhausted, dehydrated, bladder bursting, would yell out, "You've got it wrong!" DOPS would then easily pry out the whole story — the names, activities and hiding places of a clandestine group. Pee would run down the prisoner's legs.

After extracting the information, the DOPS agents would torture the prisoner anyway. "We need the practice," they would say.

CHAPTER SEVEN

I

At 2 in the afternoon I taped my drawings to the long wall where architecture students presented their work to be judged. Three other students who also had been working on solutions to São Paulo's congestion taped their drawings next to mine. Each of us was nervous, but it was too late to regret our choice to take on such a difficult problem. I had hoped Monica would skip class to attend the evaluation of my work, but she didn't appear.

"I have deep doubts about two elements of your plan, Alexandre," Professor Corrêa Neto said. "Your park interacts with the streets in an interesting way, but the reciprocal relationships among some of your decorative elements — especially street furniture and kiosks — are overdone. Also, in such a congested area, the sidewalk width is inadequate for pedestrians. Three meters of clear walking space is optimal for a high-volume area. And you need to allow additional space for your sidewalk trees."

Professor Hashimoto paced back and forth in front of my drawings. Finally he said, "The quotations from art deco in the kiosks and curves from art nouveau in the benches ... it's a somewhat unsettling combination of vernaculars. I agree with Professor Corrêa Neto. Overall there's too much confectionery. I do find, though, that your solution to the unregulated congestion around the Teatro Municipal has some merit. Let's hear what others think."

The professors took their time judging our projects — close to three hours. I didn't feel that anyone had clearly done a better job than I. I took down my drawings, rolled them up and left them with Professor Corrêa Neto. Roberto was waiting for me outside the Architecture Building.

"How'd it go?" he asked.

"I'm relieved. Overall they liked it. I agreed with about 40 percent of their criticisms. I made a bet with myself in advance — I'd win if the bad comments outnumber the good by less than 3-to-1."

"You call that winning?"

"Architecture juries are notorious for resisting temptations to praise."

As we walked toward the Literature Building to pick up the rest of the group, Roberto told me Adolfo, the other mathematician, was in the hospital for an emergency appendectomy.

"*Merda*, why didn't you tell me? Now we don't have two cars."

"I *am* telling you. Actually, I think it's better with one car — simpler and cleaner."

This would be the first time I would meet Roberto's colleagues. César, one of the classicists, was waiting for us. He was graying prematurely and had a thoughtful expression that, as we talked, frequently dissolved in a grin. He knew Méier because his great-aunt lived nearby, the result of an "unfortunate" marriage to a husband who couldn't afford a South Zone neighborhood. César was confident that he could evade police pursuit in Méier without a second car to distract the cops.

"Where's José?" Roberto asked.

"Cinelândia. He thought it was safer than all of us meeting on the campus."

We hopped on a bus to downtown. José was waiting for us at the Cinelândia stop. "Glad to have an architect in our group," he said. "My cousin is an architect and he's very good at solving practical problems." José didn't look like the extraordinarily perceptive guy I expected from Roberto's description. He looked like a playboy — handsome, tan, suave, dressed fashionably in expensive-looking clothes. The cops certainly wouldn't take him for a student activist. The four of us paced in front of Cinelândia's seven big movie houses, commenting on what was playing while deliberating the merits and pitfalls of going forward with only one car. Darkness fell. The streetlights came on. Eventually we all agreed to go ahead with a single vehicle. We felt invincible; we had the moral upper hand. César jumped onto a bench and proclaimed something in Greek meant for José, who responded by raising a fist overhead.

"Careful," Roberto said. "What if DOPS has a spy who understands classic Greek?"

José laughed. "Let's not confuse the impossible with the merely unlikely."

It started to rain. Roberto took a bus to visit Adolfo in the hospital. César and José went to an early movie, Rita Hayworth in *Gilda*. Impatient to be with Monica, I splurged on a taxi to Leblon. It had been impossible to keep her in the dark about my plans to rob a bank in Méier. Clues piled up and, in the end, she half-guessed and I half-told her. The fragrant aroma of French cooking greeted me at her door. As we embraced, I noticed that she had arranged two black table mats, black napkins and a spray of nearly black orchids on top of the white laminate board she used as an all-purpose table.

"I thought you hated domestic life," I said after a drawn-out kiss.

"I make exceptions."

"It smells like *boeuf bourguignon*."

"My version of it. They liked your project. I know it."

"How, since you didn't come?"

"Because I liked it. I was afraid I'd make you nervous. I've never let a boyfriend attend one of my presentations."

"I wanted you to come. After Corrêa Neto's usual negative observations, he asked me to leave my drawings so he could send them to a friend who's a city planner in São Paulo. I might get some work."

"Then we should celebrate doubly," she said.

I unbuttoned her black shirt and slipped it off. We kissed for a long time.

"What about the *boeuf bourguignon*?" I asked.

"It's taking care of itself."

I took off my clothes and the rest of hers — leaving on her silver pendant necklace — and we went to bed. Reacting to the tension caused by Roberto's last-minute changes, my body failed to perform. Monica picked up my limp dick and let it flop down on my stomach as she leaned over and kissed my neck.

"You're not telling me everything."

"The robbery is tomorrow, not next week. Don't ask me any questions."

When I finally penetrated her, I ejaculated in a rush. It startled us and made us laugh. We got up, showered and had dinner. For someone who claimed she had no interest in even basic culinary arts, her cooking was surprisingly delicious. I had to leave at 11 to meet my father for a late drink. Monica made three knots in the intertwined red, blue and yellow ribbons of a *fita* and tied it around my left wrist. The ribbons were stamped with the name of the church in Bahia, Nosso Senhor do Bonfim, that distributed them for a gratuity. "For luck tomorrow," she said. Following the prescribed ritual, I made a silent wish as she tied each knot.

"My class tomorrow is in the late afternoon," Monica said. "I'll be home until 2, waiting to hear from you. Call me just as soon as you can."

"My father's going home Saturday morning. He wants to have dinner with me and Maria Rita and her husband, Paulo, at the Copacabana Palace tomorrow night. I'd like you to come."

"Are you sure?"

"Very sure."

"Alexandre ... God protect you." I put my forefinger to her mouth and she kissed it.

I left without a look backward.

II

Shortly before 9 the next morning César, Roberto and José picked me up at my apartment. César was driving a dark-blue Ford Corcel — a commonplace car on the Rio streets. Roberto slid the Colt out from under the front seat so I could see it. César had planned to steal a car for the robbery, but instead came up with an ingenious scheme to use his own car. He had taken the license plate off an Army officer's car in the parking lot of the officer's club at Praia Vermelha. When the guard watching the lot took a break, César was able to sneak in and out without being stopped. The two cars were the same make, four-door model and color. "If someone notes our license number, the military will be looking for one of its own," he said. His grin was in his voice.

I hardly recognized José. Instead of the stylish clothing he had worn when I met him, he was dressed in workingmen's clothes: drab brown synthetic pants and an ugly yellow short-sleeved shirt. Our plan was for him to enter the market and shop his way toward the bank, ending up in front, where he could alert us by rapping on the window if he saw cops coming. Two blocks from the bank he got out of the car, carrying a string shopping bag. He knew how to disappear in a crowd like a chameleon on a stick. By the time he had taken five paces into the market, I couldn't spot him anymore.

The market was operating at full throttle. We made one pass by the bank without stopping, so we could check out the street activity in front. As we circled around the neighborhood, none of us spoke. I went over my mental checklist one last time. During the last few days

I had been systematically reviewing the things that could go wrong, in the same way that I had been taught to review possible flaws in the construction documents for a building. We had picked a time for the robbery when bank business would be slow. If anyone tried to enter the bank while we were robbing it, José planned to announce that the bank was closed temporarily for an emergency.

At 10:30 precisely, César drove up to the bank. José was standing near the big dark window, eating an apple. Roberto and I had black hooded masks with openings for the eyes, nose and mouth, sewn by Monica, in our hip pockets, and we each carried an expandable, satchel-style briefcase. Roberto slipped the Colt inside the waistband of his jeans and pulled his shirt over it. I had my rifle in a duffle bag. We were two meters from the bank door when two young men on bicycles darted in front of us and stopped abruptly in front of the window where José was standing. We hesitated. They stood there, chatting. "They can't see inside," I whispered. "Let's go."

As soon as we entered the bank, we pulled on our masks and took out our guns. Roberto dashed up to a woman teller's cage where a short, wiry man was transacting business and an overweight woman waited in line behind him. Roberto yelled at the customers to sit down and put their hands on top of their heads. The woman started to complain about getting down on the floor. "I haven't got time for this!" Roberto shouted. "Sit! Now!" The wiry man extended his hand to help the woman sit down.

A second teller, a thin, bald man, was sitting at an empty window working an adding machine. As soon as he saw our weapons, he froze. I heard Roberto shouting at him while I covered the stand-up counter where a middle-aged man and frail older man in a shabby suit were filling out forms. The older man looked terrified and raised his arms in the air.

"Just follow orders," I barked. "We don't want to hurt anyone." I held my rifle under my armpit, pointing to the floor.

The older man lowered his arms. Fumbling, he held out an ancient wallet for me to take. "*Senhor*, it's all I have," he said.

"Never mind, keep it." I shouted to the other man standing at the counter, "Take your deposit to the cashier!" The man looked perplexed. "Deposit your money. After it's the bank's money, then we'll steal it. Move! What are you waiting for?" The man grasped his deposit slip and ran over to Roberto. I followed him. Roberto grabbed the slip out of his hand and passed it to the woman teller.

Roberto demanded, "Where's your money?" The man pulled a roll of bills secured with a rubber band out of his pocket. Roberto snatched it. "Process this!" he shouted to the teller. He turned to the bald teller and yelled, "Empty that drawer behind you!"

"I need a key for that one."

"Where is it?"

"In my jacket pocket." He pointed to a gray jacket hanging on a hook on the back wall of his teller's cage. Don't shoot. I'll open the drawer."

"No tricks," I said.

Roberto and I held everyone at gunpoint while the woman teller stamped the deposit slip, emptied her cash drawer and piled four stacks of bills on the counter. The second teller had already piled three stacks of bills on the ledge in front of his window. He fetched his key and emptied the locked drawer.

"Open the vault," Roberto commanded.

"We don't know the combination," the female teller said. "Only the manager does, and he shut it before he left."

"I don't believe you! Open it now!"

"It's true. He had to see the doctor very urgently. Please ..."

We scooped up the cash and stuffed it into our briefcases. Roberto and I marched the four customers and the two tellers toward the windowless bathroom and herded everyone inside. I pulled a handful of our manifestoes out of my pocket and threw them on the bathroom floor.

"Don't worry, the money's going to be used in a good cause," I said. "Read our manifesto. This door is being watched by someone with a high-powered rifle. Don't attempt to leave for precisely 10 minutes."

Roberto slammed the door shut. I carried the manager's heavy chair back to the bathroom and propped it under the doorknob. Roberto dropped his pocketful of manifestoes on the stand-up counter. After we pulled off our masks and hid our weapons, we walked calmly out onto the street. César saw us coming and threw open the car doors. José scrambled into the car after us and we took off to the north. Roberto and I crouched on the floor in the back, sweat pouring off our faces. My shirt was completely soaked. I couldn't tell whether the robbery had taken minutes or an hour.

"I'm completely pissed we didn't get into the vault," Roberto said.

"Stop driving so goddamn fast!" José yelled from the front passenger seat. "We're inviting attention!" When he turned to glance out the rear window, his face looked pale despite its robust tan. César slowed down. Roberto and I climbed onto the back seat. The briefcases were between our legs.

"Next time we need another guy in the bank," I said. "That's our big miscalculation. I had to watch too many people. What if somebody had walked in? We might not have had to buy that cock-and-bull story about the safe if we had another man."

"What was that extra man supposed to do?" Roberto said. "Crack the safe? Shoot the teller? Calm down."

For a while we headed northwest, out of town. César pulled off the main road and found a garbage-strewn vacant lot where he could change the license plate. He shoved the Army officer's plate into a pile of trash. We congratulated ourselves, sweating and laughing, and berated ourselves over the vault. Would we have enough to pay off the customs inspector and buy the Uzis? César turned the car around, got on the main road and headed back toward downtown. At my apartment we counted our expropriation: 46,000 *cruzeiros novos*, more than a customs inspector would make in years. Not a bad result, considering that we didn't get the money in the vault. We agreed that Roberto, José and I would negotiate with the customs inspector. César had an afternoon class and was more than happy not to be involved. We had five hours to kill before our appointment with the inspector at the docks. Everyone left the apartment. I stashed the money in the living-room armoire and telephoned Monica.

"Alexandre!"

"Meet me in the lobby of the Copa at 9:30. Maria Rita, Paulo and my father are expecting us."

"God, you're cool."

"Your masks were perfect."

"Oh, you liked the new costumes for the play," she said. "I'm so glad."

I had forgotten for a moment that it was wise to assume phones were tapped — though realistically, most of the phones being monitored belonged to journalists and people who had lost their political rights. "Many thanks," I said. "The play was a big success."

"How was your speech?"

"There wasn't time. But we passed out our programs."

"I was so worried."

"I know. I called as soon as I could. See you later."

91

III

Roberto had set up our meeting with the customs inspector through an intermediary he trusted. We were to meet outside Warehouse 2 at 7:30 p.m. I would have to go in clothes appropriate for dinner at the Copacabana Palace and make my way to the hotel from the docks. With time on my hands, and no desire to do anything related to school, I put on my bathing suit and went to the beach. The surf was up, so all I could do was swim the crawl for short distances and dive into waves. Robbing a bank had been so easy that, without any explicit discussion, we had all tacitly agreed we were going to do it again. As long as we could get away with our robberies, I would feel less exposed carrying on as a student than if I followed Heitor's path underground. I could even hope that taking action would distract me less from my classes than my endless vacillation about how to get involved.

At 6:45 Roberto, José and I took a taxi to the docks. José was still wearing the same shoddy clothes he had on earlier in the day. We intended to make the deal first, then arrange the logistics of payment and delivery.

The inspector wasn't at the meeting place. We paced in front of Warehouse 2 for nearly an hour.

"*Chicos.*" A short, barrel-chested man called to us in Spanish from the shadow of a nearby doorway. "*Chicos*, Fernando couldn't make it. He sent me. Do you have the money?"

"Who are you?" I said in Portuguese. "We aren't *cucarachas.*" "Cockroaches" is what Brazilians call their Hispanic neighbors when they want to disparage them.

"Sorry," he said in unaccented Portuguese, "I was expecting *chicos* from Bolivia."

"Do we look like Bolivians?" Roberto said in a disgusted tone.

"You look like businessmen," the man said with a chuckle. "Fernando can't hide 15 Uzis indefinitely. Don't worry. They're the fully automatic style."

I started to sweat. I looked around for cops. A sedan I hadn't noticed before was parked about 50 meters away at the edge of Warehouse 3. "Uzis! Christ!" I said. "We're just taking a stroll looking for pussy."

"Not here you're not, boys. This isn't pussy central."

"Can you recommend a good place to look?" José said. "We're not interested in transvestites."

"Is that a fact? You never know about taste." His tone was increasingly menacing.

I turned to face Roberto and José and smiled. "Let's go for a drink at one of those tourist bars in Mauá Square," I said. "Maybe with some charm, we can get it free."

We started to walk in the direction of the square.

"Fifty-four thousand for the shipment," he called after us. We kept walking. "That's a good price, *meninos*. Did Fernando tell you? This is a one-time opportunity."

"He's DOPS," I whispered under my breath. "Keep walking. Thank Christ we don't have the money on us."

"A car's following us with its lights off," Roberto said. "The customs guy set us up."

"I thought this was supposed to be the easy part," I said. I looked at my watch. "I'm supposed to meet my father at the Copacabana Palace in an hour. This is a bad moment for things to turn sour."

"We didn't fool him," José said. "Our story was totally transparent."

"Does Fernando know who you are, Roberto?" I asked. "That you're a student? Your school? Anything at all about you?"

"I've never even met Fernando. A law student in our group made the contact. Right now I don't know what to believe."

"Shit!"

The car was still following us.

"It's DOPS," Roberto said. "If they try to search us, act calm but be a little indignant."

"I'll speak Greek," José said.

"Don't be a smart ass," I said. "When we get to the square, head for the nearest bar. At least we should try to make our story seem consistent."

The car followed us past the deserted Touring Club of Brazil to the square. We entered the same bar I had visited the night I went to the docks looking for Celso. The same kind of crowd was there — tourists, seamen and women who hang around seamen's bars. Because it was still early, the patrons were less drunk, less desperate to make a connection. Roberto and José planned to stay in the bar for at least an hour and walk out with two girls. I waited 30 minutes. Three people — two merchant officers in uniform and a girl — got up from their table and walked toward the door. I maneuvered so I could exit the bar sandwiched between them. A line of taxis idled at the curb. I pushed in front of them and jumped into the first one. As we pulled away, I tried to scan the dimly lighted square for the car that had been tailing us. I thought I saw it parked halfway down the block.

When I entered the Copacabana Palace lobby, Monica hurried over to me, looking relieved. She wore a long, dramatic black-and-white dress. I remarked that her outfit wasn't monochromatic.

"And you're not in prison, thank God."

As we walked to the poolside café, I took her hand. My father, Maria Rita and Paulo were already there drinking Campari and soda.

94

Monica charmed my family with a virtuoso display of anecdotes: Her great-aunt's famous chocolate cake recipe that won a culinary prize in Chicago, the theatrical costumes she made that fell apart in the play's second act, her late father's fondness — acquired at age 19 on his first grand tour of Europe — for eating ortolans in Paris. "The ortolans are disappearing," she said. "You're not supposed to eat them. When he ate those delicious songbirds, my father said, he used to cover his head with a napkin so God wouldn't see his crime."

"I suppose my son has told you I like to play cards," my father said with exaggerated innocence after ordering a second round of Campari for everyone. "But did he tell you I'm learning to play the piano? Last week I graduated from school exercises to *Bagatelles, Opus 5* by Tcherepnine. Naturally I'm starting with a bagatelle that has only one flat. After that I'll try one with one sharp. I have a marvelous teacher. He studied at the Academy in Budapest."

"You never studied piano as a child?" Monica asked.

"When I was 9, my mother insisted I study the violin. I was hopeless. I tried to explain to her that since I didn't even have relative pitch, I'd never be able to play a stringed instrument. We fought."

Monica laughed. "I had the same problem. My mother made me study the cello. Her favorite music is for the cello, especially Villa-Lobos' *Bachianas Brasileiras*. I was good at drawing, but I could barely tune my instrument. There was nothing to do except become an architect."

At the table next to ours, a waiter popped a champagne cork. I jumped. Monica put her hand on my knee under the table to steady me. "I wonder what an ortolan tastes like," I said. "There must be a lot of bones."

"My father told me you're supposed to eat the little birds bones and all, everything but the head."

95

Paulo tapped his glass, waited for everyone's attention and announced that at 5 o'clock, just as he was leaving his office, he learned he had finally been assigned a foreign posting. "Third Secretary in Egypt. It's punishment for my close association with Orlando Pacheco, pure and simple. I'm going from one police state to another. I understand Nasser even opens foreigners' mail."

"I don't know, Paulo," my father said. "It would be interesting to see the Aswan High Dam and all the antiquities, of course. You have to read Lawrence Durrell before you go." He held up his glass. "To my son-in-law's first foreign posting — congratulations!"

We all lifted our glasses in a toast. My father turned to me. "You're very quiet, Alexandre. Still recovering from your presentation?" I nodded. "Your mother will want to know all the details."

"Basically they liked it, particularly my ideas about creating a small landscaped park with a subterranean garage."

Monica leaned toward my father. "He's not telling you the best part. Professor Corrêa Neto liked his work so much, he's sending Alexandre's drawings to a colleague who works in planning with the São Paulo municipal government."

"Bravo, Alexandre," Maria Rita said. "When you graduate, you could work with Lúcio Costa."

"That's the problem," I said. "Brasília was a dream project. The golden opportunity in urban design was 12 years ago."

After entrées of tournedos for my father and me and ravioli with crab for everyone else, we ordered desserts and finished our meal with *cafezinhos*. The outdoor lighting that dappled the restaurant and the pool threw long, inviting shadows. I thought of the night Monica led me into those shadows to make love behind the sentry palms and philodendron. I slipped my hand onto her thigh and felt her muscles flex in response.

CHAPTER EIGHT

I

Analyzing our failure to buy the Uzis, we questioned what had happened at the docks. We assumed that the man who met us was from DOPS, but Roberto's law-school contact said we would have been arrested on the spot if DOPS had been alerted. It was possible the corrupt customs inspector really had been busy or sick and had sent a colleague who didn't know whom or what to expect. Alternatively, the inspector could have bragged about his lucrative deal, word could have spread, and an informer could have found out and contacted customs. We had no way to find out for sure whether the car that seemed to be following us had anything to do with our intended purchase. Whatever the truth was, the opportunity to buy the Uzis was dead. Moreover, the guy at the docks had asked for more than we got from our robbery. We gave the money to Heitor. Roberto told his contact to cut all further communication with the customs inspector.

Adolfo was still recuperating from his appendectomy. Roberto remarked that his fellow mathematician hadn't lost his usual energetic gait. "Doctor's orders," Adolfo said. "I'm not supposed to lift anything heavy for two weeks — unless it's sacks full of money."

Over the next several days, buoyed by our resolve to make the banks pay for our country's liberation, and by our success, the four of us drove around the North Zone in César's Corcel to look for our next target. We crammed Adolfo in the car with us on our third scouting trip.

We surveyed distant working-class neighborhoods that were terra incognita to me and my South Zone architecture classmates. As we drove, chain-smoked and evaluated various banks, our criteria for the ideal candidate coalesced. It should be situated on a corner, like the bank in Méier, with clear access to other neighborhoods in all directions on good roads. It should be outside the circumference of banks previously robbed by other political groups. In Bento Ribeiro, a forlorn neighborhood less an hour's drive northwest of downtown, a branch of Banco Estado da Guanabara met our requirements.

Monica was alarmed by my enthusiasm. "For you, robbing a bank is like winning a big pot in poker," she said. "It's the same kind of excitement. I support what you're doing, Alexandre, but don't start having fun." I assured her that "fun" was the furthest thing from my mind. In those days I believed that my family's gambling disease was confined to cards.

Pedro and I were studying furiously when Heitor showed up with the pair of submachine guns he had promised to supply. They were handmade, with square butts. Even though they were intended only for show, Heitor had tested them on the beach at Grumari. "First time I fired a submachine gun," he said. "It practically flew out of my hands."

II

The five of us — the mathematicians Roberto and Adolfo, the classicists, César and José, and I — were becoming a cohesive group, able to make our own decisions on how to oppose the military, to choose what risks we were willing to take and to execute our plans quickly. We felt that flexibility and safety demanded we remain independent and not ally ourselves with any of the entrenched opposition organizations.

We had contemplated using two cars for the robbery in Bento Ribeiro, but abandoned the idea after our first reconnaissance trip. We noticed a place where the road curved around a graveyard for junked cars. If we were pursued, we could pull into it and hide among the scrapped cars until dark — but that would be easier with one car than with two. César agreed to let his car get dirty. Before robbing the bank, we would make it look even worse by tossing sand onto it. We doubted there would be a police chase. The cops in the impoverished distant neighborhoods had to deal with plenty of petty crime — a showoff kid trying to impress his friends with the proceeds of a purse-snatching or a desperate guy with a pistol trying to satisfy his wife's demand for luxuries. They weren't used to bank robberies.

We made two more trips to the bank. One at a time, each of us went inside and scouted the interior. I drew the floor plan. César drove all the possible escape routes several times. Monica made a mask for Adolfo and sheaths for our submachine guns that looked vaguely like viola cases. Since we had two submachine guns, I didn't plan to take my rifle. At our final meeting on the afternoon before the robbery, 10 days after our robbery in Méier, César told us his brother had borrowed his car that morning and had an accident. The car still functioned, but it needed major body repair.

"God's smiling on our enterprise," Roberto said. "Now we have the perfect vehicle to hide in the junkyard."

The following morning at 8, César picked me up in his banged-up Corcel. During the night, he had exchanged his license plate for one he removed from a car parked on a quiet neighborhood street. José, again dressed in cheap clothes, and Roberto were already in the car. Adolfo met us at the curb in front of his parents' apartment building in Botafogo. He was sweaty.

"Nervous?" Robert asked.

"I just tried to do some pushups for the first time since I had my appendix out. I had to stop. It hurt. I guess I'm not ready to play soccer this weekend."

When we arrived at the bank in Bento Ribeiro, a police car was parked right in front. We circled around the neighborhood for 15 minutes, cursing. Each time we passed the bank, the police car was still

99

there. We all agreed it was not only the wrong moment, but the wrong bank. Adolfo suggested we rob another bank instead. He knew a good candidate, Banco Nacional in Realengo.

"Are you crazy? That's where the Army has its 1st Regiment of Tanks," César said.

"At least let's have a look," Adolfo said. "Realengo's maybe 20 minutes from here. What have we got to lose?"

We were primed, ready to re-establish democracy in Brazil with our bravery and our righteousness. César checked his map. Realengo was 10 kilometers southwest of Bento Ribeiro. It turned out to be nothing like the other North Zone neighborhoods we had scouted. It was a huge military village with a few commercial blocks on either side of a commuter railroad station. The streets were lined with sprawling, buff-colored Army offices, depots, garages, rows of two-story barracks for enlisted men and substantial houses with groomed lawns for officers. Ordinary soldiers in black boots and paratroopers in brown boots walked smartly in front of the vast buildings. "If it wasn't for us opposing them, these military guys would have nothing to do but scratch their balls," José said. "It isn't like we're at war with a foreign power."

Banco Nacional occupied a perfect location for a fast getaway — a quiet corner on the edge of town, half a kilometer from a major highway. Roberto, Adolfo and I went in singly, 10 minutes apart, to reconnoiter, while José walked around the immediate neighborhood, even disappearing into a Methodist church nearby. He wanted to make sure a crowd of parishioners was not about to burst out of church onto the street. The church was empty. We had misgivings about acting with so little preparation.

While we were weighing the positives and the negatives of proceeding, an armored truck pulled up to the bank and a guard carried in two sacks of money. We couldn't resist. We waited five minutes after the truck had left.

100

José took up his position outside the bank, ready to deal with any customer who might come to the door. We went in quickly, pulling on our masks. There were five customers, all civilians, lined up at two teller's windows. A third teller was putting a "closed" sign on her window. Roberto, submachine gun in hand, ordered the patrons onto the floor. I spotted the two sacks from the armored truck sitting unopened on a file cabinet and shouted at the tellers to bring them to me. Adolfo stood next to me, holding our other submachine gun as if he were in combat. I passed one sack to him and the other to Roberto. I ordered the tellers to empty their cash drawers. As soon as the bills from the cash drawers hit the counter, I crammed them into our expandable briefcases.

Roberto handed each trembling customer one of our manifestoes and threw the rest on the counter. We marched everyone to the bathroom. The lock on the door was broken. When we opened it, a man in a suit jacket and necktie, no doubt the manager, was seated on the toilet, his pants down around his ankles. *"Minha Nossa Senhora, Mãe de Deus,"* he said, pulling up his trousers to cover his knees. There was a bad smell. He stayed frozen on the seat. Our captives tittered nervously as they filed inside.

"You might as well stay where you are," I said.

He paid no attention, stood and buckled his trousers around his waist. For a moment I feared he was going to lunge at us. On the wall over the toilet was a tiny, translucent window, too small for anyone to squeeze through. I gave our speech about having an accomplice with a machine gun watching the bathroom door.

"Ten minutes! Don't move!" Roberto shouted as he banged the door shut. Adolfo propped a large leather chair under the doorknob. I had an acute sense of time, unlike the feeling of disorientation I felt during our robbery in Méier. From start to finish, the operation took eight minutes. Our choreography was brisk and efficient, as if we were a well-practiced team. No one tried to enter the bank while we were there. It was unbelievably easy — embarrassingly so.

We piled into the car, not bothering to crouch down. César took off, heading west. I was staring at the second hand of my watch when we heard a siren. Roberto, Adolfo and I dropped to the floor. It got louder. "Don't worry, it's a *Policia Militar* car going in the opposite direction," César said, "and it's not turning around."

We raced along Avenida Brasil, a major highway, with low coastal mountains in the distance on both sides of the road. For a few minutes I was a carefree sightseer, noticing the white rock protruding near the top of the mountains and thick, dark-green bush wrapping the sides. When we were confident that we weren't being followed, César got off the highway and turned around to head back toward the North Zone. When we reached Quinta da Boa Vista Park, he drove underneath its elaborate early 19th-century entry portal and stopped near some shrubs that offered good cover. César quickly put his own license plate back on the car. Roberto and I grabbed some rags and wiped the road grime off the car. It was so dirty the dark-blue color had hardly been visible, but if a witness had focused on the damage, the Corcel would have been identifiable. It wasn't until we were on our way back to Copacabana, marveling at our good luck and laughing at the plight of the manager, that Adolfo mentioned his family's connection to the bank. When his grandfather first came to Rio from the neighboring state of Espírito Santo, he had gone there for a loan to buy a small apartment building. The bank turned him down.

"What! The branch we just robbed?" Roberto asked.

"It serves them right," Adolfo said. "Power to the people! Anyway, I only heard the story from my mother. I've never actually been in the bank before today."

"Puxa!" we all shouted at once. Adolfo laughed so hard he had to hold onto his right side where he was still tender from his appendectomy.

The next day, *Jornal do Brasil* reported on our robbery:

> Boldest robbery until now. Guerrillas struck a branch of Banco Nacional in Realengo on the heels of an armored truck delivery, less than two kilometers from Army headquarters for the 1st Regiment of Tanks.

Because of the armored truck delivery our haul was much larger than in our first robbery — 88,000 *cruzeiros novos*. We agreed to split the money three ways: 42,000 each for Heitor's and Monica's groups, with Roberto keeping 4,000 for our group. "For emergencies," he said.

III

After the Realengo robbery, I looked over my shoulder every time I stepped outside my apartment. The sight of a police car would send me scrambling behind whatever concealment was handy. Sweat would pour off my body until I was sure the cruiser wasn't stopping. I was ready to quit robbing banks and concentrate on final exams. I had done more than my duty for my country.

The consequences of my parents' learning that I had robbed two banks were beyond imagination. I tried not to think about it. Maria Rita knew nothing about my activities. My sister and Paulo were busy preparing for his assignment in Egypt, a country dealing with its Six Day War defeat. Even before they left, my mother was making preparations to visit them in Cairo. According to Maria Rita, our mother had

103

instructed Emilio, her architecture tutor, to abandon his Bauhaus and International Style syllabus and, as she put it, "set sail for Egypt."

Three days after our Realengo robbery, Pedro emerged bleary-eyed from his bedroom after an especially noisy night when his bed had thumped repeatedly against our common wall. Silvia had already left for class. "It's a month, Pedro," I said. "Aren't you getting dangerously near the moment when you normally change girlfriends?"

"Silvia came into my life for a reason. She's divine. Period. And to tell you the truth, I'm finished picking girls for their looks. Silvia is real." While I had been expropriating money from banks, he and Silvia had been meeting with his group to discuss possible and impossible schemes we all knew would never be carried out.

Late Tuesday night, five days after our second robbery, my mother telephoned. I had not talked to her since the day before our robbery in Méier. "I've been waiting for weeks for the representative from the auction house in Paris to arrive. He keeps telegraphing, 'next week, next week.' I'm so tired of our academic art and our antiques. I can't wait to see how this house will look without them."

"Did *papai* mention my friend Monica?" I asked.

"The beautiful girl you brought to dinner who studied the cello?"

"She hasn't studied the cello since she was a child, but she is beautiful. Actually, I would say more stunning than beautiful."

"He liked her very much."

"I know you're dying to interrogate me, *mamãe*."

"Both your father and Maria Rita said your friend Monica was rather spectacular. Your father thinks her career ambitions are her first priority."

"I wouldn't be interested in a woman who wasn't ambitious. Do you consider yourself unambitious?"

104

"My God, Alexandre, we're talking about a different generation. I'm already considered an eccentric because I have my architecture tutor. When Emilio is between girlfriends, he comes over in the evening to play cards with me. I won a free class last week."

"You bet with him?"

"Of course. But now I have to concentrate on my trip to Egypt. When your starting point is 3000 B.C., there's so much to study. Your father was very complimentary about your São Paulo urban-design project."

"It was well received, thank God. I was really worried."

"I hear the relief in your voice. I can always tell when you're tense. Your throat tightens and you get raspy."

Her remark was telling. Lately my vocal cords had felt raw from strain. I jumped at every unusual sound on the street. I suspected the bus drivers on my route to the university of being undercover cops. I varied my itinerary. Monica was wrong. I wasn't being sucked into excitement. I wanted out. Two things helped mitigate my apprehension: Our bank robberies had not set off police pursuits, and I was part of a group. As José had said, "It's what you do alone that's scary."

Over the next few days, I settled into my classes. Monday night, Monica slept at my apartment. I was having one of my terrible nightmares when she shook me awake. "Somebody's knocking on the door!"

Before I could fully rouse myself, Pedro ran into the living room, followed a moment later by Silvia. I started to reach for the lamp to look at my watch.

"Don't turn it on," Pedro whispered. "They'll see the light under the door."

I threw on jeans and a shirt, turned on the light in the bathroom and let it throw a small amount of illumination into the living room. "What do I do?" I whispered. "Wait for them to go away? Surrender?"

105

Pedro pointed to the small bedroom window and the sheets on my bed. For a few terrifying seconds we stared at each other in the half-light. A sheet ladder to go down four stories? No time to knot them together properly. All the places I could hide were pathetically obvious. The armoire? The bathroom? Under the bed? I tiptoed to the door and listened. Another knock. Not insistent. Not even very loud.

"Alexandre. Pedro. Are you there? Open the door. It's me. Celso."

CHAPTER NINE

I

"I need to talk to you," Celso said as I closed the door behind him.

Still shaken, I said, "Why? You already burned all my negatives."

"That's not why I'm here."

"Isn't it safer to come around 10 or 11? If a neighbor sees you, you're less likely to arouse curiosity."

"I prefer the middle of the night."

Pedro flicked on the overhead light. The color had drained from his face. Monica had pulled on a skirt and one of my long T-shirts. She sat motionless on the edge of the bed, cradling her arms at the elbows. She seemed to be concentrating on taking deep breaths.

"I prefer not to talk in front of your friends," Celso said.

"You already know Pedro," I said. "Silvia's with Pedro and Monica's my girlfriend."

Silvia said, "I have a statistics exam at 9:30. I need to be alert." She excused herself and went into the bedroom, making a show of closing the door securely. I was grateful for her considerate departure. Pedro had assured me that he hadn't told Silvia about the bank robberies, though, without her saying it explicitly, she let me know she had figured out for herself that my opposition to the military government had shifted from talk to action. I didn't confirm or deny her guess. Monica stood up and shook hands with Celso. I could see she was still unnerved. She lit the task lamp on my desk and turned off the glaring overhead light.

"What's on your mind?" I said.

Celso reiterated that he wanted to talk in private.

"Where? On the street?"

"Hell, no."

"I told you, Pedro's my cousin. We don't have secrets. The same for Monica."

Celso gave us a long thoughtful look, then said, "I guess I've got to trust you. I have to say, Alexandre, you surprised me." He leaned back against the sofa and stared at me intently. "'Boldest robbery until now.' Who's to argue?"

It took me a minute to realize Celso was quoting from the news stories about the Realengo robbery and that he was connecting me to the holdup. I was speechless. When I found my voice, I said, "What makes you think it was me?"

"One of our comrades knows César," Celso said.

"César broke security!" I said, stunned at the breach. "There's no excuse! I might as well call up Costa e Silva and confess. How do you know your guy isn't a police infiltrator?"

"I'm not in prison, so he's not. Let's just leave it at that."

"When I heard your knock, I was afraid it was DOPS," I said. "You scared the hell out of all of us."

Celso took a seat on the sofa, with Pedro next to him. Monica and I sat on the floor facing them. I described how our "bold" robbery was actually so impromptu it could have been an episode from a slapstick comedy.

"I wouldn't have done it myself," Celso said, "but what I came here to talk to you about is the opposite of slapstick. Our group's making plans to rescue some comrades from Lemos de Brito Penitentiary. We could use some help."

Monica blurted out, "No! Alexandre's done enough."

Celso continued without changing his conversational tone: "The guys we want to free are four Navy petty officers. A second lieutenant

108

in the office of Navy personnel pushing for a promotion identified them as communists, which they are. They've all been tortured. Now they're serving their sentences. They're in bad shape. Two of them were so badly beaten they may not make it. The conditions are inhuman, worse than you can imagine."

Monica and I were sitting cross-legged, our knees touching. I put my arm around her shoulder. "Monica's got a brother in prison."

"What's his name?"

"Jayme Paiva," she said. "My family hasn't been able to get any information about him since he was taken 10 months ago. He was a student in his last year of architecture at Nacional. The military police took him to Cobra Island. That's as much as we know."

"It's possible he was transferred to Lemos de Brito. One of our guys may have met your brother inside. I'll see what I can find out. I really think we can liberate these guys. If I thought it was too dangerous, I wouldn't be here talking to you."

I knew if I told Celso on the spot that I would participate, Pedro and Monica would say I was insane to consider it. When I told Celso I needed a day to think it over, Monica made a face that suggested she was asking God to restore my sanity.

Celso glanced at his watch. "I've got to go. I have to know within 24 hours."

I proposed we meet at the Scandinavia Bar in Mauá Square at 10 p.m. That gave me 19 hours to think over Celso's appeal for help. I barely slept.

I got up very early without waking Monica and took a taxi to César's parents' apartment building. His mother answered the door wearing a bathrobe. César was having breakfast. We took the elevator down to the street. "You fucked up," I said. "You've endangered all of us."

"Give me a break. I understand security as well as you do. Mauro could help us. He's got a car."

"We don't need help. You shot your mouth off. Who the hell is this guy Mauro? For Christ's sake, you could have been talking to an informer."

"No way. I've known Mauro since high school. I used to date his sister."

"I'm not impressed. What's Mauro's connection to Celso?"

"They have activities in common. I don't know details. How well do you know Celso?"

"I'm not worried about Celso. I'm worried about you."

In the end César convinced me that he hadn't acted without due regard for security. We left it there.

When I arrived at the Scandinavia, I still hadn't made up my mind what to tell Celso. Thoughts of the tortured Navy guys weighed on me. I wanted to know the precise details of the escape plan. Celso arrived half an hour late with another man.

"This is Carlos."

We shook hands. "I forgot how much it stinks in here of cigarettes and stale beer," I said. "Maybe we should take a walk."

"It smells like perfume compared to prison," Carlos said.

We walked across the square toward the port. Celso's group had bribed two *Policia Militar* guards at the high-security Lemos de Brito Penitentiary who were willing to smuggle guns to the seamen. The prisoners would pretend to overcome them and get them to open the main gate. Simultaneously, Celso and Carlos would perform the same charade with the guard posted as sentry outside on the street, who had also been bribed.

"How did you know which guards to bribe?" I asked.

"We started by bribing a guy in administration. We also paid off the officer who's going to be in the guard tower. All you have to do is wait in a car for the prisoners to appear, they jump in and you drive away. There'll be a second car, too. The plan couldn't be simpler." Celso explained that, because of the guards' schedules, the escape had to take place in exactly 48 hours. "Guards don't make anything. They're happy to take our money and do as we say. They're basically all corrupt, with greedy wives or girlfriends. Half of them are criminals themselves — burglary, petty larceny, that kind of stuff. The military prisons are different. It's not possible to bribe an officer, and the Army doesn't trust enlisted men to be alone with the political prisoners."

"What if there are two guards in the guard tower? One looks the other way, one doesn't."

"We bribed the senior officer in the tower. Thursday night he's on duty alone for one hour from 10 to 11. We move at 10:30 sharp."

"That's five guys you bribed," I said. "One of them could talk."

"We told them our group will come after them if they screw up."

"How are your Navy guys going to know what the plan is? From their point of view, it could be a trap."

"The guards we bribed are going to first say 'your friends from the Roxy Bar are coming for you' and then tell them the plan. We all got plastered one night on shore leave in Belém at the Roxy Bar."

"I thought you didn't drink," I said.

"I used to."

"Why do you need me? You've got everything figured out."

"At the moment, besides Carlos and myself, we've only got one comrade in Rio and he's our lookout. The rest of our group went to São Paulo to plan an operation there. We're short-handed. We need two drivers."

111

"Ask César," I said.

"He's already aboard. Our comrade will be loitering on the sidewalk, watching the gate. Me and Carlos will wait in the cars until he signals us the guys are coming. Then we'll run out and disarm the sentry at the gate."

Carlos said, "I spent 11 months inside. Believe me, the guards have no personal interest in who's in and who's out. It'll work."

The schedule was tight. Celso emphasized again that the Navy guys' prospects for survival were slim if they didn't get out of prison. I had misgivings, but in the end I agreed to be the second driver. Celso and Carlos were responsible for stealing our transport. "Keep Pedro and your girlfriend out of it," Celso said.

"Monica can guess my decision, without my telling her. Pedro, too."

"They don't have to know the details or what night."

"I agree about details, but they both know my schedule well enough to figure out when it will be. Don't worry about them. Monica's been active longer than I have and Pedro's completely trustworthy."

The next morning, as an exercise in pro-forma normalcy, I went to my architectural theory class. Nothing the professor said stuck. At 1 o'clock Monica came by my drafting table, glanced at my aimless scribbles and whispered, "Please don't do it." I put my hand over hers; she brushed my temple with her lips. I didn't say a word.

At 2:30 César picked me up outside the administration building. The Corcel had not been repaired. Celso and Carlos were in the back seat. Celso worried about using César's car for reconnaissance. If someone was suspicious of us checking out the prison, the license could be reported.

112

Lemos de Brito Penitentiary occupied two full blocks on the south side of Rua Frei Caneca, a narrow street in the North Zone. A thick concrete wall and a parking forecourt screened the penitentiary's complex of 10 buildings from the street. On the north side of Rua Frei Caneca, a one-way side street formed a T intersection just opposite the entrance to the penitentiary. We stopped there. César stayed with the car while Celso, Carlos and I got out to look around.

The only break in the penitentiary wall was a metal gate set into a stone portal defaced with graffiti. The metal gate was painted light blue, a color widely used in Brazil's baroque architecture. At the top of the portal, carved into the stone, was a coat of arms. Cheap lights were attached at random intervals to the outside wall. A cinderblock guard tower looked down on the penitentiary's forecourt and the street. Two hundred meters to the right of the gate was the First Baptist Church, a large, sand-colored, Greek-style temple with six enormous Doric columns. It looked incongruous next to the menace of a penitentiary. I wondered which was built first, the prison or this curious building.

Directly across the street from the penitentiary wall was a row of open storefronts including a shoe-repair shop, two small car-repair shops and storefronts that sold marble, wood moldings and ice cream. A *botequim* anchored the corner of the T intersection. Two guards in navy-blue pants and matching long-sleeved shirts rolled up to mid-biceps were standing at the *botequim* counter, each holding a shot glass of *cachaça* in one hand and dangling a machine gun from the other. They looked weary, as if they had just come off a shift. Behind Lemos de Brito was a ramshackle slum situated on a hill. Supposedly, someone standing on the hill had once shot a prisoner in the yard of the penitentiary.

César had pulled off Rua Frei Caneca onto the side street and waited for us to finish our reconnaissance. "What'd you think?" he

113

asked when we got back in the car.

"It'll work because we've paid off the right guys on the inside," Celso said. "There's not much to learn from walking around."

From the moment Celso had talked to César about the prison break, César had studied maps to familiarize himself with the adjacent streets and neighborhoods. We sat in the car while he explained his escape plan and we studied his maps. Since I would be driving the second car, I had to memorize the side streets we could use as shortcuts to main roads. While we still had daylight, I took the wheel and drove the routes to the main arteries. A wrong turn into a neighborhood of one-way streets could be disastrous. There were several alternate routes. Celso and Carlos had to know the streets, too. Celso would be in the front seat of one car, Carlos in the other, helping to navigate should a pursuit develop.

There was a tunnel connection to the South Zone near the penitentiary; it was to be avoided because the police could close it off. To escape pursuit, once we got some distance from the penitentiary we would have to make our way northwest along two heavily traveled North Zone arteries before the police could block the streets. The goal was to connect to Avenida Brasil, a major thoroughfare that had interchanges with the main highway north toward Belo Horizonte and the highway west toward São Paulo. We would keep driving until we were confident we were in the clear.

When I finally got back to my apartment, Monica was waiting for me. Pedro and Silvia had gone to the movies. I ate a cheese sandwich and fell into a tense, keyed-up sleep. Every once in a while I woke briefly and sensed Monica in the chair on the far side of the room. The desk lamp was on. I heard her turn the pages of a book. Later I heard her bite into an apple. I woke again when the phone rang.

"Pedro's at the movies," she whispered. "Is there a message?" I felt her come to bed. "Sorry the phone woke you." She rested her arm across my waist.

"Do you want to make love?" I asked.

"You'd better go back to sleep. You looked really tired."

"It will help me sleep," I said. We made love quickly, Monica on top. Her silky hair beat against my face.

At 8 in the morning I got up. Monica stirred, but stayed in bed. On the way to the bathroom, I noticed her book on the coffee table — *Palladio's Rural Villas*. I opened it, glanced at several of the impressive photos of classical pavilions and wished I had the leisure to look through the whole book. I got dressed and went out onto the street.

Rio's mornings rejuvenated me. Much of the year the sky was clear blue, the temperature comfortably warm, the smell of the ocean fresh and salty. People smiled, happy because the day's possibilities were before them. They might fall in love, learn a new joke. I sat on an unbalanced red vinyl stool at the *botequim* across the street from my apartment building, sipped a *cafe com leite* and ate a piece of French bread with guava jelly. The air, the morning light, sunbathers on their way to the beach — everything felt right. Half an hour later, Monica came out of the building. I shouted and waved to her. Assured all eyes were on her, she crossed busy Rua Barata Ribeiro in mid-block, barely acknowledging the traffic. "Pedro thinks Celso's plan is crazy and so do I," she said when she reached my side.

"Coffee?" I asked.

"I don't have time." She kissed me. "Be safe, Alexandre. I'll be waiting for you at your apartment."

We kissed again and she walked away to take the bus to the university. I watched her turn the corner. I felt like running after her. To convince her of what?

115

II

Throughout the remainder of the day — on the bus to school, during classes, having lunch, walking around killing time — I kept calculating how many hours were left until I would be sitting in a car waiting for four prisoners to bust out of Lemos de Brito. Monica sensed correctly that I did not want to talk to her until it was over.

Finally, at 10:15 p.m. César and I were parked in two stolen cars at the curb across the street from the penitentiary, headlights off, engines idling, waiting for the signal that the prisoners were at the gate. Celso, in my car, and Carlos, in César's, were armed with Thompson submachine guns, the kind Chicago gangsters used in the 1920s. We weren't worried that the sentry would be suspicious of us, because he was one of the four guards who had been bribed. Both César and I wanted to drive the Chevrolet Opala, the more powerful and faster of the two stolen cars. On the toss of a coin, I got the Opala and César got the Renault Gordini.

"There's our lookout," Celso said. He pointed to a guy standing in the shadows next to a public telephone outside the *botequim*, directly opposite the entrance to the prison.

The sentry leaned against the penitentiary wall, standing in a little pool of mercury-vapor light. Two women in tight miniskirts crossed the street directly in front of César's car. When they reached the sentry's side of the street, he gave a low, admiring whistle. The women exaggerated the swing of their hips as they walked away. The sentry stepped away from the wall and turned to watch them. He whistled again.

"Did you arrange for the distraction?" I asked, trying to lighten our jumpiness.

Celso chuckled. "Not me. Those girls probably do that every night just to tease the sentries."

116

My hands and feet were ice-cold, and I needed to pee. Celso glanced incessantly at his luminous-dial watch by holding his arm up to eye level, so he could observe the gate and simultaneously check the time. "Where the fuck are they?" he said. "They should be here by now."

Finally the lookout raised his arm. Celso and Carlos leaped out of the cars and ran up to the sentry, who threw down his INA .45. Within seconds the prisoners were through the gate, pushing two disarmed guards in front of them. There were six prisoners, not four!

César and I jammed our cars into gear and sped to the gate. The lookout picked up the sentry's submachine gun and tossed it into my car. Carlos and Celso handcuffed the guards and the sentry to the gate, hands behind their backs. I looked up at the guard tower, fearing that at any second sirens would go off and searchlights would be trained on us. Celso and four prisoners piled into my car. Carlos and the other two prisoners jumped in with César. The lookout ran across the street in front of my car and disappeared down a side street.

I headed west, slicing through a jumble of small streets, constantly checking my rear-view mirror. César followed me for two blocks before he turned off to follow a different route to the highway. When we passed under a streetlight, I took a quick look into the back seat. Two men were on the floor, the other two slouched down on the seat. The car began to smell of urine. The prisoners stank. When I went fast, Celso, sitting in the front seat, said, "Slow down. You're attracting attention."

When I slowed down, the guys in the back seat yelled, "Full speed!"

I wove my way onto BR-040, the major highway north toward Belo Horizonte. I was prepared to drive as long as it took to be sure we were not being pursued. A voice from the back seat said, "Vicente, my Navy

117

buddy in the other car, needs urgent medical help. He's throwing up blood."

Another voice said, "I've got blood in my piss and my shit."

"I thought we were rescuing four comrades," Celso said.

"We decided to take two friends from the general population."

"How much did it cost?" asked a new voice from the back.

"Plenty," Celso said, "altogether over 20,000. We had to bribe an administration guy plus four guards."

"Shuu!" It was a different voice, one of the guys on the floor. "It went down just like the guard said. I found a gun in my bedding. The worst part was waiting till 10:20 to start moving."

"How long do you think it will take for the warden's office to figure out who got bribed and lock them up?"

"Unlikely," Celso said, "not with all the corruption that goes on at Lemos de Brito. What are they going to do? Lock up all the guards?"

"For sure those guys you bribed are in trouble with the military. They could lock them up and throw away the key. Letting political prisoners escape isn't like letting general-population prisoners escape."

"If the administration suspects the guards you bribed, they can say the guns were smuggled in on the day shift. How's the warden's office going to prove otherwise? The guards put on a good show that we overpowered them."

"Stop here. Pull over. I have to shit."

Celso and I exchanged nods. "Okay, Okay," Celso said. "Wait a minute."

As I slowed to pull off the highway, a long-distance deluxe coach nearly rammed me. "Fucking driver's half-asleep," I said.

Three prisoners got out of the car and ran into the underbrush. One stayed in the car. Celso and I relieved ourselves, too. I tried again to look at my cargo, but with only a quarter-moon they were just grizzled shadows. As I pulled back onto the highway, I said, "We're not being followed. I'm ready to turn back."

I got off BR-040 at the next opportunity and made a U-turn. The stench in the car from our fear, from bodily waste, from unbathed bodies, was overpowering. Having all the windows open hardly helped.

"How's my club doing?" The voice from the floor was one I hadn't heard before.

"Which one?"

"Flamengo, man, the team of the people. I'm desperate to see them play. It's been two fucking years."

"I'm a Botafogo fan myself."

"They're doormats."

III

From the highway I drove into a North Zone neighborhood and immediately got lost. Celso's comrade, the lookout, had rented a house in Grajaú, a North Zone neighborhood nestled at the foot of a mountain. The access to Grajaú was from the east through a labyrinth of small neighborhood roads. Celso thought the relatively out-of-the way location made it a safe place to bring the prisoners. We had been so concentrated on our getaway strategies, we had not rehearsed finding our way to Grajaú. I stopped the car. Celso pulled a small flashlight out of his jacket pocket and opened a map on his lap.

"What the hell?" one of the voices said from the back. "Where are we going?"

"Grajaú," Celso said. "I need to consult a map."

"Screw the map. I know the way."

119

The Renault was already parked on the street when we arrived at the house. The prisoners stumbled out of the car. Celso had to help one of them walk the few steps to the front door. César ran out of the house. We drove off to ditch the stolen cars. I abandoned the Chevrolet near the quaint train station that carried passengers four kilometers up Corcovado Mountain to the pedestal of the Christ the Redeemer statue. At that hour no trains were running and the neighborhood was asleep. When I finally made it back to my apartment by taxi at 3 a.m., Pedro and Monica were playing casino. They jumped up and greeted me as if I were an apparition. "Alexandre! *Tudo bem*? We would have waited up for you all night." Monica said.

"Everything's fine."

I took a long, long shower before I gave them a summary of my evening.

CHAPTER TEN

I

The active life of an urban guerrilla in Brazil was short — rarely much more than a year before it was cut short by arrest, exile or death — though in mid-1969 we didn't have that perspective. All I knew was that I was struggling to keep from being overwhelmed by my own ideas and actions. Even in the midst of holding up the bank in Méier, I hadn't been able to resist thinking that this would be the most exciting, important period of my life. All of us — Roberto, César, José, Adolfo and I — were coming to believe we were too smart and too fast to be caught. It worried me.

Monica was conflicted about the risks I was taking. In the days following the penitentiary break, we alternated between fighting and making peace. She complained that women in the resistance didn't get to play central roles in formulating tactics. "I've been involved much longer than you," she said, "and I'm still in a subordinate role." She was afraid for me, proud of me and envious of my opportunities as a man, all at the same time. One minute she advised me to go underground and join Celso's group, the next she was growing weary of the fight and wanted us both to quit.

"I want to live normally," she said. "When will the gods just let us be content with each other?"

"The gods always arrange it that nobody is content very often," I said, "or for very long."

"Then why are we together?"

"We've fallen into a habit, I guess."

"Then we should break it. It's good you're going home to Bauru during semester break."

121

"You want me gone, out of your life? We can separate right now." I flung my key to her apartment onto her bed, blew her a kiss and walked out.

We had escalated our irrational quarrel to avoid facing our real fears. Even before our quarrel I had decided to go home during the July three-week winter break. Not going home would alarm my father. Rather than argue against my decision, he would probably come to Rio again to see what I was up to. I wanted to avoid that possibility. Besides, as I had told Monica and Pedro, Bauru would be a welcome diversion from my schizophrenic life in Rio. According to the newspapers, the police were still staking out embassies in Rio to prevent the four escaped political prisoners from seeking asylum. The police need not have bothered. The men were well hidden and had no intention of leaving Brazil.

I looked forward to taking walks among the coffee trees and riding with the cowhands over open range. Cows spend most of their day in a half-waking state, neither asleep nor active. "Dream time," as Maria Rita used to call it. For a few weeks I would join the Nelores in their leisurely existence and try not to dwell on the daily reminders of my father's addiction to gambling and its destructive consequences. At twilight I would sit on the west-facing veranda and drink a *caipirinha* — light on the sugar, generous with the *cachaça* and the crushed lime — and watch the sun sink beneath the horizon as flocks of noisy parakeets landed for the evening in the giant, pink-flowering *paineira* trees. In a strange way, it was comforting to know that we Barbosas were only guests on Bernardo's *fazenda*. If we had still owned the land, I would have felt myself even more acutely a hypocrite — at once a member of the ruling class and a revolutionary expropriator of its wealth.

Monica planned to visit her mother during the holiday. Monica's father, a chemical engineer, had died of pancreatic cancer two weeks

122

before she graduated from high school. Monica didn't like to talk about the crushing sadness and confusion that followed his death. Shortly after he died, her mother left Rio and moved back to her family's property in Belo Horizonte. Monica missed her mother, but disliked having to visit her in a city she found boring, despite Oscar Niemeyer's famous modern buildings around Lake Pampulha. She couldn't persuade her mother to return to Rio, to the restorative power of the beach and the ocean, to her *carioca* friends, even when Monica argued that in Rio her mother would be near her brother, Monica's uncle Maurício, who continued to press the government for information about Jayme. "Everything in Rio de Janeiro reminds me of my losses," Monica's mother would say during their frequent phone calls. The two women would fall silent to attend to their individual grief.

Ten days before my exam in architectural theory, the test I felt least prepared for, Celso knocked on our door at 3 a.m. He was full of enthusiasm for a new bank expropriation.

"A really major holdup," he said. "Downtown, in the financial center. We're going to rob two banks at exactly the same time, one across the street from the other. I worked it out. There are two reasonable escape routes without having to go through the middle of downtown."

I started laughing. "That's a ballet, Celso, not a bank robbery."

"It'll take 10 people to pull it off. The six guys we liberated, plus Carlos, César, you and me."

"Those guys we rescued must be anxious to get back to the penitentiary," I said.

"Believe me, they aren't. The more I've gone over the plan, the more I realize it will work. The banks I'm thinking about are on opposite sides of the street. It'll confuse the cops. We'll have time to get away."

"Are you kidding? It will just make it easier for the cops. It would be better to rob two banks far apart, but inside the same police district. Who are the two extra guys we took out? Is this their idea?"

Celso shook his head no. "They're common prisoners. I don't know what they were in for. Our guys got to be friends with them. They said they had been politicized in prison, so our guys took them along. Anyway, the plan is mine. We could get 200,000 to 300,000 — maybe more." Celso planned to use the money to send a contingent from his group to Cuba for guerrilla training.

I agreed with him that the only way to defeat the Brazilian military was to attack it piecemeal with a well-trained, wide-ranging guerrilla force, but I didn't like his proposal. "As far as I'm concerned," I said, "robbing two banks simultaneously just means there are twice as many ways for something to go wrong, and it doesn't add any escape routes."

Celso wasn't able to overcome my negative evaluation. He left and I went back to bed. An hour later he was back at our door. "You're right. A traffic jam in the wrong place would jeopardize the escape. But it could work a few blocks away in Lapa, where there are many escape routes and few traffic jams." In the end he swayed me.

A telephone call from my mother woke me at 8:30. She was full of her latest efforts to update the parlor. She had just had the walls painted taxicab yellow and removed various antiques from the room. "The Manueline table stays," she said. "Just one ornate 19th-century piece really complements the room. I'm sure you're going to like the parlor when you see it in a few weeks, Alexandre." But the real point of her call was to quiz me about Monica. "I'm saving the Italian candlesticks and the rosewood sideboard for you. You can have them when you marry."

"Is that a veiled question, *mamãe*?" I felt sleepy and annoyed.

"I still deeply regret Maria Rita's elopement. And I blame your father. The house will be ready for a truly elegant wedding reception.

Worthy of an architect — two architects. When will you bring Monica to Bauru? I am eager to get to know her."

"We had a fight. I'm not seeing her anymore."

"Tomorrow is another day, Alexandre. I sense you really care for her."

"I've never told her that."

"Have you met her parents?"

"Her father's dead."

"European background?"

"Are you asking if she's white going back several generations? Her nose has a touch of Africa." For a full minute I didn't respond to the silence on the other end of the phone. Finally I said, "If there was miscegenation in Monica's family, it happened in the 18th century."

"She's Portuguese?"

"Don't concern yourself. Her nose is as thin as yours."

"Certain things are important, Alexandre. We have to be frank." She was silent again. "Your father's considering involving himself in a new enterprise. Coffee byproducts. He's looking into cellulose and dyestuffs."

"I thought he was busy learning to play the piano."

"He's too young to retire to his hammock and have the piano for his only amusement. And he's set his mind on getting the *fazenda* back."

II

The simultaneous robbery of two banks in Lapa turned out to be a disaster. I entered Banco Bradesco with Celso and two of the former political prisoners. At the same moment Carlos and the two common prisoners burst into Unibanco across the street. César and the other two political prisoners were the drivers. It wasn't until hours later that I found out what happened at Unibanco. My team carried out our robbery without incident. Everyone on the floor. Cash drawers emptied. The vault was open. We helped ourselves. Celso and I filled a duffle bag with money, ran out and jumped into one of the stolen getaway cars. Right behind us the two political prisoners, carrying a second duffle bag stuffed with cash, took off in another getaway car. Our car headed south; the second car went west. We planned to lose any pursuing cops by cutting through Santa Teresa. Our driver, Nilo, one of the political comrades, had lived there and knew its hilly, zigzag streets and its secret foot trails through the mountains should we need to abandon the car.

As we pulled away from Banco Bradesco, I caught a glimpse of César idling at the curb in the third stolen car, waiting for the group from across the street. When we were positive we weren't being followed, we drove out to Barra da Tijuca to celebrate. We stopped at the end of Rio's longest beach — completely deserted on a weekday — stashed our two homemade submachine guns and the cash in the trunk of the stolen Simca, took off our jeans and shirts and ran exuberantly into the Atlantic in our underwear.

It wasn't until 2:30 in the afternoon, when we got to the house in Grajaú to add up the money, that we learned the terrible news. Eloy, one of the common criminals who had gone into Unibanco with Carlos, had taken a hostage — a young boy, maybe 7 or 8 years old — whom César and Carlos released a few minutes later. Eloy said he had panicked because he thought one of the bank patrons was an armed plainclothes cop. Our two new recruits, the common criminals, failed to understand our outrage. The rest of us were devastated. When I arrived at Monica's front door at 5, I was shaken, scared and humiliated. How could I publicly apologize for what had happened? I was desperate to talk over the disaster with her. I knew Monica had an afternoon

126

class; I would wait. It wasn't until I fumbled in my pocket for her key that I remembered I had thrown it on her bed in my hasty, angry farewell gesture.

Feeling too disturbed to hang around outside her apartment building, I went to the beach and walked through the surf from Leblon to Ipanema, making an enormous effort to concentrate on the pull of the sand as waves broke over my ankles. I was in a daze, staring at my feet. Eventually I cut across the wide beach to sit at its edge on a stone bench and consider what to do. Should I lie to Monica about what happened? From a pay phone I telephoned Pedro and, disregarding caution, told him in a rush about Eloy's having taken the boy. "It's beyond terrible," I said. "I don't know what to do."

"You're going to be crucified in the news."

"Right now I've got to talk to Monica."

I waited for her at the bus stop on Avenida General San Martin. When she got off the bus I fell in step behind her. "Do you want to have dinner, Alexandre?" she called to me from over her shoulder.

"I'm not hungry." I caught up to her and put my arm around her waist. "We've got to talk. I've disgraced the revolution."

"That's a new twist."

"I'm not kidding. I need your advice."

"I'd consider giving you back my key — if you really want it."

"I really do, but this isn't about your key."

"You know I was worried about those common criminals we liberated," I said as I paced around her chalk-white room. "During our robbery this morning, one of them grabbed a young boy as a shield. His mother was standing right next to him. Eloy jammed a Luger against the kid's neck."

"My God, I can't believe it!"

127

I told her the whole story as it had been told to me. How the terrified kid cried, *"Mamãe, mamãe, don't let him kill me!"* How Eloy had marched the kid out of the bank and into César's car. César said he wouldn't take off with the boy. Eloy took the safety off his pistol and pressed it behind César's ear. The kid was terrified and crying. Carlos and Artur, the other common prisoner, ran out of the bank, each with a duffle bag full of money. César had to speed away or they would be caught.

Twelve blocks from Unibanco at Largo da Glória Park, César stopped the car. "Carlos pulled the kid out of the car," I said. "He'd wet his pants. Carlos put a handful of money in his pocket and told him to take a taxi home. The kid was sobbing and said he didn't know how to get home by himself. There wasn't anything Carlos could do. He had to leave the kid on the street."

Monica's face was ashen. "Mao said there may be Communists in prison, but we cannot blindly empty the prisons into the ranks of the revolution."

"It wasn't my idea to free common criminals. The Navy guys should have known better. I don't care what anybody else says. We have to make a public apology."

"You should be lynched."

"Pedro said we'd get crucified. I hope we can find out where the boy lives. I'd like to do something for him — anonymously, of course."

"Like what? Send him candy? You'll scare him even more. And how do you propose to find him?"

"I don't know. I'm ashamed, Monica. Profoundly. We all are. We've got to apologize publicly."

"How? Do you think the Brazilian press will print your apology? Even without censorship, they wouldn't. You're dreaming."

128

"We can try leaving a statement at the door of Unibanco. Maybe someone in the bank will spread the rumor it was a mistake and we're sorry."

"The bank will just turn your statement over to the police. You realize you've played right into the hands of the military. Are they going to let terrorists who snatched an innocent boy make a public apology? Face it, Alexandre, all excuses for snatching a kid are unacceptable. The best thing to do is keep quiet and hope it blows over soon."

"That's what Celso said, but I have to try to do something. Maybe we could take over a radio station just long enough to read an apology."

"Oh, sure. Take it over how? At gunpoint? Nobody's going to help you. The only way I can see to publish an apology is through the foreign press. Maybe you could slip a note to one of the foreign reporters covering Nelson Rockefeller's trip."

"Rockefeller's still in Brasília, and besides, now *you're* dreaming. When he gets here tomorrow, he'll be cordoned off by military security wherever he goes. The generals are making sure Rockefeller only hears their side of the story." I persuaded Monica to help me draft an apology. We decided to leave copies on the doorstep of Unibanco's branch in Copacabana. Afterward I would try to pass a copy to a reporter covering Governor Rockefeller. We debated how to sign it.

"With some letters everyone will recognize as meaningless," Monica said. "The last thing you want is to implicate an organization that had nothing to do with your mess."

We settled on signing the apology with the first and last letters of the alphabet. Monica had lent her typewriter to her group, so we each produced eight copies by hand in stenciled block letters:

IN OUR STRUGGLE TO RID OUR BELOVED NATION OF ITS REPRESSIVE GOVERNMENT AND THE ATTENDANT CLIMATE OF TENSION, ANXIETY, INSECURITY AND VIOLENCE EXTENDING TO ALL LEVELS OF SOCIETY, WE HAVE FOUND IT NECESSARY TO ACT IN OPPOSITION. ATTEMPTING TO RESTORE OUR DEMOCRATIC PROCESSES IS TAKING COURAGE, COMMITMENT AND MONEY.

IN ORDER TO FILL THE REVOLUTIONARY WAR CHEST WE HAVE EXPROPRIATED FUNDS FROM BANKS, BUT ALWAYS TAKING PRECAUTIONS THAT NO ONE WOULD BE HURT, INCLUDING BANK OFFICIALS. WEDNESDAY, DURING AN EXPROPRIATION AT A BRANCH OF UNIBANCO, A YOUNG BOY WAS TEMPORARILY TAKEN HOSTAGE BY A MAN WHO REPRESENTED HIMSELF TO US AS A RECRUIT IN THE WAR AGAINST THE MILITARY GOVERNMENT.

IT IS NOW MANIFESTLY CLEAR HIS IDEA OF HOW TO CONDUCT UNDERGROUND OPPOSITION IS AT ODDS WITH OURS. TO THE YOUNG BOY AND HIS FAMILY, WE DEEPLY AND HUMBLY APOLOGIZE. WE WILL DEAL WITH YOUR ABDUCTOR. OUR REVOLUTIONARY GROUP LOVES AND RESPECTS CHILDREN AND WE LOVE OUR NATION.

RESPECTFULLY, AZ

At 6 a.m. we walked to Avenida Nossa Senhora de Copacabana and left 12 copies of the apology propped against Unibanco's ornate glass-and-metal door. We hoped that, when the bank opened at 9, our apology would be taken inside, read and talked about. We circled the immediate vicinity of the bank for three-quarters of an hour. Each time we passed Unibanco's door, we were relieved to see our bundle waiting, tied with a ribbon from Monica's sewing supplies. The lights blinked on inside a *botequim* diagonally across the street from the bank. We hadn't slept all night, nor had anything to eat. We sat on folding chairs at the establishment's lone table and ordered *cafe com leite* and rolls. "What if a porter just throws them away?" I said.

"He won't. He probably can't read, so he'll show them to his boss."

"I think we should hang around here until someone opens the front door and we see for sure what happens."

"Wait around till the bank opens?" Monica said. "I can't, Alexandre, I have my contracts class at 9:30. Anyway, we've done what we can. You realize this is unbelievably foolish."

We walked the nine blocks to my apartment and took a nap in each other's arms. I woke up with a start at 8:15. It took me a few seconds to realize that Monica had gone to her class and wasn't lying beside me. Pedro was making coffee. Silvia was in the bathroom. I threw on my clothes and ran to the bank. The lights were on inside and the stack of apologies was missing. I cupped my hands and peered through the glass door. A man in a short-sleeved shirt saw me and pointed to his watch. He held up nine fingers. I nodded. As I was lowering my hands I saw the pile of apologies, still neatly tied, sitting on top of a standup counter. A man in a dark suit approached it with a pocket knife in his hand.

CHAPTER ELEVEN

I

Governor Nelson Rockefeller had been sent to South America by President Nixon to assess the need for adjustments to U.S. diplomatic policy in the region. Of course, he wasn't going to hear about the change my friends and I were risking our lives to achieve — an end to our military dictatorship that, from the beginning, the U.S. had supported. Nevertheless, I had hoped our cause could get some benefit from his trip — an opportunity to pass my apology to one of the foreign reporters accompanying Rockefeller's task force.

It proved impossible to break through Rockefeller's security. At the airport, a wall of armed combat troops held the crowd back 50 meters from the terminal entrance. I overheard a guy say that when Bobby Kennedy came to Rio three years before, he had been able to shake Kennedy's hand as he went by. "Now I can't even see Rockefeller," he said.

Censors withheld the reporting of our double robbery and hostage-taking until Rockefeller departed for Paraguay. In the succeeding days, the press played the story over and over. The headlines were just what we expected and deserved:

"The Worst! An Outrage!"

"Warning to the Left: Children Are Not Fair Game!"

"Brazil's Youthful Left Loses Its Innocence to Embrace Terrorism!"

There was no word on the street about the apology I had left at the bank. I was not surprised. Just as I was giving up on finding a

132

way to circulate a public apology, Pedro came up with a useful idea. "Last year, Silvia made friends with an American reporter who spoke to her journalism class. Her friend used to work for United Press International in Rio. I think her friend just returned to Rio. Silvia could get your apology to her."

"Silvia can't know I was involved in the kidnapping."

"You weren't."

"Morally I was, Pedro. Don't ask her. I'm worried enough about security being compromised with someone like Eloy walking around."

"She hasn't said anything, but I think she suspects you could have been involved. It would put her mind at ease if she knew the whole story."

"It might work," Monica said when I discussed Pedro's idea with her. "The imperialists should be good for something besides just taking their profits out of the country."

After talking it over with Celso, I decided to take the chance. That meant bringing Silvia into my clandestine life. We didn't think there was much risk of Silvia being picked up and tortured. If we misjudged the odds, I could find myself in detention, receiving electric shocks while hanging naked from the infamous "parrot's perch" torture device with my ankles and wrists tied together. Everyone I was involved with would immediately have to go underground.

The next evening Silvia reported that she had put a copy of my apology into the hands of Kate Lawrence, her friend at United Press International, who was going to send it out on the UPI wire. More than that, Kate wanted to interview the author.

"You shouldn't lose the opportunity," Silvia said.

"You're positive I can trust her? The military watches the foreign press." I raised the possibility that an American working at a reporter's job in Brazil could be undercover for the CIA.

133

"Not Kate. She's good friends with people on our side."

Silvia told me Kate's tragic story. Her wedding to UPI's Rio news director, John Wadson, was to have taken place in early January 1969. Three weeks before the wedding, John was found shot to death in the elevator of the office building UPI shared with *Jornal do Brasil*. The police concluded it was a late-night robbery and, over the following six months, they had not found any reason to change their opinion. Kate would not discuss John's murder except to hint that she was not satisfied with the police version of what had happened. Silvia suspected John had been silenced because he was onto a story that would embarrass the military government.

"John hired Kate at UPI. It was love at first sight for both of them. I think she's come back to Brazil to follow up some new rumor about John's death," Silvia said. "Besides being a journalist, she's a poet, a really accomplished one."

The following afternoon, Silvia and I were waiting at the apartment she shared with a revolving group of university students. Her two current roommates had gone home to Santos for the weekend. The apartment, on the second floor of a large low-rise structure, had thick, whitewashed stucco walls and it felt eerie. Maybe that's because I knew the building was originally built as an insane asylum.

As soon as I heard a knock, I slipped on my mask. Silvia answered the door. I almost laughed when I got my first glimpse of Kate Lawrence striding through the door. She was a long-limbed beauty with luxuriant auburn hair, straight from Hollywood central casting. I half-expected Humphrey Bogart to follow her into the room. She was wearing jeans and a man's blue-and-white-striped shirt. I had the idea I had seen her before, but I couldn't remember where. I rose to greet her.

"Your idea to circulate an apology was unusual," she said as she shook my hand with a firm grip. "We can set our own ground rules. You tell me what's on the record and what's background." Her accent in Portuguese was quite good — not quite American and not quite anything else recognizable. I offered her a seat on the worn brown sofa and positioned myself in a straight-backed chair directly opposite. Silvia disappeared into the kitchen, offering to get Cokes. Kate regarded me, head to foot, slowly. "I like your hood. It isn't the conventional pillowcase with holes."

"My girlfriend designed it."

She smiled. "Can I say that in my article?"

"I guess I don't see the harm."

"When I lived in Rio, I was close to a lot of people who opposed the military," she said. "We may have some mutual friends besides Silvia."

"We might."

"Brazil's a private club. At least among the upper classes, everybody knows everybody. Are you a member? You shake hands and sit in a chair like landed gentry." She moved forward, sitting very erect on the edge of the couch, our knees almost touching.

I ignored her probe into my background, but I admired her astuteness. "Silvia told me about your fiancé," I said. "I'm truly sorry. You have my most sincere condolences."

"Thank you." Kate looked away. "I'm leaving Rio in a few days. I shouldn't have come back. It's too painful. I told UPI I'd do occasional pieces for them. I'm interested in your story."

"The point I want to make very forcefully," I said, "is that my group's only doing what's necessary to liberate the nation. We've used all the money we've expropriated for the aims of the revolution. That's

135

on the record. I wish we could find a political solution to the dictatorship, but we've been forced into an armed struggle. Even the old orthodox Communists would like to see a return to constitutional democracy, same as me and my friends. It's only the doctrinaire wing of the clandestine movement that advocates strict socialism."

"Isn't your group underground?"

"I'm leading a life that's unlawful, but not covert. I hide in plain sight."

I barely noticed Silvia walking back into the room with cans of Coke. She had thoughtfully put a straw in mine so I could sip it through my hood. She retreated to sit on the floor on the opposite side of the room, signaling that she was listening but did not intend to be a part of the conversation.

Kate Lawrence surprised me. Our interview lasted much longer than I had expected. I was prepared to say how deeply sorry I was about taking any hostage, especially a child, but not much more. She drew me out, got me to admit I was prepared to risk my life, but not my soul.

"When you started robbing banks ... "

I held up my hand, the way my parents did to stop a conversation that was going in a direction they didn't like. "Wait a minute," I said.

"Don't worry," she said. "I'm not asking you to admit to anything, especially details of your robberies."

"We're off the record," I said.

She nodded and started over. "I'm sure you considered the risk of capture and imprisonment. But did you think about the moral risk of what would happen if you met resistance? Some innocent person getting hurt, or worse? Someone from your group taking a child as a shield?"

136

"It was a terrible, inexcusable mistake. The apology Silvia gave you is the same one I left by the door of Unibanco hours after the robbery, way before the press called for our heads. The only reason the boy wasn't released immediately at the bank is that the guy who took him shoved the kid into one of our getaway cars, pointed a gun at the driver's head and told him to hit the gas or die on the spot. The hostage-taker fooled us. He had been incarcerated as a common criminal. Our guys believed him when he said he'd been politicized in prison. He seemed sincere."

"Since when did the criminal class join the resistance?"

"We got badly taken in."

"Will you turn him over to the police?"

"No, they'd torture him and we'd be exposed. We'll deal with him."

"How?"

"I can't say, but we will."

"Aren't you playing into the hands of the military regime by allowing yourselves to be painted as dangerous criminals?"

"It's our duty to resist our oppressors."

"Are you the leader of your group?"

"No."

"Is Carlos Marighella your leader?"

"His organization has its agenda. We have ours."

"Do you have links to China, Cuba, Russia?"

"No and no and no."

I was not in a hurry to break off the conversation, but I found myself hiding behind terse answers and left-wing cant. I wondered whether Kate Lawrence realized I was playing a role. When I resisted answering further questions about doctrine, she asked, "Do you know a song by Walter Decker that goes, 'The future is a bird that comes

137

already tired from being an airplane. It is the future of Brazil, so talked of and certain . . . '?"

"No. Should I?" I said. "Silvia told me you're a poet."

Silvia spoke up: "I've read Kate's poems. I really like them. Kate writes about Brazil, but not in the way Brazilian poets do. Hers are more interesting."

Kate smiled. "You've heard from an audience of one."

"She's being modest," Silvia said as she got off the floor to stretch.

Kate continued, "Walter's a good friend. I think you'd like his album."

"I'll be sure to look for it," I said. "I wish we could have met under different circumstances."

"Maybe someday, if I come back to Rio, we will."

"I do have a favor to ask of you," I said. "The newspapers said the boy lives in the South Zone. Do you know his name? How to get in touch with the family?"

"If I knew it, which I don't, I couldn't reveal it. He's 6 years old. His parents begged the press not to publish any information about them."

"If I gave you something for the boy, a present, could you see he got it? I was thinking he might like an electric toy train set."

"What a beautiful idea. You could leave the present with a note outside the UPI bureau. Come early in the morning, before 6 o'clock. José, our legman, is the first one in. He'll find it. One way or another, before I leave Rio, I'll make sure the boy receives it."

"The present is off the record."

"If you leave it at UPI, it won't be."

"People shouldn't be seduced that what we did was all right because of the present."

138

Silvia interjected, "Give the present to me and I'll deliver it to Kate."

"Is that okay with you, Kate?" I asked. "Do you think you can keep your bureau out of it and contact the family directly?"

"My bureau has the address. I can get it. Don't worry."

"Just tell the boy the train is from someone who thinks he's very brave."

"I will." Kate put her notebook into her purse and stood up. We shook hands. Silvia showed her out. Suddenly I remembered where I had seen her before. I had seen pictures of her in *Manchete* wearing a white maillot, dodging waves, cavorting in the surf with Helena, a famous Rio model. The magazine photos had caught my eye not only because they were of gorgeous women playfully posed, but also because they were taken by Nelson Claudio Carvalho. I had admired his photo essays on Rio neighborhoods.

Monday afternoon I gave Silvia the elaborate five-car electric train set I had bought for the boy. That evening she took it to Kate. Censorship kept Kate Lawrence's story of our apology out of the Brazilian press, but democracies around the world printed it, and word of our deep regret trickled back to Brazil.

II

After the disaster of the hostage-taking, it was a relief to take time off from activism to attend to my exams. Monica was still not sleeping with me on a regular basis, and when she did, we didn't always make love. I accused her of becoming an Indian mystic, withholding her sexual energy and rechanneling it into studying for her exams. We still had unfinished business between us.

My parents telephoned with their enthusiastic plans for my homecoming. My mother said she was instructing a new cook how to make my grandmother's mocha hazelnut torte, one of my favorite desserts. My father was preparing for a piano recital he intended to give on my return. "In your honor, Alexandre," he said. "Simple pieces, of course. Maybe a Telemann fantasia transposed to the key of C. And I've invited 24 of my closest friends to attend. Afterward we'll have dinner. I've ordered four cases of Piper-Heidsieck '59, a truly happy vintage year."

My examinations in architectural theory and in case studies in engineering went well. The academic pressure was off, though I intended to spend part of my holiday in Bauru working on my senior thesis — designing housing prototypes suitable for the Amazon. Pedro finished his exams three days before I did and left to visit his parents in Curitiba. He planned to stay away only eight days because he didn't want to be separated from Silvia. "I'm not going to let myself screw up this relationship," he had said. "Maybe I should keep a psychiatrist on call."

Monica had to take one more exam before leaving to visit her mother in Belo Horizonte. Without letting slip alarming words like "love," we agreed to postpone any serious discussion of our future until the next semester. I was rambling around the apartment, investigating forgotten piles of junk, organizing clothes and books, when Roberto came by with Celso. It did not surprise me to see the two of them together. "César introduced us," Roberto said.

"That figures," I said. "Every clandestine movement needs a social director. César's our guy. Never mind about security."

"Calm down," Roberto continued. "It's obvious we're wasting resources acting separately. It's amazing what can be accomplished in one day when you have cash. We drove here in a '66 Aero Willys we bought from a friend of Adolfo's. It's in pretty decent shape, considering it's been in two accidents."

140

"We need one more car," Celso said.

The need for instant access to reliable transportation was a leit-motif for all the underground groups. People who were underground couldn't take the chance of presenting the required credentials to a car dealer. Everybody felt uneasy being dependent on the near-wrecks we were able to purchase without documentation. It was against our principles, and not worth the risk, to steal cars except for getaways.

I hadn't seen Roberto since our insanely spur-of-the-moment robbery of Banco Nacional in Realengo. Actually, I felt enormous relief that he was joining up with Celso and that consequently my services would not be required — at least for a while. Purchasing a car in my name would expose me to less risk than robbing a bank. "I'm not underground," I said, "at least, not yet. I'm willing to buy a car in my name."

Celso went on to tell me that Eloy and Artur had disappeared from the house in Grajaú two days after the hostage-taking. The night they left, there had been a small riot. A sexy woman had shown up drunk and immediately started pounding Artur's chest with her fists and screaming challenges to his manhood. Half an hour later, another woman had walked through the front door as if she owned the house. The women lunged at each other, hissing taunts, screaming hysterically, pulling each other's hair. Artur skillfully separated the women and calmed down his drunken wife and his mistress. "He's such a pretty talker," the wife had said to the mistress as the two women walked out of the house together, holding hands.

"Artur and Eloy left right behind them, grinning," Celso said. "Those guys are hard-core criminals. Without a doubt, they'll be back in the penitentiary. We couldn't count on them keeping their mouths shut. As soon as they walked out, we immediately left the house and found another one to rent in Cosme Velho. The Navy guys went to São Paulo, but they'll be back."

141

The next afternoon, just as I was leaving my apartment to go car shopping with a briefcase full of Celso's money, Roberto telephoned. "We're planning something for this Thursday. To tell you the truth, Alexandre, I feel uneasy about it, but I can't put my finger on what's wrong. Celso, Carlos, César, José and Adolfo all say I'm worrying with no reason. Have a look at the neighborhood with me."

We agreed to meet at 6:30 in Cinelândia. I was counting on a car dealer's not finding it in his interest to report cash customers to the authorities. At a Volkswagen dealer, two Beetles were available immediately — one red, one tan. I chose the less eye-catching tan car and slipped the proprietor a substantial inducement to cut through the burdensome paperwork. At 6, I drove off into rush hour traffic with proof of ownership and permanent license plates.

Roberto was waiting for me in front of the Odeon Theater. The bank he wanted to show me was in Bangu, a neighborhood situated between mountains, four kilometers west of the bank we had robbed in Realengo. Banco Boavista was on the south side of railroad tracks that carried workers from North Zone neighborhoods to downtown Rio. Several more banks were strung out along Bangu's commercial street on the other side of the tracks. I drove around the dingy residential streets where teenage boys maneuvered soccer balls between lulls in traffic, continuing past a large textile factory, then past the high outer walls and razor wire of Rio's maximum-security penitentiary complex — another hellhole where political prisoners were sent. It didn't take me long to appreciate what was worrying Roberto. "I agree. You'd better choose another bank," I said. "The railroad tracks and the mountains block your way to the north and the south. East just takes you into dense neighborhoods with no fast connection to a major highway. The cops will figure out the only direct escape route is west on Avenida de

Santa Cruz. It would be easy for them to block the street. You'd have to shoot your way out."

"The cops haven't chased us once yet. If they were going to, why not downtown or in Realengo? Why would they suddenly get lucky in Bangu?"

"You asked for my advice —"

"I'll tell Celso and the other guys what you said."

At the same hour they were planning to rob Banco Boavista, Monica would be taking her last exam. To celebrate I decided to make dinner for her — something beyond my usual omelet. I telephoned my mother for a recipe. "How do you prepare filet of sole with wine sauce?"

"The easy way or the complicated way?"

"I want to impress Monica."

Repressing her curiosity about whether Monica and I were friends again, she explained how to deglaze a white-wine-and-butter sauce with cream. "Just don't overcook the sole. It shouldn't be dry."

"How can I tell when it's done?"

"When it's opaque. And it should flake easily. Maybe you should practice once."

"No time for that."

"Your father and I can't wait to see you."

"I shaved off my beard."

"I'm glad to hear it. Your father said it didn't become you."

"I looked good with a beard. I just wanted a change."

"In principle I dislike beards," my mother said. "Unless they conceal a weak chin, which is not your case."

I was a little dubious that I could prepare her recipe, but I decided to give it a try. Monica and I had only two more nights together before I left for Bauru. I hoped the good food, or at least the good effort, and the fact that her exams were over would lead to a night of abandoned sex. She arrived at 7:30 in a lighthearted mood. "I know I passed," she said. "Actually, I think I did very well."

We kissed for a long time before I told her about the sole I had bought for dinner. "I thought you only knew how to make omelets," she said. "I'll help you prepare it."

"No need. I have everything under control."

I prepared the sole while Monica made a green salad. We washed down the fish, which I thought was slightly overcooked, with a French pinot blanc.

"The sole was marvelous, Alexandre. Not a bit dry."

I had forgotten to buy coffee. After dinner, giddy from the wine and our four-day absence from each other, we walked hand in hand to our usual *botequim* for *cafezinhos*. "What will you do in Bauru?" she asked.

"Stop looking out for the cops. Play cards. Get reacquainted with the Nelores. They've got the life — just rumination and resting all day long. And you? What will you do in Belo Horizonte?"

"Try one more time to convince my mother to move back to Rio."

We walked back to my apartment, quickly undressed each other, then slowed down to enjoy our reunion.

The pounding on the door hadn't awakened me, but it woke Monica. She shook me. I grabbed my briefs and crept to the door. "Alexandre!" It was Celso's voice. I opened the door quickly. José was with him. I glanced at my watch — 4:45 a.m.

"We've got to get out of here!" Celso said. "Right now! The police just picked up Adolfo at his parents' apartment. While the cops were pounding on his door, Adolfo managed to tell his father where to find us, and his father took a taxi to Cosme Velho to warn us. DOPS is rolling up our group!"

"Jesus Christ! What happened?"

"You were right about the robbery. We got trapped. Our car got away because we threw money out the windows and the cops stopped chasing us to pick it up, but they must have caught the other car with Roberto, César and Carlos. We didn't see it happen. They must have tortured them to get the lead to Adolfo. We had agreed to meet at the house in Cosme Velho."

José said, "César wouldn't be able to withstand torture. He's got diabetes. He'll spill our names. We've got to leave the country! Now!"

"Where's the Beetle?" Celso demanded.

"Parked across the street."

"Let's go!"

Monica had thrown on her clothes. "I'm going, too."

I looked at her hard. "They're not looking for you. Don't be crazy."

"My name could be on their list. You never know. I want to be with you, Alexandre."

"Be rational. I don't know what kind of life I'm getting into."

"I'll take my chances."

"For Christ's sake — make up your fucking minds," José said. "DOPS is probably 15 minutes behind us."

"I don't think you should come," I said.

"You don't want me to?"

"No, I don't."

"Because why? Commitment?"

145

"I've already committed to you, Monica."

"Then I'm coming."

I threw on my clothes and snatched my wallet off the coffee table. Monica ran to the bathroom, grabbed some toiletries and shoved them into her purse as she ran to the door. Rather than take the elevator, we scrambled down four flights of stairs and out onto the street. As I started the ignition, I heard a police siren approaching. From which direction? I couldn't tell. Monica was in the front seat, Celso and José in the back. We had to get off my street quickly. I narrowly missed hitting a van that was changing lanes unpredictably. As we were leaving Copacabana, José shouted, "Look at that! Did you see that sign, 'We repair rosaries'? It's an omen!"

Without thinking, I was heading toward the André Rebouças Tunnel which would connect us to the network of major highways that lead out of town. Celso read my mind. "We'll get trapped in the tunnel. Back roads. Back roads. Stick close to the coast."

"Too slow," I said.

"Have it your way and we could get fucked."

For a second I considered turning around.

José said, "Do you know where you're going?"

"Uruguay," I said. "Have you got a better suggestion?"

"No. We aren't being followed. Take the tunnel."

Everyone in the car was silent as we sped through the tunnel, the longest in Brazil, nearly three kilometers. When we emerged, José rapped my shoulder in jubilation. Celso said, "Twenty kilometers to BR 116. We're going to make it."

I nodded. BR 116 was the major highway to São Paulo. It would take us southwest. From there I could cross the mountains and follow the coast south to Uruguay. Sunrise was still an hour off. As I raced along Avenida Brasil toward the highway, Celso said, "I left the Thompsons and an INA .45 in the bathtub."

I asked, "Did you bring any of the money from the robbery?"

"I stuffed what I could in my pockets. I'll count it when I can see."

Monica put her hand on my thigh. "How long do you think it will take to get to the Uruguayan border?"

"I have no idea."

José said, "A day and a half if we don't stop."

"Longer," Celso said.

As the lights of Rio faded behind us, I began to see the stars. I even thought I saw a meteor shower, but I wasn't sure.

CHAPTER TWELVE

I

In Rio, the winter of 1969 was a time when students, musicians, artists, writers and journalists moved and left no forwarding address. The lucky ones said they were going to India and would return enlightened. The unlucky ones left in the middle of the night. We wore the bad spirits of the time like badges on our T-shirts. I had persuaded myself to make trouble for the regime, not because I was confident that my actions would do any good but because the political situation demanded that I try. I still held on to the vague hope that the money we robbed to fund the opposition would hasten Brazil's liberation.

As the four of us drove through the cold July rain toward the Uruguayan border, I could not help thinking of what, for me, would have constituted a normal life. Whatever that was — a flourishing architecture practice, prizes, an exciting cosmopolitan existence, summers at Fazenda Maraíba — seemed forever behind me. At least I knew that if we made it to Uruguay, I would live to see my future, not die in some stinking prison. I gave myself an imagined salute. Celso counted the cash he had on him from the robbery of Banco Boavista in Bangu — 14,400 *cruzeiros novos*. Without discussion, he divided the money three ways and handed rolls of bills to José and me. I split my share with Monica.

We kept heading south parallel to the coast, changing drivers, stopping only to buy gas, maps and snacks and to use a bathroom. In Pelotas, a small coastal city 1,800 kilometers south of Rio in the state of Rio Grande do Sul, we stopped to eat in a Chinese restaurant and study a map. In the underground movement it was known that there was an easy border crossing 340 kilometers inland at Santana do Livramento, which shared a central street with the farming town of Rivera,

148

just over the Uruguayan border. Cars from both countries crossed back and forth between the two towns as one would cross any main street. We left the coastal area and headed west. A few kilometers from the frontier, I slowed down and positioned the Volkswagen between a truck hauling tobacco and another full of sheep. We needn't have worried about whether our Rio de Janeiro license plate would invite questions. The border guard in Santana do Livramento barely looked up from his lunch as he waved us through.

We ordered beer, and a Coke for Celso, at a cantina in Rivera and inquired where we could make long-distance telephone calls. At Compañia Telegráfico-Telefónica del Plata we were told all international calls had to be routed first to Buenos Aires, where connections were made with the International Telephone and Telegraph Company. Depending on traffic, it could take anywhere from seven hours to two days to get through to Brazil. If you didn't want to wait at the CTTP office, you needed to wait by a telephone where you could be notified when your call went through. We got back in the car. Monica took the wheel. From the back seat I watched Uruguay's landscape unfold in low, rolling grasslands. The pastureland looked well watered. I counted grazing sheep to doze off.

In Montevideo we checked into an inexpensive hotel. Our Brazilian identity cards were the only credentials we needed at the reception desk. After more than two days on the road, finally we could take showers, sleep in beds, eat real meals and arrange to make phone calls to Brazil, though it took 24 hours before connections were established. Even from another country, I was careful what I said to my parents. This was no time to drop our paranoia about the wrong ears listening in. Celso called a sister in Recife. Monica tried to sound calm when she spoke to her mother.

José spoke with his father — an ear, nose and throat specialist — at his medical office. "I told him my business activities demanded that

149

I go to Uruguay. I doubt he understood what I was trying to tell him," José said after he hung up. "He wanted to know if I felt depressed. He said we could discuss it tonight at dinner."

"Of course he understood you," Monica said. "Your father has to know how deeply you feel about our political situation. He was being cautious."

The day after my phone call to Bauru, my father flew to Montevideo to meet me. DOPS was known to get information about someone involved in the armed struggle by kidnapping a member of his or her family. After my call home, my father had insisted that my mother leave Brazil immediately. She flew to Caracas, where one of her cousins lived with her Venezuelan husband.

My father was pacing when I entered his room at the Victoria Plaza, a first-class hotel. He seemed more agitated than on the day when Bernardo came, legal papers in hand, to claim Fazenda Maraíba. Even before he embraced me, he made a show of taking my Brazilian and American passports out of his pocket and tossing them on a chair. For the first time in my life I was glad that, because of my father's two years at Georgetown University, I was born in the U.S. and that my parents had taken advantage of America's generosity in granting their infant son citizenship and a U.S. passport. Beyond suggesting that we go to the hotel dining room for dinner, my father scarcely spoke after he embraced me. His long, pained looks in my direction were communication enough.

I was hungry. Between mouthfuls of steak Milanese, I gave an edited account of my clandestine activities. My father barely touched his food. "Good Christ, Alexandre, you're informing me of your involvement in criminal acts ... " He struggled to continue. "You should listen to yourself. You're telling me my son is an outlaw as if you were giving me a gift. I don't consider your conduct a gift." He leaned back

150

in his chair, removed the napkin from his lap, folded it and placed it on the table, signaling he was through with dinner. "You really thought you could blend casual anarchy with your studies? Taking part in the student street demonstrations last year was one thing. That was worry enough for your parents. You truly believed you could get away with robbing banks, freeing prisoners, assaulting I don't know what? My God, Alexandre, I hope you didn't think you had my blessing! And it was completely irresponsible of you to bring Monica with you. What kind of a life do you think you can offer her?"

"It wasn't my choice. She insisted on coming."

Over the following five days, my father alternated between being profoundly angry with me and grudgingly understanding of my actions. He worried about my future and Monica's, about my mother's safety and his own when they returned to the *fazenda*, how my actions might affect Paulo's diplomatic career. He asked whether Maria Rita knew anything about my activities. I said she didn't. "You know the news will travel to Paulo's ambassador in Egypt," he said.

My father spent his time in Montevideo waiting to get a telephone connection to my mother in Caracas or to friends in Bauru, nervously consuming rare steaks and Uruguayan red wines at meals with Monica and me that were mostly silent. I knew he wanted to ask how much of the banks' cash I had in my wallet the night I left Rio, but he refrained. He simply said he regretted not having kept more of his money outside Brazil. "But frankly, Alexandre, your present situation isn't one I made plans for." We each kept our own counsel on topics that could provoke quarrels.

On the sixth day of his visit, after assurances from every prominent friend he could reach that DOPS wasn't poking around Bauru looking for me, my father was ready to go home. He spoke with Bernardo while I was in the room. "Do I dare tell Lucilia she can come home from Venezuela? I'd lose the *fazenda* to you all over again rather than

151

risk her safety. Or mine, for that matter. Alexandre is going to have to become an architect without a degree. He says Frank Lloyd Wright didn't have one either, and he did quite well. I tell you, Bernardo, in all frankness, Lucilia and I had no idea. In one week, I feel a decade older. Now both of my children will be representing their country abroad — one as the wife of a diplomat and one as an exile."

At our parting in his hotel room, my father gave me 1,000 U.S. dollars.

II

On our last night in Montevideo, the four of us drove in bright winter moonlight out along the shore road as far as Playa Carrasco, the last metropolitan beach. On our way back, we stopped at the rundown Parque Hotel near Playa Ramirez and gambled at its government-operated casino. As I strolled around the drab, smoky room to see which card games were available, I felt the tug of the family disease. The money I had stashed in my jeans and jacket pockets and in Monica's purse could have disappeared. Monica sensed my temptation. She squeezed my arm. "If you lose even one peso, I'll leave you. I'll go home."

"Will you?"

"Or I'll stay with José. He doesn't gamble."

"You find him attractive?"

"Yes, I do. Very."

"Go ahead, then."

"You think Celso will come to your rescue with money from his share if you lose?"

"He might."

"I'll wait for you in the bar, Alexandre. I don't want to watch."

"Suppose I give you all my cash except 2,500 pesos."

152

"Forty cruzeiros worth of pesos is what a hotel room costs for one night," she said. "We're in no position to lose a night's lodging. I'm in no mood for this."

"I can make us money. Absolutely we can afford to risk 1,500 pesos."

Reluctantly she nodded her concurrence, but she didn't keep her promise to hang out at the bar. It was hard to concentrate on blackjack with Monica standing behind me, fidgeting. Occasionally I would look around and notice Celso observing the action at the roulette wheel. José paced from game to game, stopping to peer over the shoulders of the few young women seated at the faded and stained gaming tables. After I had played for over an hour, I was ahead by the price of two nights in a hotel. The dealer dealt me a 10, a five and a three. I bet everything — 4,500 pesos — and lost. The dealer's hand added up to 19.

The next morning we drove west toward Argentina, following the broad span of the Rio de la Plata. Our destination was Chile, a relatively democratic country that was sympathetic to Brazilians in flight from military oppression. We were dimly aware that President Eduardo Frei, a moderate, could not succeed himself and that the upcoming election, still a year away, could take the country dramatically and inhospitably to the right, but that was too far in the future to concern us. Our immediate need was to stop running, conserve money, plan new lives and come to terms with the fact that paradise didn't exist on this earth.

The night we fled, Celso was the only one of us who had a passport with him. He always carried it in his pocket — a habit left over from his seafaring days. Monica and José would need to get passports eventually. We thought their Brazilian identity cards would be all they would need to travel across South America, but just to make sure, they had obtained laissez-passers from Uruguay. With my U.S. passport, which my parents had twice renewed, I felt the whole world was open to me.

In Mendoza, Argentina, 1,000 kilometers west of Buenos Aires, the Volkswagen malfunctioned. We waited over a cold weekend for a new distributor to arrive, watching torrential showers sweep across the foothills of the Andes. During our two-week journey, first south through Brazil and then west across South America, Monica and I had slept together, held each other, but never once made love. Nor did we discuss her hasty decision to come with me. We were robots performing simple tasks like brushing our teeth, washing our underwear at night, putting on our shoes. Monica's sunglasses broke. Finding tape to fix them was as far as our future extended.

On our first night in Santiago, Chile, Monica and I negotiated a reduced price of $100 for a double room for two weeks, including breakfast, at the second class Hotel Emperador. We finally felt free enough to make love. Afterward Monica leapt out of bed, went to the window and looked out, hiding naked behind the curtain. Across the street was the old Italian Renaissance-inspired Church of San Francisco.

"You know the saying, 'God writes straight with crooked lines?'" she asked.

"If staying across the street from a church inspires religious thoughts in you, I think we should change hotels."

"I'd like to build a house somewhere warm."

"You could in Rio. Everyone you've telephoned says the same thing — DOPS isn't looking for you. Do you want to go home?"

"Not without you. It isn't just the simple fact we love each other. We belong together because we view the world with the same aesthetic. I want our house to be our joint design. Modernist — open floor plan, clean lines, no ornamentation, lots of glass and light."

154

"I want an art nouveau house — sinuous lines, intricate wrought-iron staircases and balconies."

"I don't believe you."

"Art nouveau is having a revival," I said, smiling.

Monica dropped the curtain and came back to bed. "I'd give anything for a walk along Copacabana beach." She reached across me to the nightstand for her cigarettes. "Santiago del Nuevo Extremo — the historical name for this city says it all, don't you think? Even if the name has another context, Santiago feels like The New End. I already feel isolated here."

"Regrets?"

"Our side will win, Alexandre, and we'll go home."

"I don't think banks forgive easily," I said. "We could learn to ski. In the south somewhere, there's a volcano with a ski lift. I'll take you."

"That's perfect," she said, looking unhappy. "I'm already an expert in designing ski masks. I'd rather go up north. I think the desert must be interesting. Do you suppose it has poisonous snakes?"

"Probably not as many snakes as there are on Fazenda Maraíba. I didn't know you were afraid of snakes."

"I'm not. I'm afraid of the mice they eat."

"You sound as nutty as my father."

"I really like your father, Alexandre."

"He likes you. I think you intrigue him."

We kissed. It was an extraordinary kiss — it lasted, our lips touching, all night.

José knocked on our door at half past nine the next morning. We were getting dressed. "You should try the hotel breakfast," he said. "It's pretty decent, with lots of fruit. I've been exploring. There's a

155

Turkish bath in the hotel, but it's only for women. I wish I could go — at least I could stop shivering. I can barely get a sentence out in Spanish. It's driving me crazy. I can understand them, but they can't understand me."

"Try your Greek," I said.

"Greek's over for me. I'm thinking practically, now. My father warned me I'd end up a dilettante if I didn't get serious and study medicine or engineering. It's ironic — because of a few bank robberies I'm being forced, against my preferred interests, in the direction my father wanted me to go all along. If I'm very, very careful, my money could last until I get a civil-engineering degree in Chile, assuming the university is free. The first step is to learn Spanish. I'd rather be learning Italian or French, languages for making love."

"I'd love to learn Italian," Monica said. "Spanish lacks the poignancy and musicality of Portuguese."

"Last night I decided to stop making negative observations about *espanhol*," José said. "What's the use? I'm not running to Portugal or Mozambique."

III

None of our telephone calls to Rio — to Pedro, Silvia, other friends — had comforted us during our flight. We feared that each call carried a risk to the "clean" person on the other end. No one could find out any information about Roberto, César, Adolfo or Carlos. All of us, in our own ways, dealt with the burden of what we knew was happening to them at the hands of the police. Monica never stopped talking about Jayme. Our sense of helplessness was consuming us. Tempers flared. Silly plans were concocted, then abandoned in morning's light. We would save money by eliminating lunch, only to splurge on movies.

By asking around at various faculties of the University of Chile, we made contact with Brazilian students. It took only a few days to find our way to the Brazilian exile community. The exiles welcomed us with observations on how to navigate in a country "at the end of the road."

"Chile's an island within a continent," one of them said, "maybe with a little less bullshit than other Latin countries."

We all took the experience of being in exile as a chance to confess our dreams. Our desires came out little by little. Celso was introduced to an ex-purser who had worked for Italmar, an Italian steamship company with sailings from Genoa to Valparaíso via the Panama Canal. Celso thought about returning to sea but decided that if he did, he wanted to be a captain, nothing less. For a week he devised plans that would allow him to get the training and experience he needed to pass through the ranks to first mate on a merchant ship and perhaps, eventually, to captain. Finally one night he said, "Fuck it. I figured out how to become a captain immediately. No waiting around to move up some jerk's promotion ladder or for seniority to kick in. I'll learn to fly. I'll be soloing inside of six weeks. I can see having an air taxi company — fly capitalists to the copper mines in the north and Yankee tourists to fjords in the south. My advertising slogan could be, 'Willing to take off and land in any meadow.' Tomorrow I'm arranging with the Club Aéreo for lessons. My eyesight is perfect, my reaction time is instantaneous and, for the moment, I have the money."

Hearing Celso talk so enthusiastically about flying, I felt melancholy. I didn't know if I would ever fly a glider again. The Brazilians told José about the examination he would be required to pass to get into the Technical University of the State to study engineering. A few days later he knocked on our door at 4 in the morning, drunk, mumbling that he really had wanted to study medicine all along, but hadn't because he couldn't bear the thought of being in practice with his father. "My father's never understood my deep need for personal autonomy. So I plunged into my private joke. I read Hippocrates in the original — my way of studying medicine. I figured I could always teach Greek in a philosophy department. But tonight everything has miraculously been made clear. I'm going to marry a *Chilena* and become a pediatrician."

Monica said, "I prescribe aspirin and a good night's sleep, José."

"I'm not kidding. I just met my future wife, Maria del Carmen, at a weird discotheque — Las Catacumbas. She's a blonde. I liked her so much, I didn't even invite her to my hotel room. We have a date for tomorrow. Her father is a psychiatrist and she studies law. The only problem I see is that she wants to visit Rio with me. We haven't discussed the Brazilian military yet."

"How can you discuss anything?" I said.

"We speak in English, sort of."

The Brazilian exiles helped Monica and me locate a very small, inexpensive apartment we could rent by the month. The exiles tended to drop in on one another in the evenings to hold lengthy discussions about the political situation back home, going over the same old frustrations late into the night. Monica and I sat cross-legged on the floor, drank pisco sours and missed *caipirinhas*. At first Monica and I stayed close to the Brazilians we met in Santiago. We were homesick for the vivid and spontaneous Brazilian way of seeing the world and intolerant of Chile's somber, humorless culture and its cold winter. Half a dozen Brazilian exiles we knew participated in Communist-led protests against the U.S. Peace Corps, accusing the volunteers in Chile of spying for the CIA. Other Brazilians got caught up in Chile's debate over how fast to reclaim its natural resources from foreign interests. After a while Monica and I realized that our fellow exiles' allegiance to global Marxism and their interest in taking part in the activities of the Communist Party in Chile didn't suit us. We cared only about the liberation

158

of Brazil. Moreover, I was busy developing my own idiosyncratic plan for our life in exile.

I had been reading guidebooks and decided that the way for us to continue our education in architecture was to build a house with our own hands. I spent days researching small cities and towns in northern Chile where the climate was warm and the cost of construction would be considerably lower than in Santiago. According to one guidebook, Quillota, a "resting place" in the Central Valley, had been described by Charles Darwin as a bit of the tropics installed in Chile. At first the idea of this resort town intrigued us, but after thinking about it for a day we rejected Quillota because it was not by the sea. I bought tracing paper and two books on the work of Le Corbusier and Mies van der Rohe with the idea that we should trace the drawings and photos of their major buildings. "It's a form of self-discipline," I said. "After you trace something, it sticks in your mind forever. I want our house to incorporate the latest ideas of the avant-garde — new materials, glass sheathing, restraint — but still be our Brazilian statement."

Many well-educated Brazilians were remarkably architecture-conscious. This was not so among the Chilean students we met. I hoped that if we built a house, perhaps incorporating the two outstanding features of modern Brazilian building — *pilotis* (pillars that raise a building off the ground, creating a sense of floating and lightness) and *brise-soleils* (louvered walls to create permanent shade) — our house would attract attention that could lead to commissions. As ideas for the house solidified in my imagination, I unveiled them to Monica and she joined in with increasing enthusiasm.

Even after we found paid employment in Chile, and doing much of the work ourselves, it would take us years to save enough money to pay for the construction of a house. We would have to take loans from our parents, to be repaid when we sold what we had built. We agreed that we would delay asking them for loans until our plans were more advanced.

Together we chose the coastal town of La Serena, 500 kilometers north of Santiago, for our project. According to guidebooks and information from Chileans, La Serena overlooked the Bay of Coquimbo and was situated on a marine ledge that stepped back toward the Andes. Flowers and fruits grew exuberantly in its warm climate. Six kilometers south of La Serena was a beach resort, Balneario de Peñuelas, with extraordinary views, cabins and restaurant service.

Celso did his own research on La Serena and told us to be watching the sky because the town had a small airfield. At our last dinner together in Santiago, he promised to fly in special hardware items or fixtures we might need. José's new girlfriend, Maria del Carmen, was related to the mayor of La Serena. She and José promised to visit so they could go swimming and eat local seafood. We estimated the value of the Volkswagen and divided by three. I gave Celso and José 1,140 *cruzeiros novos* each for their shares. I was pleased to own the car.

The next day, very early, Monica and I left Santiago and its cold winter mornings and drove north. Occasionally the road took us close enough to the rugged coast and turbulent surf to catch a glimpse of the misnamed Pacific Ocean.

CHAPTER THIRTEEN

I

As the guidebook said, La Serena was situated on a series of gentle terraced hills with the ocean tumbling at its feet. Although cultivated flowers were everywhere, the ground cover wasn't lush. One sensed the closeness of the great Atacama Desert to the north, one of the driest regions on earth. The town of about 40,000 was founded in the 16th century, but only a few genuine colonial buildings remained. In the late 1940s La Serena had been rebuilt at the impetus of a native son, President Gabriel González Videla, the same man who hounded the poet Pablo Neruda into exile because he was a Communist.

We worried about money and about whether building an innovative modern house would really lead to commissions, but we genuinely liked La Serena. We had traded the tropics of Brazil for a Mediterranean climate with frequently cloudy skies, traded the repression in Rio and the student demonstrations in Santiago for lazy charm and window boxes full of pink, red and white geraniums. As I walked around the town, I felt off balance, as if one leg were slightly longer than the other, because the ocean wasn't where it should have been — to the east. I was accustomed to Rio's sunrise over the Atlantic, the sense of Africa across the sea. Now we had sunsets over the Pacific, but we didn't feel that New Zealand, directly west across the water, was part of our lives.

During the lulls in our search for the perfect property on which to build a house, Monica and I fought. We continued to feel weighed down by the burden of being separated from our families, from our country. On Wednesday afternoons we went to the CTC long-distance telephone office to make arrangements for Friday morning phone calls. I would telephone Bauru and Monica would call Belo Horizonte. After hanging up, we always felt worse than before we called. Monica

161

suggested we write letters instead of phoning. "It's a more complete communication," she said. "The phone is artificial."

Sometimes we settled our arguments by making love. It could happen any time — day or night — but after lunch was a good time for going back to our spare *pensión*, with its shared bath and lumpy bed, to try to repair the morning's hostile words. Sometimes we took separate walks. One night we had dinner at the same hour in the same restaurant at separate tables. Even though she had cash in her purse, she sent the bill for her spinach omelet to my table.

We tried to buy an awkward but potentially promising property in an exclusive elevated area called Cisternas, one hilltop down from the highest point in the city. From the site it was possible to view both the city and the sea. The property's formidable slope presented a design and construction challenge, which gave us hope that its price would be low. Two weeks were lost in disappointing negotiations. Eventually we gave up on the site, the breathtaking panorama, the marvelous house with a northwest-facing, cantilevered terrace that we imagined building there. From a distance, our house would have looked like a flying saucer alighting on the hill.

On one of my solitary walks, I spotted the house that changed our luck. It was a white authentic colonial dwelling, adobe brick, two stories, taking up nearly a third of a block. It had fine bones, but was in need of exterior reconditioning. Lonely and angry with Monica over her daily, often oblique references to how much she had given up to come with me, I stopped to talk to a carefully groomed gentleman smoking a cigarette on the sidewalk near the house's imposing mahogany doorway. My assumption that he was the owner turned out to be correct.

His face brightened when I greeted him and he heard my accent. "You're Brazilian," he said in perfectly accented Portuguese. "When I was a boy, my aunt married a Brazilian and my parents took us to visit

162

her in Rio de Janeiro every summer. I became fascinated with your strange, nasal language. When a Spanish speaker sees a Portuguese word written out, he has no idea how to pronounce it. I've always wondered which language has the largest vocabulary, Spanish or Portuguese. Do you know?"

"I would guess they're roughly equal," I said.

The man nodded. "Probably so." His face turned pensive. "I must say, decoding what I read between the lines, it's very disappointing, everything that's going on in Brazil these days. At least in Chile our press is free. Congress meets." Warming to his topic, he brought up Governor Rockefeller's fact-finding mission to Latin America. "I understand the Brazilian generals swept up all the leading dissidents so there wouldn't be any political disturbances. Our government did the sensible thing and told Rockefeller not to come to Chile. Not that canceling his trip resolved our grievances over American mining interests." He leaned against the portal of his house, smoking, clearly enjoying our serendipitous meeting. He told me that when he smoked his stinking French Gauloises, he was banished from the house by his asthmatic wife. It was a quotidian occurrence after lunch — his favorite moment for lighting up. He offered me a cigarette from its distinctive blue pack.

I shook my head. "I've always admired the design of the package," I said, "but I don't like the strong taste."

"I'm thinking of having my dining room painted this same marine blue as the Gauloise wrapper. My wife likes the color, too. She doesn't seem to associate the deep hue with the strong smell."

"It's a very handsome shade," I said. "It's sort of expected of the French, to come up with a unique color."

He nodded. "So very true. The frogs have an eye."

I asked, "Are you refurbishing your house?"

"Not the outside. The town fathers won't let me change the fenestration or even vary the color. So on the outside I retain my colonial relic, but on the inside I want the clean-lined International Style, except not all white." He inhaled his cigarette deeply, holding it between his thumb and index finger as if it were a cigar. He watched as the smoke curled out from his nostrils and disappeared against the clear afternoon sky. "I'm Juan Villalon Edwards, by the way."

"Alexandre Barbosa. Pleased to meet you."

We shook hands and I continued my walk west along Calle Arturo Prat, then across the Plaza de Armas, the heart of La Serena, with its massive trees lending their shade to numerous wooden benches. We had thought that it would be more difficult to socialize in La Serena's conservative atmosphere than in the metropolis of Santiago. I was eager to tell Monica about Juan.

II

Over the next several days I walked by Juan Villalon's house at 3 in the afternoon and twice found him there smoking. Redesigning the interior of his house was not the kind of project Monica and I had envisioned, but we decided that I should propose the idea to him. His project could launch our careers just as effectively as designing a house and we wouldn't have to ask our parents for loans.

"Are you steeped in the principles of Niemeyer?" Juan asked when I made the suggestion to him.

"Every Brazilian architect is," I said. "But I have my own ideas as well. So does my collaborator, my girlfriend Monica." I said that Monica and I had been architecture classmates at the Federal University in Rio and we were both one semester short of receiving our degrees.

"I would have to see preliminary sketches of your concept," he said. "Actually, until today, I had someone else in mind for the job, but I haven't made any commitments. I'd be willing to look at a proposal."

Although I suspected Juan had already guessed, I explained that Monica and I were political exiles. I was vague about why we had been forced to leave Brazil and Juan had the sensitivity to offer sympathy for our situation but not to press for details.

Juan invited Monica and me to his house for lunch the following day to have a look at the spaces he was considering renovating. After a heavy meal of fish soup, steak, rice and preserved papaya with whipped cream, accompanied by white and red Chilean wines, he took us on a tour of the public rooms on the first floor of the house and two large rooms on the second, then left us to contemplate what he had shown us and to take measurements. The house was configured in the shape of the letter U, with a large and deep interior courtyard mostly open to the sky. A glass roof sheltered one corner of the courtyard near a well-stocked library. "I enjoy sitting in the courtyard to read, even if it's raining," he had told us. "That luxury must remain."

The main salon, large and high-ceilinged, was nearly square. It was painted an unpleasant shade of mustard. We tapped on walls to see which ones bore the weight of the building, located the electrical outlets, listed door heights and noted the amount of afternoon sunlight admitted to various rooms. As Monica and I discussed strategies for changing the floor plan and drew up a list of questions to ask Juan, it struck me that, for the first time since we fled Rio, I had spent a couple of hours without thinking about the predicament of being in exile.

Work was the answer to our problems. I foresaw a partnership that could mesh my talents and ego with Monica's — we could live in each other's pockets without arguments. We bought drawing supplies and a piece of plywood to serve as a drafting table. Throughout several days and into the evenings, we sketched proposals for the interior of Juan's grand house. We removed walls to create a stately procession of social

165

rooms, one leading to the next, to accommodate the lavish entertaining for which Juan and his wife, Marta, were well known.

"It's both cosmopolitan and practical," Monica said, looking over our last iteration. "Drinks and canapés in a square reception room. A cube, really — with the ceiling height the same as the length and width of the room. It should be painted a soft pastel aquamarine to give prominence to their gilded antique furniture, don't you think? A dining room that can accommodate 24 at two round tables. Matching side parlors that can be used for after-dinner coffee and liqueurs. Juan should love that idea — he can reserve one parlor for smoking cigars. I think they will like the area we created in the courtyard for concerts. It's a great way to entertain."

"What about a piano?" I asked. "You can't have a piano in an exposed courtyard."

"Extend the glass ceiling."

"And how does the piano stay in tune outside?"

"I was thinking of a string quartet, or at least portable instruments."

We went back to work on our freehand drawings and designed a grand staircase leading to an oval-shaped music room on the second floor. After 10 days of refining our ideas, we presented our floor plan to Juan and Marta along with a reflected ceiling plan, interior elevations to show the walls and sketches showing furniture placement. "Stunning. I like the symmetry of the two parlors off the dining room," Marta said almost at once.

Juan pulled his round wire-framed glasses from his breast pocket and studied the plans for several minutes. "Leave the drawings with me," he said. "I can't give you an immediate answer. I see resonances of High Renaissance mixed with contemporary imagination. I like the plain round arches under the vaults in the salon and the niches for displaying our collection of religious art. What's the ceiling material in the library?"

166

"Wood," I said, "in a geometric pattern."

He told us to come for tea on Monday — five intervening days in which to imagine their every possible reaction. Juan, an ophthalmologist, was descended on his mother's side from old aristocratic Edwards bloodlines in Chile. If we could please him, word of our work would spread to the right people. "What the Chileans say about themselves is absolutely right," Monica said as we walked back to our *pensión*. "They are less emotional than any other Latins, and certainly far less than Brazilians. Is Juan comparing our design to someone else's? At least he smiled tolerantly."

"Marta reacted very positively," I said. "He'll like our plan, and if he doesn't, we'll offer changes."

"My stomach is in a knot," she said.

"Mine too."

The following morning, as we were awakening, Monica sat up in bed and announced, "See, it's a beautiful life if you want it to be. Everything is going to turn out fine." Thursday through Saturday, we went late in the afternoon to a bakery to buy beef empanadas. We wanted to buy appetizers, but everything we pointed to was pickled — fish, chicken, partridge — and not to our taste. We stopped at a street vendor to buy some of La Serena's beautiful tomatoes and papayas. Sitting on the rickety chairs in our small room, we ate the empanadas cold for dinner washed down with a bottle of inexpensive red wine from a nearby vineyard.

On Sunday, one day before we would receive Juan and Marta's decision, we allowed ourselves a proper dinner at the Hotel Francisco de Aguirre, La Serena's worn but formal four-star hotel. The sprawling neocolonial building fronted on a large park that sloped downhill, separating the town from the ocean one kilometer away. "Order what you like," I said. "How about *centolla* to start?"

167

Monica looked puzzled. "I thought those were mostly served in the south and *langosta* further up the coast," she said.

We ordered the *centolla*, a delicious, giant round crab that tastes like lobster. It was served cold with *salsa golf*, a simple mixture of ketchup, mayonnaise and lime juice. We chose another specialty from Chile's sea for our entrée — swordfish. We teased each other about who should be credited with rescuing our architecture careers. "I was the one who first said I wanted to design a house in a benign climate," Monica said.

"Your vague remark had nothing to do with La Serena. And I found Juan."

"Juan hasn't agreed to our proposal."

"He's going to accept our design," I said. "I had a dream about it."

"That's funny. My dreams aren't pleasant at all. They're mostly terrifying. I dreamt you were captured during a bank robbery. The mask I made for you disintegrated, as if the fabric had rotted through. Celso turned out to be an undercover cop. The money in the vault was Monopoly money. After that I can't remember the rest, except you were caught. Jayme was in the dream, too, showing you his plans for an aquarium."

I picked up Monica's hand and kissed it. She withdrew it slightly. She appeared to be eavesdropping on a conversation she was having with herself. Finally she said, "We need to seriously study Spanish. If we get the commission, we should take classes."

"Why did you pull your hand away?"

"Did I?"

"You know you did."

"We've lost something between us," she said. "It scares me."

"I think just the opposite. We're becoming a team."

168

"Professionally we are. In Rio we couldn't wait to make love."

"Are you saying we need to participate in a revolution to have sex? The kind you think we used to have?"

"Maybe," she said.

"Do you want to get married?"

"Not in Chile. Remember the night we had a beer at the Copacabana Palace pool? We were exhausted from studying and I dared you to make love behind a sentry palm?"

"You dared me? That's not the way I remember it," I said. "I'm ready to do it again. We can walk right out that door. There's a pool, gardens." I got up and reached for her elbow. "Come on."

Monica stayed seated and smiled. "Not in Chile."

"Why not?"

"It's too sober here. Sober and solemn. It infiltrates everything, in ways I can't explain."

"You were the one who said I was becoming addicted to danger. Do you realize I've never once played cards with you? Let's play strip poker."

"Now?"

"Yes. Right now. At this table. I'll ask the reception desk for a deck of cards." Without waiting for her answer, I got up and walked through the restaurant toward the lobby. I felt light on my feet, carefree. The desk clerk handed me a sealed box of red Bicycle cards.

"How much?" I asked.

"Compliments of the Hotel Francisco de Aguirre, *Señor*."

As I walked back to our table, I glanced at the box — "Air-Cushioned Finish. The U.S. Playing Card Co. Cincinnati, Ohio."

Monica was smiling broadly when I sat down. "Well?"

169

I pulled the deck out of my pocket, kissed it and set it down on the white tablecloth. "Ready?"

"I've never played poker in my life."

"I'll teach you. It's simple. It's mostly about bluffing."

"Like now?"

"Pay attention." I signaled the waiter, ordered another bottle of white wine and, while we waited, explained draw poker.

"*Merda*, Alexandre, that's too complicated. I'll never remember what has higher value — a royal flush or a full house. Let's play black-jack instead."

"Okay." The waiter returned with the wine and filled our glasses. As soon as he was gone, I dealt each of us three cards — two face down, one face up. "Do you want another card?" I asked.

"Yes."

"If you go over 21," I said, "you have to take something off."

"Same for you."

I lost the first hand, and took off my watch and dropped it into the pocket of my blazer. Monica put on a feigned supercilious expression. The tables immediately next to us were empty, though there were per-haps 20 or 30 diners in the large restaurant. I dealt another hand and lost again. I surreptitiously slipped off my belt and stuffed it into the pocket with my watch. Monica leaned across the table and kissed me hard on the mouth. "This is fun," she said. She lost the next three hands and took off two silver bracelets and a ring and put them in her purse. "Does a purse count as a piece of clothing?"

"Absolutely not," I said.

The waiter came over and refilled our wine glasses.

"Is anybody watching?" Monica asked.

170

I took advantage of the waiter's presence to look around. "Not that I can see." I dealt again. Monica's hand totaled 26. "It's too bad I only have two feet," she said as she slipped off a shoe.

We played until it got dangerous.

"Enough," Monica said. "We're in a foreign country trying to establish professional careers. Let's finish this in bed."

I paid the bill and, giddy with anticipation, led Monica out of the restaurant. "I hope we didn't drink too much. You know what Shakespeare said?" Monica teased.

"No, I don't."

"Wine gives the thought, but takes away the action. Something like that."

We walked the five blocks to our *pensión* arm in arm. There was a strong winter wind coming off the ocean. For a brief moment I thought back to my walks along Copacabana beach; the gentle Rio breeze often would blow the other way — from land to sea — and the air would be balmy and rapturous.

At tea Monday afternoon, Juan enthusiastically told us he accepted our proposal. Thankfully, he was not bothered by our lack of credentials. "Brazil's repression is my good fortune," he said. "My house can serve as your senior thesis for an architecture degree from the University of Chile in Santiago. Why not? It's a shame the campus here in La Serena doesn't have an architecture faculty."

I telephoned my parents with our news, and Monica talked to her mother. Monica didn't let me hear her end of her conversation. I knew it was because of her mother's reasonable concerns. Was her beautiful, talented daughter going to live an exile's life with a man who hadn't even seriously proposed marriage? Under normal circumstances, *dona* Patricia would have been extremely pleased with our union. I would have been suitable in every way, but nothing in our lives was following

171

a normal course. I imagined the conversation: "How many subtractions can a mother endure? First your father, then Jayme — by taking you away, Alexandre has removed the last ray of sunlight from my life."

We settled into a pattern of work — first refining our overall concept, then drawing details, selecting materials, finishes, colors, interviewing workmen, studying Spanish. Juan hired an elderly woman, a former schoolteacher who spoke Portuguese, to serve as our translator so we could explain precisely what we wanted to carpenters, painters, plasterers, plumbers, glaziers and electricians. We ourselves took on the job of assistant general contractor. Our architecture studio was a bedroom on the second floor of the mansion. We ordered two drafting tables from Santiago, bought a filing cabinet and supplies. Juan would stop by to chat about the work when he came home from his medical office for lunch. Occasionally we joined Juan and Marta for their hearty midday meal, though we preferred to go out for a light lunch and afterward take half an hour's brisk walk. At 6:30 Juan would bring us a tray with a pot of tea and a plate of sweet English Artisan biscuits. "Do you have something new to show me?" he would ask.

The Villalon household prepared itself to receive workmen by vacating various rooms and covering the furniture of others with sheets. The artwork, a cosmopolitan collection that included 19th-century religious art and sculpture, landscapes by lesser-known pointillists and abstract expressionism, was carefully wrapped and removed to a storage room at Juan's office. There was no need to uproot Juan and Marta's three sons, ages 13, 15 and 18. The boys lived with their maternal grandparents in Santiago, where they attended prestigious schools. Monica and I moved to a *pensión* on Cienfuegos Street on the periphery of the city's central grid, where we were able to arrange a monthly rental for a comfortable sitting room and bedroom, with a private bath and a rudimentary kitchen.

172

Although Chileans swam in the Pacific, the water of the Humboldt Current was too cold for our Brazilian blood. On Sundays toward the end of October, we took advantage of the spring weather by sitting on Peñuelas Beach — wearing our sweaters — and letting the sun tan our faces. Monica's mother visited us for two weeks, bringing Monica's passport — valid for another two years. *Dona* Patricia stayed at the Hotel Francisco de Aguirre, found the very Catholic atmosphere of La Serena to her liking and didn't disguise her intense sadness.

Monica and I did everything we could to let her mother understand that our situation wasn't hopeless, that we could finish our architecture degrees in Chile and that, relatively speaking, we had adjusted to exile. In fact, we had adapted more easily than we had any right to expect. As the three of us took leisurely walks around La Serena, visited the Museo Arqueológico, drove through the arid landscape to nearby towns of interest and enjoyed the south Pacific's bountiful harvest of fish, Monica and I were careful not to allow *dona* Patricia's conversation to veer toward a discussion of marriage.

At the end of her stay, Monica and her mother had a private breakfast. Later Monica repeated her mother's words to me: "I adore Alexandre, really I do. Charming, intelligent, handsome, a good formation, excellent family. I understand everything. I've counted, Monica, there are 26 churches in La Serena and I've prayed in nearly every one of them that you'll come home soon, knowing very well Alexandre can never return."

"That isn't all," Monica continued as she pulled a stack of American bills out of her purse. "She insisted I take it — 1,800 dollars. Officially she could only take 1,000 dollars out of Brazil, but she hid money under the lining of her suitcase."

In December the Villalon boys returned from Santiago for their summer holiday. The family had to become gypsies, moving from room to room as workmen took over the house. We were flattered when the boys asked permission to observe us as we worked. After following us around for a few days, all three announced that they wanted to become architects.

The general contractor had promised to have the renovation finished, totally, by Easter. Easter Vigil came and went, with a long list of items still needing remediation. "On my children's heads," he said, "everything will be completed by the Feast of the Ascension, May 7th." He touched the cross he wore on top of his white sleeveless T-shirt. Monica and I undertook some touch-up plastering and painting ourselves, to speed things along.

In early April, with their sons back in school and their house still not finished, Juan and Marta decamped for a month to their apartment in Paris. April 23 — the anniversary of the day my great-grandfather won back Fazenda Maraíba — passed unnoticed. It wasn't until a week later that I even thought of it. I telephoned my parents and asked if they had commemorated the date. "Under the present circumstances, there will be no more celebrations, Alexandre," my mother said, "just convenient forgetting. Your father agrees, but he isn't here to tell you in person."

With the help of Saint Vincent Ferrer — who the general contractor said was the patron saint of builders — the house was ready on May 6 when Juan and Marta returned from Europe. They moved back into the completed spaces, marveling at their openness, the light, the colors, the luxurious finishes, the improved circulation patterns that led them easily from room to room. "It's like living in a never-ending sensory experience," Juan said. "I move differently. I don't want to be less graceful than my house."

On Ascension Day, seven months after we began the project, Juan paid us the final installment under our contract. Its terms had been generous. We had no complaints.

The following Monday morning, Monica and I drove south to Santiago to visit José and shop for a few last pieces of cabinet hardware. Celso had learned to fly and was busy logging solo hours. To increase his chances of establishing a profitable air charter service, he had moved to Antofagasta at the edge of Chile's northern desert where there was less competition.

Santiago wasn't peaceful. We had read the leftist press and seen Fidel Castro's TV campaign to support Salvador Allende for president of Chile. In the close three-way race, the rightist former president, Jorge Alessandri, was expected to win against the Communist Allende and the centrist Christian Democrat candidate, Radomiro Tomic. José and the other Brazilian refugees were extremely concerned for their future in view of the increasingly violent Chilean political scene. José's situation was more complicated because he was intensely involved with Maria del Carmen and he didn't want to leave her. "Everyone I know is thinking of leaving Chile," he said. "If Allende doesn't win in September, we might as well be back in Brazil. Alessandri's as bad as our military."

"Take Maria del Carmen with you," Monica said.

"Are you kidding? Her family is deeply conservative about anything having to do with sex or family. If they knew we fucked ..."

"I thought her father was a shrink," I said.

"Knowing all about Freud makes it worse. When Maria del Carmen sleeps with me, she has to get up at 11 and go home. Her father always wants to know exactly where she's been."

"So marry her," I said.

"How can I? I've got to get my medical degree first. I don't want to live off her family. Two Brazilian guys in my faculty at the university

175

are looking into emigrating to Sweden. Sweden will pay for their education. I don't put anything past Alessandri. When he wins, he could have all of us Brazilians arrested."

"He'd need a pretext," I said.

"Let's face it, Alexandre, our sanctuary in Chile is finished. Period. Rightists don't need excuses. I know one guy who's already left for Bulgaria."

On the drive back to La Serena, Monica and I discussed our choices. "The wrong man could win," I said.

"He probably will."

"Alessandri's financed by the *gringos*. If Allende wins, the first thing he'll do is nationalize all the basic industry in Chile. Anaconda isn't going to sit back and let that happen."

"Should we leave before the election?" Monica said.

"Where to?"

"Why not Sweden? Their architecture's interesting."

"I thought you hated cold weather."

She put her hand on my prick just when I had to downshift around a curve. "We could figure out ways to keep warm," she said. "Snow might be fun."

"For a week, not for months. Besides, I like the way we build in Brazil. No heating systems or heavy insulation to worry about, no cellars. It frees up the design."

"In Sweden I bet they don't spray for mosquitoes as extensively as they do in Rio," she said. "They probably need screens on their windows in summer. I'd hate that. It complicates the window frame and makes it ugly."

We had concentrated our energies on Juan's house and put off plans to build our own. In principle, we now were ready to renew our search for a piece of property. Certainly the task was going to be much easier on a second try because we knew more about the area and had connections. But the political situation held us back. We decided to spend two weeks on a leisurely drive north, exploring the desert province of Antofagasta — reputed to have the highest solar intensity in the world 360 days of the year. We definitely had to be back in La Serena by the beginning of June to watch Brazil compete in the 1970 World Cup games in Mexico. June 3 was the opening game for Brazil.

During this period of national soccer obsession, the Villalon boys returned home from Santiago. Monica and I watched the games in Juan and Marta's music room with other family members and a large gathering of friends. At each end of the room a television set had been installed especially for the occasion. A temporary banquet table was laden with trays of sandwiches and sweets and a bar beckoned with a selection of beers and bottles of champagne cooling in silver ice buckets. After the first game, when Brazil triumphed over Czechoslovakia, 4 to 1, I bet Ivan, Juan's oldest son, 50 *escudos* (worth $4) that Brazil would win the Cup. Three games later, after Brazil had beaten England, Romania and Peru — even before the semifinal against Uruguay — I couldn't contain my excitement. Juan offered me the use of his telephone so I could call my parents. "It's miraculous," my father said. "Pelé not only scores goals, his passes and headers have been phenomenal. To think he grew up and mastered the art of *futebol* in Bauru. Never mind that he was born in Minas."

When Brazil defeated Italy in the final game on June 21, 4 to 1, we were delirious with joy and pride and momentarily distracted from our concerns. Juan again offered us the use of his phone. This time we called not only my parents, but also Monica's mother, Pedro and our Brazilian comrades in Santiago.

By July, with civil-liberties violations mounting all over Chile, the polls continued to indicate that Alessandri would defeat Allende in the

177

September 4 election. In the leftist press and on television, Castro stepped up his anti-U.S. message. The Army mobilized to support the police against protesting students. Amid speculation about cataclysmic consequences if Allende won, Juan told us he and his wealthy friends were sending their money abroad.

José left for Sweden to continue his medical studies in Stockholm, without Maria del Carmen. Her family forbade her to join him; she was afraid to defy them. Celso discovered he had a taste for flying in desert country. He said he considered its monotony both beautiful and forbidding. He spent two days with us in La Serena before leaving for Algeria — and the possibility of flights above the Sahara. Several Brazilian exiles we knew were already living in Algiers under the protection of the Front de Libération Nationale. "I'll get an Algerian pilot's license," Celso said. "There's got to be money flying workers to the oil and gas fields. Who knows, maybe I'll marry a dark-haired Berber. I used to only worship blondes. What the hell, we all have to adjust." He wasn't smiling.

In Chile's northern desert cities and in Santiago, students were being shot during large youth demonstrations for Allende. In La Serena, at the local campus of the University of Chile, the student manifestations for Allende were insistent but less violent. Monica and I feared a repressive regime was coming that would sweep the whole country. We had not fled the Brazilian military dictatorship only to live under a Chilean model. Monica and I argued, tried out one idea after another, didn't talk to each other for two days and finally settled on a plan that called for compromises neither of us would have believed we would ever consider. We sold the Volkswagen and flew to Santiago to make arrangements for our departure. Juan used his influence to help Monica with her visa.

Upon our return to La Serena, Juan and Marta hosted an elaborate farewell dinner for us. Between champagne toasts, Monica and I

178

stared at each other, plainly wondering if we had made the right decision. Maria del Carmen's relative, the mayor, was there. Other distinguished guests milled about the rehabilitated rooms, which were aglow with tall candles and filled with yellow and white orchids. Most of the guests had already seen the interior transformation of Juan's house; they took the opportunity to come up to us to express their admiration for our work. A cardiologist told us he would have liked to offer us a commission to renovate his house, "but my money is in Panama. The electoral uncertainty, you understand. Unfortunately, at this precise moment it's impossible to plan."

Four days later, after one last walk around the Plaza de Armas, Monica stopped in front of the cathedral. "Wait a minute, Alexandre. I want to light a candle."

"You sound like your mother."

"I need to ask forgiveness."

We took a taxi to the airport and flew to Santiago, waited four hours and boarded a Braniff flight to New York — the headquarters of the imperialists, the country where I was born.

CHAPTER FOURTEEN

I

The morning we arrived in New York, we checked in to the Tudor Hotel on East 42nd Street. Our room, on the 15th floor, was small and square. A hole had been punched in the wall to accommodate an air conditioner. French doors opened out onto a brick terrace, nearly as large as the room. The view of midtown Manhattan was astonishing. Our money belts lay on the dresser and the rest of our material possessions — three large suitcases and a cardboard tube full of architectural drawings — took up most of the available floor space. Monica draped her clothes over a chair and stretched out naked on the bed, fanning herself with a Braniff airline magazine in the intense heat of the July sun streaming in through the glass doors. "Thank God it's hot, Alexandre. The decision to come here was easier because I knew it would be summer when we arrived. I can do anything when it's warm."

"Enjoy it while you can."

She put down her magazine. "We're spending too much on this hotel room."

"We'll look for something cheaper tomorrow morning."

We made up our minds to unpack only what we needed for the night. I felt sticky, bathed in nervous sweat; I began to undress.

"I'll shower with you," she said as she rose from the bed. "Then let's explore. I wonder if we're near The Museum of Modern Art."

"Hungry?" I asked.

She nodded. "I get more homesick every time we move. Now we're further from home and I'm dependent on you for English. Thank God my father insisted I start English in grade school even though my school steered students toward French."

"Repeat that in English," I said.

She translated haltingly, pausing to find English cognates for Portuguese words.

"You just lack confidence," I said, "and practice. From now on, I'm going to speak to you in English."

Before we left our aerie, we stepped out onto the terrace for another dazzling glimpse of the city. I took Monica in my arms and led her into a waltz. Our music was the energy and the possibilities of the street.

Juan had told us that on a trip to New York he was surprised to find a block full of tourist shops and restaurants that catered to Brazilians. "What caught my eye was all the Brazilian flags displayed in the windows," he said. "Up and down the whole block, store after store, Brazilian flags everywhere. It's near Fifth Avenue. It shouldn't be hard for you to find."

We located the block on our second morning in New York. It wasn't far from our hotel — West 46th Street between Fifth and Sixth Avenues. We moved our belongings to a small budget hotel on West 46th that attended to the needs and wants of Brazilians in New York. We got a good monthly rate. We set about gathering information from immigrant Brazilian shopowners about how to navigate and survive in the city. I even got a haircut from a Brazilian barber.

Eight days after we arrived, still adjusting to the wondrous shock of New York, I telephoned the Madsens, my "American family" in Minneapolis. The following weekend, Tom Madsen flew to New York. On a rainy Saturday afternoon we reminisced about the year I spent living with his family and going to high school in Minneapolis. In our smug adolescent years, when Tom was 17 and I was 15, teaching each other our languages and sports, we thought we were two of the cleverest kids alive.

Tom said he had managed to stay out of the Vietnam draft by going to law school. "Afterward I took the course of least resistance and joined my dad's firm. It's not a bad life, Alexandre. I enjoy the law."

I filled Tom in on my career as an architecture student and bank robber expropriating money for the cause. "*Puxa vida!*" he said, shaking his head in disbelief. "What a story. I'm speechless."

"Do you remember any more Portuguese?" I asked.

"Sometimes I surprise myself when I remember Portuguese words." He took a minute to process my revelations. "I guess my first reaction to your story is that I'm available for legal advice if you need it. Second, I'm impressed. Third, you were crazy."

Monica shifted uncomfortably in her chair. "We couldn't just study and go to classes and watch what the generals were doing to our country," she said. "We had to resist them. I was a lookout for a group that was liberating guns from government installations."

"You're both crazy." Tom smiled and shook his head. "Does your family still celebrate on April 23rd?" he asked. "My father likes to tell that story to our developer clients. They're all gamblers at heart."

"Are you ready for another shock?" I asked.

"Besides robbing three banks and freeing prisoners from a penitentiary?"

"We no longer own Fazenda Maraíba. My father lost it last year in a poker game."

"Double — no, triple — *puxa vida!*"

"Very appropriate," I said, laughing.

When we got around to discussing our plans, Monica said, "We need to complete our architecture degrees. It would be great if we could find a program in New York. I'm already falling in love with the city."

182

"You should look into the City College of New York," Tom said. "As far as I know, CCNY doesn't charge tuition. I have no idea if they offer a degree in architecture. How are you fixed for money?"

"Our families have helped, and we have a little money left from a robbery."

Tom laughed. "You should only admit that to your lawyer."

I laughed, too. "Don't worry. It was from a robbery I didn't take part in."

"You're in receipt of stolen funds, but I think you're safe. And if not, I'm a good lawyer."

Our conversation continued over the drizzly, hot July weekend. When Tom left to return home to Minneapolis, he reached into his back pocket for his wallet and pulled out four $50 bills. I placed my hand over his as he tried to give me the money. "Many thanks," I said, "but really, we won't starve."

"It's no problem for me," he replied.

I told him how grateful I was for his friendship.

II

The morning after Tom left, we took the subway uptown and found our way to the admissions office at the City College of New York to investigate its curriculum. CCNY did have a school of architecture and the tuition was free, but we came away from our interview depressed. To be considered for admission as transfer students into CCNY's program, we had to submit our university transcripts together with our student portfolios. "What do we do now?" Monica said. "I can't see Nacional supplying transcripts for a bank robber."

In New York, unlike Santiago, we had not encountered a community of exiled Brazilian political activists to offer us advice and companionship. After our year of exile in Chile, we felt practiced in suppressing our feelings of displacement and anxiety. In La Serena we had recognized an opportunity and had been able to seize it. Now, almost 8,000 kilometers away from a home we couldn't return to, inhabiting an exciting but competitive city, we had no choice but to improvise.

We tried to get around CCNY's requirements by submitting our presentation renderings, construction documents and extensive photos of the Villalon Edwards house, before and after its renovation. Although the chairman of the School of Architecture and Environmental Studies was sympathetic to our situation as political exiles, he said our materials from La Serena were not sufficient to determine our academic standing.

It took several collect telephone calls to Brazil to locate the student portfolios we needed and arrange for their delivery to New York. After we fled, Monica's mother had gone to Rio to retrieve her belongings and release her apartment back to the landlord. Pedro had assumed the full rent for our apartment, incorporated my clothes into his wardrobe and my records into his collection. He paid a student who was driving home to Londrina to make a detour to Bauru to deliver my portfolio, drafting supplies, books and miscellaneous drawings to my parents. Our parents shipped our portfolios to New York. Tom's father, Bill Madsen, and my art teacher from the high school I attended in Minneapolis wrote letters of recommendation. Pedro filled out the forms asking Nacional to send our transcripts to CCNY. I could only hope DOPS didn't have an agent there reviewing its paperwork for wanted persons.

There was one requirement we could fulfill even before our materials arrived from Brazil — the Test of English as a Foreign Language. We arranged to take it the first week in October, which gave Monica

184

only seven weeks to study seriously the English grammar books we had bought. She was nervous that she might not pass. My score was high; Monica's was one point above the minimum score that CCNY required. We celebrated her achievement with an ice cream cone and a leisurely walk from the southern end of Central Park to its northern boundary.

While we waited for an admissions decision from CCNY, we found cheap lodgings in a rooming house in a working-class neighborhood on 14th Street between 8th and 9th Avenues. Our furnished room on the second floor was long and very narrow with, at one end, a large closet, a private bath and what was called a Pullman kitchen. The three-quarter bed was somewhat concave, barely big enough for the two of us. The management supplied maid service once a week, along with a change of sheets and towels. Since we had brought nothing with us to New York besides our clothes, the arrangement suited us, including the price of $27 per week.

In early September, two months after we left La Serena, Salvador Allende won the presidential election in Chile by a very narrow plurality. We were shocked. Since none of the three candidates had a majority of the popular vote, Chile's Congress had to choose one of the two leading candidates to be president. Its decision was delayed when, one month after the inconclusive election, the commander in chief of the Chilean Army was shot resisting a kidnap attempt and died of his wounds.

Monica and I followed the unfolding story in *The New York Times*. Finally we read that, as the presidential sash was being draped across Allende's chest in Santiago, Chilean Catholics in Rio distributed pamphlets asking Pope Paul VI to oppose the installation of the first Marxist president freely elected in a non-Communist country. Our fears of a rightist takeover of Chile turned out to be wrong, but we didn't regret our decision to leave. In Chile we felt annoyingly outside our culture, but we were still in South America and therefore not really abroad.

The chairman of the Department of Architecture at CCNY had suggested during my interview that I look for work at Edward Larrabee Barnes Associates, a distinguished architecture firm known for its meticulous details in both small- and large-scale projects. I was hired to work four mornings a week in a technical position, constructing architectural-study models out of chipboard. Monica's visa status didn't allow her to work legally, but "off the books" she was a waitress at Max's Kansas City. Like everyone in New York who was caught up in pop art and pop life, she was excited by Max's chic, decadent atmosphere where she not only received a small unreported salary and tips, but also got to meet avant-garde actors and artists, writers, models, politicians and the musicians who performed there. "It's like being in a place where someone lights every firecracker in a pack all at once and then tosses it across the floor," she said.

On November 4, one day after Allende assumed office, we each received a letter stating that we had been admitted to CCNY's five-year professional architecture degree program. Classes for the spring semester would begin on January 18, 1971. With our transfer credits from Nacional, it was going to take us two-and-a-half years to receive our degrees.

Even after receiving our degrees, we wouldn't be able to set ourselves up to practice as architects in the United States. First we would each have to complete a three-year internship with a licensed architecture firm and then pass a series of examinations for licensure as Registered Architects. The exams are notoriously difficult. Quite a few interns don't pass them, even on repeated tries. Without passing the exams an architect can still work, but he isn't authorized to provide the state seal required on drawings submitted to public officials. These strictures in the U.S. were supposed, in theory, to protect the public from the failure of buildings designed by incompetent architects.

We put one foot in front of the other, worked at our jobs, cooked black beans and rice in our Pullman kitchen, visited with our neighbors in our rooming house (one was a former ship's captain who told us fascinating stories about his life at sea, another was a painter with real talent) and tried not to think about home, especially when winter arrived. I developed friendships at the Edward Larrabee Barnes firm; Monica got to know some of the regulars at Max's. "You can't tell the real women from the fakes," she said. "Everyone is beautiful."

My parents' resources allowed my father to wire me money from time to time. Monica's mother continued to be well-off in widowhood. While the Brazilian Central Bank imposed a limit of $300 per month per person on how much money could be sent to those living abroad, her mother managed to send Monica amounts over the legal limit using dollars she bought on the black market.

One Saturday in early December, after waiting tables at Max's, Monica came home at 4 a.m. and woke me. "Maybe it's better I have a job where I don't do intellectual work," she said. "I can think about the thesis project I want to do at CCNY." She took a joint out of her purse and put it on my chest. "Want it?"

"Not now. Where'd you get it?"

"One of the social curiosities at Andy Warhol's round table gave it to me with his tip. The guy just sat there all night drinking Calvados, staring at another guy's eye makeup."

Monica liked marijuana more than I did. She was happy to bring home an occasional "gift" from one of her customers. When I smoked, thoughts of Adolfo, Roberto, César and Carlos would flood my mind. And later, when I went to sleep, I would have anguishing dreams in which I was paralyzed, unable to take a step, unable to rescue my comrades from DOPS. I would wake up in a cold sweat.

187

For me, the best part of Max's was the free hors d'oeuvres offered every day between 5 and 6. I would meet Monica there, take full advantage of the fried chicken, meatballs and cheese platter and call it dinner.

III

Finally, in January, Monica and I started our classes at CCNY. It was a long subway ride, some 125 blocks, from our rooming house to the CCNY campus in central Harlem. We had adjusting to do. Now that we were in school full time, we had to cut back on our employment. I barely managed to find the time to work at the Barnes firm from 5 p.m. to 7:30 p.m. Wednesday and Fridays. Monica was a waitress at Max's two weekends a month. Between Max's free food and eliminating all luxuries, like movies and the occasional steak, we survived.

We knew that for the next two-and-a-half years of school, the character of our daily lives would change — predictability would replace urgency and risk. We wouldn't be morally challenged. Although the dictatorship would still be running Brazil, we would be on the outside looking in. I never stopped worrying about the fate of my group. Where were they? Were they alive? Pedro wrote that Heitor had left Brazil and was living in Sweden. "At least he's safe," he said. "His days to evade arrest were numbered, and he knew it."

We were surprised by our fellow students. At Nacional our architecture classmates had been the sons and daughters of the upper middle class. We never thought of our free federal university in Brazil as a bargain. College tuition in the U.S., on the other hand, certainly wasn't free for most Americans. CCNY was unique — founded to provide a free education to all. Our fellow students came from the American melting pot; they were strivers from diverse, often very poor, backgrounds. Similarly situated students in Brazil would not be found studying architecture, even though their tuition would be free. Their deficient high schools could not have prepared them for the rigorous entrance exams. While our CCNY classmates didn't have the social polish we were used to, they were talented, hardworking and friendly. And they were just as desirous as Monica and I of impressing our professors. CCNY made us rethink some of our ideas about the U.S. From afar, we had seen the U.S. as rich and entitled. We had not appreciated the opportunities it offered the less fortunate.

Both our lecture and studio classes were smaller than at Nacional. In our studio classes at CCNY, each student was assigned a desk for the duration of the class. This was not possible at Nacional; there simply were not enough desks to go around. Our CCNY professors were involved in our design projects. They would stop by our desks to look at our work and offer criticism and suggestions for improvement as often as three times a week. These faculty-student relationships were informal and intense. In Rio our design professors reviewed our projects only a few times a semester and interactions were formal.

Gradually, I let my life of predictability settle over me. It was a relief to know what lay ahead as long as I was in school: the required classes I had to take, the senior thesis I would have to produce, the employment I had to maintain to supplement the money we received from our parents. That is what I knew. The things I did not know couldn't be revealed except by the passage of time. Would Monica and I get prestigious internships, the kind that advance careers? Was my commitment to Monica going to last? Or hers to me? With Fazenda Maraíba gone, what would happen to my parents? Would their money last? There was so much at stake. As far as I could tell, my father's realism about his financial situation was like the passing illumination of the moon — it waxed and waned. Would he give up gambling? Would I give up gambling, not necessarily with cards, but with my life? Could I become a successful New York architect with the kind of distinguished practice I used to dream of establishing in Rio?

IV

For some months after my father's poker disaster, he played with fanciful ideas of forming a venture to exploit coffee byproducts. He envisaged building a plant to make cellulose and plastics from coffee hydrocarbons. He was enthusiastic about the potential of coffee protein to modify certain oils and tars. "Believe me," he said, "the sky's the limit in the byproducts business."

He was incapable of facing the fact that he lacked the capital to seed his ideas. Even though many small industries around the city of São Paulo had sprung up utilizing the byproducts of coffee, my father was, as my mother said privately, "a man trying to sail a boat against opposing winds." Nevertheless, she didn't dismiss his ideas altogether. "He's being a bit grandiose, Alexandre," my mother said out of my father's hearing. "More than a bit. But this isn't the moment to inject reality. It could kill him, and I don't want to be responsible for murder."

After my father halfheartedly came to terms with the consequences of his calamitous wager, he had become restless managing the *fazenda* for Bernardo. As he put it to me in a phone conversation eight months after we arrived in New York, "Thank God I'm not an Anglo-Saxon, Alexandre, with a moral structure to protect. I'm finished with feeling guilty. In fact, I feel lucky that everything happened the way it did."

I had refrained from mentioning my own ambivalence to him. My feelings had changed since I became an exile. I still felt relieved that my architecture career, if I could still have one, was not about to be disrupted by family obligations to the *fazenda*, but I also had an acute sense of being rootless in New York. The *fazenda* was home. There were days when I was overcome with *saudade*, that special Brazilian feeling of deep yearning for something — a person, a place, a state of

190

mind, a lost love. In trying to describe to foreigners the significance of *saudade* in Brazilian culture, I came to the conclusion that not only was the word untranslatable, but so was the sentiment.

The series of events that really did put my father back on his feet, both psychologically and financially, could not have been predicted. In June 1971, one of my father's closest friends, Augusto Faria, was killed in a traffic accident. Augusto's only son, Roberto, had left Bauru when his father, a well-off coffee farmer, opposed his plan to become an opera singer. Roberto returned home, after many years living in the U.S. and Europe, to attend his father's funeral. My parents invited Roberto to the *fazenda* for dinner.

As it turned out, Roberto's career had not included grand opera. Instead he had become wealthy writing soap operas and mysteries for radio. Procter & Gamble loved him. In the late 1950s he shifted to television, but his heart was in radio, "the theater of the mind." He was especially partial to suspense dramas and detective shows.

Roberto found himself tied down in Bauru by what promised to be a protracted legal dispute over property. His mother had died two years earlier, and there was no will dividing the estate among the children. Squabbling immediately broke out between Roberto and his two sisters over management of the family *fazenda* and its effect on their proportional shares of the estate.

Roberto was restless while he was forced to wait for various documents to be drawn up; he cast about for something to do. He had the idea to secure a concession for a new regional radio station. All radio stations in Brazil required sanction from a state legislature. My father was friendly with every politician in the area. Roberto proposed that, for a one-third interest, my father help him secure a license.

In early April 1972, the São Paulo State Assembly voted to approve Roberto's radio permit, and OPERA7 went on the air, competing with

191

Bauru's two popular stations — PRG8 and Auriverde Radio. Roberto originally planned to hire an experienced general manager to run the station while he continued to reside alternately in New York and Paris. He never got around to interviewing anyone, however, and it soon became clear he had no intention of leaving Bauru.

V

One year after we started school, Monica and I moved to a one-bedroom, fourth-floor walk-up apartment on Sixth Avenue near Houston Street in Greenwich Village. It was 520 square feet — smaller than the apartment I had shared with Pedro. Monica bleached her hair honey blonde and wore only white clothes and white boots. "My revenge against this goddamn gray winter," she said. In March she started attending anti-Vietnam War rallies organized by architects concerned with social responsibility. Many of the big names in architecture were active participants. They gathered in Bryant Park behind the New York Public Library, held up handsomely lettered posters and, on one occasion, released hundreds of black balloons. I didn't go. I was afraid that, if I were arrested, I'd be sent back to Brazil to face charges. Because I didn't totally trust American sanctuary, I missed the opportunities Monica had to rub elbows with important architects who might one day be our employers.

At one of the rallies, Monica offered the architect Sam Brody her services to help make posters. She went to his office dressed so elegantly in clothes of her own design that, except for her age, she might have been a partner. Davis, Brody & Associates' two partners had a reputation for innovative low- and middle-income housing projects. Monica made a point of getting to know the firm's hiring associate.

On days when we felt particularly irritated by some American be-havior, Monica and I would play the game of contrasting Brazilian attitudes with American. It was not a healthy activity.

"You have to lay 500 years of history side by side," I would say, "to understand how Brazilians think and act compared to Americans."

"All this planning Americans do for their leisure time, it drives me crazy," Monica often said. "How do I know if I'll want to go out to din-ner and the movies 10 days from now? And they have so many ridicu-lous rules. Notices everywhere: No spitting. Curb your dog. Don't touch. Forbidden this, forbidden that. Form a single line. Americans have no spontaneity and they can't dance."

We were still going through the four recognized stages of cultural adjustment: First excitement about the new culture, then anger about the differences from our own, then trying to adjust to the new culture and finally retaining the good things from one's own culture and adopt-ing the good things from the new. I believed I was at stage 3 — adjust-ing. Monica's progress doubled back on itself. She would briefly enjoy the balance that came with stage 3, then slip back to anger and make comments about how hard it was to navigate U.S. bullshit. She said it wasn't fair to judge her experience against mine. Wanting, but failing, to be helpful, I suggested it was taking her longer to adjust because my English was better.

"I notice people say you have a Minnesota accent," she snapped. "Of course a year of high school in the U.S. makes a big difference."

When Monica was at stage 3, she would agree with me that it was impossible to become blasé about New York and its marvelous quirk-iness. Even in my most intense moments of longing for Brazil, there was always something to catch my attention and make me laugh — like signs I noticed in the spring popping up on trash cans: "If you litter, we'll send you to Utah!"

193

For my fifth-year independent work project at CCNY, I had designed an exuberantly landscaped affordable-housing community in Flushing Meadows, Queens, formerly the site of the 1939-40 and 1964-65 New York World's Fairs. Because CCNY required each student's project "to identify an actual architectural problem in the City of New York," my previous senior thesis idea to design utilitarian housing in the Amazon had to be abandoned. I didn't resist the change of direction that was forced on me. Monica was enjoying her tutorial "Discovering Forms in Nature." Her professor found her work to be "original, mature and confident."

VI

Roberto's radio station became profitable very quickly — only nine months from licensing approval and startup to advertisers writing substantial checks. With his 33 percent interest, my father had become a paradigm for one of Brazil's fundamental economic principles: You can lose money very fast in Brazil but, in the right circumstances, you can make it fast as well.

Roberto's station was distinguished from his competition by the detective shows he wrote and produced, modeled on popular U.S. radio programs from the '40s and '50s. He even used the titles of the American shows. One was called "The F.B.I. in Peace and War." Another was "This is Your F.B.I." Whereas the U.S. originals had little sex, Roberto's Brazilian versions, set in exotic Miami, had plenty. They played twice every night for 15 minutes — at 9 and 11 — sandwiched between music shows to which people called in their requests.

My father sent me cassettes of some of the shows. The theme music, composed under Roberto's supervision, was memorable and the numerous sound effects were very professional. My father said most of the sound effects came from a turntable, though the station staged pictures for its newspaper advertising featuring beautiful "sound women" (in reality, there were no women in the business) holding pistols, surrounded by the equipment of the trade — thunder sheets, telephones, buzzers, doors, chains, breakable boxes, plungers and tubs of water, dishes and glassware.

The sophisticates in the audience were convinced that "The F.B.I." really stood for DOPS and that the programs were a clever ruse to get around censorship. Unsophisticated listeners just liked the idea of gritty stories about agents working their beats in the big city. Everybody had a theory about the shows' real message. My father thought teenage boys masturbated to them, experiencing a combination of lust and small-town blues.

"Bauru is a mediocre city," Roberto had told my father, "but it has everything." In fact, he found managing the station satisfying. Ten months after OPERA7 went on the air, Roberto inaugurated, with my father's help, another radio station in nearby Araraquara, a town of some 70,000. By then it was 1973 and I was in my last semester at CCNY.

195

CHAPTER FIFTEEN

I

In mid-March 1973, my father had a mild heart attack. From thousands of miles away all I could do was worry and telephone every few days. He was ordered to stop smoking and told to appreciate Bauru's dramatic sunsets. I was astounded by the discipline he imposed on his daily routine: At 8 a.m. he went downtown to the OPERA7 radio station to supervise the advertising staff, then home for lunch at 1, afterward a nap. He woke at 3, took a brisk walk up and down the rows of coffee trees, played the piano at 5, drank one *caipirinha* with double crushed ice at 7 and had a light dinner with one glass of wine at 8. "I've decided it's not good to go to bed on a full stomach, Alexandre. It puts a strain on the heart."

Six weeks after his heart attack I inquired, "What about your gambling, *papai*, speaking of putting a strain on the heart? Are you playing cards?"

"Just Wednesday nights, my regular game, but not every Wednesday. I don't have time. The radio stations have taken over my life 100 percent. I haven't even inquired about my adorable Nelores in weeks. You'd be impressed by my transformation, Alexandre. I'm no longer a man tied to the land. I'm a man selling suspense."

I was struck by my father's remarks and surprised by my reaction. It seemed the *fazenda* was not in the forefront of his concerns, but it wasn't far from the forefront of mine. I was glad to learn he was energized and busy but, at the same time, disappointed that he didn't even dream of recapturing ownership of Fazenda Maraíba. I felt condemned to my mix of feelings.

On Saturday, 15 days before Easter, I got up at 6 and made coffee. The newspaper predicted a high of 72 degrees Fahrenheit with cirrus clouds. A day to relax, enjoy the fleecy white clouds against a bright blue sky and not obsess about schoolwork. I shook Monica's shoulder. "The weather is perfect. Let's take the subway down to Bowling Green and walk north, the length of Manhattan."

"How about walking across the Brooklyn Bridge?" she said, still sleepy. "We've never done it."

Over coffee we agreed to take the subway to Brooklyn Heights, walk across the bridge, have lunch in Chinatown, walk up Fifth Avenue to the Metropolitan Museum and tour its Greek and Roman collection. At 5 we would see a movie and finish the day with an Italian dinner somewhere on the East Side. We were learning how to inhabit New York with purpose and joy.

The view over the water toward the skyscrapers of lower Manhattan was spectacular. We came to the end of the bridge and walked up to Canal Street. The small, humble shops selling watches, cameras, jewelry and cheap clothes had very few customers. I pulled Monica to the edge of the sidewalk and kissed her — a long, tense kiss.

"I used to think we had different fates," she said as we continued walking. "I don't think so anymore." We stopped and kissed again. I felt her relax in my arms. When I looked into her eyes, they were unguarded.

"If we got married ..." I said, slipping my hands inside the rear pockets of her jeans and holding her against me. "It's the fast lane to a green card," I said.

She smiled. "Married? Not in the U.S."

"Last time I asked, you said not in Chile."

"Are you seriously asking?"

For a second I was so sure of my urge to marry Monica that I thought I had responded yes, but I could see her face was still expectant. "It's a sincere proposal," I said out loud in a confident voice.

She ran her finger across my lips. "I accept, Alexandre, with sincere pleasure." We laughed and hugged. "Have I been difficult?" she asked.

"Should I tell you the truth? Considering all the difficulties we've been through, I think you've dealt with exile better than I have." At that moment I felt that whatever bad luck or bad choices we had made, or been forced to make, were pouring off us like sweat on a hot day.

"Do you still want to have a Chinese lunch or should we go home?" she asked.

"We can call your mother and my parents tomorrow," I said.

She laughed. "That wasn't what I was thinking we'd do." She initiated a long, open-mouth kiss, then stepped back to look into my eyes. "I want a ring."

"Right now? One from Canal Street?"

"Let's look. These shops are so funny, who knows what they have."

In a state of excitement and astonishment at the commitment we had just made, we browsed in three stores and looked at a succession of gaudy rings. "How about this?" Monica pointed out a particularly garish band — all swirls and diamond chips set in an excess of pink gold.

"I'll take you to Tiffany," I said.

"I'm hungry."

This day, this moment, had been a long time coming. I wanted to celebrate with a grand lunch. Where? We weren't dressed for a formal restaurant. I remembered one of my professors talking about his lunch at the Brasserie in the Seagram Building. "It was marvelous," he had said. "And I'm not even talking about the food. You get to experience two giants of architecture at once. Mies, who designed the building, and Johnson, who did the restaurant." Should we go home and change clothes? I didn't want to break the spell. Our jeans would have to do.

"I have the perfect plan for lunch," I said, "but I won't tell you where until we get there."

"No hints?"

"Think glass and bronze."

We took the subway uptown. Walking on Park Avenue toward the bronze Seagram Building, Monica guessed our destination and squeezed my hand. "Is it going to be lunch with Mies?" she said. "How perfect, Alexandre."

We saluted our engagement with sparkling wine and quiche Lorraine. After lunch, feeling exhilarated, and helped by buzz from our wine, we decided to resume part of our original plan for the day. At the Metropolitan Museum we rushed past the colonnade with the Greek and Roman sculptures to examine the rings in the ancient Egyptian jewelry collection. When we got home, we made passionate love.

Sunday morning we called Monica's mother. My parents weren't home. "We should have waited to tell my mother until we made our plans," Monica said. "I'm afraid she's envisioning a wedding at St. Patrick's Cathedral." Two days later, to assuage her conscience, she telephoned St. Patrick's and was informed that its two side chapels used for smaller weddings were fully booked for the next two years.

Over the next few weeks, there were moments when everything we said to each other was under pressure and disturbingly irrational. At other moments, I instinctively understood that there was no easy way out of love and accepted both its burdens and its joy and I thought Monica did as well.

"I'm a coward," Monica said.

"If I'm not what you want, say so," I said. "I'm not interested in complications."

199

"Neither am I, Alexandre. Have we been through too much with each other?"

"What's that supposed to mean?"

"I wish I could be like my father," she said. "He didn't allow annoyances, big or small, to enter his spirit. He used to say, 'I do my best with the things I can control. For the rest —'" She flicked the back of her fingers against the fingers of her other hand several times, the gesture Brazilians use to show lack of interest in a topic. "My father was able to keep his good spirits, even when he was very sick and knew he was dying. Imagine." She walked into our bedroom and came out smoking a joint. She held it gracefully in the V of her fingers and took a deep toke. I noticed that she looked slimmer than usual.

"You need to take time to eat proper meals, Monica," I said.

She examined her well-proportioned derriere in our full-length closet mirror. "Am I losing my appeal?"

"Not yet."

"I found out that to get married in church, you're supposed to answer a standard questionnaire and then a priest interviews the couple separately," she said.

"To find out if someone's being coerced? The Church has more sense than I gave it credit for." I joined her at the mirror and embraced her from behind. "When did you know for sure you loved me?" I asked.

"From our first conversation in design studio in Rio," she said, turning inside my arms to face me.

"I don't believe you."

"And the first time we made love, I felt tremendous sadness," she said. "I thought only after profound intimacy can you experience grief."

"You felt grief? You never told me."

200

We discussed children. I wanted two. Monica didn't want any. She was afraid child-rearing would end her career. "We'll import a nanny from Brazil," I said. "She'll take care of us."

"That's a typical male attitude."

We let the matter drop.

II

Nothing sharpens the edge of desire like the possibility of loss, which is why it is easy to make passionate love when a relationship is new, exciting and uncertain. Monica and I had gone through months of dailiness when our lovemaking was more practiced and perfunctory than amorous. Now, since our official engagement, when we made love there was often an added nervous ache. One day Monica would tiptoe to the precipice of happiness and we would go around our apartment declaring our love for each other and leave mawkish poems in each other's dresser drawers, shoes and books. The next day she could be bent over in pain, longing for Brazil. It wasn't that the repression had faded from her memory, or mine. She remembered the warmth of friends, the beach, the cheerfulness of Brazilians who, every day, dealt with dashed hopes with a shrug and a joke.

"You can be depressed in Rio," she said, "but it can't last long with all that sun."

The academic demands of our final semester at the CCNY School of Architecture and Environmental Studies were grueling. We were both scrambling to complete the models, drawings, diagrams and photographs for our independent work projects. Monica's project, an aquarium in Battery Park at the southern tip of Manhattan Island, was a tribute to her brother. Jayme had been six weeks away from submitting his aquarium project when he disappeared.

201

In 1973, April 23 fell on a Monday, one day after Easter. Once again the date didn't register with me until my father telephoned late the following evening to catch me up on the state of his health, which was good, and the exuberant good health of the radio stations. I was concentrating so intently on a paper due the next morning for my class on strength of materials that I hardly had time to talk to him.

We had given up sleeping our usual six or seven hours at night, instead catnapping as our schedules permitted. Over our meals together at CCNY's student cafeteria, Monica, bleary-eyed, assessed and reassessed the advantages and disadvantages of Brazilian and American architecture. At the cashier's stand she bought Toblerone bittersweet chocolate bars to bolster her energy. "In Brazil we can put up buildings that would be considered much too experimental in the U.S.," she said. "The zoning laws here are ridiculously restrictive."

"I can't believe you're in favor of unrestricted land speculation," I said.

"Of course I don't like misuse of Brazil's natural assets. I'm talking about not having to give in to the prejudices of neighborhood committees and their lawyers, whether they know anything about architecture or not. The freest, happiest people in Brazil are architects. In spite of everything, they get commissions and flourish."

"Past tense," I said.

The following weekend Monica slept all day Saturday, woke up at 5 in the afternoon, fixed herself breakfast, worked at her makeshift drafting table until 10 p.m., took a shower and suggested that we both needed a break. "It's Ricardo's birthday. He's having a party. Let's go."

There were more than 40 people in Ricardo's railroad flat in Little Italy. Ricardo, a Brazilian painter who was finding success in New York, was not in exile. He had left Brazil to expand his commercial opportunities in February 1964, one month before the military took over the country. Ricardo was well known in the Brazilian émigré community for his parties, which invariably attracted interesting people. He was in a jocular mood when he greeted us at the door. We wished him a happy birthday as we embraced. "Here we all are," he said, "immigrants in the imperialist camp, and we're on our way to becoming rich." He gave each of us a second embrace. *"Tudo bem*? Everything is good with both of you?"

"Tudo bem, Ricardo," I said, smiling.

The apartment's series of shoebox-shaped rooms were enveloped in clouds of marijuana smoke that floated out of the open, double-hung windows. Ricardo's front door was held wide open by a stack of *Time* magazines jammed underneath. No one worried that a cop would come to arrest us, especially in Mafia-run Little Italy. I certainly wasn't expecting to see Kate Lawrence, the UPI reporter who had interviewed me in Rio, walk through the door. She had the same colt-like grace I remembered, the American movie-star looks. I moved to the edge of the close packed bodies and watched her embrace Ricardo, chat with guests she appeared to know, refuse a toke of someone's joint, make her way to Ricardo's improvised bar, pour herself a glass of white wine. "Hello, Kate," I said as I came up behind her. She looked at me, trying to place my face. I let her struggle.

"Do I know you? From New York? Brazil?"

"Rio."

"Sorry, I'm usually pretty good at faces ... "

"Last time we met, I was wearing a hood."

"My God, you're the guy whose group took that little boy hostage! You're Silvia's friend." She shook her head slowly, warily, as if looking in on her own thoughts. "Every reporter in Brazil is haunted by the same problem — it's hard to reveal information about the resistance without sending someone to prison."

203

"You managed."

"Sometimes I filed half of what I knew."

"Did the boy like the electric train set?"

"He could hardly believe his good luck." Kate held me in a steady gaze. "You know how some intellectuals like to say there are only 400 people in Brazil who care what's going on politically? The boy's father was one of the 400 — a university professor who had openly supported the opposition movement."

"Christ! I hope what happened during the bank robbery didn't change his mind."

"I don't know. Naturally, the parents were outraged and frightened. The gesture of sending their son the train astonished them." Kate took a sip of her wine. We were appraising each other.

"I did get Walter Decker's record," I said. "Remember, you recommended it? I liked it."

"I'm glad. Can I know your name?" she asked.

"Are we off the record?"

"I don't work for UPI anymore, but even if I did, I'd consider our conversation to be off the record."

"Alexandre Barbosa. Pleased to meet you again." We shook hands.

"I love the way Alexandre sounds in Portuguese — *Al-is-shon-dré*. It's musical." She paused. "I have a Brazilian friend with the surname Barbosa." She looked down at the drink in her hand with a pensive expression. "I've lost track of him," she said, shaking off her reverie.

"You have lots of Smiths in the U.S." I said. "We're overpopulated with Barbosas in Brazil. I tell Americans to call me Alexander. It's easier."

Kate looked up at me and smiled. I smiled too. "Have you been in New York long?" she asked.

204

"I've been in exile here for two years, nine months, two days, and" — I looked at my watch — "11 hours and 15 minutes."

"You count the minutes?" Kate's smile was warm. "I hope my question wasn't the cause for painful calculations."

I shook my head no. "It depends on my mood. Sometimes I totally forget how long I've been in the U.S. I was in Chile for a year, too, after I left Rio. For the Brazilian exiles, Santiago was like a migrating wake. Every night we used to get together at somebody's apartment and talk about what our underground could have done differently, should have done, to be more effective against the military. It got really tiresome. I needed to get on with my life."

I told her about moving to La Serena, remodeling Juan and Marta's house, my fear that Alessandri would be elected president, my decision to leave Chile and come to New York, my struggles to transfer academic credits from Nacional to CCNY's School of Architecture. "I graduate in June," I said.

"Congratulations." She continued to stare at me.

"The irony is that two months after I arrived in New York, Allende won. I haven't had time to follow the situation in Chile since he took office. I hardly have time to keep track of what's going on in Brazil. It's true when people say architecture school in the U.S. is the most demanding next to medicine."

Kate asked, "Why La Serena?"

I remembered Silvia's telling me that Kate was an accomplished poet. Disingenuously I answered, "Because Gabriela Mistral was born near La Serena. Do you know her poems?"

Kate examined my face, acknowledging my game. "I do. They all deal with the aftermath of her lover's suicide. Gabriela never married." Kate suddenly looked sad. I presumed she was thinking of the death of her own fiancé. I touched her shoulder. She responded by moving

205

closer to me. Then she said, "The only thing I know about northern Chile is that people believe the sky is full of UFOs."

"And the only Chilean poet I've actually read is Pablo Neruda," I said.

"While you were in La Serena, did you see any UFOs?"

"Constantly. They used to do docking maneuvers on the hill above my apartment. It got to be quite a nuisance." We continued to look at each other intently. "Now that we've talked for a while, do you think you would have recognized my voice if I hadn't told you I was wearing a hood when we met?"

"I might have if you'd greeted me in Portuguese. You have a nice voice. It's very mellow, very Brazilian."

"Very Brazilian?" I asked.

"There's a kind of promise in your voice," she said, smiling, "the allure of the tropics, something like that."

"I think that's a poet's way of describing a very normal voice, like mine."

Monica came up to us and I introduced her to Kate. For a few minutes we talked about Rio, the irony of Brazil's remarkable rate of economic growth — the highest in the world — in an economy plagued by high energy costs, runaway inflation, a large balance-of-payments deficit and intensified repression.

"Brazil's borrowing a lot of money," I said, "and putting it into megalomaniac projects. Let's see if they get finished." There was no need to mention the continued prohibition on political activities, censorship, torture, the far-off dream of electing a civilian president — old stories — so I changed the subject. "They say President Médici plays gin rummy with his wife every night and he gets annoyed when he's interrupted by matters of state."

206

"It's late," Monica whispered into my ear, "and I have to be at Max's tomorrow at noon. Let's say goodbye to Ricardo and go home."

Later, in bed, Monica got up and turned on the overhead light just as I was drifting off to sleep. "Tell me about your friend Kate," she said. "She's the reporter you talked to in Rio. When you introduced me, you didn't say that I'm your fiancée."

"I told her about you before you joined us." It was a lie.

"Have you seen her in New York before?"

"After she interviewed me in Rio, I never saw her again until tonight."

"There was something going on between you."

"Are you crazy?"

Monica wouldn't let me sleep. She wanted to know everything Kate and I had said to each other. I had never seen her really jealous before. She plumped a pillow and leaned her elbow on it. "When you're in Rio, you don't have any sense of the vast interior of Brazil. No sense of the Indians."

"I'm tired, Monica."

"In their blood, Indians like bright things. I think black Americans like noise and white Americans like speed." Monica lit a cigarette.

"I'm not in the mood for comparisons coming out of nowhere, thank you. If you've got something on your mind, say it."

"Do you think your friend Kate ever interviewed a Brazilian Indian?"

"She's not my friend. I've met her twice in my life." I got up, snapped off the light, lay down and put my pillow over my head.

"I'm not trying to be argumentative, Alexandre. I just wondered. Maybe we should have children."

"Since you think all the work of raising a child would fall on you, you decide."

CHAPTER SIXTEEN

I

Months earlier, Monica and I had decided we couldn't hope for better internships than with the firms where we were already known. While working at the Barnes firm as a part-time model builder, I had created opportunities with the staff "to make charm" as we say in Portuguese. Making charm came quite naturally to both of us. Monica and I had the luck to have been born into the right families, we knew how to dress, how to walk into a room, how to circulate with ease at a party. We made the most of being exiles from an "exotic" country that had a tradition of being architecture-conscious. We could tell vivid stories about famous Brazilians like architect Oscar Niemeyer and landscape designer Roberto Burle Marx, or about curiosities like Bauru's unique, widely-known brothel, Casa da Eny, which provided not only the usual delights but also a country-club atmosphere, complete with swimming pool and restaurant.

By the time I let the Barnes firm know that I would like to serve my three-year internship there, I was already known to the associate who did the hiring. In late April I was informed that they would take me on after I graduated. Monica was similarly successful at Davis Brody. As students at CCNY, not a prestigious school like Yale or Cornell, we had each leapt over a high fence by being offered these prized positions.

During the frenetic month leading up to our commencement on June 11, we had to finish our independent work projects, present them to a panel of critics consisting of CCNY faculty and outside judges, have our final design portfolios approved and complete our work for three other demanding courses. The commencement ceremony took place in the evening under the lights of Lewisohn Stadium. We wore black gowns and black mortarboards with lavender tassels. Halfway through the uplifting speeches, I found myself wondering what commencement would have been like at Nacional. Did the architecture graduates wear tasseled mortarboards? I had no idea.

Monica and I began our architecture internships on the same day, June 18. We worked 12-hour days, getting oriented to our new responsibilities, striving to please our senior colleagues with our performance. After a month, we had settled into our internships securely enough that we could give some attention to wedding plans. We joined our local parish, Our Lady of Pompeii, an Italian immigrant church staffed by the Scalabrini Fathers, arranged for our wedding banns to be read, scheduled our Pre-Cana (marriage preparation course) and selected for our reception Chez André, a top-rated French restaurant on King Street, three blocks from out apartment, that had a graceful garden patio.

Dr. Martins, my father's cardiologist, said that he thought my father would be fit enough to attend our wedding on September 8, but that the family should not count on it. My mother tried to hide her nervousness at the prospect that she might have to travel to New York alone. Her voice on the phone was halting. Paulo's posting in Egypt was ending at the beginning of September and he and Maria Rita planned to return to Brasília by way of New York so they could attend our wedding.

Monica's mother wrote that she was elated with our news and that she planned to arrive in New York one week before our nuptials to help with last-minute details. But she also let us know she was disappointed that her daughter's wedding could not be in Rio at Nossa Senhora da Glória do Outeiro Chapel, the marvelous, gleaming, white baroque church where she was married.

"I told you," I said to Monica, "we should have had a civil ceremony and informed our families we were married. Look what we're letting ourselves in for — church banns, Vatican rigmarole, an undercurrent of regret that we can't go home to get married."

210

"Don't, Alexandre."

"No, your mother's right to want to see you married in Rio. Frankly, I'd rather be designing an elaborate heating and cooling system, not my favorite kind of work, than trying to accommodate everybody's needs and wishes over this wedding."

I was glad our wedding was six weeks off, not only because it gave my father more time to recover from his heart attack, but also because Monica was in a strange mood. And so was I. I felt as if I were walking backward into an abyss. Pre-marriage nerves on both our parts? I considered confronting Monica with my feelings of anxiousness. Should I say, "Why haven't you said you love me in weeks? Just plainly said it?" I decided to wait.

Meanwhile, I couldn't stop thinking about Kate Lawrence. I didn't want to.

II

On Monday afternoon of my sixth week as a neophyte architect at Edward Larrabee Barnes Associates, I called Kate and invited her to have lunch with me. "How's P. J. Clarke's?" I asked. Kate hesitated. "I don't insist on Clarke's. Anything in midtown is fine with me."

"No, P. J.'s is fine. I've been avoiding going there."

"Bad food?"

"Bad memories ... Or, at least, memories."

"Suggest something else."

"My mind's a blank at the moment. You're now an official architect?"

"Yes, thank God."

"Congratulations."

211

"How about lunch tomorrow?" I said. "Noon sharp. P J's gets crowded by 12:15."

Kate laughed. "Noon sharp? I don't think of Brazilians as being punctual."

"I am."

I hung up the phone without allowing myself to think about what the hell I was doing.

I got home late that night. Monica was still at her office. I fixed myself a cheese-and-tomato sandwich and went to bed. In the morning, without waking her, I put on freshly laundered and pressed chinos and my best blazer, carefully arranged a Liberty silk paisley pocket square in my breast pocket so it looked slightly foppish — the cosmopolitan architect's de rigueur accessory — and went to the office. Kate and I both arrived at P. J. Clarke's five minutes before 12. I couldn't stop looking at her.

"Tell me, do you miss your life in Rio?" I asked after we ordered mushroom omelets, small Caesar salads and iced tea.

"Constantly." Kate seemed to lean in on her thoughts, just as she did at Ricardo's party. "The last four years have been painful. I'm not quite a widow, not quite recovered, not quite a published novelist."

"You never found out what happened to your fiancé?"

"John ...His name was John Wadson. It's still a mystery who killed him and why. When José, our UPI legman, found him in the elevator early in the morning, he'd been shot in the chest. The expensive watch I'd just given him for Christmas wasn't on his wrist."

"Silvia said you worked for him."

Kate nodded, then smiled. "I did. He was the one who taught me how to be a reporter." She played with the straw in her iced tea. "From the moment I heard John was murdered, I've had theories. The

212

police investigation hasn't turned up anything besides robbery. It's complicated. I don't think I'll ever know."

"You're gorgeous, Kate. You should have a life."

"I didn't mean to imply I don't. Poets overstate. It's a professional hazard."

We talked about the novel she was working on, *Kingdom of Gestures*, inspired by her time in Brazil. "Is it your story?" I asked.

"I'm not a confessional writer. Some of my characters, though, are modeled on real people I met in Rio."

"Are you seeing anyone right now?" I asked.

"Not exactly."

"What does that mean?"

"Nobody I'm serious about. What about you?"

"I'm engaged."

"To the girl I met at Ricardo's party?"

"Yes. When I had to flee Brazil, Monica left with me."

"Lucky for you."

"I think so, too."

"When are you getting married?"

"Early September."

We had finished our omelets. I put my hand on top of Kate's. "I'm being honest," I said. I looked into her eyes.

"Do you collect odalisques, Alexandre Barbosa? I'm not available for a harem."

"I don't want you for a harem."

"You're not really being honest. You're not getting married, are you? And I think subconsciously you know it."

"You're wrong, Kate."

213

She smiled and tossed her head as if to clear the air of incongruity.

"Believe me," I said, "it's a knot too tangled to untie." I looked away. "Should we get out of here?"

"To where?" she asked. "From a certain slant of light …" She dropped her chin and regarded me intently. "You remind me of someone."

"You're very secretive," I said.

"'There's a certain slant of light' — it's a line from an Emily Dickinson poem."

"I've never read her poems, but I'll start immediately. You've just told me it's important to you. Who do I remind you of?"

"Sérgio, a Brazilian friend."

I didn't quiz her about Sérgio. I paid the bill and we got up from the table. I put my arm around Kate's waist as we walked to the door. On the street, before parting, I kissed her behind the ear. Her hair smelled of Cape jasmine.

I was ready to suffer the consequences of desire. Was Kate? I didn't want to hurt her. Friday, three days after our luncheon at P J Clarke's, we made love. The summer sun of early evening streamed through the south window of her apartment on East 56th Street. Undressing her, with her skirt pulled up over her shoulders, I nearly said we should stop. I felt her vulnerability when I entered her.

III

Late July was hot, sultry — my kind of weather. Rio weather. Monica and I were acutely aware of being in the world's center of architectural dialogue and excitement. At night the city offered an array of lectures and symposiums on the future of architecture. We drank in the intellectual fervor along with architects in all phases of their careers. The established architects had just the right eyeglass frames, the right suits, the right silk pocket squares, the right haircuts, the right swagger. With the demands of our hectic final semester at school behind us, we had more time to take advantage of the lectures at the Architectural League on Madison Avenue and at the Institute for Architecture and Urban Studies on West 40th Street. We started with a series, "The Challenge of Bringing Good Design to Subsidized Housing," presented by architects rooted in the modernist movement.

During the day I was doing what all new architecture interns do — drawing. I drew details of bathrooms and staircases. I corrected blueprints where errors had been marked in red. There are no shortcuts to becoming a competent architect. Having, or not having, design talent is altogether a separate matter. It was next to impossible to pass the exhaustive, three-day licensing examination without observing actual construction and knowing every aspect of the process, from functional requirements to the early design concept, to schematics, preliminary drawings and final working drawings.

At Davis Brody, Monica was fitting out kitchens for a high-rise housing complex on Third Avenue that stretched from 90th to 92nd streets, learning from other jobs the firm had done. Sometimes when I had dull work, such as reproducing a section of a drawing, I would picture Monica pausing at her drafting table to peel and lick a banana the way she used to at Nacional. She laughed when I reminded her. We were talking about moving to a larger apartment in an elevator building, now that we had money from two regular salaries.

I waited a week to call Kate. Before she could say anything I said, "I'm used to taking risks, Kate, but usually I calculate the odds beforehand. With you, I have no idea what they are. What I know is that I want to be with you."

She didn't respond right away. Finally she said, "When you didn't call, I wondered if I would ever see you again. Last Friday, with you, I was giving myself permission to start letting go of John."

It was clear we were going to continue seeing each other. The reasons didn't matter. I changed the subject. "Have you heard from any more publishers about your novel?"

"Not yet. It could take months."

"I'm sure your novel will be accepted, Kate."

"You haven't read it."

"I want to."

Three days later we had lunch at P.J. Clarke's again. She brought her manuscript for me to read. "Some publishing professionals only read the first two pages of a manuscript, the last two pages and two pages in the middle to decide if it's worth reading more," she said.

"I'll start on page one and go to the end. Promise."

We looked over our menus and ordered lunch.

"Don't you have to worry about supporting yourself?" I asked.

"Not for a while longer. John left me money in a Swiss bank." Kate leaned back in her chair and appraised me. "You realize, don't you, that our relationship is based on situations that are unfinished, in my life and yours?"

"I come from a half-finished country."

"Very true." She smiled and I kissed her hand.

That was as far as we were ready to go. We changed the subject. After lunch I went back to my office. Kate went back to her writing.

I didn't meet Monica for a lecture that evening. I telephoned Kate and we took a walk. We found ourselves on East 52nd Street where it dead-ends overlooking the East River. We sat on a bench to talk. There was still enough light to make out the swift current. "Before I went to Rio, I used to spend time late at night on this very bench brooding about Sérgio," Kate said.

After a while we walked to Kate's apartment. She apologized because there wasn't much food in her refrigerator. She poured two gin and tonics and handed one to me. She raised her glass in a toast, "To Summer." I saluted her with mine. I liked the taste of juniper in her mouth. We undressed quickly. Nothing mattered — not the fact that I was cheating on Monica, or that Kate and I came from different worlds, or that she was seven years older than I, or that I didn't know why she would have me. Perhaps she was right, even though I wouldn't admit it to myself — Monica and I were losing each other. Monica wanted desperately to live in Brazil and I couldn't.

A week later Dr. Martins declared that my father had completely recovered from his heart attack and could attend our wedding. My father was ecstatic on the telephone. At 7 the following morning, a telegram was delivered to our front door:

JAYME RIO MORGUE. DEATH CETIFICATE SIGNED PHYSICIAN PATHOLOGY SECTION, CENTRAL ARMY HOSPITAL. FUNERAL CANDELÁRIA CHURCH SOON AS YOU ARRIVE RIO. MÃE

Monica collapsed in my arms. We were both speechless. Finally, through tears, she stammered, "I'm leaving today on the first flight I can get. I don't care if my name is on all the lists in the world. If someone from my group was tortured and gave my name to the police, it doesn't matter now."

"I'm the one they want, Monica, not you," I said.

"Maybe, maybe not."

217

"You'll get your passport stamped without raising an eyebrow. Straight through the line. You'll see." Her face was anguished but resolute. We knew that when she handed her passport to the control agent, she was stepping into the unknown. Would she be in danger? I had to think it was unlikely.

I helped her pack. All day we discussed what she should do if she encountered trouble at Galeão International Airport. We never came up with a plan that comforted either of us. That evening, she flew to Rio.

Had Jayme been incarcerated in Rio for five years — ever since 1968? Or held in some remote place? Student demonstrators who were arrested on the streets of Rio were usually broken by intimidation and released in a matter of days or months. Dissidents with a police dossier, on the other hand, were tortured. Scores died at the hands of their torturers and became "the disappeared." Some detainees went through a legal process. After they were sentenced, the family could usually get information about the prisoner. Jayme had been a demonstrator, not a known dissident, but in spite of repeated inquiries, he had vanished without a trace.

Monica telephoned me the morning after she arrived. "They weren't looking for me," she said. "Nothing but the usual formalities at passport control."

"I told you it would be okay, didn't I? But thank God."

We talked for nearly half an hour. Her uncle Maurício had received an anonymous phone call informing him that the body of Jayme Paiva could be picked up by the family at the morgue. As her mother and uncle waited in the front seat of a hired hearse, a mortuary attendant handed them a death certificate stating that Jayme had died of internal bleeding while in the custody of army police. That was all, one sentence. Maurício's attempts to get a further explanation of his confinement and death were futile.

218

"My mother and my uncle are out of their minds thinking that Jayme might have been here in Rio all this time and they couldn't find out anything. At least we can bury him. It's more than most families of the disappeared get to do. My mother is in total despair. I won't be able to leave her for a few weeks. I'll call my office." I could hear unbearable agony in her voice.

"Is there something I can do?"

"I wish there were. Jayme was alive all this time. I can't stop thinking about how he must have suffered in prison and how he must have been desperate to let us know where he was. That's the hardest part. I didn't really expect a different outcome. I mean, I hoped . . . "

When we spoke again three days later, I heard the voice of a woman who was slowly rediscovering what it meant to be home — to hear the sensuous cadence of Portuguese all around her, the music, the food, the fragrance of the ocean just outside one's doorstep, the self-deprecating jokes, the crazy irony, the florid descriptions, the delirious joy, the saddest longing.

At the office, while making formulaic drawings at my drafting board, I turned off the radio and paid attention to the turmoil spinning in my head. Everything in my life was suddenly very tense once again, the way it had been in Rio when I was working on a project for design studio, writing papers, taking exams and simultaneously robbing banks, terrified that I would be caught. I was anguished over Jayme's torment, almost wishing I could strike back by taking up my old life as a guerrilla with all its suspicion, tension and fear. At the same time, I wanted Monica to truly embrace the reality that marrying me meant permanent exile.

CHAPTER SEVENTEEN

I

Two days before I expected Monica to return, her phone call woke me at 6 in the morning. "My mother's in the hospital. She fell and broke her ankle last night. She was in such pain in the emergency room, the doctor said she should stay in the hospital overnight."

"She's going to be all right?"

"She is, but she'll be on crutches for six weeks. A walking cast isn't possible. She may find crutches too difficult and have to use a wheelchair. I don't see how I can leave on Thursday. She's not herself. Neither am I. We keep going over the same ground about how we couldn't help Jayme, or even get news of him. Both of us are having a series of mishaps. I scraped the whole side of my uncle's car when I was leaving his garage. It was so stupid."

"You haven't driven since Chile. You're out of practice."

"It's not that . . . It's very hard to explain everything from here. Do you think we should delay our wedding?" Her voice was low in her throat, the voice of someone hiding from herself.

"Let's not decide that right now," I said.

"I love you, Alexandre."

II

On the phone a few days later we made the decision that, under the circumstances, we had no choice but to delay our wedding. We thought the weather would still be warm enough in early October for a champagne reception and luncheon, outdoors on the French restaurant's garden patio, as originally planned. By then Monica's mother would be

220

out of her cast and able to travel to New York. Our Lady of Pompeii Church and the restaurant on King Street were accommodating. I kept our invitees up-to-date on our plans. Moving the date forward four weeks did not inconvenience my parents or the Madsen family. Maria Rita and Paulo, however, were unsure whether they could attend an October wedding in New York after they had already returned to Brazil from Egypt. Our guest list had grown to 45 people, including colleagues from our two offices as well as friends and professors from CCNY. Finally, with new arrangements in place, I could tell everyone that our wedding would be on Saturday, October 6.

While Monica was away, I kept on seeing Kate. In mid-August I finished reading her novel. I was impressed by its language, its plot, the characters. I took it for granted that Kate shared my political views because she had portrayed the resistance and the underground movement with understanding and sympathy. I had missed some subtleties, as it later turned out.

Under Kate's direction I read contemporary American poetry, spending languorous nights at her apartment. She went with me to architecture lectures. When I encountered colleagues who might mention her to Monica, I introduced Kate as a friend whom I had met in Brazil and went on to say how surprised we all were when Monica and I ran into Kate at a party in New York. Kate was exactly like many educated Brazilians I knew. She had strong opinions about modern architecture and was able to speak with assurance about the balance of solidity with transparency, spatial experience, architecture's uplifting purposes. Sometimes instead of eating a sandwich at my drafting board, I would slip away from my office at lunchtime and make love to Kate. The Barnes office on East 62nd Street was just eight blocks from her apartment.

I began to recount to Kate details of my adventures as a bank robber — the outrageous chances I took. When I told her about my father's loss of Fazenda Maraíba in Bauru, we got a shock. "My God, Alexandre!" she said. "Is your father Jorge Antônio Barbosa?"

"He is. How would you know that?"

"John and I were planning to interview him for a story. We had an appointment to visit Fazenda Maraíba — it would have been the week after John was killed. Not only that, you must be a cousin of Sérgio Barbosa!"

"Jesus, Kate, I can't believe it. Were you Sérgio's American fiancée?"

"I was."

"Sérgio is my father's first cousin."

Kate studied my face. "To tell you the truth, you've been reminding me of Sérgio," she said. "Little facial expressions, the unexpected way you have of expressing ideas. Now I understand why."

We sat staring at each other, not knowing what more to say.

Two days later, looking out over the East River at twilight from Kate's bench at the end of 52nd Street, I said, "You might be interested to know what my father said when he heard that Sérgio had broken off his engagement — his American fiancée was lucky not to have married him."

"It cost me a lot of heartache to reach the same conclusion. Sérgio's the reason I went to Rio. It's a long, sad story, as love affairs that end badly usually are. He accused me of having an affair with one of his subordinates at the Brazilian Consulate in New York. It wasn't true, except in his mind. I knew Sérgio was neurotic and difficult, but also brilliant and exciting. After he ended our engagement, I thought I could understand him better, and the hold he had on me, by visiting his country. I was able to convince a travel magazine to let me write an article on Rio's 16 beaches."

"Did it work? Visiting Rio to understand him?"

"As you can guess, yes and no. I'll never regret my decision to go. My life has taken a direction I never could have imagined."

"I want to remind you that I'm not Sérgio."

"I'm reminded."

I had accepted that I could never take the place of John and that there were parts of Kate I would never know — that she had been my cousin's fiancée raised too many complications for either of us to work out. For the next week I caught her glancing at me warily, but eventually she seemed satisfied that I wasn't a copy of my cousin. After a couple of weeks, I had convinced myself that I could handle her past and its ghosts without feeling jealous.

III

Monica didn't return to New York until August 30. In one of our tense telephone conversations, she had wistfully mentioned that she saw opportunities in Rio to do design work and thereby jettison the three years of drawing and copying that her U.S. architecture internship required.

Our embrace at the airport was mechanical. Immediately I felt a change in her. Our familiar invitations to lovemaking felt childish and awkward. When I was inside her, Monica's body didn't yield to mine in the same way. The transformation was unmistakable. Was she responding to subliminal signals in my behavior? I toyed with the idea that she had had an affair in Rio. Of course, there were a lot of possible reasons for Monica's demeanor to have changed.

Two days after she returned, Saturday of Labor Day weekend, having slept until noon, Monica and I strolled among the sculptures and brightly colored flower beds at the United Nations garden. Sunday we took a picnic lunch to Roosevelt Island, a sliver of land two miles long and only a sixth of a mile wide in the East River between Manhattan and Queens. We welcomed the small adventure. The weather was hot on Sunday. Non-threatening clouds offered moments of shade.

Philip Johnson and John Burgee had designed a master plan for a mixed-income community on the island, where vehicular traffic was to be minimized. Construction of the first residential complex was well under way. We were curious. A Swiss company was building an aerial tramway to connect the island to Manhattan. In 1973, the only way for us to get to Roosevelt Island was by subway to Queens and then by bus across a lift bridge; its main span could be raised straight up to allow ships to pass underneath.

"What a relief we're finished with school," Monica said as we spread out a blanket on the weeds and straggly grass at the southern end of the island. "Every other time we've taken a day off to explore around New York, we've had some huge unfinished project hanging over our heads."

We ate pâté and Brie on fresh baguettes, hard-boiled eggs, oranges and chocolate cake, drank a fruity white wine and stretched out to get a tan. Without opening my eyes, I reached for Monica's hand and held it. She moved closer to my side. I felt reconnected to her at last. Guilt overwhelmed me. I suppressed a wave of compulsion to confess. "If we moved to Roosevelt Island, it wouldn't take long to discover all the secrets of this very, very small paradise," Monica said.

"It wasn't paradise for Mae West," I said. "In the mid-'20s she was incarcerated here in Blackwell's Penitentiary for a scandalous play she wrote."

I opened my eyes and watched Monica sit up and look around. "What a scary name for a prison — Blackwell. I don't see a penitentiary. Where is it?" She leaned over me and brushed her lips against my cheek.

"The city razed it when the jail complex on Rikers Island opened," I said without moving, except to shield my eyes from the glare of the sun. "I told one of the associates at my office we might come here over the weekend and he launched into the Mae West story. Roger's hobby is curious facts about New York."

"We haven't done anything scandalous for a long time, Alexandre." She stretched the full length of her body against mine. We were alone in an open field. The only thing within 200 yards of us was a shabby-looking city hospital that appeared deserted, even though I knew it wasn't. Monica was playful, daring me. I was tempted. "I won't invite you twice," she teased.

I reached over and ran my hand along the curve of her hips. She moved away. Her sudden change in mood seemed to come out of nowhere. It was as if the wind had shifted. I kissed her. A long, open-mouthed kiss. "What's wrong?" I asked.

"Let's not start this now."

"Scared?"

She nodded. "On two accounts. Being interrupted," she said, pointing in the direction of a nearby broken-down bench. "Somebody could come along." Suddenly her voice was low in her throat again, the way it was on the telephone from Rio. "And getting married."

"For Christ's sake, Monica!" I removed my hand from her hip. I looked for a squall in the sky, but the clouds had scattered. The sky was cerulean. "Everybody gets nervous before their wedding. It's normal." I tried not to sound impatient.

"Don't treat me like a virgin bride. You know what I'm talking about."

"I'm not sure I do."

"We've been drifting apart."

Certainly it had crossed my mind that Monica and I might be heading into a marriage neither of us was sure about but neither of us had the will or capacity to stop. I sat up and played for time with a couple of deep breaths. "You've only been home for four days. You've been through a lot —"

"That's the trouble, Alexandre, I'm not home."

"Home isn't with me?" She stared at her hands in her lap. "I didn't force you to run away from Brazil, Monica — just the opposite."

"I know."

"I've asked you dozens of times if you regretted your decision. You always said no."

"It was no, for a long time."

"I can't force you to love me."

"That's the trouble. I do love you. It would be easy if I didn't." She had let her spine, normally erect, sink into a deep curve.

"Easy to do what?" I asked.

"Easy to go back to Rio."

"You know my name is on the control list. You don't think I can just slip back into Brazil?"

She reached for my hand on the blanket. I covered hers with mine. "Of course not, Alexandre." Her voice was almost a whisper.

"I love you," I said. "I'm sorry you don't love me enough ..." Monica continued to stare into her lap. At that moment, I wasn't ambivalent. I wanted our marriage. I wanted children with her. Was it a matter of pride? Habit? The arrangements we had made?

"Is there someone else?" I asked. "Someone you met in Rio? Let's be frank with each other."

"Should I ask you the same question, Alexandre? Have you met someone?" Then, hearing herself, she was silent.

"Men are men," I said.

"Especially Brazilian men?" she said.

"I can't say I've always been faithful."

"Good."

She stood up, gathered the remains of our picnic and folded the blanket. The tension between us was unbearable. We retraced our trip back to Manhattan in silence.

Everything was closed on Monday, Labor Day, even my newsstand. New Yorkers had evacuated the city to celebrate the end of summer elsewhere. It started out to be a beautiful day, then it rained on and off. Monica and I felt trapped in every way possible. I felt sick watching her pack. "Where are you going?" I asked.

"Nowhere at the moment. I'm just organizing my clothes." I opened our front closet and took out an umbrella. "Where are you going?" she asked.

"To a hotel for lunch. Nothing else is open. Come with me."

"No thanks."

"I wish you would. I love you, Monica."

"I'm not hungry. I'm glad you had an affair, Alexandre."

"Why? So it's easier to leave?"

"Not at all. I'm glad for you."

"What hurts is, I believe you."

Over breakfast the following Wednesday, we pored over the shocking news from Chile. President Allende had committed suicide in the course of a military coup. Chile, which had been polarized by Allende's socialist agenda, would now be in the grip of a military junta.

Brazilian exiles in Chile were taking refuge in the Argentine Embassy in Santiago. My personal anguish was coinciding with the sad events in Chile. "September is an adverse month," I said. "Jimi Hendrix died in September — two months after we arrived in New York, remember?"

On September 12, three and a half weeks before we were to be married, Monica bought a ticket for Rio. "Did you have to choose the 13th to fly?" I asked in the taxi on the way to Kennedy International Airport.

"I'll take out flight insurance, with you as the beneficiary."

And since we had an awkward hour to kill, in a forlorn little ceremony of love she actually purchased a half-million-dollar policy from a vending machine. "I intend to have a 13th floor on every building I design," she said.

"So do I," I said. "No skipping."

"You aren't really superstitious," she whispered into my ear just before she handed her ticket to the Varig agent at the gate.

"You know I'm not. At least I hope you do."

"I do know you, Alexandre. I love you."

"Different fates?" I said. "No way to reverse the inevitable? I hope to God you aren't leaving because you're jealous."

"Rivalry is dangerous," she said. "You only nominate your successor." She turned around to face me. "I'll write."

But she didn't.

And neither did I.

CHAPTER EIGHTEEN

I

I wanted comfort from my lover. I recognized Kate's hurt to be greater than mine — John could never come back — but my pain was immediate and acute. Two days after Monica's departure, I wasn't ready for a cultural comparison of Brazil and the United States. But that's exactly what Kate and I got into over dinner at the San Remo, my favorite Italian bistro, a short walk from my apartment, where abstract expressionists would still occasionally drop by to drink and argue. Kate had begun the discussion by saying that everything in Brazil is the opposite of the way it is in the United States. I didn't agree. I was in no mood for poetic hyperbole.

"Americans and Brazilians are both quick studies," she said, "but Americans exaggerate what they know. They say they've read a book when they've only read the review. Brazilians use charm. They'll say something like, 'I never read the book, but I didn't like it.'" She leaned forward in her seat. "If a Brazilian wants to complain about stupidity or inefficiency, he becomes instantly vehement. He yells. It doesn't work with Americans. An American is likely to say to a hysterical person, 'I won't talk to you if you don't calm down.'"

"I never yell at anybody," I said. I refilled our glasses with Chianti. The San Remo's inexpensive wine never cheapened its sautéed veal dishes or its pasta.

"Do you complain in a loud voice?"

"Exiles don't bother about complaining. They're just waiting to go home."

"Is that what you want to do?"

"I don't let myself think about it anymore. If I could go home, after two weeks I'd probably get as fed up with Brazilian bullshit as I

229

get with the American. At which point, according to you, I'd not only be free to yell, I'd be obliged. Did you learn to yell when you lived in Brazil, Kate? Did John?"

"I never heard him raise his voice," she said.

"Really?"

She paused. "What you should know about John is that he was audacious. He took risks. Of course, he calculated the odds. His biggest risk was being honest with me."

"About his feelings? Is that what this roundabout conversation is leading up to? John was able to express his feelings and I'm not."

"No." She said it firmly. "John was fearless like you, but he had an unusual history — and it included being a sniper." Kate pressed her hands together in front of her, carefully matching fingertip to fingertip. Finally she said, "That's what I wanted to tell you, Alexandre, and I can't tell you more than that." She watched me for a moment until she was sure I had taken in what she had just said. Then she looked away toward the crowded bar while I gathered my thoughts.

For an instant I felt all my senses leave me, then rush back all at once. "Your fiancé didn't come to Brazil to be a reporter, did he? What was he really doing, Kate? Training DOPS? Christ! Spying on the underground movement? Was he a sniper in Rio?"

"Categorically no to everything you just said." She leaned her elbow forward on the table and cupped her chin in her hand. "Please don't look at me like I'm an iceberg."

"How should I look at you? Reporters report, Kate. They don't carry guns and shoot people, even in Vietnam. Brazilians know the CIA played a major role in our '64 coup, and the CIA has been supporting the generals ever since. I risked my life to oppose the military dictatorship. Your fiancé was on the wrong side. To say the least, I have a complicated mix of thoughts and feelings right now. You should know me well enough to understand that."

"Let me put your mind at ease on one point. John wasn't in the CIA. He was a Canadian citizen and as far as the Brazilian resistance is concerned, he sympathized with your side. He could see plainly enough what the generals were up to. John was a thoroughly honorable man. You'll just have to believe me. I loved him deeply. And he was a damn good reporter."

Kate refused to answer any more of my questions. We finished our entrees without speaking. "I need some air," I said. "Let's get out of here."

"I remember you said 'let's get out of here' midway through our first lunch together at P. J. Clarke's. I was still eating my omelet."

"I wanted to make love to you, desperately."

"But we didn't. A kiss behind my ear is what I remember. What about now?"

"Yes. Right now."

I paid the bill and we left the restaurant. I put my arm around Kate's waist in our now-familiar way of walking as we covered the few blocks south along MacDougal Street, then one block over to Sixth Avenue. She had never seen the apartment where I lived with Monica. I turned on the lamp in the hall and led Kate through the dark living room to the bedroom. The sheets on the bed were clean; the set Monica had last slept on was still piled in a hamper, waiting to go to the laundry. I didn't want to think about what my reluctance to take them meant.

We undressed silently. It was a kind of feral lovemaking, almost unkind, and over quickly. I went to the kitchen and brought back a Coke, which we shared. We made love again, each of us indulging in our individual yearnings and pieties. Was I sleeping with the widow of my enemy? I perceived a new and disturbing guardedness in our

231

behavior. Perversely, I felt even more drawn to her, my sense of reck-lessness and danger stronger than when I had been seeing her furtively while Monica was still in New York.

As she fell asleep in my arms, my first thought was that she had tested me and I hadn't passed. Her timing was opportune. Monica was gone, and the possibility now existed that our relationship could develop into something more enduring than sex and exploring the for-eign worlds we brought each other. I recalled that Monica had given herself to me wholly only after I proved my commitment to the as-pirations of the underground movement. I didn't believe Kate's test was political. She understood my views well enough. I had heard her expound my arguments more eloquently than I could, and she had dra-matized them in her novel. Hadn't she been a trustworthy ally in the matter of the apology and the gift to the boy? I remembered friends saying that the most dangerous time in a relationship was when all the perceived external problems disappear.

After a few minutes, Kate woke and spoke into the middle distance without looking at me. "Did you know Gabriela Mistral was the princi-pal of a school in Temuco, Chile, where Pablo Neruda was a student? She was already a gifted poet, and she encouraged him. It's so unusual and surprising, really — the only two Chileans ever to win a Nobel Prize, both poets, and one was helped by the other."

"Fuck it, Kate! Don't play games with me. Talk about something serious."

"All right. After Gabriela's lover killed himself, the focus of her poems was thwarted motherhood. Did Monica want children? Was that one of your problems?"

"Exactly the other way around. I did. She wasn't as sure. I thought we loved each other enough that we'd work it out. Our problem was that I couldn't go home, and she could. Kate, do you think we're on opposite sides?"

232

"Only about children. I used to want children. Now I'm not certain."

"That's not what I meant."

"I'm happy to talk about my political views, but John's views are off the point. This is between you and me, not you and him."

It had started to rain heavily and water from the open window was starting to splash onto the parquet floor. I got up and closed the window. Across Sixth Avenue I saw a male neighbor, also naked, closing his. When I got back into bed I said, "Do you want to stay the night?"

"Yes." She rested her head on my chest and put her forefinger to my lips to quiet me. We fell asleep until morning.

For the next day or two, we said very little to each other, both of us pretending that silence was not unfavorable to our continued relationship. Then, over a late meal at her neighborhood diner, Kate brought up politics. "Do you think it's worth it — discussing politics seriously?" she said. "We've barely talked about what I think."

I was eager for an explicit rapprochement, though I wasn't ready to say, "Politics be damned, Kate, I'm falling in love with you." I had begun rereading several of Kate's poems in the light of what I considered my well-founded suspicions about John. I was intensely curious about him and the extraordinary charisma he must have had. Kate gave me no help. She would only insist that her poems, like her novel, were the product of her imagination.

We talked about the left's agenda in Brazil and elsewhere. She didn't hide her skepticism. "Do you really believe their solutions can do anything about the world's problems? I'm saying that as someone in great sympathy with your views."

"Do you think you're talking to a communist?" I asked.

"Of course not. I'm talking to a member of the ruling class."

233

Occasionally we leaned on a Campari and soda or two before dinner to refocus and lighten our evening. One time Kate joked that perhaps she was too old for me. I responded that from the day I met her in Rio at Silvia's apartment until that night, she reminded me of a *potranca*, a filly, moving lightly in a pasture. "That was my first impression of you, Kate — spirited and not appreciating your own grace."

She feigned wonder over my metaphor. "You really did grow up on a *fazenda*," she said, smiling. "I doubted you."

Secretly, and only because of her remark, I examined her body for signs of aging. Her auburn hair was shiny and lustrous, no suggestion of lines at the corners of her eyes, no hint that gravity would concern her anytime soon. Monica's figure was lean, but curvaceous around the hips. Kate's, at age 34, was angular and athletic. She reminded me of Katharine Hepburn.

When I pressed her again about John's mysterious history, she offered, "John never would have become involved with me if he hadn't been convinced I would keep his secrets. He dealt out his confidences, always watching how I handled one before he ventured another."

Kate's reserve grew. So did mine. Our sex, though, was free and abandoned. After three anguished weeks we reached an unspoken understanding. It came down to an awareness that we were strongly attracted to each other, that we both were convalescing from losses and that we wanted and needed each other's company.

Whom had John killed? Why? Where? Who had killed him? I was convinced Kate carried heavy secrets. She had made an opening to me, her lover, a person she hoped she could trust. I was coming to see that my failure with Kate was in not rising to her challenge with empathy and receptivity. If I now suddenly tried to respond to her closely guarded confidences with loving sympathy rather than with political doctrine, I worried that she would see my shift as insincere. I didn't like this distance, this caution between us. One night when we were playing double solitaire on her bed, I summed up our situation in gambling terms. "You offered to raise the ante, but I couldn't stay in the game. So we've agreed to play for lower stakes."

"That's an interesting way to put it, Alexandre. I rather like it." Her neat displays of alternating red and black cards scattered onto the floor as she leaned across my losing game to kiss me.

II

After my day of drawing plans at the office and her day of writing, Kate and I would often meet in front of the Architectural League of New York to attend lectures. I taught her how to draw freehand perspective. We went to movies and saw plays more to her taste than mine.

New York City was sliding toward financial crisis — we didn't notice. Kate wrote book reviews for *The New York Times* and *Saturday Review* and worked on a new novel, which she wouldn't show me. She was still hoping to hear from her literary agent that he had sold her first novel, *Kingdom of Gestures*. The waiting took its toll on her nerves. She showed me by example that poets and novelists are empowered equally by ambition and despair, and by lives of loneliness and adventure. She typed out a quote from Proust and gave it to me:

When we discover the true lives of other people, the real world beneath the appearance, we get as many surprises as on visiting a house of plain exterior which inside is full of hidden treasures, torture-chambers, or skeletons.

Whenever I tried, obliquely, to explore John's background, she was evasive. "Was he in the Bay of Pigs invasion?" I asked. "That was a

CIA operation. You never know about the CIA, they might have accepted a Canadian." It was a cruel remark that I immediately regretted.

"At that moment John was living in a charmed city where a dramatic mountain range descended to the sea."

"Rio?"

"No. Beirut."

"I give up, Kate."

"Haven't you ever had a mysterious girlfriend?" she asked.

"The first woman I ever screwed was very mysterious. She was a prostitute in Bauru who spent her off hours reading Aeschylus because, she said, he was the father of tragedy. Supposedly I was the one with every advantage to get an education, and I'd never heard of Aeschylus. I was not quite 15. After I visited Sandra, every boy in my class lost his virginity to her, and we all ended up reading Aeschylus I never knew if her reliance on Aeschylus was an intriguing device to augment her business or her way to deal with a disaster in her life. It would be easy to spin out stories either way. Sandra was not forthcoming. She hid behind a shy smile and said simply that her father was in the Soviet Union."

"What a story! You took my breath away, Alexandre."

"Good. We're even."

III

Roberto Faria's two radio stations continued to thrive, and my father's 33 percent ownership had become a reliable source of income. His health, though, was not flourishing. I increased my phone calls to Bauru to twice a week. Too often the connection was poor, but even when the line was free of annoying echo, his voice sounded so weak and fatigued I would hang up ready to fly home. Paulo's ministry had

236

delayed his departure from Egypt until the end of the year, so he and Maria Rita could not assess the situation firsthand. I called Pedro to get his counsel. "I need an independent opinion about what's really going on with my father. I'm not getting a clear picture with my phone calls."

"Knowing your father, I'm sure he has his own interpretation of what the doctors are telling him."

"That's the point, Pedro. I don't trust my father's health reports, and he intimidates my mother to go along with his views."

Pedro offered to fly to Bauru to check up on his Uncle Jorge Antônio and I accepted his generous proposal. His report was somber. My father had congestive heart failure, a chronic condition brought on by his heart attack, with well-recognized symptoms: shortness of breath, edema in his ankles, occasional trouble summoning the energy to walk across a room. His doctors recommended medication and a pacemaker. My father took the drugs, but refused the device. He had been meticulous in following the advice of his cardiologist when it came to his heart attack, but my mother couldn't persuade him to deal with this new condition in the same sensible manner. He had developed an elaborate set of responses to ward off her entreaties.

After Pedro left Bauru, my father telephoned. "Really, Alexandre, implanting a pacemaker in my chest? An electronic object that could stop on any pretext — faulty manufacture, a magnetic field, an electrical storm. Then what? I trust my own God-made heart a hundred times more than a secular device. I prefer His science, thank you."

"He has no intention of dying," my mother whispered to me on the phone when my father left the room. "We just have to be a little patient with him. His partner Roberto is no help at all. He likes to believe your father is as strong as a fighting bull."

I had not seen my father for five years — since his trip to meet me in Uruguay. My wedding was to have been the occasion for my

237

parents' grand trip to New York. Now it seemed he might never be able to travel. For several weeks I thought about trying to arrange to meet my parents on the Argentine side of Iguaçu Falls, or just over the border in Paraguay — the closest places to Bauru I could visit while keeping my feet outside Brazil. "Is it safe for you to even fly over Brazilian territory?" my father asked. "What if your plane had to make an emergency landing? They'd arrest you on the spot."

"You could fix your heart with a pacemaker, *papai*. Then you could travel. There's an architect in my office who has one, and he's flourishing. And he's about your age, too."

"Is my son trying to kill me?"

When I hung up the phone, I was disappointed and a bit angry with my father's intransigence.

IV

In early March 1974, Kate heard from her literary agent that Harper & Row had bought *Kingdom of Gestures*. To celebrate, I took her to the Russian Tea Room for champagne and caviar. Only later did she tell me that she and Sérgio had often eaten there. Our wounds were healing. My work at the Barnes firm grew more interesting and challenging. I worked long hours. Sometimes I didn't get home until midnight, and I had to be back in the office at 9 a.m. Kate was busy, too, working on her new novel. We were seeing less of each other.

On a Tuesday night I got home late from the office. I fixed myself a tuna sandwich and went to bed exhausted. I was the junior member of the team responsible for designing an American Savings Bank branch on Steinway Street in Queens. The presentation of our preliminary concept before the bank's board of trustees was scheduled for Thursday, and we were behind in our work. The irony of my working on a bank design amused me. Kate said I should tell Ed Barnes that

I was ideally suited for the project because I had experience entering and leaving a bank quickly.

Just as I was ready to leave for another long and tense day at the office, there was a knock on the door. When I opened it, Monica stood in the hallway, two huge suitcases grazing the hem of her coat. She flung herself into my arms. "You win," she said. She burst out crying.

We held each other in the open doorway — I don't know for how long.

CHAPTER NINETEEN

I

I arrived at my office nearly two hours late and left for home at 3 in the afternoon, despite the formidable amount of work that still remained for our meeting with the American Savings Bank officials. When I mentioned that Monica had unexpectedly arrived in New York, my colleagues at Barnes consented with genial smiles to take up the slack. She was waiting for me in bed, reading a magazine from the stack piled on the nightstand. "I haven't unpacked," she said. "Should I?"

"Are you planning to leave again?"

"Not this time."

I quickly undressed and joined her in bed, where we stayed making love and talking, oblivious to the bedroom's afternoon light fading to shadow. I hadn't forgotten what the fire of passion was like with Monica. One minute we were athletic together, the next tender and solicitous. How could we have failed so miserably with each other? "This isn't just reliving what we had," I said. "At least it isn't for me."

"What we had never went away, Alexandre."

"Why didn't you write me? I waited for a letter."

"You know the answer. I was in conflict about making the commitment to live outside Brazil."

"You saw it as irrevocable," I said.

"Well, isn't it? Going home to attend Jayme's funeral reminded me of what I was missing. I didn't write because I didn't have anything new to say."

I said I didn't write because I was angry and hurt that she hadn't resolved her dilemma long ago, when her leaving might have been less painful.

If she'd had a boyfriend in Rio, she didn't let on. This wasn't the moment to mention my affair with Kate, which was clearly now at an end. I was more than ready to start over with Monica. Finally, at dusk, exhausted, our explosion of passion suspended, it was time to confront the evening and beyond. We realized we were hungry. We decided on Max's. "For nostalgia's sake," she said.

After we ordered dinner, I adjusted my chair and leaned forward. "I thought I was the gambler," I said.

"You mean my coming to New York without calling or writing first?"

"Do I have to ask you again to marry me?"

"No," she said, with a warm smile.

"I'm not interested in going through religious rigmarole like last time."

"Neither am I."

"I have a crazy idea," I said. "Let's get married in Las Vegas."

She laughed. "You mean before we have time to mess things up again? Okay, but it has to be in one of those tasteless, over-the-top wedding chapels." She looked down at her plate and fiddled with her fork. "I have to say it, Alexandre. I'm sorry."

"For what?"

"For everything I've put you through. Even before Jayme's funeral, I was distancing myself from you. I was scared of spending the rest of my life in exile. You picked up on my mood and reacted. Then, all of a sudden, the funeral put me back in Rio and I was feeling that home is home even when there are things about it I don't like. It's not your fault we can't live in Rio. But I'm sure now — I'd rather be with you than live in Rio. Home is with you. I got on a plane hoping it wasn't too late."

"Let's not talk about it. You're here. I love you, always have."

She leaned over the table and kissed me. "I called Davis Brody from Rio. They'll take me back. I really didn't expect that they would. Remember we were talking about moving to a larger apartment in an elevator building? We should do it now."

"We're back on track," I said.

"Just slightly delayed."

I didn't need time to think through a whirlwind marriage to Monica. I'd had years to contemplate our ample supply of worries. The next morning, we bought plain gold wedding bands at Tiffany & Co.

II

Two days after Monica arrived in New York we flew, lighthearted and exhilarated, to Las Vegas and checked in to the Tropicana Hotel. The hotel was a suggestion from my colleague, Roger Lynch, who had told me the story of Mae West's imprisonment on Roosevelt Island. "Enjoy it," he'd said. "Las Vegas is an affront to everything we've been taught in architecture school, so don't come back with any crazy ideas."

The acceptably unctuous front-desk clerk handed us a roll of 20 quarters along with our key. "We're having a promotion this month," he said. "See, you've already won, compliments of the hotel."

The next morning, Saturday, I woke Monica at 9, eager to explore the property. We showered and dressed quickly and set out to wander among the games vying for our money in the hotel's vast casino. A waitress came by with a tray of complimentary glasses of orange juice. Monica took a sip and made a face. "There's vodka in it. It's too early for that. Let's have a real American breakfast."

"Indulge me," I said over a breakfast of silver-dollar pancakes. Monica looked as if she knew what was coming. I continued, "No,

242

not gambling. I want to walk around the property and just let the ambience soak in without making a single aesthetic judgment. I want to see if I can do it."

"It's going to be a challenge. I'll try, too."

The hotel's theme of tropical artifice was everywhere — our room, our bathroom, the manicured gardens, the scalloped-edge swimming pool, the fern-laden bars, the restaurants, the shops selling everything from pricey furs to penny candy. I started to say something derisive, but Monica put her finger to my lips. We kept to the game for two hours. Finally, Monica said, "Are you ready to give up? I am."

"Definitely."

"I suppose we should try the casino," she said. "We might even win."

We walked to the casino cage, where I bought $65 worth of chips. "I'll quit when it's gone," I said.

"Let's play as a team," she said.

"I was expecting you to say 'I'm not going to watch.'"

Monica collected the chips and walked to the nearest blackjack table, where we played several rounds, alternating places at the table. When she lost, she asked for advice. When she won, she declared that she was a natural player and wasn't it appropriate that she was marrying a Barbosa. We stopped when we were ahead $22.

The temperature was 70 degrees Fahrenheit, cool for outdoor swimming, but we decided to try the heated pool. Monica looked ravishing in a white bikini, diving off the low board. When I swam the sidestroke, there was no way to miss the underwater Muzak. We floated in each other's arms, enjoying the feel of our intertwined bodies in the water and the weirdly opulent surroundings.

We decided that our wedding ceremony should be at midnight. The hotel concierge assured us that on weekends the Marriage License Bureau was open from 8 a.m. Friday until midnight Sunday. On Saturday afternoon we took a taxi downtown to the courthouse and paid $6 for a license. "How convenient," Monica said. "No blood test, no waiting period like in New York. They didn't even ask if we were American citizens."

"Why should they? By accident of place of birth, I am. They knew that."

"They're so intelligent in Nevada."

"They're used to foreign accents," I said. "Didn't you see the sign?"

"What sign?"

"The one that said 'Requirements for Non-U.S. Citizens to obtain a license are the same as those for U.S. Citizens.'"

Riding in a taxi along the Strip back to our hotel, we looked over the list of wedding chapels we'd picked up at the license bureau. "I guess we have two choices," I said, "a ridiculous wedding chapel with some sort of gimmick or someplace absurdly romantic."

At that moment, I noticed the garish neon sign for the "World Famous" Chapel of the Bells. I told the driver to stop and wait. "It's your dime, mister," he said. "There are something like 30 wedding chapels in Las Vegas. Take your time, plenty to choose from."

"Is Chapel of the Bells popular?" Monica asked.

"It's been here for 15 years. In a competitive business, that's not bad."

"Do you recommend it?" I asked.

"Never been inside a single one. Almost got caught a few times, though."

As we got out of the taxi to investigate, Monica said, "Our luck — a helpful philosopher."

244

In our high-spirited mood, the Chapel of the Bells, with its excessively plush ivory decor and its atmosphere of faux romance, seemed just right. There was no need to look further. We selected a wedding package that included use of the Candlelight Chapel, silk floral arrangements, a photographer, intimate soft lighting, a witness (legally required by the State of Nevada), background music and a minister. "I can hardly believe this," Monica said in the taxi on the way back to the hotel. "It's holy matrimony, Disney style."

We took a walk, hand in hand, along the four-mile Strip, passing the three-month-old MGM Grand Hotel — with over 2,000 rooms, the largest hotel in the world — continuing as far as the Dunes, with its giant onion-shaped neon sign evoking an adventurous night in Arabia. Our walk gave a new sense to my father's fey statement that Las Vegas was his "dream city." Gaping at the phenomenal, playful roadside signs and the grandiose porte-cocheres, Monica said, "The Americans understand excess better than anyone. All this exuberance is calculated by clever businessmen to make you gamble more than you planned."

In the low humidity and bright midday sun of the Nevada desert in winter, we strolled back to the Tropicana. I was completely in love with Monica. Everything else in my life, especially our surroundings, was surreal.

Over cocktails Monica suggested we think about establishing our own architecture firm in New York. "I loved working with you on the Villalons' house. Juan and Marta were really pleased with the result."

"We're going to have our own firm some day, but let's just get through our internships and pass our exams before we start making plans." I suddenly remembered that, just as we were boarding our plane to Las Vegas, the yellow-and-green presidential sash was being placed on the shoulder of Ernesto Geisel, the fourth army general to rule Brazil since the 1964 coup. "You realize," I said, "yesterday was Inauguration Day. Maybe it will bring us luck. It's possible Geisel

245

could turn out to be less of a monster than Médici. By the time we're ready to establish our own firm, it could be in Rio instead of New York."

"Don't bet on it, darling," she said. "I'm too happy to think about what's happening or not happening in Brazil. Right now, I'm thinking about us. Anyway, we won't know about Geisel until he's been in office for a while."

"We haven't discussed children," I said. "We've talked about everything else."

"We'll have children."

"And a nanny," I added.

"I love you, Alexandre."

"You're absolutely certain you do?"

"I am. I've had six months alone in Rio to think about it."

As we entered the Chapel of the Bells at the appointed hour — midnight, March 16, 1974 — we were nervous, giddy, delirious. I whispered, "My life is yours, Monica." The ceremony took 11 minutes.

III

Sunday evening, as soon as we got back to New York, we telephoned our families. Although my father had met Monica in Rio and again in Montevideo, my mother had never met her. When I telephoned my parents, my mother spoke first. "I've heard so much about Monica, I feel like she's been in the family for years. We can't wait to embrace both of you. I think, even without a pacemaker, your father can manage a trip to the Argentine side of Iguaçu. It's certainly a romantic spot — the cascades, the iridescent butterflies, the birds. You know what

246

Eleanor Roosevelt said when she saw Iguaçu? 'It makes our Niagara Falls look like a kitchen faucet.'"

My father took the receiver. "Your mother is crying with happiness. We give both of you our blessings. I'm still afraid to have you fly over Brazilian territory to Iguaçu."

I promised to send photographs of our wedding and to think about another way for us to get together.

My mother spoke again. "I have a pearl necklace and a sapphire ring that belonged to my maternal grandmother. I want to present the jewelry to Monica in person."

"Tell her yourself."

I handed the phone to Monica. She spoke with both my parents, adding humorous details of our Las Vegas wedding. No one mentioned that we would be settling down to married life thousands of kilometers from home, with no way for me to return.

Monica's mother was delighted by our news, though not completely surprised. Not very successfully, she tried to hide her disappointment that her daughter had not waited to be married in church by a priest. I overheard Monica say, "Don't worry, *mamãe*. God recognizes and has special blessings for weddings in Las Vegas."

With a reception in Brazil to celebrate our nuptials out of the question, we thought again about having one at Chez André's lovely outdoor patio. "It's sad about your father," Monica said, "but I hope our mothers will come. We'll invite all our New York friends and colleagues. Let's start making plans."

IV

I telephoned Kate, 12 days after I last saw her, to invite her to lunch. "I have some news," I said.

"Tell me."

"It can wait."

"You're not mad at me?" she asked.

"Of course not. Why would you think that?"

"I've been so busy with the demands of my publisher I haven't been giving you much attention."

"Isn't preoccupation obligatory for famous authors?"

Kate walked into P.J. Clarke's lively and spirited as ever but, I knew, not yet at peace with herself. We ordered precisely the same lunch we'd had at our first meal together — mushroom omelets, small Caesar salads and iced tea.

"Does it have something to do with Monica?" she asked.

"How did you know?"

She leaned away from me, looking for something in my face. She continued her inspection, then burst out laughing when she noticed my wedding ring. "You're married. I knew you were going to marry her eventually — even when she left New York."

"That's the opposite of what you said at our first lunch."

"When I got to know you better, I changed my mind. I couldn't be happier for you, Alexandre. For you both. Congratulations."

"It's taken us by surprise."

Kate listened intently to the story of our trip to Las Vegas. "The Fates hurried you," she said. She stirred the ice in her glass with her straw, engrossed in thought. I took her hand, held it against my cheek. "I'm envious of your happiness, Alexandre. Sometimes I think I should go back to Rio and live there. Sit on the beach in the morning, write in the afternoon, see friends at night."

"I don't allow myself thoughts of the beach," I said. "It would just remind me I can't go back. Anyway, politically Brazil continues to be a graveyard. The sunshine is the one thing the military can't suppress."

Neither of us ate much of our lunch. Finally she asked, "Can I ever be really happy again? I wonder."

"You absolutely will be, Kate. Everything's going to change for you once your book is launched and everyone's reading it. You said so yourself when you were making the final revisions, that publishing your novel was helping you put your demons to rest. Your book is going to be a success. I can't believe a woman with your beauty, brains and courage can keep on being at odds with herself."

She looked up at me and broke into a broad smile. "I'm sorry, Alexandre. I really meant it when I said I was happy for you. I didn't have much of a chance to talk to Monica when we met at Ricardo's party. Maybe when the time's right, we'll have a chance to really meet."

I paid the bill and we went out onto the street. "Which way are you going?" I asked.

"Home, back to galley proofs." She cupped her hand to shield her eyes from the late winter afternoon sun and studied my face. "It could never have been, Alexandre — you and me."

"I know," I said, "have known from the beginning, but that didn't make me want you any less. Or admire you any less. Even when I was sitting on Sylvia's sofa and you were interviewing me, there was a moment when I wanted to rip off my mask and kiss you."

"You should have. I wouldn't have betrayed you." For a moment she let her gaze follow the traffic moving uptown on Third Avenue, then she looked directly into my eyes. "Finding you in New York has meant a lot to me. Some important things got clearer." She smiled. "I'm working on being brave again like I was in Rio, taking chances, not looking back."

"I'm your friend and your servant always, Kate."

I took her in my arms and held her, feeling her lithesome figure under her coat. I realized how much I admired her resilient honesty. I felt her shiver against me. Then we parted and walked quickly away.

I was afraid to dwell on our farewell. Kate and I had shared our witness of Brazil's repression and our pain at losing John and Monica. Tantalizing as it had been, the ardent phase of our relationship had faded into friendship — unguarded friendship. I felt dazed, reviewing bittersweet memories as I walked toward my office.

CHAPTER TWENTY

I

I telephoned Tom Madsen with the news of our wedding and said we hoped he and his parents would come to a reception we were planing for June 8. "Am I supposed to be surprised?" Tom said. "I've been wondering why it took you two so long to come to your senses."

Bill Madsen, Tom's father, called back the following day. "If your father had been well enough to make the journey to New York, I'm sure he would have wanted to host your celebration. Betty and I would be pleased to step in with something more elaborate than you and Monica have planned. We'll pick a nice hotel. I'll leave it to the women to work out the details."

I handed the phone to Monica so she could join me in saying that we were thrilled by their generous offer and pleased to accept it. Betty telephoned a few days later to suggest having a reception and buffet dinner at the St. Regis Hotel. We thanked her effusively.

Monica and I met after work with office colleagues and friends who toasted us and wished us the best. We called Pedro and wrote to Celso in Algeria and to friends in Brazil, Chile and Eastern and Western Europe, recounting our amusing wedding in Las Vegas. I made Monica the beneficiary of my life-insurance policy. And we started to think about where we wanted to live — Greenwich Village or near our offices, located just blocks apart in midtown on the east side.

II

Thirty-two days before the reception, my father called to say that he had had a pacemaker implanted in his chest and that his doctor declared him fit to travel to New York. Not only that, but he had already purchased plane tickets and made reservations at the St. Regis. For a few seconds I wasn't sure I had heard him correctly. "The procedure went perfectly," my father continued. "There was no pain. Of course, I was asleep throughout. I'm not exactly my old self, but I'm a very good replica. You see, my son, everything happens in life at the right moment."

"More stamina?" I asked.

"More energy, I hope, for all the wrong things."

The weather was sunny and warm at 7 in the morning on Sunday, June 2 when Monica and I took a taxi to JFK Airport to meet my parents after their overnight flight from São Paulo. Patricia, Monica's mother, had arrived a week earlier and was also staying at the St. Regis. As my parents exited the customs area, it was apparent that our five-year separation and my father's heart problems had taken a toll on both of them. My father waited patiently for my mother to release me before he grabbed me in a huge hug. "I hardly recognize you," he said. "You've become a man, my son." He embraced Monica, then stepped back, held her outstretched arms and admired her, before embracing her again and kissing her on both cheeks. "Your recent photographs don't begin to capture your beauty, my dear. I told Lucilia you would be our daughter-in-law one day. And I was right."

The Madsens had sent a dozen roses to Monica's mother's room at the St. Regis. When my parents arrived, roses were waiting for them, too, with a note: "A warm welcome to Alexandre's parents. With affection, good wishes and *abraços*, Betty, Bill and Tom Madsen."

252

My parents took a long nap to recover from their trip. At 1 o'clock, Monica and I went back to the hotel and had lunch with them. "You'd better start practicing your English," I said.

"My English is perfect," my father said with a wink and immediately switched languages. I had never heard him speak more than a phrase now and then. I was astounded. His English was very good. So was my mother's.

"Two years in Washington at Georgetown University, and many years before that studying English. French, too." He tapped his temple with his index finger. "I'm an elephant - I haven't forgotten."

My mother said, "I've been practicing with your Aunt Claudia. Do you remember that she lived in Boston for a year?"

I shook my head no.

On Tuesday morning Monica and I accompanied my parents while they shopped at Brooks Brothers and then we all set off to tour the city. They wanted to see Grand Central Terminal, The Museum of Modern Art, the Metropolitan Museum. As we turned the corner toward MoMA onto West 53rd Street, my mother and I fell a few paces behind. "Your father's frightening me again," she said.

"I thought his pacemaker was the solution."

"It's not that. He isn't content with just the success of one radio station in Bauru and another one in Araraquara. He and Roberto are determined to build an empire. They've taken out a big loan — he won't tell me how much — to launch another station in Campinas and other stations I don't know where. I'm terrified he's going to bankrupt us."

I told my mother I would talk to him about his business plans, but we both knew our ability to influence him, no matter the subject, was limited.

That evening my parents hosted a formal dinner for Monica's mother, Patricia, and Betty, Bill and Tom Madsen. My father was his usual charming, unpredictable self. "My son is what you are now calling a baby boomer. Isn't that right, Bill? Clogging the system — a python swallowing a calf. I would apologize to President Nixon for my addition to the U.S.'s demographic burdens, but the aftermath of the Watergate burglary seems to be keeping him very occupied these days."

Bill Madsen exploded in laughter. "I'm sure, Jorge Antônio, a short note of apology would be much appreciated, even at this busy time."

Betty and Bill suggested several Broadway shows that we might like to see together. Everyone settled on *A Little Night Music*. Monica and I rarely had time to attend the theater, nor could we often afford Broadway tickets. Work be damned, at least for the nights our families and close friends were in town. My father recalled that in 1948 — on their only previous trip to New York — he and my mother had gone to see *A Streetcar Named Desire*. "I remember the story very well," he said as he lit the cigar Bill had offered him. "Pretense versus fact, a universal theme."

"A very good summary of Tennessee Williams," Betty said.

At the reception, Monica wore both of my mother's gifts — the pearl necklace and the sapphire ring. As I surveyed the line of guests waiting to greet us, I was astonished to see my sister and Paulo in the queue. In mid-May Paulo had been told he was being posted to Madrid. He and Maria Rita had expected to be busy preparing for their move and had doubted they could attend our reception. When I saw her, for a moment the New York hotel ballroom receded and I was back on Fazenda Maraíba, strolling with her along the avenues of coffee trees. I had to make an effort to shake off my *saudade*.

"Did you bring Isabel and Tomás?" I asked.

"We left the children with Paulo's parents. We just decided to jump on a plane and come. It's been too long since I've seen you."

"It's fantastic Paulo has been posted to Madrid," I said. "Not a bad second post for a diplomat whose brother-in-law is on the wanted list."

"It doesn't seem to have hurt his career, thank God. I really liked Monica when you introduced her to us in Rio. You should be married. I'm happy for you."

"I'm happy, too."

"Completely happy?"

"That's not a good question to ask an exile who still loves his country."

After the celebration and with everyone departed, Monica and I got back to work. I threw my energy into an exciting project at my firm — the Bass Library at Yale University. At Davis, Brody & Associates, Monica was working on a residential complex of apartments and offices built on concrete pilings sunk into the bed of the East River. One of Monica's colleagues told us about a highly desirable two-bedroom apartment in Greenwich Village that wouldn't be on the market for long. In the midst of our hectic schedules and long hours, we moved into it and bought furniture. We loved our new home on the ground floor of a 19th-century town house with access to a small garden. We ate out less and made other sacrifices to afford the rent.

III

Monica and I postponed having a child until we felt our careers were solidly launched. There always seemed to be another professional hurdle we wanted to clear before she got pregnant. Finally, we agreed in January 1976 that she should stop taking the pill.

I passed the examinations for licensure as a Registered Architect in July. Monica wasn't eligible to take them until October. She was notified the day before Thanksgiving that she had passed.

Our son was born on Christmas Day. We named him Antônio after my father, Jorge Antônio, and Monica's father, Luis Antônio. We hired a Portuguese nanny, Nélia, who came to live in our apartment in a small room we created by rearranging inefficient hallway and vestibule space.

While we were preparing for our licensure examinations, we were hard to live with. I tried to respond with sensitivity to Monica's mercurial moods and food cravings, and she was sympathetic when I railed about having to study half the night after putting in a 10-hour day at my office. "Jesus Christ, we don't even have these fucking examinations in Brazil," I said one night when I was utterly exhausted. "In Brazil it's enough for an architect to have taste and talent."

Deep down, though, I knew more and more I was feeling myself to be an American, or more precisely, a New Yorker. I took the local mores for granted — professionalism, organization, punctuality, casual friendliness, commitments made in the mutual expectation that they would be fulfilled, without relying, as we Brazilians do, on excuses or last-minute scrambling. I knew that if I ever returned to Brazil, I would have lover's quarrels with my homeland — that I would be frustrated by its disregard for punctuality, its unfulfilled promises, the constant need to make little "arrangements" to accomplish ordinary things like opening a bank account or renting an apartment.

In the fall of 1977 Monica and I started our own firm, in partnership with my Barnes colleague Roger Lynch. I admired Roger's design talent and, considering that all architects have outsized egos, I had always

256

found it congenial to work with him. Roger had prestigious degrees, which would be a plus for our new firm. He had graduated from the College of Architecture, Art and Planning at Cornell and had received his Master in Architecture from Harvard. Although the architecture school at CCNY didn't have a comparable reputation, Monica and I had been interns at highly regarded architecture firms and our being Brazilian and having attended architecture school in Rio brought a certain exotic glamour to our enterprise. We flipped a coin to see whose name would go first. I called tails and won.

Roger and his wife, Sara, came to our apartment for a celebratory dinner. We toasted Barbosa Lynch Partnership with champagne. Roger teased me that when I got frustrated with an unrealistic plan, I would say it was annoying to Brazilians to make long-range plans and they should be left to God.

I smiled and said, "I think I also added that, from the Brazilian point of view, agendas are arrogant. But don't worry, Roger, I've come to embrace American arrogance."

Even before we gave notice to our employers, we had two commissions lined up. Dining Inc. was ready to hire us to design the interior space of its new project, an Italian trattoria on the ground floor of a glass-and-steel office building on Sixth Avenue. The other job, for a prominent attorney and his wife, was to remodel a Long Island beach house. The lawyer, Bob Wall, told us his house in Southampton was regrettably bland. "I want to feel elevated," he said, "when I open the front door."

In its current configuration the house barely acknowledged the presence of the ocean. Our design "celebrated" (in the lingo of our profession) the magnificent setting by replacing cottage-size windows and large sections of exterior wall on the water side of the house with a sweep of gigantic double-pane windows and two sets of nine-foot French doors opening out onto a large, newly created brick terrace.

We had to conform to local zoning ordinances by not changing the window placement or size on the street side of the house. Both of these commissions led to referrals and other work. Neither Roger, Monica nor I took vacations. My parents suggested reviving my idea of meeting them on the Argentine side of Iguaçu Falls, but I never could find the time to go.

On January 6, 1978, our daughter, Beatriz, was born. Our life was full.

CHAPTER TWENTY-ONE

I

I hadn't realized that my father was gradually drifting back into playing poker for higher and higher stakes. I was astounded when he telephoned Wednesday evening, February 22, 1978, to tell me he had just won back Fazenda Maraíba.

"My God, what did you put up?" I asked.

"My interest in the radio stations and the Ford dealership. It's a shame it didn't happen on April 23rd."

"I'm speechless, *papai*. I can't even imagine what *mãe* must be feeling — were you prepared to have her leave you for good if you lost? You were taking a crazy chance!"

"God saw fit to give me a deceptively powerful hand. I've been waiting for an extraordinary hand for nine years. Bernardo, Renato, Fausto and I were just settling in for our regular Wednesday night game of seven-card stud. Renato and Fausto dropped out in the third hand when I was showing the nine of diamonds, the nine of spades and the seven of diamonds and Bernardo was showing the 10 of spades, the 10 of clubs and the queen of clubs. I had the seven of hearts and the jack of diamonds in the hole. From just what was showing, Bernardo would beat me."

"What was the deception, *papai*? You had two pairs."

"Just listen. I knew exactly what I was doing when I made my final bet. It looked like the strength of my hand was in my two pairs but, in the end, I didn't even use them. I got the 10 of diamonds face up and Bernardo got the king of clubs. We both stayed in. When the last card was dealt face down, Bernardo began to bet vigorously, and I kept raising him. At the showdown, it turned out Bernardo's last card face down was the 10 of hearts. He had the queen of diamonds in the hole, which gave him a full house. He would have beaten me, even if I also had gotten a full house. But listen to this! In the last round I got the eight of diamonds. Imagine! I completed an inside straight flush! It was a once-in-a-lifetime hand! We raised and raised again until the pot was what I just told you — Fazenda Maraíba against my interest in the radio stations and the Ford dealership. Well, what do you think?"

"I really don't have words ... "

"Bernardo said I must have cheated."

"That's what you said about him when he won Fazenda Maraíba."

"Did I? I must have been right. The *fazenda's* profitable, too. Bernardo's been selling beef abroad. Coffee prices are up."

"Now what?" I asked, still unable to take in the full import of his news.

"My empire is back, that's what. April 23rd is back on the Barbosa family calendar."

My mother got on the telephone. She had been asleep when my father walked into the house, triumphant, with his news. "I'm happy and I'm furious," she said, barely able to speak. "When your father lost the *fazenda* but canceled our debt, we had a setback. This time we weren't canceling a debt. If your father had lost, he would have been canceling our future."

I suspected my mother would have liked to say a lot more, but she pleaded shock and I didn't press her to sort out her feelings. She did manage to say, "Since your father won, thanks be to God, we'll celebrate on April 23rd again. It will be unbearable that you won't be here."

"By April, who knows what could happen?" I replied. "He could lose it again."

"He says he's giving up poker." She handed the phone back to my father.

"That's right, Alexandre," he said. "I've played my last hand of poker."

"I don't believe you."

"From now on my game will be canasta. And, as you know perfectly well, canasta isn't a game for betting."

I hung up the phone dumbfounded. At least Monica and the children could attend the April celebration. She had run out to the drugstore for a prescription she'd forgotten to pick up. Antônio, 14 months old, was asleep. I tiptoed into his bedroom to whisper the news. "Your crazy, rash, addicted grandfather has won back your birthright, my son. Maybe someday you'll be more interested in farming than I ever was. I pray your grandfather will be able to manage Fazenda Maraíba until you are old enough to take over."

Only seven weeks old, Beatriz was in her bassinet in our bedroom. I crept into the room and gave her the same news. When Monica arrived home a few minutes later, I greeted her at the door with champagne. "Are we celebrating something?" she asked.

I told her the story.

"It's unbelievable, Alexandre. Not that he won back the *fazenda* — that he's played his last game of poker. Do you believe it?"

"In a funny way, I do," I said. "I don't think I fully appreciated how much that loss has disturbed his mind all these years. He's always pretended to make light of it, even though I knew it must have wounded him deeply. We're landed gentry again."

"And you're potentially burdened again," she said.

"I've already said a prayer for my father's health. I hope the burden, if it comes, will be many years in the future." I reminded Monica that, in addition to having been lost twice at cards, my family's *fazenda* had been imperiled many other times by bad markets, competition, pests and weather. "You know as well as I do," I said, "that in my crazy family, nothing is ever for sure."

II

By the first week of March, my parents were already planning their grand weekend celebration to commence on Friday and conclude with an impressive banquet on Sunday, April 23. I was in anguish that I couldn't attend. By the mid-1970s, absolute control by the Brazilian military was beginning to relax somewhat. President Geisel had announced a period of "decompression" — gradual steps toward restoring democratic rule. Perhaps I could enter covertly, stay just long enough to attend the festivities and retrace my route to leave. I had been able to escape from Brazil even though the police were looking for me. They wouldn't be expecting me now. I mentioned this idea to my father.

"Are you crazy?" my father said. "Trying to reverse your escape across the border? Just because your scheme is plausible in theory doesn't mean it will succeed in practice. You are asking a father to support a gamble that could put his son in prison. I don't want to even think about everything they could do to you."

Monica agreed with him. "At a minimum, you would need false identity documents that you have no way of getting," she said. "For the sake of Antônio and Beatriz, if nothing else, I beg you not to pursue this idea."

She had a point about the false passport, but I chose to overlook it. The revolutionary organizations in Brazil that in the past created false documents had become infiltrated by spies. In effect, they no longer functioned. But even if they had, what good would they do me since I had no way to contact them? I had no idea how to get a passport

262

in a false name. I had been extraordinarily lucky when I fled Brazil. I didn't want to push my luck by relying again on inattentive border guards.

Murilo, a fellow Brazilian exile in New York who had become a close friend, had grown up on a cattle ranch in Mato Grosso do Sul. He suggested a plan.

"It's easy to cross a dry frontier," he said. "There's no way to patrol it. Pedro Juan Caballero in Paraguay shares its main street with Ponta Porã in Brazil. The two towns straddle the border. The drug smugglers cross wherever they want. If the border guards are looking for anything, it's contraband. They won't be on the alert for a returning exile. There's a totally simple way to cross. It's a five-block trip between the two countries. You could take a taxi from Pedro Juan Caballero and just nod at Brazilian control and customs."

"Taxis? In the middle of nowhere?"

"They're there — at the bus station in Pedro Juan Caballero. People use them."

"Have you ever tried it?"

"Driving my own car, lots of times, but not since my status changed from citizen to subversive."

I rejected Murilo's idea of taking a taxi. Too many things could go wrong. The safer way to cross the border was on horseback, well away from the main road. Once I reached Ponta Porã in Brazil, I could fly from the airport there to Presidente Prudente, a farming town 230 kilometers due west of Bauru. It would be a direct flight to a small, out-of-the-way airport. For this flight within Brazil I wouldn't need identification, only a ticket that I could buy in New York. My father could send a car to meet me in Presidente Prudente. Monica and the children would fly directly from New York to Bauru via São Paulo. Nélia, our nanny, would accompany them. Monica would take my

263

luggage with her, so all I would need was a small knapsack. I wasn't sure who would have the more stressful journey, Monica, managing the children, or I.

I surprised myself by the depth of my feelings about my father's winning back Fazenda Maraíba. Time had not diminished my nagging sense of rootlessness. The *fazenda,* though unavailable to me, was psychologically my home. I missed my parents, the land, the spectacular sunsets, the avenues of coffee trees, the Nelores. I was determined to be present for the celebration. After the festivities, I would reverse my route to leave Brazil.

III

On Thursday, April 20, I flew to Asunción, the capital of Paraguay, where I boarded a bus with inferior shock absorbers for the eight-hour trip to Pedro Juan Caballero, a cattle-raising, coffee-growing area. Along the highway near Asunción, small markets popped up here and there, where women smoking big cigars sold farm products and hand-made spider-web lace. Farther on, the road crossed bush forest and then endless plains and hills. The only distractions were narrow valleys carved by tributaries of the Paraguay River. I opened a book to direct my thoughts away from my uneasiness about crossing the border, but reading on the winding road gave me a headache. Instead, I struck up a conversation with my mestizo seatmate. His native tongue was Guaraní, an indigenous language, which, for my benefit, he mixed with Spanish. I could barely follow what he was saying. After a while I stopped trying and simply stared out the window.

I was weary and apprehensive when I got to Pedro Juan Caballero at 8 in the evening. I knew that the town's only overnight accommodation was a hostel. The three or four modest hotels that served the area were on the Brazilian side of the border, unavailable to me. Pedro

Juan Caballero had one advantage over its Brazilian neighbor — the Paraguayan government permitted casino gambling, long banned by federal law in Brazil.

The town had two casinos, one downtown and one on the outskirts. I told myself that half an hour at a blackjack table would help calm me. I bought the equivalent of $10 worth of chips at Palacio Corina, the downtown casino, and took a seat to play. Three-quarters of an hour later, distracted and out of practice, I was out of chips and quit. I ate a steak sandwich in a simple canteen and went to bed. Polka music from somebody's phonograph kept me awake until well past midnight.

Murilo had arranged through his father for a local businessman to help me enter Brazil. After I met him at breakfast, he introduced me to a farmer who was happy to take my money for the short trip across the border. "With the morning sun in our eyes, Brazil will be straight ahead, *señor*," the farmer said as we mounted our horses. "We will ride without danger through coffee fields."

I felt instantly at home riding between rows of coffee trees. The harvest was just beginning on the Maracaju hills. Coffee workers went about their task of collecting the deep-crimson, mature fruit and took no special notice of us. We dismounted at the tiny Ponta Porã airport. The farmer shook my hand, wished me luck and departed for Paraguay with my horse on a lead.

IV

I arrived in Bauru on Friday afternoon. Monica and the children were waiting for me. My parents were beside themselves with joy. At 1 o'clock on Saturday, all the out-of-town family and guests — some 60 adults and children — gathered at the *fazenda* for *caipirinhas* and *feijoada*. After so many years abroad, I had to adjust my appetite to Brazil's heavy but delicious concoction of black beans, air-dried beef, sausage, tongue and pig's ears and tails served over rice. By evening, everyone was still full from lunch and, for the moment, more or less talked out. People retired early.

On Sunday, my parents walked at a stately pace down the main aisle of the Church of Santa Terezinha for the noon mass, my mother's hand resting lightly on my father's arm. A family midday mass, the customary inaugural event for the April 23rd celebration, had formerly been held at Fazenda Maraíba's private chapel. In one of his few breaks with tradition, my father decided to invite all their guests to mass and to replay his entrance into the church where, three days after losing the *fazenda,* he had had to face his friends at the funeral of Bernardo's mother. I had been so absorbed in my own anger, I hadn't considered how humiliated he must have felt. His swagger had been complete and convincing.

The church was full. Maria Rita and Paulo, now assigned to his ministry in Brasília, came with their two children. Aunts, uncles and cousins of all degrees were in attendance. Pedro, Silvia and their 4-year-old daughter came. Heitor's Swedish wife came with their two blond sons, but Heitor, more cautious than I, stayed in exile in Stockholm. The pews were filled with family and friends I had not seen since I was in my teens.

Antônio, now a fully rambunctious toddler, sat on my lap, mercifully quiet and content. We had left Beatriz with Nélia at the *fazenda.* Monica looked serene, like the daughter of a monarch, ready to reclaim her rightful prerogatives and position. In his homily, *Padre* Eugênio was able to make the Gospel reading of the day fit the occasion.

High summer was over. The noonday sun was bright, the temperature mild, as we filed out of the church. The celebrants got into their cars to continue the festivities with lunch at the *fazenda.*

The governor of the State of São Paulo arrived at the *fazenda* in a limousine. The verandas quickly filled with members of Congress and the state legislature, lawyers, physicians, notaries, my father's radio-station partner, Roberto, and the stars of all three stations, other business associates, the mayor, the Bishop and *Padre* Eugênio. Whole families attended, including cousins, widows, divorcées and divorcés. Bernardo Fernandes and his family came, as well as my father's other poker cronies — men who had met to play nearly every Wednesday night for 40 years.

You might think Bernardo would have been morose. He wasn't. Neither did he look relieved to be quit of his responsibilities as owner of the *fazenda*. For most of the first five years after he won it, Fazenda Maraíba was paying off debts it owed him. Then, in 1975, the *fazenda*, like much of Brazil, lost half of its coffee crop in the severe frost. But in the last three years, thanks to improved efficiency and the worldwide boom in coffee prices driven up by the frost, he had been pocketing profits.

People helped themselves to the lavish buffet and drank *caipirinhas* and my favorite soft drink, Guaraná, which was hard to find in New York. After lunch, there were tours of the property. Some people returned to their homes or hotels for naps; others napped in the *fazenda's* guest rooms. Fewer people smoked than in the past, but some things don't change. It was impossible not to notice the flirtations of certain cousins, bored with their rural existence, admiring another's partner. No doubt some of the dalliances ended in assignations.

The evening's festivities began with cocktails at 6, followed by dinner at 8:15 sharp under an enormous white tent festooned with glowing Japanese lanterns. The climax of the weekend celebration would be the recounting of my father's jubilant game. I had urged my father to condense his recitation of our family's previous gambling saga, when great-grandfather Machado had won back Fazenda Maraíba.

We showed off Antônio and Beatriz at the cocktail party. Then Nélia put them to bed. Maria Rita's 5-year-old son, Tomás, and her

7-year-old daughter, Isabel, were allowed to stay up for the dinner. "I want them to remember this evening," Maria Rita said. "I don't think our family will ever have a celebration quite like this one again."

Monica was a sensation at dinner. She wore a long red chiffon dress, deeply cut in the back. At precisely 9:35, the exact time of my father's victory, dinner was suspended after the main course as my father rose from his place of honor at one of the large banquet tables, tapped his glass and ascended a makeshift raised platform. Tomás and Isabel were still wide awake at their places. My father invited them to join him on the platform. "First things first," he said. "Please raise your glasses. A salute to my wife, Lucilia, a woman of moral courage who has twice lived to see Fazenda Maraíba lost on the turn of a card — first by her grandfather, Raimundo Machado, and then by her husband."

The guests saluted her with their freshly-poured glasses of champagne and shouts of *"Hurra!"* *"Viva!"* wondering, I'm sure, at my mother's fortitude. My father raised his glass again, looked around at his smiling guests and said in a conspiratorial tone, "I must assume we are among trusted friends." He paused. "A warm welcome to my son, Alexandre, and his wife, Monica, who are visiting only briefly from the United States of America."

Once again the crowd responded with *"Hurra! Hurra!"* A few people shouted in English, "Hear! Hear!" I froze in my seat. During the festivities, people had asked me about my life in New York, but no one had questioned me about my legal status. I hoped and believed the guests assumed that whatever the government had against me was settled. Naturally no one connected to the military had been invited, but my father's calling special attention to my presence could turn out to be a disaster. Monica looked terrified. Half-expecting a DOPS officer to grasp my collar from behind and drag me off, I got up, walked to the rococo easel on the raised platform and, with what I hoped was the right amount of flourish, removed its covering. While guests were touring the property in the afternoon, I had drawn all the hands of the four players as they were dealt on the night of my father's triumph. I had placed my full-color renderings on the easel and covered them with an antique blue velvet cape.

"How could he?" Monica said when I sat down. "Is your father becoming senile? You'd better leave immediately."

"It's too late. I have to assume he knows what he's doing." I tried discreetly to wipe the sweat from my forehead.

Monica said, "I'm going to be on edge until you get back to that town in Paraguay."

"Me too."

My father began narrating, with grand elaboration, the particulars of the winning game — all the cards that were showing and hidden in each hand when Fausto and Renato dropped out in the third round of betting. My father admitted that he didn't need to use strategy to keep Bernardo in the game or to escalate the betting. "When God sends opportunity, it's best just to seize it and not be too clever." He related how he and Bernardo had stared each other down, matching bets through three more rounds. The amount of the bets increased wildly in the last round until, at the showdown, it was Bernardo's full house against my father's straight flush.

Just as my father reached the climax of his story, Tomás interrupted him to whisper loudly that he had to go to the bathroom. Maria Rita turned crimson and quickly whisked both her children away to be put to bed by Nélia. My father continued with a wink: "I've been waiting a long time, nine years and one month, for a miracle — two superb poker hands, but mine the winner. Gambling is a vice and a temptation but, after all, what good is life if you can't be fanatical about something? Now let's have Lucilia's wonderful dessert, my favorite and I think Alexandre's too — mocha hazelnut torte."

269

After the dessert plates had been cleared, my father rose once again. In another break from tradition, he didn't mention the 1937 poker game in which my great grandfather won back the *fazenda*. Instead, he invited Bernardo to join him on the dais to say a few words.

Bernardo began, "Perhaps you think, all of a sudden, I became an overconfident bluffer, a bad poker player."

A few people called out, "*Não! Não!*"

"I thought so myself for a few days. But a week after my miscalculation, by God's grace, Jorge Antônio agreed to play one last game of poker with me, on the proviso that we bet no more than my favorite record album against his favorite book. Well, I'm here to tell you, I now own his treasured edition of *War and Peace*. But the best part was our hands. Did he tell any of you?"

This time, a roomful of "*Nãos.*"

"I thought not." Bernardo looked at my mother. "I'm well aware, Lucilia, that after Jorge Antônio won back your *fazenda*, he promised you he would never play poker again. In that last secret game, Tolstoy against my recording of Villa-Lobos' *Bachianas Brasileiras No. 5*, I bluffed Jorge Antônio into folding when he had two pairs. I took the pot with one pair. I re-established my confidence. I know how to bluff."

Bernardo turned to my father, walked across the platform and kissed him on both cheeks. "My old and dear friend, Jorge Antônio, I treasure your book. Now treasure your *fazenda*. I never felt I really owned it. Let's say I borrowed it for nine years."

My father embraced him. "Bernardo, my old and dear friend, for those nine years you have been a good steward, better than I."

CHAPTER TWENTY-TWO

I

While I retraced my circuitous route through Paraguay, Monica, Nélia and the children flew home. After our return from Brazil, the Barbosa Lynch Partnership entered an open design competition for a library on the campus of a preparatory school in Massachusetts. In an invited competition, only a handful of qualified firms are asked to submit, but in an open competition there can be so many submissions that the odds of winning are very small. Even though we worried that it didn't make business sense, we decided to commit the requisite resources to enter. Our design was an octagon with a dramatic central skylight that flooded the core of the building with natural illumination. In the eight corners in the outer ring of the building we created private study areas.

Snow clouds were gathering over New York when we heard that our long shot had paid off. Announcing the award, the chairman of the jury wrote: "The symmetrical exterior proposed by the Barbosa Lynch Partnership will be an elegant good neighbor to the school's Georgian classroom buildings. Furthermore, the interior spatial experience as conceived by the firm expresses a library's ennobling and uplifting purposes." To celebrate, the Barbosas and the Lynches, children included, went to Martinique for a four-day weekend.

On the last day of December 1978, the first step toward a miracle took place in Brazil. President Ernesto Geisel, responding to widespread civilian pressure, repealed the extraordinary powers decreed by the notorious Fifth Institutional Act. It was one of Geisel's last acts before leaving office. With this decision, the government relinquished its powers to shut down the Congress, dismiss elected officials, overrule the courts, deprive citizens of their political rights and jail them without cause.

Over the first week in January, I had excited conversations with my parents, the Madsens, Pedro in Rio and all the exiles I knew in New York. I wrote to Celso, who was still in Algeria, and to José and Heitor in Sweden. I even got a call from a former professor at CCNY.

On Saturday morning, January 6, Monica and I bundled up Antônio and Beatriz, grabbed a taxi and went to West 46th, now commonly called "Little Brazil Street," to soak up the atmosphere. From an engaging vendor we bought our children tiny white T-shirts with the Brazilian flag emblazoned across the chest. In a restaurant next to the hotel where we had first stayed in New York we ate Bauru sandwiches — roast beef, melted mozzarella, tomato and pickled cucumbers in a French bun with the soft inner part removed, named in 1934 after a law student from Bauru invented them. Although the Bauru sandwich is popular all over Brazil, my father found its oozing cheese messy, so my mother rarely served them.

During that winter I felt my world changing on all fronts. I had one eye on the architecture practice we were working to build, the other on the news from Brazil. Barbosa Lynch lost a chance for a commission to design a dormitory for a small college in Pennsylvania. A larger firm got the job. Roger and I scrambled to find other business. In mid-March, President Geisel chose military leader João Baptista Figueiredo to succeed him in the presidency. It was widely believed that Figueiredo would not only continue Geisel's decompression process, but expand it. As the political process was opening, a movement advocating amnesty for political activists was gaining nationwide support in Brazil.

This news mesmerized me and worried Roger. "Is the military really going to restore elected government to your banana republic?"

272

he asked. "Sorry, Alexandre, I shouldn't be flippant about something so important. Seriously, what if they decide to let you return?"

"Don't worry, I don't know if I will ever be allowed back. So far, they're only letting certain well-known exiles return."

"But what if you *are* allowed? I'd be surprised if this amnesty momentum lets up."

"It's too late for me. Monica and I have built lives in New York. I'm having too much fun working with you, building our practice ... I can't see us leaving."

When I thought about the prospect of a safe return, I was filled with a mix of feelings: anger, relief, sadness, apprehension, *saudade*, fear of my reaction to living in Brazil after 10 years abroad, reluctance to disrupt the careers Monica and I had worked so hard to build, loyalty to Roger. My parents called me every few days, or I called them. Monica concentrated on work and taking care of the children as a way to calm her conflicting emotions.

II

In June, the Brazilian Justice Minister began drafting an amnesty plan. It specifically would deny amnesty to those, like me, who had held up banks to finance political activities.

Roger saw my turmoil. "I know this amnesty business is very distressing for you," he said. "Anytime you want to talk about it, you have my ear."

"It's still so much in flux, I hardly know what to think. As it stands now, I'm excluded."

On the telephone, my parents tried to hide their disappointment. Even Antônio seemed to catch my sadness and held back tears when he was tempted to cry. Instead he threw me infectious smiles.

273

Two months later, the Brazilian Congress enacted the final version of the amnesty law. The clause denying amnesty to bank robbers had been removed. I was included after all!

My father telephoned. "Thank God!" he said. "Thank God, Alexandre! You can come home! Of course, every atrocity perpetrated by the military was as if it never took place. No investigation! No uncovering of the truth! Blanket amnesty for acts of torture and disappearances! No compensation to victims or their surviving families! Officially, nothing is remembered."

"Did you really expect a different outcome, *papai*?"

He took a moment before he replied. "It was obvious from the beginning that the generals were afraid to mouth any placating words without first protecting their own from prosecution. The bastards were forced to include amnesty for guerrillas to make their self-serving pretext palatable. But never mind President Figueiredo's intentions — the fact is, you can come home! My son can come home legally. I wasn't sure I'd live to see this day."

I wept as we spoke.

I didn't immediately jump onto a plane to Rio. After a week, when our uncontrolled joy and excitement moderated, my father grew circumspect. He said he was going to hire a lawyer to contact the administrative branch of the state court of Rio de Janeiro to be absolutely certain I was free to enter. "Just a precaution, my son. I want a certificate that says there is nothing against you."

III

It took several months for my father to secure the state court certificate stating that there were no charges against me. To this day, I don't know if there ever were. It depended on what the captured members of my group had revealed under torture.

The Barbosa Lynch Partnership was extremely busy with new commissions. As our business expanded, we gradually added professional and support staff. It wasn't until the 1980 Christmas holiday that Monica and I could find two weeks to get away to Brazil. I was in a state of delirium when we arrived. One minute I felt like kissing the ground, the next I felt like shaking my fist. It wasn't as if I were coming home to a democratic country. The generals were still not ready to entrust the choice of president to a supposedly backward people who, as President Figueiredo put it, "did not know how to brush their teeth or bathe."

Pedro met us at Galeão Airport in Rio. "You've changed," he said, surveying me from arm's length after our long embrace, "even more than when you were here for the celebration at the *fazenda*." He tugged at the sleeve of my Brooks Brothers seersucker jacket. "You look like a Yankee. It's going to take some getting used to."

Pedro was tan and had grown a mustache, carefully trimmed. I told him it made him look dashing. "A civil engineer has a duty to go against stereotype," he said. "Especially now that I'm single again."

"I was sorry to hear about that," I said.

"Don't worry. I'm fine, and Silvia is happy with her new husband. She's eager to see you. Our daughter looks more and more like a Barbosa."

Pedro took us to our hotel on Avenida Atlântica in Copacabana, eight blocks from our old student apartment. Monica's mother had come from Belo Horizonte to stay with us. She welcomed the opportunity to look after Antônio, now 4, and Beatriz, nearly 3, whenever we needed a babysitter.

Out on the street, the familiar sensuous, humid smell of Rio enveloped us. I felt intoxicated by the music of my language all around me, the unique light of summer, the rhythmic sound of the ocean waves breaking on the beach, the undeniable magic of the tropics. I squeezed Monica's hand, overcome with the ecstasy of being home.

Our five days in Rio were a whirlwind — not always happy or care-free — of visiting friends from school and comrades in the struggle, sunbathing, playing in the surf with the children, visiting old haunts, eating crayfish and South Atlantic sole. We went to dinner at the Yacht Club with Professor Corrêa Neto.

Monica and I were so involved with finding our old friends that the only time we were alone was when we went to bed, usually around 3 in the morning. Comparing impressions, she said, "Pedro's right — you have changed. You're punctual. You make plans. You've lost your Brazilian spontaneity."

Her remark didn't strike me as a compliment. It made me think of her disparaging cultural comparisons when we were trying to adjust to New York. "Brazilians know how to enjoy life," she had said back then, "even with its difficulties. Americans feel they have to achieve their lives." Had I become an American for whom life is a duty rather than a pleasure? It wasn't the moment to start an argument.

We found Adolfo's mother, *dona* Marian, in the same apartment building in Botafogo where César had picked him up on the way to rob our second bank. "Excuse me," she said, pulling a satin robe tight around her, "I was taking a nap. I'll just tell the maid to prepare *cafezinho*. I'm sorry Adolfo's father isn't here to meet you. He's in São Paulo. Adolfo spoke of you. You were studying architecture?"

"I was. At Nacional."

She told us that Adolfo and Roberto had been held in prison for two years and released with no explanation. She didn't know where Roberto went after he was freed. "My son didn't want to talk about his experience," she said, "but finally he broke down and told his father he was stripped naked and bound by chains and cuffs to the floor while first an alligator and then a police dog were introduced into his cell." She struggled to contain her composure. I moved to sit next to her

276

on the sofa and took her hand in both of mine. "Under those circumstances, Alexandre, you'll say anything." Her face had become ashen. "He confessed to one bank robbery and breaking into a government building to steal blank identification cards. I have a picture of Adolfo taken after he got out of prison."

She got to her feet unsteadily, went into another room and returned with a picture of a gaunt, hollow-eyed man I hardly recognized. There was no trace of the strong young mathematician who could do pushups and play soccer not long after having his appendix removed. "Where is he now, *dona* Marian?" I asked as gently as I could.

"West Germany. Two weeks after he got out of prison, a priest posed as his uncle and took him across the Argentine border. He says he's not coming home until there's a civilian government in Brazil."

"Your husband saved my life," I said. "After DOPS came here for Adolfo, *senhor* Octavio went right away to warn our group at their house in Cosme Velho. It was a selfless, courageous act. At that moment, you and your husband must have been in unbearable fear and shock. I've been in exile for 10 years, but I've wanted to thank *senhor* Octavio in person from the bottom of my heart."

In our attempts to discover the whereabouts of César and Carlos, we spent hours on the telephone and canvassed their former haunts. Eventually, following one lead after another, I found out that César had died in prison. Without medical care, his diabetes had killed him. We couldn't uncover any information about Carlos.

The day before we flew to Bauru, Monica pressed me to drive past the banks I had robbed. The idea made me uncomfortable. "Why?" I asked.

"Remember how you compulsively made drawings of a bank robbery in São Paulo? I'm trying to visualize —"

"Is that necessary?" I interrupted. Finally, I agreed. "Okay," I said. "Maybe I can even laugh at the chances we took."

Pedro drove. We took the children with us.

The former Banco Boavista in Méier had become a branch of Unibanco. When Monica noticed its large front window, she shook her head. "You were crazy."

"Get out and look more closely," I said. "You can't see inside. This one was actually less dangerous than the others."

By the time we got to Banco Nacional in Realengo, Beatriz was getting fussy. "Let's go in," Monica said.

"No, thanks."

Monica got out of the car and reached inside to take Beatriz out of my arms. Reluctantly I got out, too, and followed her into the bank, holding Antônio's hand. "How does it feel to be standing here?" she whispered.

"Disturbing," was all I could manage to say. I could feel sweat forming on my upper lip. I had indulged her curiosity. I wanted to leave. I glanced at a man standing behind one of the tellers and nearly jumped. "My God, Monica! It's the same manager!"

"The one who was on the toilet?"

"I can't believe it."

Antônio was tired and started to cry. My attempts to quiet him weren't working. The manager looked up, smiled at Antônio, came around the counter and walked over to us. He pulled a red lollipop out of his pocket and gave it to my son. I didn't have the nerve to thank him. I was afraid he might recognize my voice. As if I were watching a play, I heard Monica being gracious.

278

On the way downtown, Pedro detoured past the forlorn walls of the Lemos de Brito Penitentiary. Celso's comrades had escaped through the main gate, which now looked abandoned. I peered through the old gate, still painted light blue, an incongruously pleasant color for such a savage place. Inside the penitentiary's forecourt, I spotted two guards monitoring an interior gate, well back from the street. By the time we pulled up in front of Banco Bradesco, I'd had more than enough.

"I'm not going in, Monica."

"I am. Don't let Antônio eat that entire lollipop."

She went in with Beatriz. Antônio squirmed in my lap while Pedro idled the car. I was squirming inside. When Monica reappeared, she admitted that the afternoon's project had shaken her. "You were ridiculously brave," she said.

"You were brave, too."

"Being a lookout in front of an arsenal isn't the same as robbing a bank or rescuing prisoners."

On the plane to Bauru, I thought about my few days in Rio — so long and earnestly awaited. Monica read my mood, patted my hand and didn't say anything. For me, Rio was a kaleidoscope of memories, longings and new impressions. I had to make an effort to adjust to Third World nuisances — temperamental phone lines, dirty streets, an electrical outage just when you needed to turn on a light, bad smells of garbage left to rot, municipal water that I dared not drink. Still, there was an inner satisfaction to being in my own country, sharing these sensations and inconveniences and Rio's intense summer heat with my own people. The poverty was, as always, heartbreaking and inexcusable. When approached on the street, Monica and I gave money to beggars, knowing it did nothing to ease an endemic problem.

IV

When I had slipped into Brazil to celebrate the return of Fazenda Maraíba to the Barbosas, I hadn't had the leisure to explore my surroundings. Now, walking around Bauru after so many years in exile, I felt like a foreigner in the place where I was born and raised. Even the familiar features of the *fazenda* seemed altered — the long avenues of evergreen coffee trees, the endless pasture created from cleared forest for our lovely Nelores. I watched, full of emotion, as my children scampered on farmland that had belonged to their ancestors.

Our aging *administrador*, Mario, greeted me like a long-lost son. "Thank God, I have lived long enough, Alexandre" he said, sweeping his arm to encompass a vast expanse of row upon row of ripening coffee trees. "I had my doubts you would return."

"I had my doubts, too, Mario. I'm home now."

The house definitely had changed. From the day the property was back in Barbosa hands, my mother had made plans to transform it into a showcase. Now the rooms were all soft whites and pastels. "I gave up on the taxicab yellow in the parlor," she explained. "It got tiring."

Small windows had been removed and replaced with walls of glass looking out at *paineira* and *ipê* trees and the rows of coffee trees beyond. Recessed shelves had been built into walls to display indigenous pottery and wickerwork from the northeast of Brazil. Early 19th-century religious paintings had been replaced by contemporary Brazilian abstracts. Cream-colored Italian leather sofas were combined with the best of the family heirlooms. When Monica and I entered a room or turned a corner, we smiled with delight. "I wanted the house to reveal itself," my mother said, "becoming richer as you move from room to room."

"It's a triumph, *mamãe*."

Monica said, "I love what you've done. You really should have the house professionally photographed for a magazine."

My mother had instructed the cook to prepare all my favorite dishes. Bernardo invited us to a traditional Saturday *feijoada* lunch. Roberto had recently married Regina, a beautiful concert pianist who was born in Bauru but had studied abroad. They entertained us at an elegant dinner party, followed by a recital of arias from Mozart operas. Roberto's rich baritone voice was impressive.

My father took Monica and me on a tour of his radio station in Bauru and the one in Araraquara, an hour and a half away. We had to skip the more distant one in Campinas. With obvious pride he introduced us to the on-air personalities. In our eight days in Bauru, we didn't have time to accept all our invitations to dinners and luncheons. Everywhere we went, my father was sure to mention that his beautiful daughter-in-law was a distinguished architect. Underneath all the social activities, I knew my parents were overcome with emotion at having me and my family home.

The atmosphere in Bauru was very different from Rio's. It lacked both the highs of the nightlife, the cultural institutions and the beach and the lows of abject urban poverty and the reservoir of grim stories of people who had disappeared. I suggested to Monica that we go for a glider ride. "Is it safe?" she said. "We have children to think about."

"It's safer than driving a car or flying a plane with an engine."

My father had sold my glider when I went into exile. I rented one from the *Aeroclube* and went up with a friend for a short flight to make sure I hadn't forgotten my skills. It was as if I'd never stopped flying. The proprietor, Hans, insisted I take up a new Schleicher glider he had just received from Miami. "No charge, Alexandre. We're old friends. Just be careful about a hard landing."

With Monica aboard, I had us towed to 3,000 meters. We would be able to stay up for half an hour or more, depending on the currents.

Monica loved sweeping over the countryside, seeing the avenues of coffee trees stretch out rhythmically beneath us. I pointed out fields growing pineapple, and orchards of mango and avocado trees. "Some pasture is very green," she said, "but in other places, it looks almost bare."

"That's because ranchers graze their cattle around a circle to give the pasture time to recover."

I made a few tightly banked turns. "It's amazing," I said, "what these aircraft can do without an engine. They're incredibly aerodynamic." I couldn't resist pushing the stick forward, letting the nose head straight toward the ground until I built up my airspeed to 90 mph. Then I did a loop, up and over.

"Oh my God, Alexandre!" Monica said. "My insides have to catch up with the rest of me."

I caught one more thermal before letting gravity return us to the airport. I surprised myself by managing to land at barely more than a walking speed. Hans and the ground crew jogged alongside the glider as I came to a stop.

When we got back to New York, I felt freer than ever to be professionally adventuresome. Returning to Brazil, being at home with my parents in an easy, relaxed way, gave me a check on my inner reality. It is a bourgeois thing to say, but the truth is you have to be at peace with yourself. As an exile, unable to return to my country, I had been forced to convince myself that I was content with my circumstances. Now I had a bigger problem — I really had a choice.

CHAPTER TWENTY-THREE

I

In the weeks following our return from Bauru, Monica and I thought seriously about what it would mean to relocate permanently to Brazil. We had to think of Roger. The three of us had worked hard to build our practice and we enjoyed our partnership. The more I ruminated on our situation, the more I came to realize that, if we remained in New York, we would have to change our narrative of who we were and why we stayed. As I put it to Monica, "Up to this point we've been deeply committed to being political exiles. It would take an adjustment to think of myself as an immigrant."

In the end, we realized that our daily activities already reflected an unspoken decision. We found ourselves plunging eagerly into work on new commissions. Our conversations about returning to Brazil tapered off. What excited and challenged us was to design good buildings and satisfy clients. Gradually Roger relaxed his vigil of our moods.

We were busy enough to hire a project architect, two additional intermediate-level architects and more support staff. Our practice covered a wide spectrum, from commercial and educational commissions to restoring and converting older structures. To a limited extent, we also designed custom residences and second homes for the well-to-do. Our residential work gave us a chance to flex our design muscles, though it hardly paid, because the many hours spent working intensely with clients on their homes took time away from more remunerative projects. All our clients were demanding, but we were even more demanding of ourselves. When one of us got frustrated over some annoying obstacle, we invoked the office mantra: "Never compromise." But, of course, we had to compromise constantly, for all sorts of reasons.

In late August, eight months after we got back from Brazil, Monica and I were taking a Sunday afternoon stroll in Central Park with the children when we ran into Kate Lawrence and a friend whom she introduced as Dr. Peter Fall. A year after our marriage, Monica had been surprised when one day she found Kate's novel, *Kingdom of Gestures*, among our books. Kate had sent me the book as soon as it was published, with a rather mysterious inscription:

> To Alexandre –
> Was I self-absorbed? Writers must be forgiven.
> Kate

"Should I be worried about this?" Monica had asked.

"No, you shouldn't," was all I said.

Did Monica suspect I'd had an affair with Kate? Had she read Kate's book? Monica never said. I was grateful that she had let the matter drop.

By 1981 Kate was becoming known in the literary world, with two successful novels and two collections of poetry. I had kept up with her career and bought her books, though we had not seen each other for seven years, ever since our parting shortly after I married. "Sooner or later we were going to run into the famous Kate," Monica said as we walked out of the park toward our apartment. "I remember her from Ricardo's party. There was a time when I felt jealous of Kate, but not anymore. We should make arrangements to see her sometime."

Monica's statement shocked me. Should I feel guilty that I had not been forthcoming about my relationship with Kate? Whatever the answer might have been, now it was too late.

The following week, I telephoned Kate and invited her to lunch at "our" restaurant, P. J. Clarke's. She strode in as usual, spirited, all eyes on her.

284

"My stepmother introduced me to Peter Fall several years ago and I've run into him now and then, but we've just begun dating," she said as she glanced at the menu. "Peter's English. He's a neurosurgeon and he teaches at Columbia. He keeps the most amazing journals on his patients' lives. It's literature, really. I told him he could make some alterations, change the names and publish them as short stories. Every day is an adventure for him. Imagine confronting patients on the operating table who have more than dying at risk. One mistake and Peter could take away their intellect — who they are — but they'd still be alive. He's so courageous."

"So are you, Kate."

"So are you, Alexandre. Peter thinks I was half in love with you."

"Is he right?"

She touched my elbow, but didn't answer. After a while she said, "Love always has an element of tragedy in it, don't you think? I like Borges' description: Love is a religion organized around a fallible god." She hesitated for a moment, reached for the sugar, put some in her iced tea, and stirred it before she continued. "I'm serious about Peter, Alexandre. I think we'll get married. At least, that's how I feel. When I'm with Peter, Brazil — even John's death — seems distant. All the could-have-beens and the desolate feelings fade."

"They didn't with me?"

"You're Brazilian, my darling."

"You remember when you asked me if I thought you could ever be really happy again and I said you absolutely would? I knew you didn't believe me."

"In a way, I did."

I took Kate's hand and kissed it. Her eyes filled with tears. The moment passed. "Do you still play solitaire for answers to your questions?"

285

"I still have questions," I said, "but no time for card games. I make private dares with myself instead."

She turned to me. "It's really much better the way things turned out," she said.

After Kate married Peter, we occasionally got together with them for dinner. It was plain that neither Kate nor Peter was focused on the trappings of success. Even so, they lived stylishly in a handsome apartment on East 75th Street. They had no children. I suspected they didn't want any. Kate had chosen for herself a husband who was her soul mate. In their separate ways, they both explored dangerous territories and investigated unconventional lives. I realized I had not understood Kate's relationship with John and consequently had missed a deeper friendship with her. I had been both jealous and suspicious of John, presuming he was likely a CIA agent. I had indulged my own longings and appetites without properly appreciating her highly nuanced view of Brazil or John's story, the part she was willing to share.

II

Our children were developing their own differing interests and personalities. Neither Antônio nor Beatriz would speak to us in Portuguese, though they understood it well enough, especially when we didn't want them to. Neither showed any affinity for agriculture, not even an interest in pets. I was convinced Antônio was going to be a lawyer. He debated everything. Beatriz liked to draw, and I set aside time with her before she went to bed to review her day's output. At 5 years old she had already sketched, numerous times, all the rooms in our three-bedroom apartment on East 86th Street and the views outside the windows. Her precociousness was scary.

Three years after our Christmas trip to Brazil, my parents visited us in New York. Monica and I took a taxi to the airport to meet them. New York was turning green, preparing itself for St. Patrick's Day. A double stripe had been painted in green along the Fifth Avenue parade route. In spite of the March temperatures in the low 40s, my parents insisted on walking everywhere, exploring parts of the city they hadn't seen on their previous visit.

My mother didn't look her age of 67, but she reported that her friends who'd had face-lifts were inquiring when she planned to have hers. "I thought about it," she said as we ambled along the edge of Gramercy Park. "I even made an appointment with Dr. Pitanguy, but then I canceled at the last minute. Why do I have to take on this obligation to be a youth impersonator? My friends are getting the illnesses of the old and they act completely surprised because, when they look in the mirror, their faces are 15 years younger than their interiors."

My mother was still actively engaged in making plans for herself. "Finally," she said, "I can study architecture and still live with your father at home. The Universidade Estadual Paulista has just established a Faculty of Architecture, Arts and Communication in Bauru."

Monica asked, "Why not enroll for a degree?"

"If they'd accept me at my age, I would. At least I can look forward to attending lectures and maybe participating in a class that interests me." My mother smiled. "You know, of course, your husband's and your daughter's design talent comes from Alexandre's maternal side."

On Fifth Avenue my father took note of the green median stripe. "Green, but no yellow," he said, smiling. "Half of our national colors." He turned to my mother and said authoritatively, "They can't paint the yellow line until the green one has had time to dry."

I had to admire my father's charm and idiosyncratic observations and also — no longer a surprise — his business acumen. Fazenda

Maraíba was profitable. It was plain, though, that the social and psychological consequences of winning back the *fazenda* were more important to him than the money. Over the years, coffee production had become much more mechanized. The international markets for coffee and beef were bringing dollars to the farmers in Bauru. When Mario retired, my father hired a new *administrador* with a college degree in agricultural engineering. "Today it's all about genetic engineering, artificial insemination, frozen embryos," he said over dinner at our apartment. "Our Nelores are starved for love. At least sometimes they should be allowed to be naturally aroused. They look sad."

The three radio stations also continued to thrive. Roberto and my father had added a fourth station in São Carlos, playing a mix of music ranging from classical to Michael Jackson to close-harmony singing duos — the backbone of Brazilian country. Listeners called in their requests to the minor gods, the on-air personalities spinning the records. Roberto's old standbys — big-city detective shows and suspense dramas — had been completely eclipsed by television soap operas, but they still had enough of an audience to be reprised on Sunday afternoons in Bauru, right after the religion shows. On all four stations, news bulletins were broadcast on the hour; the morning news in depth included crop and cattle prices. It wasn't hard for the stations' sales forces to sell ads.

My mother had one more very pertinent story to relate, out of my father's hearing. "He's driving a used car," she said. "Your father won Renato's 1980 Mercedes at one of his Wednesday night canasta games. He's absolutely incorrigible. He's managed to turn a social card game into an opportunity to gamble. I actually prefer Renato's four-year-old car to our new Mercedes, but I'd never tell your father that."

Later, alone with Monica, I said, "With the old man, there's no telling what he might do. I won't know until he dies whether Maria

288

Rita and I will inherit Fazenda Maraíba or not. He could be gambling on his deathbed."

<h1 style="text-align:center">III</h1>

By 1984 we knew that Brazil's generals were ready to accept a civilian president, but only through a vote by a government-dominated Electoral College consisting of the members of the National Congress and some additional representatives chosen by state legislatures. So on Wednesday, March 21, the day before my parents were to leave New York, Monica and I were electrified by news from Rio. A parade of 200,000 people had formed downtown from Candelária Church to Cinelândia to support a movement that had been gathering nationwide steam for months — a return to choosing the president of Brazil by a direct popular vote rather than indirectly through an Electoral College. Diverse elements of Brazilian society were letting the government know that they were united in common cause. A constitutional amendment calling for direct election of the president had been pending in Congress for a year.

After dinner, we rushed to my parents' hotel room as they were busy packing.

"Did you hear the evening news?" I asked.

"We did," my father said. "It's just what I said 15 years ago, Alexandre. The military would eventually lose its prestige with the public and disappear into their barracks to complain to each other about their general discontent, their stupid superiors and what inflation was doing to their wages. Of course I support the movement for direct elections, but I don't see our Congress approving the amendment. There are too many pro-government deputies to let it pass."

"I disagree," I said. "There are big names bringing pressure on Congress. This movement isn't going away."

289

"There's something else to consider," my father continued. "Look what happened last year in Argentina. A civilian president was elected by popular vote, and five days later he set up a commission to investigate the disappeared. There's no doubt that, over time, hundreds of Argentine military personnel will go on trial. You think our generals don't fear something like that happening to them?" As my mother dithered with her packing and my father looked on, he said, "Well, do you want to come home and get involved with the campaign for the direct vote?"

"I wish I were free to."

Monica chimed in, "Me, too. I wish I could help."

"Ah, but your architecture clients await," my father continued. "That's what happens, isn't it? You're young, you take big risks, you face up to the consequences of those risks, then you mature, move on and before you know it, with hard work and maybe some luck, you have built a life with a family and have responsibilities that you can't so easily push aside for another risk. I know a little about that progression."

The next day at the airport, the Brazil-bound passengers at the gate were reading newspapers, chatting with each other about what had happened in Rio and predicting that within days, millions would march all over the country demanding that the president of Brazil be elected by direct popular vote.

IV

After my parents left, Monica and I talked about what it would mean to live in Brazil if it were to become a truly democratic country. The temptation to go home would be there, but our lives were bound up in New York and we both knew it. Twenty-one days after the first demonstration in Rio, there was a second that drew a million people.

Six days later, in mid-April, a million and a half people demonstrated in São Paulo. Monica and I were convinced that democracy was just around the corner. We followed the news as the widespread demonstrations in Brazil continued. Finally, when the constitutional amendment came to a vote in the Chamber of Deputies on April 25, it lost.

"Your father was right. Congress wasn't about to capitulate to the demonstrators," Monica said.

"It didn't lose by much. Just 22 votes shy of the required two-thirds majority." As disappointed as I was by the failure of the amendment to elect the president by a direct vote, I confessed to Monica that I was also relieved that I could stop thinking about returning home. "The generals still pull the strings," I said. "It reminds me why I'm angry at my country. The defeat gives me an excuse to resist my *saudade*."

Brazil's generals had their candidate for president picked out, a civilian politician named Paulo Salim Maluf. Opposing Maluf was Tancredo Neves, the governor of the State of Minas Gerais, a skilled politician, a moderate, who knew how to forge alliances to win. With the opposition effectively closing ranks behind Neves, the armed forces let it be known they were unhappy at the prospect of his victory, but they gave no signs of refusing to accept their anticipated defeat.

On January 15, 1985, Tancredo Neves was elected Brazil's first civilian president in 21 years, but the drama was just beginning. On Inauguration Day, March 15, less than 12 hours before Neves was to receive the sash of office, he was rushed to a São Paulo hospital with severe pain requiring immediate surgery for an abdominal illness he had endured for several months. In Brasília, his running mate, Vice President-elect José Sarney, was sworn in before the assembled National Congress and designated interim president.

Monica asked, "Did you notice that Vice President Bush attended the ceremony?"

"I wouldn't put it past the U.S. to say they want to see democracy in Brazil, but secretly they're worried to see their staunch anti-communist military pals out of power. I'm still bitter about the disappearances and a lot more, and that feeling is never going to leave me."

General João Baptista Figueiredo, our last military president, literally left the Presidential Palace by the back door, without formally passing the yellow-and-green sash of office to Sarney. The armed forces had exhausted their ambition for power.

Over the next 29 days, Neves underwent seven surgeries for an acute inflammation of the intestine. The political life of Brazil was in paralysis, traumatized by his deteriorating health. When Neves died on April 21, Sarney, the former head of the pro-military Democratic Social Party, became president.

Within weeks of Sarney's accession to office, Brazil's intellectuals began a debate on how to deal with past human-rights abuses — something both the old government and the new one had hoped to avoid.

V

On September 7, Brazil's Independence Day — equivalent to the Fourth of July in the U.S. — our family joined thousands of Brazilians on West 46th Street to celebrate both the 163rd anniversary of Brazil's independence from Portugal and six months of civilian rule. Boisterous joy filled the street. Antônio and Beatriz were thrilled by the glittering Carnival costumes imported from Rio, the huge yellow-and-green banners, the balloons, the samba and bossa nova music, the aromatic food stands selling Bauru sandwiches, black beans, *farofa* and rice, manioc fries and Bahian shrimp stew. Even the weather cooperated to make Brazilians feel at home — hot sun and a slight breeze. A Portuguese-Brazilian church choir sang the Brazilian national anthem.

Our political troubles had finally unwound. I felt I had become a traveler in a safer world.

CHAPTER TWENTY-FOUR

I

My mother's phone call woke us early in the morning of October 23, 1987. My father had dropped dead of a heart attack in his bathroom while shaving. "There was no warning," she said. "I waited for him at the breakfast table, and when he didn't join me, I went to see where he was."

Monica and I left for Bauru that evening with the children. Overcome with sorrow, I stared out the window at the green navigation light on the wing-tip of the plane. I refused the dinner being served. When the children fell asleep, we discussed the many arrangements we would have to make immediately upon landing. I wasn't mentally prepared for a world without my father. I had always thought my father denied the possibility of death. I expected that my mother would be immobilized by shock and grief and that it would be up to me to make all the decisions for the family. I was wrong.

A few hours after we arrived, my mother said, "Don't worry, my son. Everything is taken care of, and has been ever since your father had his heart attack 14 years ago. But since his pacemaker was working so reliably, we didn't think this day would come so soon. Even his cardiologist told us he could look forward to many more years of vigorous health."

My father, far from denying death, had faced it with admirable courage. He and my mother had made it their responsibility, not their children's, to attend to its practical consequences. I had expected him to die intestate. I had been prepared for chaos, costly years tied up in court trying to settle his estate. He had never mentioned that he and Mother, over the last few years, carefully considered the organization

of their affairs and had legally registered their wills. He had had his notary double-check the filings of all his deeds, his accountant had been
directed to draw up a plan to pay any outstanding debts and his lawyer
had been told to reach an agreement with Roberto Faria that spelled out
how the ownership of the four radio stations would be divided upon the
death of either partner.

The funeral at the Church of Santa Terezinha, the same sanctuary
where my father had publicly confronted both loss and triumph, over-
flowed with mourners. In his homily, expressing gratitude to God for
my father's life, *Padre* Eugênio ended by saying, "Truly, Jorge Antônio
Barbosa was a man who persisted in faith, accepting that the struggle
to believe is the story of our lives. Too many people, when they encounter life's setbacks, defend themselves by developing mean, dried-
up hearts. They act out of anxiousness, not out of trust in God's loving
mercy. This was not the case with Jorge Antônio. He never allowed
himself to become blind to God's availability, even when life seemed
to go against him."

After the requiem mass, with my family gathered at the portico,
Padre Eugênio embraced me. "The grand gesture died with your father,
Alexandre. There will never be another like him."

In the following days, my mother's bearing was a renewed demonstration of her strength. She told friends she was comforted believing
that, at his final moment on earth, the grace of the Spirit was with him.
"I tried to breathe life into his mouth," she said to Bernardo, "even
though I am not trained in resuscitation, but it was already too late."

Five days after the funeral, my father's battery of lawyers, notaries
and accountants came to the *fazenda* with all the necessary beribboned
and authenticated documents to ensure that his testament could be settled in a matter of months, rather than years. My father's will was

295

clear and unequivocal: His entire estate was divided among his "necessary heirs" — fifty percent to my mother, the remaining 50 percent divided equally between Maria Rita and me. Bernardo Fernandes' son, Gilberto, was one of the assembled lawyers. He handed my mother, Maria Rita and me sealed letters from my father. "Jorge Antônio wrote these three letters on March 15, 1985," Gilberto said, "the day the military government stepped down. I don't think he had any intention of ever revising them."

It took me a day to open my father's handwritten letter. It was hard to bear the thought that it would be his last communication.

15 March 1985

My beloved son, Alexandre,

I wanted to write you this letter on a happy day, a day you paid a deep personal price to help bring about. The military government is gone. Only Brazilians at least 45 years old could, in their lifetimes, have voted for a President. For most Brazilians, there is hardly any memory of democracy left in this country.

Although some say the new system is the old system with a face-lift, I believe the country will move in the correct direction. The tradition of political parties will reappear and our democratic memories will be reborn.

Your parents, too, have paid a price for your courage. How many times has your mother held back her tears when she talked to you on the telephone in Chile and then later in New York? Countless times, my son. Men don't like to talk about the pain of separation from someone they love deeply, but your father has entered your old bedroom more than once wishing he could see your clothes in the armoire and your architecture books spread open on your nightstand.

You know the story of the Fates? The three stern god-
desses who determine human destinies? One spins the thread
of life, one dispenses each person's lot and the third wields the
dreaded shears to cut the thread at the appointed time.

Since you were a young boy, you told me you planned to
be an architect and live in Rio. Despite the obstacles you have
encountered (some, let's be honest, of your own making), you
have held to your plan and achieved much of it; even though
the Fates tugged at the thread of your life along the way and
wove it into unexpected and unforeseen patterns.

But I feel compelled, at this late juncture, to suggest you
allow your life to come full circle. Although you would never
know it from my actions, I have long hoped Fazenda Maraíba
would stay in the Barbosa family and not be sold off at my
death. Am I an old, unrealistic man dreaming of his grandchildren growing up on the *fazenda* and loving the land as he did?
I can say, for my part, that being the patrão of Fazenda Maraíba
has not prevented me from pursuing other interests. The radio
stations prosper. Perhaps you will see a way to be both the
fazenda's patrão and also a working architect. My hope for
the fazenda is not to be taken as an order. In truth, even in my
darkest hours of humiliation and loss I never stopped believing
that Fazenda Maraíba belonged to the Barbosas, always would,
and you would one day return to care for it.

I hope you can forgive your father his weaknesses, which
I do not need to enumerate here. (Everybody in Bauru knows
them and probably everyone in the State of São Paulo as well.)
And finally, though I know I don't need to say it, comfort and
protect your mother should I depart this earth before she does.
Stay close to Maria Rita and her family.

Wherever I'm going after you read this letter is known only to God. Every Sunday at mass, Padre Eugênio promises eternal this and everlasting that. Who knows? I hope he's right, but I also am prepared that he might be wrong. I always liked Pascal's flip of the coin: If God does not exist, a skeptic loses nothing by believing in Him, but if He does exist, the skeptic gains eternal life by believing. An interesting wager. So much of life is a gamble and, now that I think of it, so is death.

Mourn me, but not for too long. Get on with life. Bring beauty into the world with your talents. Cherish Monica, Antônio and Beatriz. And know you brought joy to your father's life. I am more proud of you than I can say.

I trust you will find my estate in good order. My aim was to relieve you of as many burdens as I could.

I embrace you.

Your loving father,

Jorge Antônio Barbosa

II

Monica and I wept over my father's letter. I never asked my mother or my sister what my father had written to them, nor did they inquire about his letter to me. In a separate package, my father left my mother the deck of playing cards that were used the night he won back the *fazenda*.

I always thought of my father as a man unwilling to admit the truth when it didn't suit him, too often teetering between good fortune and calamity. After he was gone, reviewing his correspondence, his papers — his empire, really — I saw that he hadn't talked to me about many things that really mattered to him. I loved him, but I didn't fully

appreciate his depth. I should have probed deeper. I took his easy pro-
nouncements about life's eternal verities as his last word on a subject.
He had more to teach me, and now it was too late.

Two days after I first read his letter, Monica and I went for a walk
among the coffee trees. Spring maintenance of the trees was beginning. We stopped to watch laborers with hoes cleaning out debris from
around the bases of trees. We came to the end of one avenue of trees
and started along another. "Sometimes there are snakes in there," I said.
"Rattlesnakes and *jararacas*. The workers have to be careful. Remember what you said to me about snakes when we were trying to decide
where to live in Chile?"

"No."

"You said you weren't afraid of snakes. You were afraid of the
mice they eat."

"Did I?" She smiled. "Anyway, it's still true."

III

Back in New York, suddenly rich, we both understood that our new
wealth carried obligations. I asked Bernardo and one of his sons to take
over management of the *fazenda* while we pondered our future. Some
things were clear. My mother wanted me to return home and manage
the *fazenda* and Roberto wished I'd take over some of my father's responsibilities at the radio stations, although I had the contractual right
to remain an inactive partner. No one expected or wanted Paulo to
give up his diplomatic career so Maria Rita could remain in Bauru and
share in management responsibilities. Roger hoped, at the very least,
that Monica and I would continue our relationship with the firm even
from afar, but better yet, he hoped we would stay in New York.

We had the money to experiment. For nearly six months, Monica
and I debated. The easiest course would have been to sell the *fazenda*

299

(but not the house, if my mother wished to live in it), but neither Monica nor I was content with that solution. At crucial times in my life I had taken big chances and, despite some setbacks, it hadn't worked out badly. We both felt ready for challenge and adventure. "Now we have possibilities we never had before," I said. "We need to use them well."

We shut the door on our apartment and left New York to spend one year in Bauru. We had no idea what the consequences would be. The day after I arrived at the *fazenda*, Bernardo invited me to take my father's place at the Wednesday night card game. "We're playing poker again," he said, "but no large bets." I was pleased to accept. We settled into the manor house with my mother. The children were happy, and suddenly willing to speak Portuguese. Roberto had hired a manager to perform my father's duties at the radio stations.

After talking with the household help, Nélia, our nanny, announced that Brazilians were uneducated. "They believe in witches and strange cures and magic words and I don't know what," she said. "Brazil isn't anything like Portugal." Nevertheless, within two weeks she had found a Brazilian boyfriend. And six weeks later she said that Antônio, age 12, and Beatriz, age 10, were old enough not to need a nanny, that we would always be her family, but that Luis, her boyfriend, had asked her to marry him and she had accepted. She was right. The children were beyond needing a nanny. Nélia moved with Luis to São Paulo, where he had found a job as a bookkeeper for a trucking company.

I bought a glider, and to the delight of the children, took them up. Antônio wanted to know if glider pilots got half-wings to wear on their lapels instead of full wings. Beatriz loved flying over Bauru's agricultural fields. She was fascinated by their rhythmic patterns. On her second glider flight, she took her sketchbook.

When we left New York, we had agreed with Roger that one of us would fly there every month for ten days to meet with clients, inspect

300

sites and give guidance to staff. As it turned out, I made these trips more frequently than Monica. We equipped the manor house's atrium as a studio with drafting tables and a fax machine. Roger was skeptical at first, but we were making the long-distance arrangement work. The three of us talked about making the Barbosa Lynch Partnership international and setting up an office in Bauru.

IV

In December 1988 we invited Marcelo Coutinho, a publisher who was visiting Bauru from São Paulo, to dinner at the *fazenda*. Marcelo was an old friend of Monica's from high school. After dinner we went out on the veranda to enjoy the evening and drink liqueurs. It was a warm, crystal-clear summer night. Monica left us to supervise the children's bedtime. I liked Marcelo. We were having an interesting conversation about how life can constantly confound us. I told him something about my history. He thought my story would be an interesting book. "From robbing banks to designing one! It's a great story, Alexandre." I told Marcelo I had no experience with that kind of writing, and doubted I could do it. Further, much of what I would have to say was too private to be published. "Write it for yourself," Marcelo suggested. "Then make up your mind about whether or not you'd like to see it in print."

I thought, at the very least, such an analysis of my life might offer a helpful perspective as I pondered the choices Monica and I still had to make. I began writing, unbeknownst to my family. The effort took on a life of its own. The airplane between Brazil and New York became my private study. Toward the end of our year in Bauru, Monica and I made the decision to continue to divide our energies between Fazenda Maraíba and our architecture practice.

301

By this time Roger was content with our working arrangements. When my fellow poker player, Renato, hired us to design an eight-story commercial building to house his family's expanding business interests, Roger chose the occasion for his first trip to Bauru. After a tour of the building site and other rapidly developing areas downtown, he agreed that the time had come to open a second office in Bauru and hire local staff. While we took Roger and his wife on a tour of the region, his two teen-aged children preferred to spend their time exploring the *fazenda*. One at a time, I took each of the four Lynches up in the glider.

Marcelo visited the *fazenda* several times. Only once did he ask me if I was writing. My answer was equivocal. First, because Monica was in the room. But second, and more significant, because I had no idea if I could sustain my scribbling and actually finish the book. As the new decade began, I laid my fountain pen to rest in my briefcase and I had time to read books and magazines on my trips between hemispheres.

Finally I felt ready to send Marcelo this letter. There was nothing accidental about my decision to mail it on April 23, a day of such consequence to my family.

23 April 1991

Dear Marcelo,

Your suggestion that I make the stories I told you during your first visit to Fazenda Maraíba into a book surprised me. As I said then, when I was a young man, I resented the expectation that I would be the *patrão* of my family's *fazenda*. That was what we architects call the "parti" — the guiding concept — of my life as my family and their friends understood it. I had other ideas. My actual life has too often seemed a series of accidents in which little turned out as I anticipated. Yet here I am

302

managing Fazenda Maraíba and going back and forth between New York and Bauru to sustain my architecture practice.

I appreciated your encouragement to write down my history. Many pages were composed on long plane trips. The exercise has made me see that I can't claim to have a heroic imagination. Rather I have been an odds player, courting risk. I count my decision to immerse myself in agriculture and still hold onto my architecture practice as another throw of the dice. Two years of writing have helped me fit the pieces together, feeling that there are still interesting and surprising things to come. As I thought from the beginning, much of what I have had to say concerns private matters between myself, my wife and a dear friend, which it would be shameful of me to reveal. Perhaps one day, when everyone mentioned in my manuscript is too old to take offense, or when we are all gone, my children will read it.

The other day I recalled a quote from Frank Lloyd Wright: "The truth is more important than the facts." I have tried to record both.

Yours in friendship,

Alexandre Machado Barbosa

V

Nothing about Brazil's past has been settled yet; there are still wrongs to be righted. Nothing about my future is settled, either. I am almost 45 and I know the Fates are far from through with me. If my life so far has been haphazard and risky, it is because I come from a haphazard country that has never had a sense of a common good, and because I'm descended from irrational gambling families on both sides.

Antônio, a teenager now, likes to follow our *administrador* around, asking question after question about the workings of the *fazenda*. Beatriz, at 13, enjoys sketching the Nelores lazing in the pasture. I am still amazed by her prodigious talent for drawing.

At sunset, Monica, my mother and I like to drink *caipirinhas* on the veranda and watch the swarms of parakeets settle for the night in the *paineira* trees. Often we sit in silence, admiring one of Bauru's magnificent sunsets, listening to the birds squawk, each of us lost in his or her own thoughts.

My father said the Fates had woven the thread of my life into some strange tangles. There are times when I feel seduced by the idea of returning permanently to the urban excitement of New York, or of Rio. But, in the end, the risks and failures and hard work I've borne have brought me close to the life my father envisaged for me — a love of the land and a desire to commune with and care for it. I am sure my country will continue to challenge and surprise me. Like my ancestors, I will remain a gambler to the end.

DISCLAIMER

All the main characters in this novel, their actions and Fazenda Maraíba are creations of my imagination. Several real New York architecture firms and their principals are mentioned in the story, but the characters' interactions with them are entirely fictional.

This story is set against veridical descriptions of places in Bauru, São Paulo, Rio de Janeiro, Montevideo, Santiago de Chile, La Serena and New York. The historical descriptions of Brazil's period of dictatorship are intended to be accurate. Many of the Brazilian students who took enormous risks to oppose the military dictatorship became prominent citizens in later years, including Dilma Rousseff who suffered imprisonment and torture. She was elected President of Brazil in 2010, the first woman to hold that office.

ACKNOWLEDGMENTS

I am grateful to Peter Kaufman for his astute editing and to Patricia T. van der Vorm, Ph.D. for catching my mistakes in the final galley. I thank Ambassador Marcio de Oliveira Dias and Ambassador Marcelo O. Dantas for their insightful comments on the manuscript.

For stories about the resistance to the Brazilian military dictatorship and for helping me understand the North Zone of Rio de Janeiro I am grateful to Leoncio de Queiroz Maya and Rogerio de Queiroz Grillo. For information about Bauru and its surrounding *fazendas* I am indebted to Ambassador Fausto Godoy, Counselor Renato de Assumpção Faria, Rosa Ranieri, Maria Lucia Ranieri Previdello, Ambassador Eliana Zugaib, Carolyn and Thomas Kunkel, Lars Krook, Joseph K. Obeid, Francisco Ourique and Giuseppe Granchelli Filho. For information about Chile I thank Counselor Maria del Carmen Dominguez. I owe thanks to Theodore Liebman, Stanley Hallet and Roger Lewis for helping me understand the study and practice of architecture. I am grateful to Donna Lomangino for helping me refine the design of the book cover.

This novel would not exist without the patience, intelligence and encouragement of my devoted husband, Bernard. Always willing, day or night, to take out his red pen, he has read, commented on and edited more drafts than I care to count.